having
hope

having
hope

terri ferran

bonneville books
springville, utah

The views expressed within this work are the sole responsibility of the author and do not necessarily reflect the position of Cedar Fort, Inc., or any other entity.

This is a work of fiction. The characters, names, incidents, places, and dialogue are products of the author's imagination, and are not to be construed as real.

ISBN 13: 978-1-59955-233-0

Published by Bonneville Books, an imprint of Cedar Fort, Inc.
2373 W. 700 S., Springville, UT 84663
Distributed by Cedar Fort, Inc., www.cedarfort.com

LIBRARY OF CONGRESS CATALOGING-IN-PUBLICATION DATA

Ferran, Terri, 1962-
    Having hope / Terri Ferran.
        p. cm.
    ISBN 978-1-59955-233-0
    1. College students--Fiction. 2. Mormons--Fiction. I. Title.

    PS3606.E734H38 2009
    813'.6--dc22

                                    2008048216

Cover design by Angela D. Olsen
Cover design © 2009 by Lyle Mortimer
Edited by Natalie A. Hepworth

Printed in the United States of America

10 9 8 7 6 5 4 3 2 1

Printed on acid-free paper

For Brianna Faith,
who allowed me to experience Romania vicariously
through her journal,
and motherhood firsthand,
to which no journal could do justice.

chapter one

I haven't had too many perfect days in my life. I've had high hopes, but it seems like they rarely work out the way I plan.

June twelfth was a day like that. It was *the* day. By that I mean it was the day Adam Bridger, the guy I adored and was dying to see again, was actually coming home from his mission.

It had been nearly eleven months since I'd seen him. It should have been two years, but Adam had come home last July when his sister, Janet, died unexpectedly in a car accident. I was in the car with Janet; my injuries were serious and left me with a scar running down the left side of my face. It was a constant reminder of the loss of my best friend.

Losing Janet and having to tell Adam good-bye again were two dreadful events I would never want to relive. After almost a year had passed, I could say that the experiences strengthened me; but at the time, I thought I wouldn't make it through.

I joined the Church just a few months before the accident that had shaken my faith. I felt like both my faith and testimony had grown since then. I knew I had changed in the last year and I was certain Adam's mission had changed him, too. Would the changes be too great?

I also worried about more mundane issues. What if my face broke out with huge zits? I obsessed about sleeping in past my alarm, so I set another as backup. I had my clothes picked out and had even planned the clever things I would say when I saw him again.

What I didn't plan on was waking up at five AM, dashing feverishly for the bathroom. I hardly ever got sick, and to have it happen on this of all days was devastating to me. I prayed it would pass, and it did—every fifteen minutes or so.

My mom came in to see if I needed help. I tried to convince her I would be fine by the time the Bridgers picked me up at nine to head to the airport. She tried to humor me, but at 8:30 she made the phone call I refused to make. I heard her voice penetrate my wretched, or should I say retched, state.

"Barbara? This is Nora Matthews." She paused. "I'm fine. Apparently Kit isn't, though. She's been up for hours with some sort of stomach flu. She isn't going to be able to go with you this morning." I was ready to crawl to meet Adam, if only I had a port-a-potty to bring with me.

"Oh, I know. She is so upset." Upset? My stomach was upset; I wanted to scream in frustration, but didn't have the energy.

"No, there's nothing you can do. Well, maybe tell Adam that she would be there if she could." Another pause. "All right, I'll tell her. Drive safely. Bye-bye." I heard her hang up. I groaned in frustration then turned my attention back to my porcelain pal.

I spent the morning switching between cursing my existence, wanting to die, and praying for a speedy recovery. I had planned this day for months. What would Adam think? That I didn't even care enough to come greet him at the airport? Of course, if he saw me in my present condition, he would run screaming back to the plane.

Adam's flight was due to arrive in Salt Lake City at 10:45 AM, and I knew they were planning on going to lunch down there. That meant I couldn't reasonably expect them back in Cache Valley before 2:30 at the earliest. Knowing how they all loved to talk, it would probably be closer to 5:00.

Thanks to my mom's willingness to wait on me hand and foot, I was able to drag myself to the bathtub by early afternoon. By 4:30 I actually resembled a human being again, and although I still felt ill, I managed to eat a little bit of toast and keep it down. I napped on the couch with our home phone and my cell phone right by me. By 6:00 I was a little irritated that Adam hadn't called me yet. Seriously—he must have noticed I wasn't there. He had to know I was really sick to miss his homecoming. For all he knew, I could be dead by now. He didn't even bother to call. It would serve him right if I did die from this miserable flu bug—if he even made it to the funeral!

After wallowing in self-pity for awhile, it occurred to me that maybe something had happened to Adam. Maybe he was the one lying near death, wondering where I was. I started to feel sick with worry. I mentioned my fears to my mom and she assured me that someone would have called if there had been a problem, and they were probably just caught up in the excitement of the day.

My brother Dave strolled in as I was voicing my concern and had to add his two-cents worth (which was worth about half a cent). "Don't worry, Kit, I'm sure Adam's just fine. They just probably have to hold him back from all the women he can check out now that he's done with his mission. If I were you I'd worry about getting your beauty sleep—you need a lot of it! See ya later, barf bag." He pulled the pillow out from under my head as he passed the couch.

"You jerk!" I yelled as I flung the pillow at his back. I wished I could hurl on him at that moment. Every time I thought Dave's immaturity level had peaked, he proved me wrong. He was about to turn seventeen and was going to be a senior in high school; it was looking to be a long year.

Finally, the phone rang. I checked the caller ID. Hal Bridger. I felt a surge of light-headedness that had nothing to do with the virus I was fighting off. "Hello," I said breathlessly.

"Hi, Kit. It's Lily." Disappointment flared, but I recovered myself before I responded to Adam's fourteen-year-old sister.

"Oh, Lily, I wasn't expecting you." I heard her laugh on the other end.

"I'm sure you weren't. You thought it was Adam, huh? Well, don't shoot me, I'm only the messenger. How are you feeling? Still got the turkey trots?" Lily had as much subtlety as Dave sometimes, but I liked Lily a whole lot more.

"I'll live. I can't believe I got sick today. How was everything? How's Adam? Is everything okay?"

"Everything's fine. Yeah, Adam couldn't believe you called in sick today, either. He's beginning to wonder if you still care. I told him about that one guy you've been dating pretty seriously and he—"

"What?" I yelped. "What guy? I haven't been seeing anyone else!" Lily laughed even louder.

"Kit, you're such a sponge. I was just messing with you. Seriously, Adam knew you must be really sick not to come today. We all went to lunch and then after that we went to the Joseph Smith Memorial Building. We just got back and Adam had to go meet with the stake president, so he asked me to call to see how you're doing and to let you know that if he can't call tonight, he will tomorrow."

"You're a little creep, do you know that? I'm sicker than a dog all day long and you just call and hassle me. I can't believe you!" I tried to sound mad, but it was kind of funny how she sucked me in so easily.

"Well, you should count your blessings that you got so sick!"

"How do you figure that, Lily?"

"I don't think you could have kept your hands off Adam, which would have been a problem because he is still officially a missionary until the stake president releases him tonight. I think maybe the Lord was protecting an innocent missionary from your worldly ways, and that's why you were struck down with a terrible sickness this morning! You were smote, Kit!" Lily cackled at her own cleverness.

When Lily was on a roll, she would twist anything you said, so I ignored that comment and went for the sympathy ploy. "I'm feeling really lightheaded and nauseated again. I think I'd better go and lie down." She didn't know I was already lying down. "Tell Adam I'll talk to him later. Thanks for calling, Lily."

"Oh, well, I hope you feel better tomorrow. I'm sorry if I teased you too much. I was just kidding about you being smote," Lily sounded contrite and I smiled, knowing that she felt a little bad for teasing me.

"I know. I'll probably see you tomorrow if I'm not too sick. Bye." I hung up, glad to know Adam was safe, but a little disappointed that I wouldn't see him until tomorrow. It was enough to make me want to throw up again.

chapter two

Adam called the next morning. When my cell phone rang and I saw the caller ID, I let it ring three times before I answered it. After all, I didn't want to appear to be waiting.

"Hi, this better be Adam Bridger calling, or I'm coming right over to wring his neck," I answered, blowing my plan of not appearing too eager.

I heard his laugh before he replied, "Put your wringing tools away, Carson, it's me. Sounds like you're feeling better. Lily said you still felt pretty sick last night." I liked it when he called me "Carson," which was his nickname for me. Since we first met he has called me "Kit Carson" and I have called him "Captain Bridger;" it's corny, but very endearing.

"Sick of Lily's teasing and sick of waiting for you; but whatever I had has passed. I can't believe it hit me yesterday, of all days. I'm sorry. Did you miss me?" I wanted to hear him say it.

"Only for the past two years of my life! Of course I missed you. My day probably wasn't as big a drag as yours though; I was surrounded by the clan."

"So was it fun to see everyone?"

"It was great. I can't believe the changes. They're all growing up; it's weird."

It was silent for a few seconds and I didn't know what to say. Adam filled the void. "So when can I see you? I want to talk to you

5

face to face. I need to see my favorite scout." His words thrilled me. Maybe he was as excited to see me as I was to see him.

"I can come over now, if you want. I don't think I'm contagious. Anyway, I'm feeling much better." I didn't care if he knew how antsy I was.

"Then come and pick me up and we can go to the park for a while to have some time alone. I promised my mom I wouldn't disappear for too long, and the family is probably more eager to see you than me, anyway."

"Let me just touch base with my mom to let her know where I'm going. I'll be there in fifteen minutes!" So what if I let my enthusiasm show—it was Adam and he was home! I had every right to be excited.

After we hung up, I told my mom I was going to see Adam. She fussed over me a little to make sure I was all better from my flu bug. Even though I didn't feel 100 percent, I was going to see Adam, no matter what. Besides, my fluttery stomach was more because of anticipation than illness.

When I pulled up to the Bridger house, I considered honking to see if Adam would just come out so we could see each other without a big audience; but I figured that might be a little tacky. Besides, it was going to be a little weird, seeing him again for the first time since his mission. When he had come home for Janet's funeral, I was so foggy from the pain meds I was on for my own injuries, that I couldn't remember much about it.

I figured I couldn't really count the two days of seeing him after the car crash as really seeing him. So it had actually been two years since we had really talked, face to face. Suddenly, doubts assailed me. What if his feelings had changed? I didn't think they had; his letters and tapes had been reassuring. But what if he didn't feel that same excitement when he saw me again? What if he didn't like the way I looked anymore? Maybe it was best if we saw each other again with the horde around—just in case.

The door opened and Lily came flying out. Although she was only fourteen, she looked sixteen, and she was definitely boy crazy. She was already beautiful with long brown hair nearly to her waist and big blue eyes. She also had a flair for the dramatic.

Lily and I have shared a special closeness since Janet died. I think she saw me as a surrogate sister. She sure teases me like a sister.

"Kit! You're here!" Lily flung her arms around me in a huge hug. "How are you feeling?" She stepped back, but held on to my hands. "You smell good. You're all dolled up for Adam, huh? Too bad he gained, like, forty pounds on his mission. He's a chunky monkey, now! Oh well, more of him to hug, right?" She laughed and it dawned on me what she'd said.

"What do you mean he gained forty pounds? Really? It's noticeable?" I'd never thought about Adam gaining weight, although I had teased him about losing his hair on his mission.

Lily reassured me. "Don't worry about it, Kit. He is pretty tall, so he carries it well. Anyway, I already told him that you gained about thirty pounds. You two will make a nice, chubby pair!"

"That's not true! Why'd you tell him that?" What was she talking about? Then I realized she had sucked me in again with her tall tales. "Adam didn't gain forty pounds, did he?"

Lily was laughing at me. "Of course not! I was teasing you; but his hair is a little thin on top!" She darted away as I tried to kick her in the behind. She disappeared around the side of the house.

I was distracted by the front door opening again, and there he was—in person! Adam Bridger, giving me that heart-melting smile of his; flashing his cute little dimple. I stood still for a second, just drinking in the sight of him, then before I knew it he closed the space between us and I was wrapped tightly in his arms.

I inhaled the scent of him as we hugged. We didn't say a word, just stood there, holding each other; as if we were giving each other the embraces we had stored up for two long years. I would have liked to freeze that moment in time, but too quickly we were interrupted by a nine-year-old voice chanting, "Kit and Adam, sitting in a tree. K-I-S-S-I-N-G!" With the voice came his sister Sarah's unmistakable giggle. I looked over Adam's shoulder to see his brother, Travis, standing with Sarah in the doorway spying on us, with Lily egging them on.

Adam stepped back and turned towards the perpetrators. "What are you guys doing? Travis, I thought you were old enough to know the difference between hugging and kissing. That was hugging. This is kissing." He turned back to me and demonstrated the difference right in front of his little brother and sisters.

My concerns evaporated as I felt the familiar rush of being kissed by Adam Bridger. He slowly drew his head back and looked me in the eye. "Kit, can you tell the difference between a hug and a kiss?" he asked softly.

"I'm not sure," I whispered, "You'd better show me again, just to make sure." He quickly complied and his brother and sisters heckled us in the background.

As Adam and I reluctantly stepped apart, we kept holding hands and looking at each other. "Welcome back, Elder Bridger," I said, giving his hand a big squeeze.

"That's Cap'n Bridger to you," he grinned, "or, you can call me Adam." He led me into the house to let his family know we were leaving for awhile. I knew once I went inside it would take a few minutes to get away again. I was right.

Adam's brothers and sisters all talked at once to tell me about picking him up the day before. It was chaotic, but in a good way. I loved being at the Bridger home.

Adam's mom, Barbara, came in the room. "I could tell you were here by the way the crowd went wild," she joked as she gave me a hug. "How are you feeling? Your mother said you were pretty sick." I was still surprised by the changes in her since Janet's death. Barbara had always been a little on the heavy side. Over the past eleven months, she had not only lost the extra weight, but now she looked almost emaciated. She used to joke about "being the first to the table and the last to leave," but now she always says "I just don't have much of an appetite, I guess."

She usually looked tired and a little bit sad. She was still the kindest person I knew, but she didn't joke as much or have much energy. I knew that her husband, Hal, had been very worried about her.

I assured her I was better, and we visited for a few minutes. Adam stood up first and tugged at my hand. "C'mon, Kit. Let's go play in the park." He stopped to give his mom a hug. "We'll be back in a little while, Mom." Barbara beamed when he hugged her.

We went to Adams Park (We considered it to be our park and

called it Kit and Adam's Park.) and played on the jungle gym, went down the slide, and pushed each other on the swings. Then we found a soft, grassy spot in the shade and watched a little girl stand under a big willow tree trying to catch the little leaves that occasionally swirled to the ground.

"So how does it feel to be home? Are you running wild, able to stay up late and sleep in till noon? Got a bunch of women lined up to date?" It was so great to have him back. My jaws were beginning to ache from constantly smiling.

"Well, I did stay up until about midnight last night, but still woke up early. I have a whole 'kit and caboodle' of women to date. Well, actually just a Kit to date." He stretched out resting his head on my lap. "It's a pretty great life so far, this running wild stuff. How 'bout you, how does it feel to have me home?"

I pinched his cheek then leaned down to give him a quick kiss. "Mmmm, yeah, it feels pretty good to have you home. So what are your plans? Besides dating me, that is?"

"I need to get a job. I have a little money left in the bank, but not much. I've got to make sure I have enough for tuition by fall, I'd like to get a car, and even though you're a cheap date, I expect I'll have to spend some money on you."

"You're right about that. When winter comes, this park will be mighty cold for hanging out. Also, I really like ice cream, and that addiction ain't exactly cheap." I leaned back on my arms, marveling at how beautiful the day was, and how wonderful it felt to be there with Adam. I closed my eyes for a few seconds to let the delicious moment sink deep into my body and soul.

Adam reached up and touched my cheek. "You're smiling. Thinking about ice cream?" I wasn't aware that I was smiling again. I felt content; it had been a long time since I had felt so . . . complete.

"No, that wasn't an ice cream smile. That was a smile for enjoying the moment. I'm just so glad you're home." I plucked a blade of grass and tickled his face with it. "Do you know I was afraid it would be kind of strange between us? I mean, of the two and a half years we've known each other, we've really only dated for about four months. And it's been two years since we actually dated. A lot's happened during that time." I didn't know if I was expressing my thoughts coherently.

"And is it strange?" Adam asked.

"No. And that's what the smile was about. I was enjoying the moment of non-strangeness. It just feels complete." I hoped Adam got what I meant.

"I worried about the same stuff, Kit. I wanted things to be the same between us, but I knew the past two years would change us. I was afraid to hope we would feel the same connection we'd had. But hanging out here with you feels really good. It just feels natural."

I could only take so much seriousness at one time so I had to lighten up. "But you still need to find a job. I'm not the same cheap date you left two years ago. I have expectations now. And standards. I'm not going to lower them just because some good-looking former-missionary begs me for a ride to the park and then tells me how beautiful I am. You did tell me how beautiful I am, right?"

"Did I mention that you're beautiful?" He said without missing a beat. "If I promise to buy you ice cream, will you give me a ride home? Oh, and will you take an IOU?"

When we got back to his house, we hung out with his family for the afternoon. Adam's older brother Justin was coming over for dinner with his wife Michelle. Everyone assumed I would stay, too. I didn't have to be asked twice, but I was quieter than usual, mainly because of a slightly queasy stomach. I enjoyed watching Adam interact with his family. I'd spent a lot of time at the Bridger house, and I realized I had probably spent as much time with Justin as I had with Adam, yet I had never really seen them together.

I always thought Justin and Adam looked a lot alike and I'd heard it from other people as well. As I studied them, side by side, hearing both of their voices, I was amazed at how striking some similarities were.

Their hair was the same rich deep brown color; Justin still maintained the shortness and style of a missionary cut, even after being home for almost two years. The dark chocolate eyes were also a match. They each had a strong, square jaw line, and although they were the same height, Justin had put on a little weight since his marriage.

Adam and Justin had the same timbre to their voices. They really could pass for twins. No wonder I had sometimes felt a thrill when looking at Justin (of course that was before he was married, and only because Adam was on a mission). I was still a little embarrassed when I remembered how Justin had reprimanded me for acting like I was coming on to him a year ago.

The differences were more apparent when Adam and Justin smiled. Although they both had those brilliant Bridger smiles, Adam had the little dimple in his left cheek. Adam laughed more readily; Justin was more reserved.

As I pondered on the two brothers, my thoughts turned to their choice of women. Justin's wife, Michelle, was a former beauty queen and looked every inch the part. I used to refer to her as Lexus Barbie (okay, sometimes I still did, to myself). She had blonde, flowing hair, big blue eyes, a flawless complexion, a tiny waist, a big chest, and long dark lashes. I sometimes wondered how much was natural, but I knew it was jealousy feeding those thoughts. Oh yeah, her parents were rich, too, so Justin married into the Lexus. They lived in an apartment in her parents' basement that was almost as big as the Bridgers' entire house. Maybe he married her for her money. Oops, there was envy rearing its ugly head again.

By contrast, Adam's woman—me—was sorely lacking. My light brown hair was thick and hung past my shoulders, with natural (yes, they really were natural) blonde streaks. My face wouldn't scare small children, but neither did it invite many double takes. If I were totally honest, I thought I had great cheekbones—I had been complimented on them more than once and it puffed up my vanity a bit. My brown eyes were ordinary, as was the rest of me, and I would never be mistaken for a Barbie doll. Being tall, when I stood next to Michelle, I felt like an Amazon woman. I was on the thin side—I liked to call it "willowy." I thought that sounded better than skinny.

The scar on the left side of my face was three and a half inches long—I know; I measured it. It was close to my hairline, so most people didn't see it unless they were next to me. I forgot about it most of the time, until that moment in a conversation when the person talking to me noticed it. Most people tried not to stare, but their efforts made me even more self-conscious and I refused to explain unless I was asked about it directly.

Poor Adam. I hoped he didn't make the same comparisons between Michelle and me. What did he see in me, anyway? I didn't have a Lexus, I drove a Chevy. I wasn't even a sweet spirit. I depressed myself so much with my thoughts that I couldn't eat Lily's homemade chocolate cake.

Lily wouldn't let that pass. "You must still be sick if you're turning down cake. Someone call 9-1-1." Everyone laughed and I tried to go along with it. My attempt was half-hearted though.

"Yeah I guess I'm not doing as well as I thought I was. I'd better head home." As I got ready to leave, Adam walked me out to my car.

We sat outside for awhile talking, mainly about school. I was taking classes during summer semester. I had also taken CLEP tests and satisfied a lot of my general ed requirements already. I only needed thirty-three more credits to graduate. That practically made me a senior. When I told Adam, he was suitably impressed.

"I can't believe you stuffed three years of college into two. Brains and beauty! How lucky can a guy get?" Adam's words lifted my spirits again. The kiss he followed up with helped as well.

"So, you don't feel like you got the raw end of the deal? I mean, I'm no beauty queen, like some people." Yes, I fished for compliments. But being around Michelle seemed to make me need them.

"Hey, you're not comparing yourself to Michelle, are you?" Adam knew my insecurities well, it seemed. "You've never had anything to worry about there, Kit, don't you know you're beautiful to me?" He stroked my face, lightly tracing my scar with his thumb. "Even this scar makes you more beautiful, because it reminds me of your faith; how hard you've struggled, and how much you've overcome. Don't compare yourself to anyone else. You are who you need to be."

If the glow I felt inside at Adam's words had reflected on the outside, the night would have lit up like a sunny day. Adam made me feel so special; maybe there was hope that I would get over all my self-criticism.

had class the next day, so I couldn't spend it all with Adam. It was probably just as well, because we both had things we needed to get done. I wasn't so smitten that I would throw away all my plans—especially the ones involving school. I felt driven to do my best, and when I got less than an A, it was hard not to beat myself up about it.

I was majoring in Accounting. I liked it when things worked out neatly and I could quantify everything; it felt safe.

Last year when I was learning about the gospel, I had come to terms with the circumstances of my birth—which to my knowledge consisted of being abandoned shortly after birth in a public restroom. My adoptive parents had always treated me like their own child. I had no complaints on that issue; rather, I struggled with feeling worthless, having been discarded like garbage by the one person who was supposed to love me no matter what.

When I gained a testimony and knew that I was a daughter of God, it changed how I thought about a lot of things. I had been rather self-centered (and probably still was), but through gospel teachings and the example of others—Janet was the best example I could have had—I thought a lot about how I could make a difference in the lives of others.

Last October, when I really felt the seeds of faith finally swelling inside of me, I thought about serving a mission. I asked Barbara about it, feeling kind of silly because she was Adam's mom, but she encouraged me to pray about it. I did, but I really didn't feel the burning desire that I thought I should feel if I was supposed to serve a mission. Still, it was there in the back of my mind, and I considered discussing it with Adam.

I didn't want to talk to him about it through letters though, so I decided to wait until he got home. I wondered what he would think. Would he wait for me? I calculated that I wouldn't turn twenty-one until Adam had been back for almost a year, then I would be gone another eighteen months. Even if he would wait, was that what I really wanted?

As I thought more about it, I realized I didn't really want to serve a mission. I still wanted to do something—something that mattered. I was talking to my friend Tara Knight about it. Tara and I were in the same student ward and had become friends when we were both put in charge of the Linger Longers, the ward socials for students, and we discovered we were both waiting for missionaries (luckily not the same one!).

Tara lived at home, too, but she was majoring in Family, Consumer, and Human Development. She convinced me to take a couple of classes with her. We took the Marriage and Family Relationships class together in the spring and I took a human development class as well. I was surprised at how much I liked it. I found out I could minor in FCHD, which I decided to do.

We were taking Family Crises and Intervention together during summer semester, and I was excited to see Tara. Of course, she knew all about Adam from my constant rambling about him. I slid into the seat next to her.

"So, how did it go? How was the big day? Is he as wonderful as you remembered?" Tara peppered me with questions. "Tell me all about it!" (As if I needed encouragement to talk about Adam.)

"Okay, so you know how I missed class so I could go to the airport with Adam's family? Well, I woke up so sick, you wouldn't believe it!" I gave her all the gory details of my illness and the tragic result of not being able to meet Adam at the airport.

"I'll just die if I can't meet Eric at the airport when he comes home." Her missionary wasn't coming home for eight more months;

she had a while to wait. "I'm sorry you were sick. Did you get to see Adam yesterday?"

I told her how much fun it was to be with Adam again. I tried not to go on and on, because I remembered all too well how irritating it could be to have someone gush about their boyfriend when yours was far away on a mission.

Tara wanted to hear more, though. "So did he pop the question yet?"

"Tara! He's been home for two whole days—that's just a little premature, don't you think?" I didn't mention that my brother, Dave, had asked me the very same thing last night.

"Well, you said you guys have talked about it. I just wondered if you'd set a date yet. It's never too early to plan!"

I decided to turn the tables on her. "Have you and Eric set a date? He'll be home in only eight months. I hear it's never too early to plan!"

She laughed at me. "As a matter of fact, we have. Well, sort of. He'll be home in February, and we think a June wedding would be super. That way we'll have the summer to honeymoon! That is if I haven't 'Dear Johned' him before then!" Tara was always joking about not waiting for Eric. She was a big flirt and I wouldn't be surprised if poor old Eric did receive a "Dear John" letter from her sometime during the next eight months.

We stopped talking as our professor began her lecture. Before she got into the class material, she made an announcement about a special lecture that would give us extra credit. My ears perked up at that; I liked extra credit. The lecture was that evening and a professor from BYU was coming to speak.

Before I could say anything, Tara leaned over and asked, "Will you go with me tonight? It's that lecture I was telling you about. Remember?"

I vaguely remembered Tara trying to get me to go to something with her, but I hadn't committed because it was set for a couple of days after Adam got home. Between Tara's urging and the lure of extra credit, I agreed to pick her up later that night.

After class I called Adam and we talked for awhile. He had been searching the "help wanted" ads for a job and had put in his application at a couple of places. I told him about the lecture and that I wanted to go with Tara.

"I think you should go," Adam said. "My dad has called a family council tonight, so this will work out fine. Will you come over afterwards?" I agreed to stop by when the lecture was over. I was glad that he had plans so he wouldn't feel like I was ditching him.

When I picked Tara up for the lecture, she was excited. "Guess what? I talked to my cousin Amanda this afternoon. She's the one who goes to BYU. Anyway, she's majoring in FCHD, too, and she has a class with this professor who's speaking tonight. Well, she's going to do her practicum in Romania, under a program this guy has set up. She's going for three months to work with the orphans and stuff there. It sounds so cool. This lecture tonight will tell us all about it. I think I want to go. Amanda and I are both so excited! They only take, like, ten people a semester, but wouldn't that be so awesome?" Tara could hardly sit still. She usually only got this excited about guys—mainly Eric, but guys in general worked, too.

"Romania? Why would you go all the way there? Can't you do your practicum right here?" Ugh, I sounded like my mom.

"Kit, you don't understand. It's a chance to put to use all the stuff I've been learning about. To really help somebody who needs it. There are tons of orphans in Romania. They need volunteers and you can get college credit." Tara was really into this Romania thing. "Just pay attention at the lecture. We'll find out all about it. I don't know that much, just that it sounds so cool."

There were maybe thirty-five students at the lecture. In spite of my reserved response to Tara, I was interested in hearing more about the program. For the next ninety minutes, I turned my full attention to the plight of orphans in Romania. I was prepared to be touched and to be asked for donations to help "Children Far and Wide," the organization behind the trips.

What I wasn't prepared for was how I felt at the end of the lecture. Tara started talking immediately after it ended, but I couldn't really focus on her. All I could feel was my own heart pounding like it was going to explode, and that strong feeling that I wanted—no, needed—to go to Romania.

I grabbed Tara's arm and demanded to know, "Are you really going to go?"

"Yes, Kit, I'm going. Come with me."

"Come with you? What do you mean?" Had she read my mind?

"Come to the front with me to talk to Professor Lowe. Now. I want to find out what I need to do to get signed up. Hurry up."

I kept quiet about how I was feeling as I followed Tara to the front of the room. We had to wait for a couple of other girls to finish asking questions. As we waited my thoughts ran wild. *What in the world are you thinking Kit Matthews? Adam just came home. You've been waiting for two years for him. This isn't your field of study. Why are you even considering it?*

When Professor Lowe was available, Tara did the talking. He gave her a handout that explained the program costs, dates, and everything involved. He pointed out the web address as he handed one to me, too. I took it, not saying a word.

The last thing he said was, "The application deadline for the fall semester is June 30th. So if you're serious, you'll need to move quickly."

As we walked to the car, Tara asked me what I thought. I told her about the feeling I got during the lecture; that I needed to go to Romania.

"What?" she squealed, positively giddy. If I thought she was excited before the lecture, it was nothing compared to the way she went on after I told her what I felt. "Are you serious, Kit? That would be so great if we could go together! Oh, say you'll go!"

"You're forgetting a couple of things. First of all, Adam just got home. I can't leave just after he got back. There's no way. Not to mention, I don't need a practicum. I'm majoring in business. This would in no way further my academic or personal plans. It just doesn't make sense for me to go." I could talk myself out of this wacky plan.

"Hello? You just told me that you felt a strong impression that you needed to go to Romania. How can you say it would 'in no way further your academic or personal plans?' Kit, you're always lecturing me on faith! Yet when you get a little personal revelation, you just rationalize it all away because it doesn't fit into your plans! You need to pray about it. That's what you'd tell me to do."

Tara was right. I was trying to rationalize. I tried some more. "It doesn't work for me to go and it makes no sense. I'm afraid I was just caught up in the emotion of the moment."

She challenged me. "If that's all it was, it will pass. If it's something more, it won't—unless you force it away. Pray about it. You'll get your answer. As for me, I already know I'm going. If they accept me, that is."

As I dropped Tara off at her house she reminded me, "Don't forget to pray about it." Why did I surround myself with all these spiritual people? Why?

chapter four

Although it was late, I still really wanted to see Adam. I called him to make sure it was okay if I still came by. He said he definitely wanted me to come over.

I tried to clear my mind as I headed over to see Adam. When I got there he gave me a tight hug, but he looked really somber. I knew something was wrong.

"What's the matter? Has something happened?" I was worried; Adam always had a big smile for me, but not tonight.

"Let's go sit in the swing out back," he said, "I'll tell you what's going on."

I felt a little panicky as he led me to the backyard. Was someone sick? Was he going to break up with me? I couldn't imagine what the problem could be, but I was sure it wasn't good.

"So what's going on?" I needed to know before I gave myself an anxiety attack.

"You know how I told you my dad called a family council for tonight? Well, he just found out he's losing his job. His company's been bought out by a bigger company who's using their own management team, so they let him go."

"Oh, Adam, I'm so sorry. Do you think he'll be able to get another job soon?" I was relieved that no one was sick or dying and that Adam wasn't breaking up with me; but I remembered that my dad losing his job was what caused my family to move from

California to Utah to start with.

"He's pretty discouraged. He's worried about getting another job at his age and he's been out of the job market for a long time. He was at his company almost twenty years. He's really stressed." Adam's look mirrored those feelings.

"So your dad had the family council to let you guys know what was going on?" I still didn't understand all the things the Bridgers did.

"Yeah, so there's basically no income in the household now. My dad will get some unemployment money, but that's barely enough to make the house payment, which still leaves utilities, food, insurance and everything else. You've seen our food storage, so at least we won't go hungry."

Adam was right about that. There was a big storage room in their basement with shelves that had rows and rows of canned goods, and boxes and bags of stuff. I used to joke that you could go shopping from their food storage. If my own family had to live off what was in our house, we would last maybe two weeks—with a lot of whining. I would guess the Bridger family could make it at least a year.

"That's true you have plenty of food. And knowing your parents, they probably have some money saved. That'll help now, right?" The Bridger family was a pillar of strength in my opinion. Something like a job loss wouldn't shake them.

"You've probably figured out that our family doesn't have a lot in the way of material things. I know you're not after me for my money, at least." He forced a smile. "My parents never had much in savings, but what they did have was wiped out by the expenses of Janet's funeral, plus a lot of the money was already spent on her wedding. Then they had Justin's wedding, and, of course, my mission. They don't have anything in savings. As a matter of fact, they had to take out a second mortgage to pay for some of the bills."

"Is there anything I can do?" I really wanted to help.

"I don't know right now," He shook his head in discouragement. "Do you have any idea how expensive health insurance is? I know I didn't have a clue until my dad told me. It will cost nearly a thousand dollars a month to keep health insurance coverage on the family while he's out of a job. A thousand dollars! I've just taken so much for granted."

"That's horrible! But you don't have to pay it do you? Can't you just go without insurance?" I knew that was stupid as soon as it came out of my mouth, but I didn't know what else to say.

"My mom's sick. I'm sure you've seen some of the changes since Janet's death. She's really struggling with depression and is on medication for it." The porch light caught the tears in Adam's eyes. "She sure doesn't need any more stress like my dad losing his job. I'm really worried about her, and so is my dad."

"I've been worried about her, too. What can we do? There must be some way we can help." I felt like I was part of the family and I needed to pitch in too.

"Kit, I have to tell you something. It sounds so selfish to say this right now when my parents are struggling so much. But I had plans." He turned to me, his face inches from mine. "I wanted to come home from my mission, get a job, go back to school, and ask you to marry me. Not this way—I'd planned a romantic proposal, and I wanted to make sure I had a way to support you. I also figured I had a few weeks or months for us to have fun together and just be young and happy."

My heart leaped at the thrill of his near-proposal and declaration that he wanted to marry me. I sensed he had more to say, though.

"It's hard to adjust to life in the real world when you get back from your mission. It's just too soon to have problems like this thrust on me. But, Kit, I'm telling you now—I love you and want to marry you."

I wanted to shout with joy at his words. Somehow I knew there was another "but" coming, and it did.

"But, I'm just worried about my family. They need my help now. That means you and I have to sacrifice for a while longer." Adam leaned in and gave me a long kiss.

He suddenly pulled back and before I could say anything he said, "Unless you want to elope tonight?" He grinned to let me know he was joking.

All kidding aside, I wanted to run away with him then; just the two of us, without complications and responsibilities. Instead, I gave him the answer I knew he really wanted. "I'll only elope with you if it's to the temple, at the right time."

"I knew I could count on you when I got weak, Carson." He took my hands in his then raised them to his lips and kissed each one of them. "But I definitely heard a yes in there."

"When the time is right, and the place is right, you'll hear a yes in there," I said. "But it sounds like right now, you need to be there for your parents. I'm sure you have a new plan, to replace your old one." I struggled not to let my disappointment sound in my voice. Would there always be something to come between us?

Adam told me that he and Justin stayed after the family council to talk to his parents. They had each offered to help out during the time their dad was out of work. Justin said that he and Michelle could give a little bit of money each month until their dad got another job.

Adam had committed a third of whatever he earned to go to his parents. He still wanted to start school in the fall, if he could save enough for tuition. He also still needed to find a job.

"Can I keep paying the fifty dollars I've been paying towards your mission?" I asked. I had taken over Janet's contribution after she died; it made me feel closer to both her and Adam.

"I don't think my parents would accept it. But thanks for the offer."

We sat out on the swing a little while longer, not really talking, just holding hands. I loved Adam so much, and although I knew it could be quite awhile before he "popped the question" for real, and I was disappointed, I was impressed with his reasons for the delay.

Later, as I was getting ready for bed, I realized that Adam had driven all thoughts of Romania out of my head. I felt kind of silly thinking about it now. It had seemed so important earlier in the evening, but as I brushed my teeth I wondered if I even needed to pray about it. I didn't want to leave Adam, I knew that much. What if the Bridger family needed my help?

There were so many reasons not to go, but once it was back in my mind, it wouldn't leave. I knelt down and said my prayers, asking a special blessing on Hal and Barbara, and said all of the other things I usually prayed about. I climbed into bed and tried to clear my mind. I wasn't going to go to Romania. I didn't need to ask, I already knew.

An hour later, when it was clear that sleep was no closer than it had been an hour earlier, I resignedly got out of my bed and back onto my knees. I knew what I needed to ask. Then I could go to sleep. As I prayed, asking the question I had tried to avoid, my heart started pounding like it had earlier that evening.

I didn't want to go and it was against my better judgment, but as I crawled back into bed, I knew I was going to Romania. I still couldn't sleep, but it was for an entirely different reason this time.

I climbed out of bed again and found the paper I'd gotten from Professor Lowe. I booted up my laptop and logged on to the Internet. I found the site easily with the web address on the flyer. I read everything possible on the site, going to every link. When my eyes burned too much to continue, I crawled back into bed. I felt a sense of peace, and as I drifted off, I had the thought that I wasn't trying to counsel the Lord anymore—I was ready to let Him counsel me.

chapter five

In the light of day, I had to face some realities. The program would cost about thirty-five hundred dollars. I also had to find out if I could get credit from USU for going.

Because I had concentrated so hard on going to school, I'd only worked part-time and had very little in savings. My parents covered my tuition and books, and I lived at home rent-free. I figured they would be more likely to back me up in this plan if I could get college credit for it.

I wanted to talk to Adam as soon as possible, yet I also felt reluctant to tell him so soon after he got home. I considered just signing up to make the deadline, and then telling him in a few weeks when we were more settled. That was very tempting but it didn't feel very honest, plus I really wanted Adam's approval.

My thoughts turned back to the money issue. I could ask for more hours at work and scrimp on my spending, and save up at least half of the program costs myself. If I showed my parents I was willing to put that much into it, they would probably take the news a little easier. If they wouldn't pay for half, maybe they would lend me the money and let me pay them back.

I thought I would handle the college credit issue first. I called to see if my advisor was in, and she actually had a time she could meet with me that morning. Then I called Tara and told her I had decided to go to Romania. I had to hold the phone away from my ear to keep her screeching from damaging my ear drum.

"I'm so glad you're going! What made you decide? Have you told Adam? What do your parents think?" She didn't give me a chance to answer any of her questions before she continued. "My mom had a fit about me going overseas. She kept telling me all the bad things that could happen to me. I finally asked her to call Aunt Sharon, Amanda's mom. That calmed her down, because Aunt Sharon had already researched the whole program and feels good about Amanda going. So did your mom freak out like mine?"

"I haven't talked to my parents or Adam yet. You're the first person I've told. I figure if I can still get college credit, then maybe my parents will take it a little better. Will you come with me to talk with my advisor?" I needed someone who would support me in this scheme.

"Of course I will. When did you want to go?"

Feeling relieved, I arranged to pick her up in an hour. I had just hung up the phone with Tara when it rang again. It was Adam.

"Hey, Carson, it's your favorite scout," He sounded pretty upbeat.

"Hey, Bridger, what's up?"

"I've got a job interview this morning and wondered if you could give me a ride. Our Suburban is out of commission too—it needs a new transmission. Perfect timing, of course. If you could give me a ride I'd be eternally in your debt."

"Eternally? Just for a ride? I like the sound of that. What time is your interview? I need to meet with my advisor this morning and I'm leaving in about an hour."

"My interview's in an hour, too. I can just ride my bike, and we can catch up later."

"Don't be silly, Adam. I can drop you off on my way. Where is it?"

"It's at the home improvement center where I used to work."

"How come you have to go through an interview again? I'd think they would hire you, based on the fact you already worked there."

"Yeah, it's pretty lame. I already know how to do the job, but they've changed some hiring procedures, so I have to go through the interview process again. Are you sure you don't mind dropping me off on your way?"

"I don't mind a bit. I'm not sure how long I'll be at my appointment with my advisor, but I'm guessing about half an hour. If you don't mind hanging out after your interview, I'll come back and pick you up." I knew Tara wouldn't mind if I had to drop her off in a hurry; she would understand.

"That'd be great, Kit. Can you pick me up in about forty-five minutes?"

"I'll see you then." I hung up and really had to hurry to get myself ready to go.

I was about five minutes late for my meeting, and quickly realized I could have just gotten my answer over the phone. It took less than ten minutes to realize there was no way I could get college credit for going to Romania. My major didn't require a practicum, and I didn't meet the prerequisites necessary to take one in the FCHD major.

My advisor asked me why I wanted to disrupt my education path. "If you want to travel to Europe, why don't you go over summer break? If you stick with your current track, you'll graduate next May. Why don't you wait until then to go to Romania?"

It made sense. Why was I set on going to Romania in September? If I went in the fall, it would set my graduation back by a semester. My parents would never understand. I didn't understand why I was even considering it.

As we drove back to Tara's house she asked, "Do you want my opinion?" She usually didn't ask me, she just gave it.

"Yeah, I do. What do you think?"

"You know I want us to go together, but I don't want you to go just for me. I don't blame you if you wait until you graduate. I think if you wait until then, you'll never go. You and Adam will get married, and you'll miss out on this experience. I know it goes against all your practical, planning ways, but if you felt the impression to go, then maybe there's a reason for it."

"Thanks, Tara. I'm just afraid I'm not really being inspired." I felt afraid—period. I was afraid of losing Adam and fearful of what lay in store for me in Romania. "It doesn't make any sense to me.

If I really am being inspired, that's even scarier, because it means I have to go. I'm not sure I can overcome all of the obstacles to get there. I felt kind of stupid when my advisor told me to just wait until I graduate. That makes the most sense. That, or not going at all." I was as confused as I sounded.

"I think you're afraid to tell Adam and your parents. Why don't you talk to them and get their input? They might be more supportive than you think." Tara was right. Talking to them was one more thing I was afraid of.

"You're right," I agreed out loud. "I'll talk to them. Maybe I just need them to talk some sense into me."

"Let me know how it goes. You know I'm hoping you'll come with me, but I totally understand if you can't. But don't talk yourself out of it before you even talk to them. Promise?"

I promised. Then I dropped her at her house and went to pick up Adam.

I got to the home improvement center before Adam was finished so I just waited in my car for about fifteen minutes until he came out.

"You're looking at a man with a job! The pay isn't great, but they'll give me forty hours a week and I start tomorrow! Let's celebrate; I'll buy lunch! What sounds good?"

I suggested pizza, so we went to our favorite pizza place just off campus. It was a perfect place for a conversation. It was clear he was relieved to have found a job so quickly.

"So what did your advisor have to say?" Adam brought up the subject before I got around to it.

"Well I asked to meet with her because I had a question about fall semester. I wanted to talk to you about it. You'll probably think I'm really weird when I tell you."

"I already know you're weird, Kit, that's part of what I love about you! What was your question?" Adam's teasing was reassuring, so I went on.

"Okay, it's kind of a long story, but I think if I start at the beginning, it'll make more sense. Or at least it will sound less crazy." The waiter came with our drinks and I gratefully took a big swallow.

"We've got lots of time, Kit. Fire away."

"You know I've really struggled to gain a testimony and to have faith, right?" Adam nodded and I went on. "Only you and Janet really know how I've struggled. There were so many times I wished I could talk to Janet, or to you, face to face. Well I didn't have either one of you close by where I wanted you, and now I think, in a way, it helped me to turn to the Lord. My faith grew when I had to rely on it—even when I thought it didn't really exist."

Adam nodded. "We do grow the most when we have to rely directly on the Lord. I think that's one of the reasons missionaries are called to serve away from their homes and families; the one constant is the Lord. He's there no matter where we go, or how far away we are; it's just up to us to seek Him."

"See, you understand it. When you left to serve a mission, I couldn't figure out why you would do it. I couldn't see what would drive you to leave everything that you cared about to go among strangers and serve them. After Janet died, I prayed to know that God was real, and I got an answer. That was when I caught a glimpse of what motivated you; why you would be willing to give up so much to serve. I started to feel like I wanted to do something, but I didn't know what I could do."

Adam had been listening attentively, and I saw a look of understanding cross his face. "Kit, are you telling me you want to go on a mission?"

His question caught me off guard. "Oh, no, that's not what I'm saying. I did think about a mission; I even prayed about it, but it didn't seem like the right answer for me. I just really envisioned you coming home, and you and I, well, you know . . ."

"Are you proposing to me, Kit? Is that what you're saying?" Adam was laughing at my embarrassment, and at that point I could feel my face burning and knew I must be beet red.

"No! You already proposed to me, at least I think you did. Didn't you?" Somehow this was not going the way I had envisioned it.

"Oh, so you're not going on a mission and you're not proposing to me! This isn't a 'Dear John' then is it? You didn't bring me here to a public place to break up with me, did you? And to think, just when I'd gotten a job and could actually spend money on you."

Adam's drama made me laugh. Luckily, the waiter came with our pizza, which gave me a few seconds to compose myself. While Adam dished the thick, cheesy slices I tried again.

"I'm going to try to get back to the point of the story. You're not making this easy by teasing me. I have something serious to say."

He tried to look apologetic. "I'm sorry, I'll be serious," he said with his mouth full, cheese stringing from his mouth to the piece of pizza in his hand. Of course I started laughing again, so I gave up trying to talk, and just enjoyed the pizza perfection.

After we'd each eaten a couple of slices, Adam spoke up. "Okay, Kit, you were telling me that you were talking to your advisor about serving a mission. So then what happened?"

"I didn't say anything of the sort, Adam Bridger! If you want to hear what I have to say, then you'll have to be quiet and listen. Here, have some more pizza." I shoved another thick slice onto his plate. He didn't protest.

"I told you I took a couple of classes with my friend, Tara. She's an FCHD major. I liked the classes so much, I decided to minor in FCHD. So remember that lecture I went to last night, before I came over to your house? Well, I went for extra credit and so Tara wouldn't have to go alone. The guy who spoke is from BYU and he's in charge of this program where people go to Romania to work in an orphanage or hospital for a semester. Tara has to take a practicum, which is like an internship or student teaching, for her major. Going to Romania with this program counts as her practicum. She's going to go this September, for three months." My nervousness started to fade as I saw Adam was listening attentively.

I continued. "What I didn't count on is how I would feel when I heard about the orphans in Romania. When I heard about the program, it's like I knew—I just knew—I had to go this fall. Me. Go to Romania. For a semester." I wanted to make sure I'd said it as plainly as I could. Adam seemed to understand.

"So you feel like you need to go to Romania this fall with your friend, Tara, to work in the orphanage there, for your practicum." Adam repeated back to me.

"Yeah. Only I don't need a practicum. I can't get college credit for going. That's why I had to talk to my advisor." I watched for his reaction. He seemed mighty calm, much calmer than I felt.

"Were you only thinking of going to get credit, like a study abroad thing?" Adam asked.

"No. I wish that were the only reason. I feel like I'm supposed to go to Romania. I even prayed about it. I didn't want to, but I did."

"What answer did you get?" Adam took this news way too easily.

"I need to go to Romania. Do you think I'm crazy?" I wanted his reassurance.

"I don't think you're crazy at all. Do you think you are?" He always asked more questions than he answered.

"Adam, you just got home. I don't want to leave you. Couldn't I just help orphans here at home? My parents won't understand, and I can't afford to go without their help. Another thing, I could graduate next May if I stick with my current plan. If I go to Romania, then it will really mess things up!" I wanted Adam to talk me out of it. I wanted him to convince me to stay home with him.

He didn't look happy, but didn't waver as he answered me. "Kit, I don't want to be apart from you either. But if you tell me you feel like you need to go and you've prayed about it and had it confirmed, then I'll support you. It'll work out. I know it will. So, if you leave in September, when exactly do you get back?"

"I'd be back the first week in December." With Adam's support, I couldn't use him as a crutch to back out of what I knew I had to do. I managed a smile and said, "Thanks—I think."

chapter six

We stopped by Adam's house and I showed him the website for Children Far and Wide. We looked up the program dates and downloaded the application form.

Adam read through the form and the checklist we printed off. "It sounds like they know what they're doing. Look, they even hook you up with a tutor to help you learn a little bit of the language and about the culture. I think this will be a really great experience."

"Do you think so? I don't know why I feel so drawn to it, but I do. Maybe it's because I never knew my birth parents and so I feel a kinship to these children. I'm nervous, that's for sure. I only have until the end of the month to get my application in."

"Yeah, you need to get busy. You have to get your shots and apply for a passport. You'll have to expedite it." Adam pulled up a website that had instructions for applying for passports and downloaded the application for me.

"Wow, you're in a hurry to get rid of me!" I complained. "Are you going to pack my suitcase too?"

"No, I just figured it would help you out if we printed this stuff off as we think about it. I'm a little jealous of the adventure you get to have. I wanted to serve a foreign mission, and I kind of wish I could go to Romania with you. You'll have to make sure you email me a lot."

"Don't worry, I will," I promised.

"It's kind of like we're reversing roles here for awhile. You'll be off serving far away from everyone you know, and I'll be staying here working my butt off with school and work. At least we have a couple of months together before you go." His words reassured me.

"And it's not like I'll be gone for two years, I'll only be gone for three months. It'll pass before we know it, right?"

"Right. I have a feeling the time will fly by. I'll miss you, but I think it will be a good thing overall." Adam gave me a big hug. "Just don't fall for any Romanian guys while you're over there." He followed up with a couple of kisses that left me feeling dizzy.

"That's one thing you don't have to worry about. And don't you go falling for any women, Romanian or otherwise, while I'm gone."

I left in time for dinner, determined to talk to my parents. I was glad to see that my brother was out with friends.

After we dished our plates, I jumped right into the subject. "Mom, Dad, there's something I really want to do, but I need your help."

"What is it, dear?" my mom asked. I had their attention; I think it was partially because I rarely asked for their help.

I told them about my plans to go to Romania and waited for the explosion.

My father spoke first, so it was still calm. "You mean you want to go to Romania to volunteer in an orphanage?"

"Yes." This wasn't so bad. Then my mom let loose.

"What in the world has possessed you? You're kidding, right? Do you have any idea what people in other countries think of Americans, Kit? It's just not safe. Get this idea out of your head—immediately!" Yep, that was my mom.

I wasn't giving up. "Mom, let me tell you more about it before you make a snap judgment. I've done some research—"

She interrupted me, eyes blazing. "I don't need research to know that it's dangerous going to a foreign country! What if you were kidnapped or something? There are terrorists over there! You don't even speak the language."

"I would be traveling with a group of students and they have mentors there, housing set up, and the program is already in place. I really want to go. Dad?" I looked for cooler heads to prevail, although my dad almost always deferred to my mom.

"Why do you want to go to Romania in particular? If you want to do volunteer work, I'm sure there are plenty of opportunities here in Cache Valley." At least he was asking questions instead of forbidding me to go. That was a good sign.

"I know it doesn't sound like me, and it doesn't fit into the plans I had to finish school by next spring, but I am serious about it. It's hard to explain, but I've been—I don't know—searching, I guess, for what I can do to serve others. I even considered going on a mission for the Church, but that wasn't for me—"

"Adam's put this into your head, hasn't he?" my mom accused. "Filling your head with missions and who knows what else! I don't mind you going to that church, but if they expect you to travel to the other side of the world, that's where I put my foot down!" She was starting to sound irrational. I didn't know if I could reason with her.

"Mom, this has nothing to do with Adam or the Church. It's personal. It's so personal that I don't know how to explain it to you guys. I'll try, if you'll just listen."

She started to say something, but my dad put his hand on her arm and said, "Nora, wait. Let's just hear Kit out. We need to let her finish." His touch seemed to calm her a bit.

"Okay, I was trying to tell you that I've wanted to do something meaningful to help others. I had no idea what until I heard about this program called Children Far and Wide. It touched me, and I just knew I needed to do this. Maybe it has to do with the fact that there are so many children who not only will never know their birth parents, but they'll probably never be adopted by parents who will love them and take care of them. I've been blessed with a family who loves me, and this is a small way I can share part of that blessing with others who aren't so fortunate." I desperately hoped they understood my need to go.

"When would you leave?" My dad spoke again; I took my mother's silence as progress in the right direction.

"It's a three-month program. I'd leave the first week of September and come back the first week of December. I would miss a semester of school, so I wouldn't graduate in spring, but I've already stuffed three years of college into two, so it wouldn't be like I wasn't graduating on time, it just wouldn't be as early."

"It would be worth it to you to miss a semester of college? After all, you've set this accelerated pace for yourself; it was your own goal to graduate in three years instead of four." My dad was still asking the questions, and my mom was still silent—both good signs. "And how is this program funded?"

"It is worth it to me. I know I've pushed myself to finish school early, and I'm shocked that something like this would change my priorities, but it has. It costs about thirty-five hundred dollars for the program. That includes airfare, housing, food, and allows for a little spending money. I can save half by September. I wondered if you guys would consider paying the other half. If not, maybe you could lend me the money and I'd pay you back when I get home." I realized I was holding my breath, waiting for their response.

My mother spoke again, although she didn't seem quite as riled up as before. "So you're asking us to support you in this mad scheme? You want us to let you go halfway around the world, put yourself in unnecessary danger, and pay for the privilege? I thought I'd heard everything." She rolled her eyes and let out a loud sigh—a sure sign I'd greatly disappointed her.

My dad shushed her and asked, "What does Adam think of you going away so soon after he returned from his mission? I was under the impression that you two were just waiting for him to get back so you could get married. How does this figure into your plans?"

He caught me off guard with that question. I'd expected my mom to ask about my relationship with Adam, but I didn't think my dad even knew that much about it. Apparently, he noticed more than I thought he did.

The one thing I did know was that they both thought I was too young to get married. Even though I was twenty years old and knew plenty of people who were married at eighteen or nineteen, my parents held the view that I was just too young. I realized this could play to my advantage.

"Adam and I have talked about it, and he supports me. He knows I'm not making this decision lightly. Now is the time for me to have this sort of experience, before I settle down and get married.

I waited for him for two years, I'm sure he can wait for me for three months. It's not like we're in a big hurry to get married, anyway."

I saw a glint of hope in my mother's eyes. "So you're not thinking of getting engaged before you go, are you?" She didn't mask her eagerness well.

"No, we both have things to do before we get engaged." Given the financial situation of the Bridger family and Adam's commitment to help them, I was pretty certain we wouldn't get engaged before I left.

My mom relaxed a little at that point. "Your father and I would like to see the literature you have about this program. I want your father to check out the legitimacy and safety of this whole thing before we commit to it." That was a major change of tune for her. I could hardly believe it.

My father nodded and said, "Get me the information, Kit. I want to check out this program with a couple of other faculty members. Some of these programs are excellent and some of them are scams, out to take your money. We won't send you if we don't think it's safe."

"That's great! Thank you guys so much for considering it. I know it came out of the blue, but it means so much to me. The application deadline is in less than two weeks, so can you please hurry? I have to get shots and apply for a passport and figure out everything I need to do. Do you guys want to see the website?" I knew I was babbling, but I was so relieved that they had practically said yes.

My mother reminded me that we needed to finish dinner first, but afterwards they both sat down with me and looked at the website. I could tell by the time we were finished that they were feeling more comfortable about the whole thing. Knowing my parents, I was pretty sure they'd say yes once my dad had investigated it a little more.

I went up to my room feeling elated. I couldn't wait to tell Adam and Tara. I was going to Romania!

chapter seven

My parents agreed to pay for half of my expenses, Tara and I were both accepted into the program, and the time flew by as we got ready to go to Romania.

I didn't see Adam nearly as much as I wanted to, although we did talk on the phone every day. I wished he had a cell phone so I could text him, but that was lower on his list of priorities. His parents had taught him to budget and he actually listened.

On one of the rare evenings we had together, he asked me if I had worked out a budget for Romania.

"Well, just in my head. Why?"

"Would you mind if we worked out the actual figures? I'd feel better if I knew all the bases were covered. I've got a budget spreadsheet that we can start with if you want." He was already sitting down at the computer pulling up the program.

"Sure, let's do it." Being an accounting major, I was familiar with budgets and I expected to see a simple list of expenses, like the one I had stored in my brain.

I was surprised as I looked at the spreadsheet Adam had opened up. Not only did he have a list of expenses, but he also had an income section, a variance section, and a running balance for his checking account.

He started to explain the numbers. "I know there's software that'll do all of this stuff, but I didn't want to spend money on it.

See, the income section allows you to change the pay rate or the hours and it recalculates automatically. Things that are a percentage item like taxes or tithing recalculates as well."

I gave a laugh and said, "Holy cow, Adam! You made this just for your own budget? This looks like something Justin would come up with. I don't think I need anything this complicated."

"You're right," He shrugged. "I got it from Justin. It helps me to plug in the numbers so I can figure out what I'm bringing in and what I have to pay. We'll just modify it for you and save it on your pen drive. Copy it to your laptop and update it as things change."

"Smile." I said.

"What?" Adam looked confused.

"Smile." I repeated.

Adam complied but gave me a strange look. "Why did you want me to smile?"

"You were sounding so much like Justin that I had to see your dimple to make sure it was really you!" I dodged away from him just as he lunged at me.

"I'm just trying to help you, you ungrateful wench!" He caught me before I made it out of the office door. He wouldn't let me go until I'd paid the penalty—a kiss, which was really no penalty at all.

I pulled away. "You're right, you are Adam. The lips know." I tapped my lips and smiled in what I hoped was a mysterious way.

"And how would you know the difference between us with a kiss?" Adam's dimple was not showing at that moment.

"Easy. I've kissed you a lot, and I've never kissed Justin. What did you think I meant?" I tried for an innocent look to match my tone.

"Very funny, Kit. Do you want help with this or not?" He was trying not to smile, I could tell.

"I want help. But, if I'm going to divulge my deep dark financial secrets to you, I want to see yours first. Deal?"

"Deal. Look all you want. My life is an open book; or I should say—an open spreadsheet." He moved over so I could sit down at the desk. I was curious to see the details; I knew he and his family didn't have a lot of money, so it was interesting to see how he had things planned out.

I saw he had tithing at the top of the list, followed by a third of his net pay going to his family to help while Hal was unemployed. His list of expenses was short; college tuition and books, car, and spending. I could see that almost everything was being set aside for college; nothing was going towards a car, and only a token amount was set aside for spending money.

I felt a little guilty about Adam spending any money on me at all when I saw the actual figures he was working with. It didn't take an accounting major to figure out that what little money he had, he spent on me.

"Wow. I'm impressed with how disciplined you are, Adam. You're not saving anything for a car yet. Are you discouraged about it?"

"Yeah, sometimes I get frustrated, but my main goals right now are to save enough for school, and to help my family while my dad's out of work. I'm meeting those two goals, so I'm okay. I wish I had more money to spend on you, though. I'd like to take you out more, to places other than the dollar movie."

"Well, look on the bright side," I quipped. "When I leave for Romania in September, you'll be able to save that dollar, too!" At least I didn't have to worry about Adam dating someone else while I was gone; he wouldn't be able to afford it.

"I guess that's the silver lining then." He smiled at my effort. "You know, as much as I'll miss you, you'll be less of a distraction if you're halfway around the world. I'll be busy with work, school, and homework. And checking e-mails; which I should be getting a lot of, right? Hopefully, my dad will have a job long before you get back, so that'll relieve a lot of stress."

"How is the job search going, anyway?" I hadn't been hanging around the Bridgers' house very much for the past few weeks; I had been so engrossed in my preparations for Romania that I kept forgetting to ask about Hal and Barbara.

"There just aren't very many job openings at his level. He's discouraged, and follows up on every lead he finds. He spent most of the evenings last week working on the Suburban transmission. It's running again, but it was expensive just for the parts. It was amazing, though, to see how much it cheered him up to be able to fix something. He's felt pretty helpless lately."

"How's your mom doing? I thought she seemed a little better since you got home, but I haven't seen her much lately." I realized I missed my talks with Barbara.

"You know, depression is tough to live with—for everybody in the family. My parents try to shelter us, I think. I don't know if that's the best answer or not. I talked to my mom about it and told her that I think the younger kids understand a lot more than she thinks they do. The changes in her scared me. I didn't know what was wrong at first. When I found out that she had been diagnosed with clinical depression, I was actually relieved, because it explained some of the changes."

"Lily told me your mom doesn't like to talk about it. Why is it so hard for her?"

"She's really struggled with being sick, especially because you can't see what's wrong with her. She thinks if she had a broken leg with a cast for all to see, that it would be more acceptable. I think she needs the evidence herself, not that she really cares what people think. She has a hard time accepting that she can't just pull herself up by her bootstraps and snap out of it. It took a while for my dad to convince her to try medication, but she finally did. I guess there were side effects from the medication so she stopped taking it and had to start the whole process over."

"I've never had to deal with depression, so I can't even imagine how she feels. It's hard to believe that she even has it. She's always the one doing things for others." Even when Barbara seemed really down, she always asked how I was doing.

"My mom's great at cutting everyone else slack; but she doesn't allow herself to be imperfect. It's hard. She's been through a lot, and my dad losing his job doesn't really help matters."

I felt bad for Hal and Barbara, but I also felt proud of Adam for the way he stepped up to help his family. He asked what I was thinking.

"I love the way you help your family," I told him. "I wonder if I could be that unselfish if the situations were reversed. I guess that's just one more reason I love you." I gave him a tight squeeze.

He returned the hug and said, "You're not selfish, at all. You're going to Romania as a volunteer; I'd say that's pretty unselfish. And you're putting your schooling on hold, not to mention your amazing boyfriend. But don't worry, we'll both be right here when you get back."

"You mean both you and my amazing boyfriend?" I couldn't resist twisting his words a bit.

"I meant both me and school. But now I'm hurt. Here I was thinking you thought I was amazing, and now my bubble has been burst." Adam gave an injured sniff that I'm certain I taught him.

"Wow you're pretty good at fishing for compliments. If I told you how amazing you were, what conversation would be left for you to have with yourself? Now, let's stop talking about you, and get to work on my budget."

I turned back to the spreadsheet and hit the "save as" button. I named the new spreadsheet "URamazing2" to see if he noticed. I could tell by his smile that he did, even though he didn't say anything.

We spent the next little while putting my budget numbers into the spreadsheet. It didn't take too long to drop in my numbers. It was kind of neat to see that I would meet my goal with a little bit of a cushion.

When we were convinced we hadn't missed anything, I commented on the small surplus. "I think I should take you out for ice cream, Captain Amazing."

He put up a little resistance, but I had tools to wear him down and I wasn't afraid to use them. A few minutes later, we were headed out for ice cream—my treat.

chapter eight

Adam and I were enjoying our ice cream when I heard someone—a female someone—call out his name.

"Adam!" A pretty brunette scurried over to our table. "I swear I see you everywhere!" She had bright blue eyes that sparkled when they lit on Adam. She gave me a cursory glance then turned her attention back to him.

"Hi, Ruth," Adam greeted her without a lot of enthusiasm, I noticed happily.

"How is your dad's job search going? I checked at work, and I'm sure I can get him on there; you know, until he finds something in his field." She beamed at him as she waited for his answer.

"My dad hasn't found anything yet. I haven't talked to him about your idea of him working a few hours a week, but I will." He turned towards me. "Ruth, I don't think you've met my girlfriend, Kit Matthews." Adam's introduction forced her to acknowledge me. Before he could continue, she held out her hand to shake mine. I noticed her French-manicured acrylic nails.

"I'm Ruth Randall. Just call me Ruth. You know, 'Entreat me not to leave thee . . . Whither thou goest I will go'. Get it? Ruth—from the Old Testament. That's me! Well, I'm not actually from the Old Testament, but I am named after her. And I am loyal. I'm sorry, what was your name again?" Her words gushed forth in a fountain of self-importance.

I stared at her for a few seconds as I shook her hand, and tried to absorb the stuff she rattled off. I was familiar enough with the scriptures by then to figure out that she was telling me she was named after Ruth from the Old Testament, but why would anyone introduce themselves that way? She didn't seem to notice my failure to answer her, because she kept right on talking.

"I work with Adam. I'm sort of one of his bosses, actually! I do HR for the company and I'm the office manager there. I'm also in his ward. What a small world! Of course, that's not why I hired him. My uncle is the stake president. You've probably heard of him, President Lant? I'm living with them right now. I'm working on my master's degree at USU, in addition to working full time." She sighed dramatically. "It will take me longer, I know, but it will be so worth it! Sometimes you just know you're in the right place at the right time. Life is just so busy!" Ruth took a breath, twisted a long dark curl around her finger, turned back towards Adam, and kept chattering.

"It's so fun to see you outside of work and church. Just think, we'll probably see each other on campus, too. Well I don't want to interrupt so I'll just say bye-bye and I'll see you tomorrow!" She reached out and squeezed his arm. "Don't stay out too late!"

Ruth Randall left our table without glancing my way again. I watched her bounce back up to the counter to order her ice cream. She was a curvy little thing; not chunky, but round in the right places. Her curly brown hair tumbled every which way as she smiled and greeted everyone she passed. Even from the back, she bubbled with energy. I couldn't hear what she was saying, but I could tell she was still talking—constantly.

After she paid for her order, I was afraid she might come trotting back over to join us, but luckily she just looked our way and said, "Toodles!" and left.

I turned back to find Adam watching me, watching her. "What was that?" I asked him.

"That, as you probably figured out, is one of the managers at work. She's a, um, well, how can I put this . . . ?" Adam searched for the right words.

"A motor mouth?" I offered.

He laughed. He was kinder than I was. "Ruth does talk a lot. She has a lot of energy and just really tries to be helpful. I don't think she means to come across so . . ." Adam again groped for words.

"So full of herself?" Like I said, he was the kinder, gentler half.

"It seems that way, doesn't it?" He agreed, which made that little flare of jealously I felt die down—but not completely.

"Well, she made sure I knew she was one of your bosses, lived in the same ward as you, and has an uncle who is the stake president. As if that wasn't enough to impress me, knowing that she is named after a woman in the Bible—well that clinches it for me. Color me impressed." My sarcastic tone added a bite to my words.

"Kit, are you jealous?" Adam smiled knowingly. "You can't possibly think that I would even look at Ruth that way. Besides, I made it clear that you are my girlfriend; I even introduced you that way."

"Yes I'm a little jealous," I conceded. "It doesn't matter if you look at Ruth that way or not. She reached out and squeezed your arm like it was a plump turkey leg she was testing for tenderness before she gobbled it up. She practically ignored me."

"I'm pretty sure Ruth is harmless, but I'll keep an eye out. How about you, Carson? Do you want to squeeze my arms and see if I'm tender?" He held his arms out to me across the table.

I started squeezing him all the way up his arms until I got to his biceps then I quickly tickled him under his arms. He jerked away so fast that his elbows hit the table and he almost tipped over his water cup.

"You're not tough at all! Come on Cap'n Bridger, it's time to go. You know the drill—whither I goest, you go! Plus I have the car keys!" I laughed and tried to beat him to the car.

Later that evening as I wrote in my journal, I started questioning my decision to go to Romania. This happened to me about once a week. Usually it was when I thought about leaving Adam. I also wondered if I would be able to do the actual work. I'd never even spent much time around children at all, let alone sick or abandoned ones that spoke a different language.

When I got these feelings of doubt about my decision, it seemed I followed the same pattern. I would start to worry about something then my fears would kick in. My logical thoughts would take over until all I could think of were all the reasons I shouldn't go.

After beating myself up about it for awhile, I would pray about it again, just to see if maybe I got the answer wrong when I prayed before. I'd get up from my prayer and feel strongly that I needed to stop analyzing my decision and trust in the answer I got the first time. That feeling of confirmation would stick with me for about a week, until worries and doubts crept in once more.

I sat on my bed, feeling hopeless about my lack of faith in the answers I had received. I opened the scriptures, looking for help. I turned to Doctrine and Covenants 9:8. I had marked it in an institute class. We had joked about it in relation to choosing an eternal companion. I read it again; "But, behold, I say unto you, that you must study it out in your mind; then you must ask me if it be right, and if it is right I will cause that your bosom shall burn within you; therefore, you shall feel that it is right." I read it often and it comforted me; I knew I'd had a confirmation when I prayed about going to Romania.

I felt comforted, but I really wanted more assurance. I didn't want to be afraid, I just *was*. Then my eye caught verses 13 and 14, which I had never noticed before; "Do this thing which I have commanded you, and you shall prosper. Be faithful, and yield to no temptation. Stand fast in the work wherewith I have called you, and a hair of your head shall not be lost, and you shall be lifted up at the last day. Amen."

I felt peace. Even though it was hard, and I was sometimes afraid, I was going to follow through with the promptings I had received to go.

chapter Nine

August was sweltering that year in Cache Valley. Temperatures soared, and while other people complained about the heat, I loved it. Adam and I even got to go boating at Bear Lake once for a singles ward activity.

Adam brought his brand new wakeboard that was over two years old, but had never been used. I had given it to him on his nineteenth birthday, ignorant of how inappropriate a wakeboard was for a soon-to-be missionary. I could tell he was excited to get on the lake with it.

"Hey, Bridger. You hug that wakeboard closer than you've ever hugged me." I teased him.

"This wakeboard never makes smart-aleck comments and I can stuff it in the corner of the garage when I'm too busy for it," was his comeback.

I ignored that remark and said, "I'll worry when you start kissing it."

"If that happens, I'll worry too," he said.

Adam was great on the wakeboard and he taught me how to do it. After about five tries, my brain was able to connect with what he'd been telling me and I popped right up. It was such a rush.

We had so much fun, but I could barely walk the next day. My arms and legs screeched with pain every time I moved. A lot of the stiffness had worked itself out by the time I got off work, but Adam noticed I was walking carefully when we went out.

"You know, Kit, you're going to have to wakeboard more so you don't get so sore. When we're married we're going to get a boat someday, so I don't want you wimping out on me."

"I'm not a wimp! I've just never used these muscles before, or if I have, they've forgotten what they're made for." I gave him a playful shove and noticed that he winced with pain. "Hey, Adam, you're not sore, are you? You big hypocrite!" I lunged at him again for good measure; he cringed and I laughed.

We went boat shopping the next day we had off together. Not to actually buy a boat, but it was a great, cheap date and fun to dream. We spent awhile at the boat dealership, climbing in and out of boats and looking at brochures. We tried to tell them we were just looking, but one sales guy just kept following us around, trying to sell us a boat. He wouldn't leave us alone until we sat down and filled out a credit application. When he took it back to process, he had to tell us that we couldn't be approved because we didn't make enough money. I pretended to cry and Adam put his arm around me and led me out to the car. We laughed and laughed until we thought about how we'd wasted the poor guy's time, and then we felt bad. Well Adam felt bad, and I felt kind of bad—for about a minute.

It was our summer of cheap dates and we did things that didn't cost a lot of money. We went to a furniture store that gave away free hot dogs on Saturdays and had lunch. Then we walked through the store, sitting on couches and chairs, picking out dining room furniture, bedroom furniture, and even a patio set.

Adam made us leave the departments whenever salespeople started to approach us, so we wouldn't waste their time. We didn't even get to pick out baby furniture before he made us leave! I accused him of not wanting children and he just laughed at me and offered to "buy" me another free hot dog.

Another night we went to a grocery store that had some tables by their deli section. We bought burritos, three for a dollar, and cooked them in the microwave there. We had to take turns drinking from the water fountain.

We went to a stargazing party at the Heritage Center to watch a meteor shower, which was really cool. We didn't have a telescope, but Adam brought a pair of binoculars for each of us, so we sat there wrapped in quilts, staring at the sky. They told stories while we gazed and I learned a little about meteors. It was kind of romantic, and as we walked back to the car, arm in arm, I noticed several people smiling indulgently at us.

We went back to the Bridgers', hoping to score some cake or other goody, and we weren't disappointed. Lily had made cookies earlier and the fragrance was still wafting through the house. We went to the family room where they were gathered, watching a movie and munching cookies.

As we scooped up some cookies, Lily burst out laughing. She was looking right at me. Her brother, Mark, followed her gaze and joined in.

"What's so funny?" I asked, wondering if she had put something strange in the cookies. I looked at Adam, who was trying hard not to laugh. "What's the joke?"

Even Hal and Barbara were trying to hold back smiles. "What is it?" I demanded. I knew whatever the joke was, it was on me.

Lily enlightened me. "I like your new eyeliner. It is a little heavy, but, hey if you like that look, who am I to judge?"

I ran to the bathroom and saw my reflection. I had a perfect black circle surrounding each eye, suspiciously close to the size of binocular eyepieces. I touched one of the circles and it smudged— that ratfink Adam had done this to me on purpose!

"Adam!" I shrieked. "I can't believe you did this! How long have I been walking around like this?" I grabbed a washcloth and started scrubbing my eyes.

He came to the doorway and said innocently, "Kit, what makes you think I had anything to do with it? I thought your choice of makeup was strange, but I love you anyway!" He stood there chuckling as I tried to clean up the big smears of black encompassing the upper third of my face.

"Don't you even try to lie your way out of this one, mister! What is this stuff anyway? No wonder people were staring at us. I must have looked like a clown!" I was a little ticked off, and a lot embarrassed, as I remembered the looks and smiles we received as we walked through the exhibits and crowds back to the car.

"You don't look like a clown; more like a raccoon. People smiled because you're so cute. I wasn't embarrassed to be seen with you." He still had the nerve to stand there laughing. "It's shoe polish. If you don't rub too hard, you'll buff up to a nice shine—then you'll have a couple of shiners!"

He did not amuse me. "I'll give you a couple of shiners. What a rotten thing to do!" The black was coming off, leaving puffy red skin where I had scrubbed; I wasn't going to let him off easily.

"Don't get mad, Kit, it was a joke! You're pretty good at dishing it out, but not so good at taking it, huh?" He was still laughing.

"I don't get mad, I get even," I huffed, glaring at him in the mirror.

Adam didn't look intimidated by my tirade. He kept smiling and said "I know what you mean, that's my motto, too. Let me see, does tubing at Bear Lake ring a bell?"

My memory flooded back, and my entire face flushed red. When we had gone boating at Bear Lake with the singles ward, we went tubing after everyone was finished wakeboarding. Adam and several other guys bragged about how they couldn't be thrown from the tube.

Guys being guys, they took turns trying to throw each other off the tube. One time Adam was hanging off the back of the tube, being dragged in the water. He almost made it back onto the tube when he suddenly let go, dropping off the back. It wasn't a very spectacular move and I was surprised that he just let go, until the boat circled around to pick him up and we saw him frantically looking around the water.

I realized his dilemma when I saw his blue swim trunks floating a few feet away from him. I told the others on the boat what I saw. We didn't let Adam know, and as the boat came around to pick him up about six of us jumped in for a "swim." Of course I grabbed the swim trunks, which Adam hadn't found yet, and swam away.

Adam frantically called out for everyone to stay away as he had "a swim trunk issue." I climbed back in the boat, discreetly hiding the trunks from Adam's view. We let him look around for a few minutes more, until he confessed his "loss." The guys formed a shield, and handed him a towel, which he had to wear until we got back to shore, amid a lot of teasing about losing his shorts.

When we reached the dock I held up the trunks and asked, "Does anybody know who these belong to?" Everyone laughed, except Adam, who was very embarrassed. He received more recognition that evening at the barbeque—he was given the "Truncated" award. People still teased him about it when they saw him. He'd seemed to take it with grace, but I realized he had just been waiting to get even with me. I suddenly felt fortunate it had not been worse.

I smiled at him with no trace of irritation. "So, we're even then? Truce?"

Adam smiled back. "For now," was all he would say.

I came out of the bathroom with a shiny scrubbed face and Lily was waiting to hear what had happened. "So, what are you going to do to get even with my brother? I hope it's something really good. I'll help if you want!"

"Well I'm feeling kind of forgiving tonight," I told her and watched disappointment cross her face. "I'm not going to get even with him." I smiled sweetly at Adam, and he returned the smile and his dimple flashed. I crossed the room to grab some cookies. As I passed by Lily, I said softly, "For now."

chapter ten

The summer drew to a close; Adam geared up to start classes and Tara and I prepared to leave for Romania. We had our passports ready, immunizations complete, and were eager to go.

Our tutor helped us learn a few phrases of Romanian. He told us about life in Brasov, which was the city where Tara and I were assigned to volunteer. Tara's cousin, Amanda, and Amanda's friend Kellie made up the rest of our group that would be staying together.

My mother occupied her time by researching Romania, Brasov, the orphanages, the current political climate in Romania, weather patterns, crime rates, diseases, and every other thing she could think of concerning my trip.

Tara and I each got five sets of scrubs to wear; my mother bought me five more. I couldn't find thermal underwear in August; my mother had purchased six sets online. My mom bought me a first-aid kit that included bandaids, three kinds of pain reliever, moleskin, compress bandages, a thermometer, tweezers, sunscreen, insect repellent, topical pain reliever, and a few more items I hoped I would never need. I mean, really, suppositories?

My mother came home with two huge suitcases—as she put it "designed to fit airline size limitations, yet surprisingly lightweight and durable". She wrapped the handles with fluorescent green duct tape so "they won't get mixed up with other luggage and they will be readily identifiable". I held out my wrists and asked her if she wanted to duct tape them so I would be readily identifiable as well. She ignored me and proceeded to put little "KIT" labels on all my clothing, including the thermal underwear.

I found out my dad contributed his share to my mother's overprotective attitude. She received a package one afternoon that contained an undercover money/passport belt; an over-the-shoulder money/passport neck pouch; and three pairs of zip-it socks, with places to stash cash, credit cards, and keys. The socks were "breathable and moisture-wicking."

"Where's the holster, gun, and bullet-proof vest?" I queried. She ignored me. "And why'd you get so many?"

"Your dad emailed me the link with suggestions to get a couple of items, so you can choose which is the most comfortable and usable."

"The one with the most money in it will be the most usable." I quipped and proceeded to check each one for cash. Just as I suspected—they were all empty. My mom ignored my hint, but a couple of days later, the day before I was scheduled to fly out, she gave me two cards; one was a prepaid debit card and the other a prepaid phone card.

"The debit card is for emergencies only," she said emphatically. "It has three hundred dollars on it. Only use it for emergencies." She paused, waiting for her instructions to sink in.

"Only for emergencies; it is not a toy," I repeated dutifully.

Satisfied that I understood the concept, she continued. "The phone card has one hundred prepaid minutes based on rates from Romania to the U.S. It's a lot more expensive for you to call here than for us to call there. I want you to check in by phone at least once a week, do you understand? We have a calling card from the U.S. to Romania that's much cheaper, so we'll call you when we have a number for you. You use this for emergencies as well. This card is not for you to call and chat with Adam, do you understand?" She waited for an answer from me.

"This card is to check in with you, not Adam. Call to give you my number and in case of emergency. If you want to chat with me, you'll call me. So basically; don't call us, we'll call you." Sometimes I just liked to push her buttons.

"You don't need to be a smart aleck with me, Kit. I just want to make sure you're safe. Dad and I are paying for half of this trip and we would like some accountability on your part. I'm sure you'll want to talk to Adam while you're gone, but that expense is your responsibility; I just want it to be clear." Her hands on her hips and her no-nonsense tone made it pretty clear.

I bit back the flippant response that came to my mind and tried really hard to be serious and responsible. "It's clear, Mom. I really do appreciate all that you and Dad are doing for me."

I spent the evening before my departure with Adam. We went back to our park and strolled around, holding hands. We found a bench to sit on, and Adam put his arm around my shoulder. I snuggled in close to him and rested my head on his shoulder. We sat there without speaking for a few minutes. I was suddenly hit with the realization that this was the last time I would see him for three months.

"What are you thinking?" I asked him. I wanted to know if he was going to miss me as much as I was starting to miss him.

"I was thinking I don't want this moment to end, and I want to store it up to last until December. How about you? What are you thinking?" He stroked my hair, his fingers lightly brushing my cheek.

"I'm thinking I should just stay here. I don't want to leave you." It didn't feel strange to voice my insecurities to Adam. He'd heard me whine before.

"I want you to stay, too. The only thing that makes it easier is I know how fast three months will pass. I've already been home from my mission that long."

"You're right, but I don't think I can stand it."

"It seems like it will be an eternity, but I know that school and work will make the time pass quickly. It will go by fast for you, too."

"I know all that," I yielded grudgingly. "Even if I didn't feel like I needed to go, if I backed out now, my parents would probably disown me." I tried to not be so glum. "You'd better email me every day, Adam."

"Am I hearing this from the woman who barely managed to write to me twice a week while I was on my mission? Do I detect a double standard here? Hmmmm."

"Emailing is a lot more convenient than writing. You'll be at a computer every day with classes and homework. It won't be hard for you to write me a line or two. It's not the same!"

"Oh, so now you're saying that you can only write to me when it is convenient or easy. So am I just a matter of convenience to you, Kit?" He seemed to know that lightening the tone would make our separation a little less difficult.

"I'd answer you, but it's not really convenient for me right now." I sniffed and turned my head away from him, adopting what I hoped was an indifferent air. He responded the way I hoped he would.

"Let's see if we can fix that for you!" He turned my head back towards him and kissed me. At first it was playful and teasing, like our banter had been. Then it deepened into something more passionate; an intense effort to connect and stay connected during the time we would be apart.

Neither one of us wanted to break away from the other. Adam was the stronger of the two of us. He pulled back, his breathing ragged.

"If I keep kissing you like that, I'll never let you go to Romania," he whispered, lightly kissing the top of my head instead.

"I know what you mean. This isn't making it easier, is it? It seems like I'm always the one clinging and you're always the one keeping us on the straight and narrow path. I'm glad one of us is strong."

"You're a lot stronger than you give yourself credit for, Kit. I admire what you're doing—leaving school, going to a foreign country, doing what you believe you need to do. I know it's much harder for you than just leaving me. But don't think for a minute that I won't miss you like crazy, because I will. And don't worry, you waited for me for two years; I can wait for you for three months. Now, tear yourself away from me before my resolve disappears."

After kissing him once more, lightly, I pulled back. "I love you, Adam Bridger. Thank you for being so willing to support me."

"I love you, too, Kit Matthews. We support each other." He

kissed me once more and we walked through our park for the last time for a season.

I didn't sleep well the night before my departure. My mind kept spinning and I found myself worrying about all the "what ifs." What if I forgot my passport? What if we missed our flight in New York? What if no one picked us up in Bucharest? What if I was making a huge mistake?

Fortunately the dawn breaks over the worriers and dreamers alike, and my alarm finally signaled it was time to get up. I showered and packed all the last minute things while my mom kept reminding me of everything she was afraid I'd forget.

She made me eat a good breakfast, for which I was secretly grateful, because I figured it might be the last really good home-cooked breakfast I would get for three months. I thanked her as she hurried past me to stuff a bottle of vitamins in my luggage.

My dad wasn't going to the airport with us; he had classes to teach at the university. When Mom went off to fortify my bags with vitamins, he took the opportunity to give me last minute instructions of his own.

"Kit, I know you're a sensible girl. This is a great opportunity for you to travel and learn more about the world, firsthand. Don't worry about things here at home, just focus on the experience you're having. Stick with the other girls and don't wander off alone. Remember, we love you and are here if you need us."

That was a long speech for my dad. I went over and hugged him. "I love you, Dad. Thanks for supporting me—it means a lot to me. Don't worry, I'll be careful."

My dad returned the hug then cleared his throat as he pulled back. He reached for something in his pocket and handed it to me. As I took the neatly folded cash he said, "This is a little emergency fund. Just stash it away so you'll know you have something extra, if you need it. Your mom doesn't need to know I gave you a little more. She's always worried I'm going to spoil you and Dave."

I hugged him again. "You do spoil us, but she won't hear it from me. Thanks, Dad."

My mom came back and gave instructions. "Paul, the bags are ready to be taken out to the car. Kit, Dave will be down in a minute to say good-bye. Now's the time to take care of any last-minute things you need to do. Have you used the bathroom?"

I rolled my eyes and said, "I don't know how I'm going to make it three months without you reminding me to use the bathroom, Mom. Maybe you can email me every day just to make sure." She gave me a look, yelled up the stairs for Dave, and then told me I had five minutes before we left.

I ran upstairs to brush my teeth and use the bathroom. I grabbed the backpack I was taking as a carry-on and made one last check around my room. Other than being extraordinarily clean, it didn't look like I was going away. The two pictures on my nightstand were missing; one of Janet and Adam, the other of Adam and me. They were safely packed in my luggage and the empty space on my nightstand was the only visible sign indicating my departure. Well, once the two massive suitcases on my bed were hauled out.

I headed out of my room and met my brother, Dave, going in to grab one of my suitcases. He shoved a paper at me. "Here. I did some research of some places you should visit while you're in Romania so you'll feel more at home. No need to thank me."

I looked at the pages he had printed off from the Internet. Creepiest Places to Visit in Romania; the Real Dracula's Castle. Of course Dave would give me something like that.

I started down the stairs and yelled back over my shoulder, "Thanks, Dave. I was worried about missing you, but now I know where to go if I do. You might not be there in body, but I'm sure you'll be there in spirit."

He came out lugging one of my suitcases. "Holy cow, woman! What do you have packed in this thing? Rocks? Oh wait, it's probably just your makeup! Hey, can I use your laptop while you're gone?"

"You leave my laptop alone. Besides, I have a password on it." I didn't want him rummaging around my computer files and downloading who knows what. Even though I had password protected it, I had also taken the power cord and hidden it to discourage the temptation I knew Dave would face.

Dave groaned as he lifted my suitcase into the trunk. "A

password won't stop me from using your computer." He smirked at me, then turned to look at my car parked on the side of the driveway. "But don't worry it's your car I really want."

"Leave my car alone." I turned to my mom. "You won't let him drive my car, will you? Hide the keys. And make sure he stays out of my room."

"Kit, he's just pushing your buttons," she answered.

Dave passed by me on the way back in the house and said under his breath, "I have my own key." I tried to trip him, but I wasn't quick enough, and he laughed as he went back inside.

"Well, he's one person I won't miss. Please keep him out of my stuff." My mom shook her head and motioned for me to get in the car. My dad loaded the second suitcase into the trunk and leaned in for one more hug before we left.

The ride to the airport was uneventful and I could tell my mom was worried. She didn't talk very much, and when she did, it was to ask if I'd remembered this or that. I felt a little nervous myself as it finally sunk in. I had never flown anywhere by myself and I had never been outside of the U.S. before.

I was glad Tara was going with me, but as I started to think about actually living with three girls—two of whom I didn't know at all—in a country none of us had ever been to, I started feeling a little queasy.

I texted Tara off and on throughout the morning. We met at the big world map on the floor, in between the terminals. Tara flitted about, excitement shining on her face.

"Look at my new digital camera! Amanda and Kellie will be here soon. I was so excited, I couldn't eat a bite! How are you feeling? Are you ready for a life-changing experience? Lean close to me so we can take a self-portrait." She held out her camera to take our picture. "Smile!" she chirped. I obliged and then dug out my own camera so I could take one too.

I was glad Tara was so bubbly. Her constant chatter helped ease my anxiety. A few minutes later Amanda, Kellie, and Amanda's mom showed up. Tara introduced her cousin Amanda, a sturdy, serious brunette who was a complete contrast to Tara's blonde bounciness. Kellie was almost as tall as I was, with green eyes and short strawberry blonde hair that fell perfectly into place. After introductions were made, more pictures taken, information and phone numbers verified, we departed for the check-in counter.

We checked in without incident and set off for the security checkpoint. Without her luggage hampering her, Tara was practically dancing with excitement. I don't know if her feet or her mouth ran faster. Amanda, Kellie and I exchanged looks and just laughed. I again felt thankful for Tara; I had a feeling we would need her joyful personality and happy outlook far more than we thought we would.

We arrived at the security screening lines. It was time to say our final goodbyes. I had struggled when I told Adam goodbye the night before, and I had felt emotional when my dad had given me his speech and hug that morning. I wasn't prepared to see my mom crying when I turned to give her a hug. I was even more surprised when I felt my own tears spill over.

My mom hugged me tightly. "Goodbye, Sweetheart. I love you. Please take care of yourself and each other. Call me from New York." She just kept hugging me until I pulled away first.

"I love you too, Mom. Don't worry, I'll be fine." I told her as I joined the others in line. "I know I'm always complaining, but I really do appreciate everything you do for me." She gave one last wave as the line snaked along.

The security screening went by quickly and before I knew it, I was on the plane and on my way to a "life-changing experience," as Tara so aptly called it.

chapter eleven

I was amazed at how huge JFK Airport was. We barely had
time to figure out where we were going and make it to the
correct terminal. I was really glad that Kellie was with us. Out of
the four of us, she was the only one who had traveled internationally
before. The rest of us felt like a bunch of hicks.

I quickly called my mom on my cell phone to let her know we'd
made it to New York safely. I tried to call Adam although I knew he
probably wouldn't be home. I talked to Barbara briefly and told her
to tell Adam I had called.

The flight to Bucharest was about ten hours. It was a surreal
experience to fly into the sunset, fly through the night, and into the
sunrise. It was hard to sleep, so I pulled out my iPod and worked
on a letter to Adam. During that flight it really hit me hard that I
wouldn't see him again for three months. I fought back the tears and
tried to think about other things.

When we arrived in Bucharest, we were tired and just wanted
to go to bed. We were supposed to be picked up by someone at the
airport to take us to Brasov. We held up a paper with the big letters
CFAW (Children Far and Wide) but we didn't see anyone. Tara
finally noticed a man and a teenage boy who were looking at us. She
turned the sign towards them; they nodded and spoke to each other,
then headed over to us.

They spoke a little broken English and we guessed they were

telling us it would take two hours to get to Brasov. They looked nice enough, but it was a little weird to get into an old beat-up station wagon with complete strangers in a foreign country.

The driver tailgated everyone, then I realized everybody drove that way. The roads were narrow and I was a little freaked out by the way they drove.

My eyes burned from fatigue but there was no way I was sleeping, so I tried to concentrate on my first sights of Romania. It was all pretty much a blur.

They took us directly to our place in Brasov. It was a little house that was old, but nicer than I thought it would be. We paid them for the ride and I think Tara gave them a really good tip, because they smiled and waved enthusiastically, calling "La revedere," which was one Romanian phrase I actually knew—it meant good-bye.

Our mentor and liaison, Anya, was waiting for us with the key. She led us inside the little house as she told us the rules and what came with the house. We paid her the rent in advance for the time we would be there.

Anya spoke English fluently in an abrupt, business-like manner. She was a chain smoker and Tara's loud coughing when she blew her smoke directly at us didn't faze her. She told us she would take us to exchange our money and shop for food. She was ready to go immediately, so we didn't even unpack, we just took a minute to use the bathroom. (My mom would have been so proud!)

It was a good thing Anya went with us. She was our translator and showed us how to buy tickets for the bus and how to spot the signs for the stops. She was impersonal, yet efficient.

When we returned home a couple of hours later, we were even more exhausted. Anya wasn't ready to leave yet. She explained that our tutor, Corina, would be coming over in a few minutes to meet us. We put away the few groceries we had purchased. Anya told us to save the bags to use them again.

When I met Corina I liked her immediately. She was only a few years older than we were and an aura of friendliness emanated from her. Anya informed us she would be back the next day to help us get a cell phone and to show us where to buy other things we might need, then she left.

"That was sudden," I said, referring to Anya's departure.

"That is how Anya is," Corina replied. "She likes to do her job and no more. That is not how I am. I like to talk and talk."

"Your English is so good," Tara observed. "You hardly have an accent. How did you learn to speak it so well?"

"I attended school for one year at BYU. I also served a mission in the States. I was a missionary on Temple Square. I would love to go back."

We were excited to find that Corina was LDS. She answered many of our questions. I was glad she was employed as our tutor for the time we would be in Romania.

"I have found that it works well to teach two evenings each week for a two hour period. As part of my services I like to help with shopping or going to church or other things you might need assistance with from someone who lives here."

"That's a lot more time than our tutor spent with us back home," Amanda said.

"I like to do more than the minimum," Corina replied. "My English improves when I do this, and I enjoy making new friends."

"Corina, is there a place nearby where we could make a call to our families?" I asked. "We promised to call when we got here and thought we'd have a cell phone."

"There is an internet café just a few blocks from here. I can walk with you and I will ride the bus home from there." We were glad to have her show us the way.

Corina told us more about herself as we walked. Daylight was starting to fade as we got there. We saw that there was a pay phone outside, and were glad that Corina stayed long enough to show us how to make calls using our phone cards.

Tara turned to Amanda and said, "Let Kit and I make our calls first. Then we can hurry and send our emails while you two use the phone."

Amanda protested. "You don't have to email tonight. Let's just limit the calls to a couple minutes each, then we can all go home."

"Yeah," said Kellie, "I'm so tired I'm about to lie down on the sidewalk."

"I'm tired too," Tara argued, "But I need to email Eric's family so they can send it with theirs before his next P-day. Kit needs to email Adam too. Don't you?" She turned to me for support, and of course she got it. I really wanted to talk to Adam, even if it was a one-way conversation in the form of email.

Kellie and Amanda looked at each other and sighed. Amanda spoke up. "You guys hurry and make your calls. Then if you're not ready when Kellie and I are finished, we're heading home without you. If I know you two, you won't be able to find your way home alone, so you'd better hurry."

I had the fleeting thought that Amanda was bossy, but since the clock was ticking I let it pass. Tara and I made our calls home to check in and promised to follow up with emails.

We hurried inside and Tara quickly charmed the guy at the counter, whose name was Vasilé. He spoke English quite well, although his accent made me smile. He sounded like one of those people who tried to speak with an exaggerated Italian accent. When he said "Let me show you" it sounded like "Letta me showa you." I kept expecting him to burst out laughing, but to him, it was his way of speaking.

Kellie and Amanda came inside faster than I thought they would. They came up behind us as Vasilé was showing us how to log on to the Internet.

I made the mistake of saying to Kellie, "Letta me email-a you." She gave me a look that was not amused and said, "At least he can speak two languages. How many can you speak?"

Wow! I thought. I guess Amanda is the bossy one and Kellie is the one who can't take a joke. She was right, though; I shouldn't have made fun of his accent. I'd meant it in fun, but didn't attempt any more of that type of humor.

I paid attention closely enough to figure out how to log in to the server. I was thrilled to see I had access to Instant Messenger, but disappointed to see that Adam wasn't online. It was just as well; I felt like Amanda and Kellie were timing us.

I quickly logged on to my email account. I saw that I had an email from Adam so I opened it.

To: kitcarson@yahoo.com
From: bridgerman123@hotmail.com

Subject: Hey Kit!

I wanted to send you a short email to say welcome to Romania and to tell you I love you and I already miss you. I hope your flight was good and you got there safely. One day closer to you being home! I love you.

Adam.

That brief email made my day. I typed a quick message back to Adam.

To: bridgerman123@hotmail.com
From: kitcarson@yahoo.com
Subject: Hey Bridger!

It's me, your world-traveling girlfriend! I'm really here in Brasov. It has been an exhausting 24 hours. I want to tell you all about it, but I only have a couple of minutes before Amanda and Kellie leave Tara and me to walk home by ourselves. I'm not sure I could find the way right now.

It's ten hours later here so I know you're still in class. I have access to IM so we'll have to set up a time we can chat online. I don't know for sure what my schedule will be like right now, but I'll let you know as soon as I find out.

We don't have the cell phone they told us we would have at our house. I guess the girls who lived here last semester made the landlord mad and he confiscated it along with a bunch of other stuff I'm sure we'll figure out in the next few days.

It's so weird to be half a world away from you. I miss you so much. I started a letter to you on the plane when I couldn't sleep that I'll finish up and send when I can figure out how to mail a letter.

I love you. Don't forget about me while I'm gone. I hope my roommates and I can stand each other for three months. Right now we're a little snappish, but I think it is because we're all so tired.

They are eyeing the door like they're going to leave me. I'd better go. I'll send you an email tomorrow and hopefully will have some news about our phone. I'll also send you our address. I forgot to write it down.

Remember I love you! I hope you still miss me, cause I sure still miss you!

Love, Kit.

I logged off about the same time Tara did; Kellie and Amanda were already heading for the door.

I was glad the four of us walked home together. Everything looked different after dark and the sounds and smells were strange. We saw at least five different stray dogs on our way home. They seemed to be everywhere; sniffing around and barely moving out of the way as we walked by them.

I could tell that the others were as glad as I was when we reached our little house. The key got stuck in the lock and we tried for a minute to open it, but it just wouldn't work. I felt a sense of panic and wanted to sit down and cry.

My eyes met Tara's and she looked like I felt. "What are we going to do?" she asked.

"We could break a window and one of us could climb through," I suggested.

"We could just huddle here and sleep in the doorway," Amanda offered.

"We could walk back to the internet café and call Anya," Kellie, our voice of reason, said.

We agreed that calling Anya was the best solution. Then we realized none of us had thought to bring her number with us. It was inside, on the table. We tried the key again, but it still didn't work.

I sat down against the house and put my head down on my knees. I was cold, tired, overwhelmed, and ready to give up.

Kellie spoke first. "I'm ready to break a window. Help me find a rock." It seemed even the voice of reason had her limits.

Tara grabbed her arm and said, "Wait a minute. I think we should say a prayer." As soon as she spoke the words, they made perfect sense. I felt ashamed I hadn't thought of it.

The four of us knelt down in front of the dark doorway. Tara offered to say the prayer. She humbly asked for help, remembering to give thanks for our safe travel. I felt a sense of peace as I added "Amen."

We stood up from our prayer and Amanda tried the key again. I expected it to miraculously open. It still wouldn't budge. I think Amanda started crying, judging from the sniffle I heard coming from her.

Kellie said, "Let's find a rock. I'm serious."

An idea suddenly came to me. "Let's try the window to see if maybe it's unlocked." I walked over and tried to open the window. It was stuck firmly shut.

Tara found a rock and handed it to Kellie. "I'm with you, let's break the window."

Just as Kellie drew back her arm to throw the rock, a light came on and the door opened. Tara screamed and we all joined in.

A strange man was at the door, yelling at us in Romanian. We nearly fell over each other backing away. Who was he?

Amanda realized what had happened first and spoke loudly through the din. "I think we're at the wrong house. Kellie, I told you it was the next street." The realization suddenly dawned on all of us and we took off running.

We didn't slow down until we turned the corner and were halfway down the next block. We quietly crept up to the house we all thought was ours, silently slipped the key into the lock and it opened easily.

Our prayers were answered all right, just not the way we thought they would be.

chapter twelve

I woke up to sunlight streaming through the thin curtains on the window. I looked over at Tara's bed. She was still asleep, covers pulled up tightly with only tousled blonde curls showing.

I looked at my travel alarm clock which I had managed to set to the local time before collapsing in exhaustion the night before. It was just after noon and my stomach growled as if to remind me that it had acclimated to the local time even if the rest of my body hadn't.

I remembered the night before, looking at the mattresses that were stained and lumpy. Kellie had wondered aloud if they had bedbugs. We were glad we had our new flannel sheets even if we didn't have pillows. As I crawled between my warm sheets, I fought the urge to scratch. I hadn't even thought about bedbugs until Kellie had brought them up. In spite of my fears, I fell asleep quickly and didn't stir all night long.

Although I'd slept so long, my eyes stilled burned. I contemplated whether to sleep more or to get up and find food. I could smell something cooking and my stomach won the battle. I went to the kitchen to find Kellie and Amanda both at the table, eating toast that smelled burnt. I knew I must be really hungry when burnt toast smelled that good.

"We have a toaster?" I looked around the kitchen. The countertop space revealed no toaster; I wondered where it was hidden.

Kellie enlightened me. "Yeah, it's called the oven. We set it on broil and watched it very closely. The black part can be scraped off, but it's better if you don't burn it to start with." I saw the pile of black scrapings in the sink. I decided I would just eat the bread without toasting it.

I ate two pieces with jam; it was a little dry but it took the edge off of my ravenous hunger. We only picked up a few groceries the day before with Anya, so there wasn't a lot to choose from.

I went back to my room and dug through one of my massive suitcases. I knew my mom had packed a box of instant oatmeal packets. Triumphantly, I took my find back to the kitchen with me. "I guess a microwave is out of the question, huh?" I said more to myself than anyone else. Amanda and Kellie laughed at me.

"Finding a pot to boil water in appears to be out of the question," Kellie quipped.

"If you let the water run long enough, it might get hot; we didn't get past lukewarm. We didn't resort to toasting bread in the oven because we thought it might be fun. It was an act born of desperation and hunger." Amanda's comments were not what I wanted to hear.

Tara wandered in about that time sniffing the air. "What's that smell? I'm starving."

"Toast." Kellie and Amanda said in unison, laughing.

"I have some dry instant oatmeal." I offered. "Wait, I'll be right back." I raced back to my room and dug through my suitcase again. I found a box of granola bars and silently thanked my mom.

I took it back to the kitchen to share with the others. Kellie rummaged through her carry-on and found a box of crackers. Amanda contributed trail mix and Tara pulled out a bag of chocolate kisses. It was an interesting meal, but we were truly thankful for it.

Anya was due back around three, so we all had to get ready. I was done a few minutes before Anya was expected, so I finished my letter to Adam.

I told him about our knocking at the wrong door and filled him in on our first breakfast. I sealed the envelope, looked to make sure no one was around, and gave the envelope a kiss. That was the closest I was going to get to Adam for three months. Feeling a little discouraged by the thought, I kissed the envelope again.

Anya arrived on time. Before we left, she explained to us more about the work we would be doing. We were scheduled to work at the hospital in the mornings from 9 AM to 1 PM; and the orphanage from 3 PM to 6 PM She told us the orphanage was not far from the hospital.

Anya drew a map showing how to get to the hospital and orphanage from our house. Tara asked if the bus route ran there. Anya told us that since it was less than two kilometers away we could walk there and back. She said it with such authority I felt like a slacker for even considering taking the bus.

Anya explained that we would be expected to help wherever needed. It might include changing diapers and bedding, teaching the children English, playing with the children, or simply holding the babies to help stimulate them. She made it clear that we should be prepared to work. Her tone made me wonder if the girls before us had given her trouble.

Anya stopped talking and pulled out her cigarettes. She took one from the pack, lit up, and took a long drag. Tara once again coughed and waved vigorously to get the smoke away from her.

Amanda spoke up. "Anya, you know that smoking is bad for you, don't you?" Anya gave her a look that would have stopped a more cautious soul, but Amanda was on a crusade. "You've heard of second-hand smoke, right? Well it's almost as bad as smoking, and I would appreciate not having my lungs polluted. Would you please refrain from smoking in our house?" Amanda's tone was firm and she didn't cringe at Anya's fierce gaze.

I expected a blow-up as they stared each other down. Anya blew her smoke directly at Amanda, but then suddenly turned towards the door. She opened it and said as she went out, "I will not smoke in your house; you do not give me lectures about my smoking. I know about Mormons. Let's go!"

We hurried to grab our jackets and ran to keep up with her. I thought she might hold a grudge, but she continued to talk to us in her same no-nonsense way, as if Amanda had not rebuked her. I was glad for that; I didn't want to make an enemy of our liaison on the second day.

We got a cell phone and then stopped at the post office. I bought ten stamps, which cost about a dollar each. I mailed my letter to Adam and noticed that Tara had one for Eric too.

We purchased hot buttered corn from a street vendor. It was so delicious we all bought a second ear. The breakfast we'd had made us appreciate the corn even more.

As we returned home, Anya reminded us that our duties would begin on Monday. That gave us a couple more days to relax and adjust to the time change. She left with instructions to call her if we had problems.

We needed to get more food, so we decided to walk the few blocks to the store. Because we had no translator and couldn't read most of the labels it took us a long time to shop. Some things were obvious like bread and eggs, but we were a little confused about which milk, butter, or flour to get.

We forgot to bring our bags so we had to buy more. The money was also confusing to us, although Amanda took charge and assured us she knew what she was doing. We ended up with several bags of groceries and didn't want to walk home, especially because it was dark by the time we left the store. We couldn't find a taxi though, so we ended up trudging home again after dark, although this time we paid closer attention to which street our house was on.

After a simple dinner of hot buttered noodles, we headed to bed. After brushing my teeth, I wrote in my journal and read scriptures. As I settled into bed, I felt wide awake and feelings of loneliness and homesickness crept in. After tossing and turning for half an hour, I pulled out some paper and started another letter to Adam.

> *Dear Adam,*
> *What in the world am I doing here? I don't understand the language, I'm confused by the money, I'm exhausted, and I miss you! I have never been so tired in my life. I don't know if I can do this. I just want to cry . . .*

chapter thirteen

We awoke sometime mid-morning to loud knocking on our door. Amanda got there first and found Corina with a bag in her hand and a smile on her face.

Amanda invited her in and we all wandered in to the living room. Corina offered the bag. "My mother sent me with some bread and cheese. I had some time so I wondered if you would like me to show you more of Brasov and we could work on language. Would you like to?"

We thanked her for the food, and Amanda took the bag to the kitchen. Since it was only about eight steps away, she was able to hear the conversation.

"We just woke up. It'll take us a little while to get ready," I spoke up for all of us. I'm sure I looked pretty scary.

Tara added, "We'll hurry. Do you mind waiting about half an hour?"

Corina said she was happy to wait and we hurried off to get dressed. We skipped the showers and quickly pulled our hair back. I looked at Tara and she looked totally cute, in spite of the fact she had just crawled out of bed. Some things were just not fair.

We each grabbed a piece of fruit and a granola bar, then put on our jackets.

Corina suggested we ride the bus to the church. I was surprised that they had a building of their own; Corina told us there was only a branch, no ward. All the way there she chattered, pointing out things that might interest us and telling us how to say things in Romanian.

We walked around the outside of the church building. It was smaller than the buildings I'd seen in Cache Valley. It was surrounded by fencing with a couple of locked gates. Corina told us the meetings started at 10:00, which relieved me; I couldn't imagine all of us up, ready and at church by 9:00. I should have held that thought; as soon as I had it, Corina was also inviting us to come early for choir practice at—you guessed it—9 AM.

I would have chosen to sleep the extra hour, but apparently my three roommates were all songbirds and they quickly agreed to join the choir. What could I do? I opted to stick with the crowd.

We rode the bus to the orphanage to see where we would be working. Again, we only walked around the outside, but it was interesting to see where we would be spending our time. It consisted of three buildings and had an air of neglect about it. A fence ran around the perimeter and there were a few kids playing outside.

Corina pointed out the hospital, which was just down the street. It was a gray, two-story building that looked depressing. I felt downcast looking at this lonely little piece of the world. I wondered if we could possibly make a difference at either place.

We decided to walk back to our house from the hospital so we would be familiar with the route. Corina told us the bus would take us most of the way there if we wanted to ride it. We told her how Anya seemed disapproving of using the bus for a distance of "less than two kilometers." Corina laughed and said, "That is just Anya's way. Her words are sometimes sharp."

Corina continued her tutoring as we walked. We would ask her to repeat what she said in Romanian. I found that I was picking up more words than I thought I would. Corina was careful to repeat the phrases slowly so we could understand them.

As we stopped by our house for a bathroom break, we discussed what we should eat. Corina spoke up and invited us to her house for dinner.

I didn't know what to say. Tara didn't have the same problem.

"That sounds great to me!" Kellie and Amanda exchanged glances. I saw one of Amanda's eyebrows go up and an almost imperceptible nod by Kellie. They seemed able to communicate with each other without speaking sometimes.

Amanda asked, "Corina, there are four of us. Won't your mother mind if you bring all of us home with you for dinner? Wouldn't she like some notice first?"

Corina shook her head. "My mother loves to cook and always makes more than we need. She told me to ask you to come. She loves to meet people." She frowned for a second. "My father, he is sometimes grumpy, but he will not mind. My brother is always happy to meet people from America. Come home with me."

Tara repeated, "Sounds great!" Kellie and Amanda both seemed convinced, so I went along with the group. I was curious to meet Corina's family. She was so friendly and helpful, I was sure her entire family would be the same way.

They weren't exactly like Corina. Her mother and grandmother were very happy to see us. They hugged us and carried on a lively conversation in a language I didn't recognize. We must have looked puzzled because Corina explained that although she lived in Romania most of her life, her family was Hungarian.

Her grandmother only spoke Hungarian. Her parents spoke some English, but her dad mainly just watched TV and smoked. Corina's brother was fascinated by us because we were Americans. He spoke English very well and asked us if we knew any celebrities.

Corina's mother started dishing up the food. It was authentic Hungarian food. I was nervous at first because I like to be able to identify what I eat before I eat it. They served some kind of soup that looked like chicken broth with three or four fist-sized clumps of egg-y stuff in it. It was actually pretty good. We each had a big slice of bread with it.

I thought that was the meal but then they brought out some mashed potatoes and some chicken that was just plain yummy. They poured us a glass of orange drink and gave us another slice of bread. I was so full, I thought I might explode. Then Corina's grandmother brought out little muffins and pretzels. I didn't think I could eat another bite, but the grandmother kept shoving a muffin at me and jabbering in Hungarian. I gave in and took one so she would leave me alone.

We all wanted to stop by the internet café on the way home, so we kept our after-dinner visit short. As we walked to the bus stop, we laughed about all the hugs and kisses we got from the grandmother and how the father just ignored us.

At the internet café we had to wait for computers to be available. When it was my turn, I logged on and eagerly checked my email. There was a message from my dad, asking me if I was okay and telling me to write my mother, who was going crazy. I privately thought it could be a short trip for her, but dutifully sent a quick reply to my dad assuring him I was fine and promising a letter soon.

Then, there it was—an email from Adam! I quickly clicked on the message.

> To: kitcarson@yahoo.com
> From: bridgerman123@ hotmail.com
> Subject: I miss you!
>
> I can't believe it's only been four days! I feel like it's been an eternity since I've seen you. I've been trying to get all of my reading and assignment due dates figured out so I can get everything done. I forgot how hard it is to go to school, study, and work. I keep wanting to call you or come over to see you. On the plus side, staying so busy with work and school helps the time pass. Not much has changed except you're not here and I am. I miss you so much. Please write when you can and give me all the details of life in Romania. Well I'd better go, I have to be at work in twenty minutes and I need to grab something to eat. I love you, Kit! Don't forget it!
>
> Love, Adam.

Short but sweet; it felt good to know he was thinking about me and missed me too. There was also an email from Lily.

> To: kitcarson@yahoo.com
> From: lilyofthevalley16@hotmail.com
> Subject: can I come to Romania with you?
>
> Okay so now I wish I came to Romania with you. Why, you ask? Because my family is driving me nuts! I can usually stand them but right now I am ready to scream. Beth always has her nose in a book and Travis

is always playing stupid practical jokes and Sarah copies EVERYTHING I do. I never see Adam since you left and when I whined to Mom about it, all she said was that it's normal to be irritated by your brothers and sisters. Okay, so if that was it I could probably deal with it, but get this—that Ruth girl that is Adam's and Dad's boss at work—she lives right down the street. With the Lants, who she has to make sure we know is the stake president. Like I haven't lived here my whole life. Well she came over last night "just to say hi and share some yummy chocolate cake that she made." She brought chocolate cake, like I don't make the best chocolate cake around! I'm not saying that to brag, but you and I know it's true. Of course my mom invited her in so she sat and ate cake with us—which was NOT as good as mine! She talked, talked, talked about herself the whole time she was there. When she left my mom invited her back anytime, which means that annoying person will be back a lot! Mom kept going on about how nice she was; kind of bubbly like Janet. She is NOTHING like Janet. I know I'm whining but she bugged me big time! I personally think she has her eye on Adam—but don't worry; you're way cuter and nicer and you are LIKEABLE! I'll guard him for you. Email me back, okay; I need to hear about something good so maybe I won't be so grouchy. Love, your sister (I hope soon!)

Lily.

I laughed as I pictured Lily writing the email. She was usually pretty easy-going, but clearly Ruth had rubbed her the wrong way. I could sympathize as I recalled the one time I had met her. I felt a flare of jealousy when I thought about how she probably was trying to snag Adam. Then I realized he didn't even mention her in his email so I figured it was no big deal.

I replied to Lily's email, telling her about our house, Corina, and Anya. I also assured her that her chocolate cake was the best. I hurried through so I would have time to devote to my reply to Adam.

To: bridgerman123@ hotmail.com
From: kitcarson@yahoo.com
Subject: Four days down . . .

Hey there awesome boyfriend! I'm so glad there was an email from you. I really miss you too. I don't think Kellie and Amanda understand my pining away for you because they didn't leave boyfriends behind. Even Tara has been away from Eric for a long time so it isn't the same. I try not to whine too much to them about missing you, but let me tell you, my journal hears it all! I'm glad you're staying busy. I think that will be the key to making the time fly by.

Today we went to Corina's house and met her family. They are Hungarian and fixed us a ton of food. Her grandmother kept talking to her mom and dad in Hungarian about us and we didn't understand a thing. Corina said it was all good though. She said her grandmother kept saying how healthy we looked. I wonder if that is a nice way of saying we're fat! Corina brought us some bread and cheese this morning that her mother sent over. The bread was good, but the cheese nearly made me throw up. I wasn't the only one, so it found its way to the garbage can. I asked Corina later what kind of cheese it was (so I can avoid it in the future) and she said it was sheep's cheese. Yuck!

We took the bus to the orphanage and hospital to check it out. We didn't go inside but at least we know where to go on Monday. We also checked out the meetinghouse. There is only one branch that meets there and they have their own building.

I'm glad Tara is with me. If I had to room with Kellie or Amanda I don't know if I could do it. They are super bossy, that's for sure. I don't think they get my sense of humor. Oh well, they are pretty smart, I'll give them that. Well they're giving me the eye so I should probably sign off. I don't think they'll want to come to the internet café as often as I want to, so hopefully I can drag Tara here with me. I don't feel comfortable coming by myself. Tara's over flirting with Vasilé, the guy who works here. No one can resist Tara; she's just too cute.

By the way, please make sure you tell Lily that her chocolate cake is THE best. I think she's feeling a little lost and out of sorts lately. So take a minute to see how she's doing. Tell your family I said hi and give your mom and Lily a hug for me. Then hug yourself two or three times for me! And give yourself a kiss . . . oh wait, I'm getting carried away. If I kiss the computer screen, they'll probably kick me out–plus I might catch something disgusting. This is not the cleanest place I've seen.

Drill sergeant Amanda has spoken. We are leaving. I love you! Write back soon.

Love, Kit.

I signed off, then remembered I hadn't given Adam or my dad our cell phone number. I asked the girls if they minded waiting while I signed on again to send it. Amanda rolled her eyes, Kellie sighed, and Tara didn't even hear me; she was still flirting with Vasilé. I took it as a yes and hurried to log on to send an email to Adam and my dad.

Of course I didn't have the cell phone number written down so I called to Kellie and Amanda to ask if they had it. Amanda came over with a piece of paper that she slapped down in front of me. She said in an exasperated voice, "Kit, you're helpless. You should write things down. We won't always be here to rescue you."

I smiled brightly and said, "Thanks, Amanda. I know you won't always be here, that's why I'm trying to get the most use out of you while you are here." She must have heard my sarcasm, because she turned in a huff and snatched the number away. Luckily for me I can type and be sarcastic at the same time, so I'd already typed the number in. I added myself to the email so I wouldn't have to ask her again for the number.

I hit send and quickly logged off. I went to the counter to collect Tara. Vasilé looked longingly at Tara as I led her away. I don't think Tara realizes the effect she has on guys. It didn't take a psychic to figure out there would be a poor sap with a broken heart when we left Romania, courtesy of Miss Tara Knight.

chapter fourteen

Somehow we made it to choir practice on time. I was pressured into joining the choir, I mumbled my way through it. The old lady next to me was as tone deaf as I was, yet she could hear me well enough to know I wasn't singing the correct words. She moved closer to me, shoving her hymnbook close to my face. I caught a whiff of body odor, which I had discovered was pretty normal in Romania.

It was difficult to sing while holding my breath; but it was hard not to smile back at that little old lady who kept beaming at me while she belted out the hymn. After the song was over she reached over and squeezed my hand and said something I couldn't understand.

The choir director wasn't too happy with how we sounded and she made us sing the song again. The second time I actually managed to sing a few words correctly and since I was familiar with the hymn, I even figured out what some of the words meant. This could actually help me learn the language. Maybe choir practice wasn't a total waste of good sleeping time.

Sacrament meeting started about ten minutes late. It seemed that Mormon Standard Time was alive and well on both sides of the world. I understood very little. Corina tried to give us a quick summary of each talk, and I understood the "amens" at the end. I was grateful for the familiarity of the sacrament service itself. I felt a pang of homesickness as I thought of Adam and my family. I missed them.

I shifted on the hard wooden bench and noticed my shoes scraped the bare floor. The chapel was tiny compared to the ones I'd seen in Logan. The branch presidency sat in metal folding chairs and shared a hymnbook between them. The tinny sounds of the portable keyboard interrupted my thoughts and I realized the meeting was coming to a close.

After the closing prayer the branch presidency came up to greet us. Close behind them were two sister missionaries, Sora Campbell from Richmond, Virginia, and Sora Barnes from Boise, Idaho. I recognized that Sora meant "sister." They helped in translation as we spoke with the branch presidency. President Barbu spoke some English, but his counselors did not; they all greeted us with enthusiastic handshakes.

Sora Barnes and Sora Campbell asked us to attend Gospel Principles with them; they had an investigator they would like us to share our testimonies with. Tara told them she couldn't speak enough Romanian to bear her testimony, and I quickly echoed her reply. My first thought was: *There is no way I can bear my testimony in front of people—no way*; but the language barrier card was easier to play and would most likely achieve the same results.

I was wrong—the sister missionaries had a trump card to play. Sora Barnes was first to use it. "You don't need to worry about speaking the language. We'll translate your words, and the Spirit needs no translation; it can be felt in any language."

How do you fight that? I'd tried fighting the spirit of testimony before and it was tough, as I'd found out when the sister missionaries taught me. I was able to ignore the Spirit somewhat when they gave me the discussions, but when they bore their testimonies I could not deny what I felt.

That feeling was also what prompted me to sign up for this Romanian service trip to start with. So as I fought the urge to walk out the door and keep on walking to avoid having to bear my testimony, a thought came to me that maybe this was why I needed to come to Romania.

Could my testimony touch someone else? It seemed farfetched

and highly unlikely, yet I did know there was a reason I had to come to this country at this time. My heart beat so rapidly I thought it might leap out of my chest. My hands felt clammy. No one else seemed to be affected the way I was. Everyone else appeared to be just fine.

Even the investigator looked calm. She was an older lady, missing a tooth in the front, just off to the side. She smiled and nodded as Sora Campbell made the introductions. Sora Pavel was the investigator and Sora Milcu was the instructor.

I wiped my palms on my skirt and sat down on a folding chair. The four of us doubled the class size.

The sister missionaries worked together like a well-oiled machine—a bilingual machine. As Sora Milcu taught the lesson basics, Sora Campbell spoke mainly in Romanian to Sora Pavel, and Sora Barnes translated to us in English. Comments we made were translated by Sora Barnes back to Romanian. It sounded confusing, but I was amazed at how much we understood.

Tara, Kellie, and Amanda made several comments, but I kept quiet. Whenever I heard comments made in Gospel Doctrine or Gospel Principles, I was always amazed at how much other people knew and how little I really knew.

I would celebrate the second anniversary of my baptism in less than six months, yet I still felt so ignorant. I read the scriptures, prayed regularly, attended my meetings, and now I could even add singing in the choir to my list of "choosing the right," but I still felt like I would never get to the level of fitting in with "life" members of the Church. I absorbed the lessons and commentary like a sponge but felt like I could never gain the depth of understanding that others had.

As I pondered my own feelings of inadequacy, the pain of missing my best friend, Janet, pierced my soul. If I could just talk to Janet, I knew she would reassure me. It wasn't just because she was the kindest person I'd ever met, but she always seemed in tune with the Spirit. She could find strengths where I could only see weaknesses, and she helped me feel like maybe I wasn't so hopeless.

Janet was gone. It had been more than a year since she passed away. I didn't think I would ever comprehend why she died in that accident, and I lived. It was one answer I longed for, one nobody could give me. My prayers regarding that had gone unanswered. Well, I can't honestly say they weren't answered; I felt peace when I prayed about Janet, but there was no answer as to why she was taken, and I really wanted to know why.

Tears filled my eyes and threatened to spill over. I didn't want to cry so I forced my thoughts in a different direction. I studied Tara; I was thankful she was my friend. Her bubbly, carefree attitude had lifted me out of discouragement; usually by making me laugh.

Tara seemed like a stereotypical blonde to some people, but I admired that she wasn't afraid to speak out loud the things she thought. She shared that trait with her cousin Amanda. The similarity ended there, however. Tara seemed full of good humor and laughter; Amanda had a look about her that suggested she perpetually smelled some disagreeable odor.

It suddenly occurred to me that maybe she didn't look like that when she was back home. Some of the smells of Romania made my own nose wrinkle. It was apparent that bathing or showering did not share the same level of priority here as it did in America. I guess it was her bossiness that made me more critical of her.

I still didn't know Amanda or Kellie very well and felt a touch of guilt at my judgmental attitude. Sometimes my thoughts just got in the way of my good intentions. I resolved to try harder to think kind thoughts about Amanda and Kellie during the upcoming week—or at least the rest of the day; I should keep my goals realistic.

When church was over, we rode the bus home. We talked about cooking dinner together on Saturday and Sunday since those were the days we wouldn't have to work at the hospital or orphanage. We decided to pair up—Tara and I together, and Amanda and Kellie together. We would alternate Saturday and Sunday every week. We decided to each handle our own meals the other days since we would all be tired from working and none of us would feel like cooking.

We all pitched in for that first Sunday dinner. We had a disagreement almost immediately. Amanda wanted to keep the Sunday meal simple, because it was the Sabbath and Tara wanted to have a big dinner—like a family meal.

They argued more like sisters than cousins; Kellie and I wisely stayed out of it. They ended up compromising on letting those in charge of cooking for the day determine what to cook and how simple or fancy it would be.

I hoped Tara could cook better than I could, because we would have soup and sandwiches a lot if it were left up to me. That's exactly what we ended up having that first Sunday; tomato soup and grilled cheese sandwiches. We were hungry enough, it tasted like manna from heaven.

Amanda brought up the subject of riding the bus to church on Sunday. She felt like it was breaking the Sabbath to take the bus. Kellie agreed, of course. I pointed out that it was too far to walk, and Tara agreed with me.

Kellie calculated that it was about four miles away and we could walk it in an hour if we walked briskly. She actually said "briskly."

My resolve to think more kindly of them was quickly fading away. "It's bad enough I'm losing out on an extra hour of sleep by going early for choir, when I'm much better at sleeping than singing. I am not going to walk briskly, four miles to church. I don't think it's that big a deal to ride the bus."

Kellie looked offended. "It was just an idea. Does anyone have any other ideas? I'm not saying anyone has to walk."

Tara furrowed her brow as if in deep thought then said, "Why don't we buy our tickets on Saturday, so we aren't actually spending money on Sunday. The buses are going to run whether or not we ride them, and we'd only ride the bus to and from church—it's not like we're sightseeing or anything. What do you think?"

Amanda actually agreed. "I think that's a good solution. We really can't walk that far each way, especially when it gets cold. And we should all stick together, I think that's important." Kellie nodded as well.

I personally thought it was a perfect example of letter of the law versus spirit of the law that I had learned about in a Sunday school class; but I saw no point in arguing it. At least we weren't going to be hoofing it to church on Sunday.

chapter fifteen

To: bridgerman123@hotmail.com
From: kitcarson@yahoo.com
Subject: the first day is finally over

Dear Adam,
It has been an amazing couple of days. I had to beg Tara to come with me to the internet café. We are all so tired. I told you about church in the letter I just mailed so I won't repeat myself. Today was our first day working at the hospital and the orphanage. I knew things would be different here, but I had no clue just how different.

We got to the hospital this morning, and Anya took us on a tour before we started working. If I had to describe the hospital in one word it would be "smelly." It doesn't smell sterile—it's kind of gross. It's also really dim and depressing. There aren't a lot of lights and even though the windows are pretty big, the view from them is so dreary, it's depressing. The babies are on the first floor and the children are on the second. Tara and I chose to work with the children, mainly in the play therapy room. Kellie and Amanda chose to work with the infants.

It's so sad to see the children in the hospital. A lot of them are from the orphanage and so they never have visitors. They don't laugh or interact very much. I worked with a two-year old boy named Alin. He doesn't walk or crawl or even sit up. He's from the orphanage and is in the hospital because of an infection. He is so tense and his leg and arm muscles have sort of wasted away. Anya told me it is called "failure to thrive." Alin doesn't respond to normal stimulus so it was really hard to get and keep his attention. He's very traumatized by change because he's used to just being in his crib all the time.

It took him awhile to get used to me. He was shaking and crying at first and it made me so sad. I wanted to cuddle him but he was so stiff. I kept talking to him and trying to get his attention and it took a long time for him to warm up to me. Regular toys don't keep him entertained so it was hard to think of things to do. I worked with him for about two hours. When I put him back in his crib he was screaming and crying so loud–I thought my heart would break. It made me wonder if it was better not to get him attached to me, I don't want to make it worse for him.

Kellie and Amanda told us about the babies. They only get changed twice a day so they're all messy and wet until it just drips. Yuck. When they put the babies back in their cribs they all screamed and cried, so pretty much there was crying going on all the time. They were both dying for a shower when we got home, so of course I couldn't convince them to come with us to send emails. I wanted a shower too, but I wanted to email you more. Besides you can't smell me in an email! Give thanks for that!

I am so thankful for Tara. Of course she is over flirting with Vasilé as I write this to you, so I don't think it is that big of a hardship for her! She didn't shower either, but Vasilé would never notice because people over here just don't bathe very often.

Oh yeah, I don't think I mentioned that the hospital is a children's hospital. When Anya showed us around, she showed us the new emergency room that was recently added on. It's weird because they ran out of money before they got equipment for it. So it's there, practically empty. I shudder to think of children needing emergency care. Just imagine, these people live with stuff like this.

We went to the orphanage this afternoon from 3–6. It was a real eye opener. We had learned a little from CFAW about why there are so many orphans in Romania, but I didn't know that parents come and drop off their children sometimes just because they can't take care of them. Maybe that kind of thing happens in the U.S., but I'm just amazed that someone could just walk up to the orphanage, drop off their little baby, and leave again. Wow, I can't believe I just said that–coming from a person who was left in a garbage can after birth. At least the orphanage is better than the trash. It just makes my heart hurt to see it.

I met a supervisor at the orphanage, her name is Ileana. She is so nice and speaks English pretty well.

She told us a lot about how the orphanage is run and how things are in Romania.

The babies are kept upstairs in one huge room with rows and rows of cribs. I think I counted thirty cribs. They lie in their cribs most of the day, some of them just staring and not making a sound. Some babies self-stimulate; maybe they play with their fingers or rock back and forth if they're strong enough to sit up by themselves. We saw one baby who just laughed and laughed, which was really weird because there wasn't anything that we could see that made him laugh like that.

This is really hard. It's hard work physically and so draining emotionally. How do these people have hope in circumstances like these? It makes me glad of who I am and that I have parents who love and care for me. Most of these children in the orphanage will never get adopted or picked up by their real parents. Most of them will live there until they are old enough to take care of themselves. For a lot of them, they'll end up begging or living on the streets.

I miss you so much. I wonder why I am here. My little effort seems so puny. How will it make a difference in the lives of these children?

Wow, I'm a real downer. Sorry this email seems kind of negative. I'm just really tired, discouraged, and I really, really miss you. I can't wait to talk to you. I hope the cell phone works when you try to call. I am dying to hear your voice. How did we go two years without talking to each other?

I love you, Adam. That thought is holding me together right now. I can't wait to come home, but I guess for now I'm committed to staying here. Don't forget about me! Email me, call me, write me!

Love, Kit

I sent the email and glanced over at Tara, who seemed to be having a good time with Vasilé. It looked and sounded like they were giving each other language lessons. I figured I had time to email my parents.

As I was writing to them, the IM icon showed up telling me that Adam had signed online. I was ecstatic! Before I could send him an instant message, his conversation popped up "hi. r u there?"

Yes, I was! I quickly started chatting with him. It wasn't quite the same as hearing his voice, but it was actually real time. How amazing to be able to type in a conversation from half-way around the world and have an instant reply!

Actually, not a lot had happened at home in the week since I left. Adam was still busy with school and working. Since I had just sent that long email telling him about my day at the hospital and orphanage, I told him we had to talk about his day. When Tara wandered back from her visit with Vasilé, I reluctantly told Adam good-bye.

Before we logged off, we set up a time for him to call me on the cell phone. We decided on one day a week when he could go home between classes and call me. It wasn't much, but given the financial situation of the Bridger family, I understood. It gave me something to look forward to.

Tara and I walked home quickly since it was getting dark and it was only the two of us. We joked about going to the wrong house again, but we were both careful to pay attention to where we were going.

I teased her about Vasilé. She took it well and even laughed about it. "You never know, Kit, I might just dump Eric and stay here with Vasilé. Of course, he would have to convert first. I think I'll give him a Book of Mormon."

"Are you serious? You like Vasilé that much?" I was shocked that Tara was thinking anything remotely like that.

Tara laughed at my reaction and said, "Don't worry, I'm kidding. I like Vasilé, but Eric's the one for me. I just like to get to know people. Especially cute male people! I am going to give him a Book of Mormon, though. You never know when someone is ready to accept the gospel."

"You had me worried for a minute, Tara. I just can't imagine living here permanently. It's just so different. Be careful that you don't break poor Vasilé's heart." It was probably too late for that; guys seemed to fall for Tara pretty easily.

When we got home Kellie and Amanda had showered and changed. Corina had stopped by to see how we liked our first day and offered to work on the language a little. I wanted a shower and some dinner more than I wanted to visit and speak Romanian.

Tara voiced what I was thinking, and Corina quickly offered to leave. Kellie and Amanda urged her to stay and told us they had left some rice and vegetables warming in the oven for us. What a nice and unexpected gesture!

We wolfed down the food, which was quite good; apparently Kellie's cooking ability exceeded the rest of ours. As we ate, Kellie and Amanda told Corina about our first day of volunteering. Corina told us how poorly staffed and underpaid the workers at the orphanage were.

"There are two kinds of workers there," Corina informed us. "Those who love the children, and those who just need work and aren't able to find anything better. There are not enough of the ones who really love the children. It is a hard job. No one thanks them for their work. They know that most of the children will end up in the streets when they leave the orphanage. It is good that you come to volunteer. It helps to make the load not so heavy on the workers."

Her insight helped us understand the need for volunteers. I felt a glimmer of how important service to these children was—maybe not to their earthly parents, but to their Heavenly Parents. Maybe my little effort was enough; it was hard to know for sure.

chapter sixteen

The week flew by. One highlight came when Adam called me on Wednesday and I heard his voice for the first time in more than a week. We had to limit our time on calls, which was hard, but it was so good to talk to him.

Another exciting thing happened at the hospital on Friday morning. I was in the play room with the children reading books to them in English. They didn't understand the words, but seemed mesmerized by my voice and the pictures.

Alin was brought in after a breathing treatment. He was lying there on the floor next to some blocks staring into nothingness. I kept an eye on him as I finished the book I was reading aloud. He didn't move or focus on anything. If his skinny little chest didn't rise and fall rhythmically, I would wonder if he was even alive.

I handed the book to one of the older children and moved over by him. "Alin. Alin." I tried to get his attention. He didn't turn towards my voice but his frail arms twitched and his fingers moved.

I moved into his line of vision. I started singing songs, smiling and gesturing as I sang. He shifted his head slightly.

"Alin, it's Kit. I know you can hear me. How are you, sweetheart? Can you look at me?" I took his hands in mine and played Pat-A-Cake. I kept looking at him and smiling. His head turned again and he focused on me. He looked in my eyes and smiled! It was fleeting, but I was certain he recognized me. It made my day.

When the weekend came all four of us were exhausted. None of us was prepared for the week we had just experienced. Even bubbly Tara was subdued. We just wanted to relax.

I fixed a simple dinner of soup and toast then curled up on my bed to re-read the letter I'd received from Adam. I reached over and touched his smiling photograph, willing him to feel how much I missed him and longing to feel his presence beside me.

Amanda stuck her head in my room to see if I wanted to play cards with them. Usually I liked to play games but that evening I just wanted to wallow in my fatigue and my homesickness. I didn't want to be cheered up.

I thought about starting another letter to Adam but didn't have anything new to tell him since I had emailed him earlier that day. I found there was time after the hospital and before the orphanage to stop by the internet café for a little while. It was better than coming home after dark and Tara usually seemed happy to accompany me.

Tara wandered in after a few minutes and settled down to write a letter to Eric. Since she couldn't email him, she had to content herself with snail-mail. She hadn't received any letters from him since we had arrived in Romania, but said she didn't expect any yet. She told me her mom would send any letters on to her until he received her new address and started using it.

I pulled out my iPod to listen to while I wrote in my journal. I tried hard to write in it regularly, but I'd skipped the last couple of days because I was so tired.

I wrote a little about the hospital and the orphanage then my thoughts turned to Adam. I shared my insecurities with the blank paper, filling the white space and relieving my tired brain and lonely heart.

I try so hard to remember I am here to help. This place is so depressing. There are so many children here without parents. They have no one to love them or look after them. It seems like a lonely, lost, forgotten place. I used to wonder why I was so unlucky to be thrown away by my birth mother; now I'm thankful it happened in America. I really miss my family. I miss Adam most of all. Here I feel isolated and like I could just disappear and no one would notice. What if Adam forgets about me? What if he changes his mind about me? I'm not strong in the Gospel like the Bridger family. I think he deserves better than me. I just wish he were here right now, to hold me and comfort me.

I set my pen and journal aside and closed my eyes. It didn't take long for me to drift off to sleep.

It seemed like moments later that the sun shining through the window woke me. I hadn't moved all night long; my journal was still by my side. Tara must have thrown a blanket over me, and I guessed she was already up, judging from her neatly-made bed.

I staggered into the kitchen and found all three of my roommates there at the table, finishing breakfast.

"Good morning, sleepyhead," Tara said, mid-chew.

"I made pancakes. There are some in the oven if you want them," Kellie offered. They smelled heavenly so I got a plate and helped myself to a stack of three.

"Thanks," I mumbled between bites. I was famished. Kellie looked pleased as I gobbled down the three I took and went for two more.

"We think Kellie should be the designated cook," Tara announced as she rinsed off her plate. "My pancakes are always rubbery or gushy in the middle."

"I told you how to tell when they're ready to turn," Kellie said. "You wait until the edges start looking dry and bubbles appear in the middle. And you don't beat the batter to death; you just mix it until it's all moistened."

"So are these from a mix?" I wondered aloud. I guess I shouldn't have because Kellie looked offended.

"They're made from scratch. That's why they're so light and fluffy."

I didn't know anyone under the age of forty who made pancakes from scratch. Actually I didn't know anyone over the age of forty who did either. My mom sure didn't and I'd always liked her pancakes just fine.

Tara laughed and said, "Kellie, you're such a Molly. You probably make your own clothes and bake your own bread."

Amanda jumped into the conversation before Kellie could reply.

"What's wrong with that? Being self-reliant is important. Kellie does sew really well and I haven't heard either of you complain about her cooking. It just irritates me when members make fun of other members for being self-reliant. It's bad enough when non-members do it, but we don't need contention amongst ourselves."

Contention amongst ourselves? I swear Amanda talked like a dictionary sometimes. I didn't care for her member vs. non-member talk; I remembered too well when I was labeled as a non-member, and how it was said in such a way that I felt inferior and like I was being judged and found lacking.

I decided to just keep quiet and concentrate on finishing my pancakes, which were quite delicious. Tara laughed again and said, "Lighten up! I wasn't being contentious. You Happy Valley Mormons take life way too seriously. I don't think being a Molly is bad, but even Mollys can have a sense of humor."

"You're not funny, Tara," Amanda grumbled at her cousin. "You are far too irreverent about sacred matters."

Tara snorted. "Since when are pancakes 'sacred matters?' I'm not irreverent about things that really matter."

Kellie stood up and started clearing the table. "You two argue about the dumbest stuff. I really don't care if you think I'm a Molly. I take it as a compliment."

I swallowed my last bite and said, "Those were really good, Kellie. Thanks." I was proud of myself for staying out of it, but then I just had to add, "What are Happy Valley Mormons?"

That triggered Tara's laughter again and made Amanda look like she was going to bite my head off. Kellie came to the rescue before Amanda could let loose on me. "Happy Valley is what people outside of Utah Valley call Utah Valley. It's usually people who are just jealous of BYU." She gave Tara a pointed look.

"It's called Happy Valley because so many people there are caught up in their own narrow view of the world. They think their way is the only way and are happy in their tunnel vision. Oh, and most of those people go to BYU." Tara stared her down.

"There you go again!" Amanda huffed. "Treating sacred things disrespectfully! You drive me nuts, Tara." She was riled up.

"Happy Valley is not sacred, Amanda," Tara said slowly as if speaking to a child. "That's the problem with Happy Valley. The people all think it's sacred. It's the true valley." She rolled her eyes as she said it.

Amanda was sputtering and I thought she might smack Tara. Tara kept smiling at her, and I realized I'd never seen this part of her. I never thought she would deliberately taunt someone, but that's what she was doing.

Kellie stepped forward and took Amanda's arm. "Just let it go. You know she's just doing it to get to you. Ignore her." Amanda let Kellie lead her out of the kitchen, and I could hear Amanda murmuring furiously in the other room.

I turned to Tara and said, "Wow, you were pretty brutal to her. I've never seen this side of you."

Tara tossed her blonde curls and said, "Amanda drives me nuts sometimes. She really acts self-righteous. I should probably apologize, but I'll do it later. I'm going to go shower now."

I stayed in the kitchen and did the dishes. I didn't know what to say or do, but I hoped it would all blow over. I didn't want to live in a war zone.

A couple of hours later, the confrontation seemed to be forgotten. We were all dressed and ready to go exploring. We walked down to catch the bus to Strada Republicii, the main marketing street in Brasov. We passed a dark little man selling fruit.

We passed this man every day on our way to catch the bus. When we bought fruit from him once, he stared at us as he counted back our change and I thought the way he looked at us was pure evil. Since then, we wouldn't stop. He yelled things at us in Romanian that gave me the creeps even though I couldn't understand what he was saying. I'm sure he could tell how uncomfortable I was because he gave a nasty little laugh after he yelled. I wanted to go a different way, but it was the shortest way to the bus stop and the others thought I was overreacting.

We hurried past him and he called out who knows what to us and cackled. I tried not to look at him, but wished I could push him and his little cart down a steep hill.

We rode the bus down to the central square and met Corina where the pedestrian zone began. She walked with us, telling us good places to shop and giving us a language lesson along the way. She seemed to have plenty of time for us and I wondered what kind of job she did besides tutoring.

"I'm still going to university here in Brasov. University Transilvania of Brasov. I am studying nursing. It was my dream to finish school at Brigham Young University, but there is never enough money and my family is here. So I am here. I earn some money tutoring students like you and I work some shifts selling cosmetics at the mall."

We must have looked surprised because Corina laughed and said, "Yes, Brasov has a mall—two malls. I work at the Brasov Mall. I have not taken you there yet, but we can go. I thought you had seen enough malls in the United States and would not be interested in them here. It is not so big as your malls there, but it has a cinema and it is near the railway station."

I was impressed. Brasov was beautiful and seemed like a little city set back in time, so I was surprised when I realized many of the modern conveniences—like malls, were available to us there.

Corina got my attention again as she pointed to a huge church with black walls looming over us. "Biserica Neagră," she announced. "The Black Church. It is the largest Gothic-style church in Transilvania. You will like it. Did you bring your cameras?"

We dug through our backpacks and found our cameras. We toured the church and it was amazing to stand inside a church over six hundred years old. I wished those walls could talk to me. Although Biserica Neagră dominated the square, there were other beautiful old buildings that were worth photographing as well. Several were museums and we spent a very pleasant afternoon wandering through them, learning more about Brasov's history.

As evening approached we discussed what we should do for dinner. Corina suggested a small Mexican restaurant that she knew of called Bella Musica. The food was good, but too expensive for us to go to very often.

Corina told us about more places she thought we would like to see in and around Brasov. She told us about a couple of great places to hike and suggested we go on a hike the following Saturday.

After dinner we took our time walking along Strada Republicii.

It was so nice to have Corina with us. I worried that we were monopolizing her time, because she spent so much more time with us than a language tutor normally would. When I brought it up, she told me not to worry, she was having fun showing us her city and country and it helped her keep her English skills polished.

We left Corina when we got to the bus stop. She reminded us of choir practice the next morning. We called "La revedere" as she climbed on her bus and then went to wait for our own. As we were standing there, a guy came riding by on a rickety old bicycle. He was somewhere between thirty and fifty, it was hard to tell. He grinned at us, showing stained teeth with a gap where a couple were missing. He was another one of those that gave us the heebie-jeebies, so we kind of turned to each other to avoid eye contact.

Amanda was standing at the end of our group, and as the man pedaled by he reached out and grabbed her chest. Amanda screamed in outrage and disbelief. The pervert groped her right there, in public, and no one stopped him! He kept on riding like it was something he did every day, which it probably was.

We were stunned, but Tara sprang to action first. She looked down and found a couple of rocks, scooped them up, and ran after the guy. She threw them at him in quick succession; unfortunately, they both missed. She called him a name I didn't know she knew. He pedaled on, unfazed, getting away with his crime.

We turned our attention back to Amanda, who was crying. Kellie had her arm around her and Tara and I reached out to her in solidarity. She was upset and furious; but insisted she was not hurt. The bus came and we helped her board, surrounding her, as if we could form a protective shield around her.

The bus ride home was very quiet. None of us talked about it until we were safe in our little house with the doors locked. Amanda cried again as she recalled the feeling of being violated, but her tears turned to laughter as we recounted Tara's rock-throwing and name-calling.

Amanda blew her nose and said, "Tara always was the feisty one in the family. She would always defend your honor if she perceived injustice."

That caused Tara to sniffle and she went over to Amanda and

hugged her. "I'll always stick up for you. I love you." That was followed by another hug. "I'm so glad you're all right. I'm sorry I was being rude to you earlier today."

"I'm sorry I take offense at everything. I don't mean to sound self-righteous." Amanda's apology set off another round of hugs between the cousins.

Although Amanda and Tara's reconciliation came about because of the disgusting act of a stranger; the spirit in our home that night was one of thanksgiving and love. All contention between them had passed and the day ended on a much sweeter note than it had begun.

chapter seventeen

At choir practice the next morning I found it was still a challenge to sing the hymns in a different language—who was I kidding, it was a challenge for me to sing in any language.

I stood next to Kellie to share her Romanian hymnbook. I think she cringed as I attempted to hit the notes and failed more than half the time. Oh well, I tried to warn them! If they insisted on dragging me out of bed an hour early, they would have to pay the price.

After sacrament meeting, Corina introduced us to Danielle Porter, an American woman who had two young Romanian children by the hand whom she introduced as her children, Tomas and Alexi. The sister missionaries joined our little group, I think it was to remind us to go to their class with their investigator.

Danielle greeted them and reminded them about coming to dinner at her house later that day. Then Danielle turned and invited the four of us—actually the five of us, including Corina, and we enthusiastically agreed.

This time when we attended the Gospel Principles class I was not quite as nervous. I had pulled it off last week without having to comment. Amanda and Kellie were both ready to give input, so it was easy to go unnoticed.

Sora Barnes and Sora Campbell did their translation routine rather flawlessly, as far as I could tell. If they made mistakes, their confidence masked it. I was impressed by how fluently they spoke

Romanian; they both were just over a year into their missions.

Sora Pavel, the investigator, seemed to agree with all that was said. She didn't ask questions on her own, but she responded when the missionaries or Sister Milcu asked her something directly.

I followed the discussion fairly well; they were talking about the importance of baptism and how it should be performed in the proper manner with proper priesthood authority. My mind wandered a little as I thought about my own baptism and how Adam's brother Justin had baptized me because Adam was still on his mission at the time.

I was brought back to reality when I realized that Sora Barnes was speaking directly to me. "Sister Matthews, we understand you are a convert to the Church and were baptized not too long ago. Would you be willing to share your feelings about your baptism with us?"

I probably looked like a deer in the headlights, caught unaware and frozen in fear. Who told them? I looked at my roommates to see if I could tell who was guilty, but they all looked at me encouragingly as if they couldn't wait to hear.

I was not particularly willing but, like Sora Pavel, I was trained to answer when directly addressed. "Uh, I was baptized about a year and a half ago by my boyfriend's brother. He has the priesthood." I sounded like a moron.

Sora Barnes smiled kindly at me as Sora Campbell translated my brilliant speech to Sora Pavel. "Can you tell us about how you felt when you were baptized, Sister Matthews?"

I struggled to gather my thoughts. Why was this so hard? I realized that I hadn't shared my feelings about being baptized with anyone besides Adam and Janet. I didn't know if I had the words. I worked up the courage to try.

"When the sister missionaries taught me, they asked me to pray about getting baptized." I took a deep breath to calm my nerves. My heart thumped in my chest. "I prayed about it, but at first I didn't really want the answer because I knew in the back of my mind that it would be yes. I wasn't sure I wanted to admit that God really existed, so I wasn't looking very hard for an answer."

I took another breath. Sora Campbell kept translating. Sora

Pavel nodded, but looked alert, like she cared about what she was hearing. I felt the sweat trickle down my back. "I finally agreed to be baptized; I wanted so much for it all to be true. It felt right. I know I was baptized by one who holds the authority from God. I felt the Spirit so strongly when I received the gift of the Holy Ghost. I knew it was the right thing to do. I knew the Book of Mormon was true."

My voice quavered and I felt the tears well up in my eyes and spill over. Tara passed me a tissue. I wiped my eyes and finished sharing the words which now seemed to come forth from my heart—I could not hold back. "I received a witness at my baptism that my Heavenly Father approved of my decision. But I was not perfect in my faith. I still wondered. Did He hear me? Did He know me? Was He really there for me? It wasn't until after I lost my best friend, Janet, in a terrible accident that I turned to Him and honestly, honestly asked Him for help. I received my witness." I turned to face Sora Pavel. "I know He lives and loves me. He loves me, Kit Matthews; and if He loves me, I know He loves you. He knows you, Sora Pavel. He does."

The tears flowed freely down my face and Tara perceptively handed me another tissue. When the blurring cleared, I dared to look around at the faces of my roommates. They all sniffled into their tissues. I'm pretty sure they felt what I did.

The class continued on, and my heart went on beating, although not nearly as fiercely as before. At the end of class, Sora Pavel came over and gave me a kiss-kiss, which we had learned was a traditional greeting. She beamed at me and jabbered something in Romanian.

Sora Campbell translated. "She says, 'Thank you for your beautiful testimony. I can see that God smiles on you. I love you.' Thank you, Sister Matthews. It was a beautiful testimony."

After church, we went directly to Danielle Porter's apartment. It was small by American standards, but it felt like it could have been in any city in the United States. Danielle helped her children get changed from their Sunday clothes. I guessed Danielle was in her early thirties, judging from her appearance. I saw several family pictures on a bookshelf; two or three of Danielle and the children, but no evidence of a Mr. Porter. I tried not to be nosey, but I wondered.

Tara wondered the same thing, out loud. When Danielle came back out with her children, Tara asked, "Are you married, Danielle?"

"No, I've never been married. I came over to Romania three years ago to teach English at the University. I loved it here so much. Like you, I spent some time volunteering in the orphanage. I fell in love with this one." She ruffled Tomas's hair. "He was two years old and I felt like he should be my child. I checked into adoption requirements. Adoption is made so much easier if you have residency here. So I renewed my teaching contract, which was originally for only two semesters, and I brought Tomas home with me. A year later, his little sister Alexi was brought to the orphanage. She wasn't his birth sister, but I knew she belonged in our family. That was a year ago."

Danielle hugged her two children to her and kissed them lightly on the head. "They are my children now, as much as if they had been born to me. Tomas is four and Alexi is two. I don't know if we will add more to our little family. Right now, we're pretty happy with the way things are."

"Don't you have family in the U.S. that you miss?" Amanda asked. "It must be hard to be away from them."

Danielle looked a little wistful. "My mother and sister are in Phoenix. They talk about coming to visit, but airfare is so expensive. I may go back to the States someday, but for now, I'm needed here."

Tomas squirmed away from his mother and demanded food. "I want pizza, Mommy."

Alexi echoed, "Peetcha, peetcha."

Danielle laughed and told them to hold on, offering them each a cracker to hold them over. She then excused herself while she stepped in the kitchen to order the pizza.

My roommates and I exchanged looks. "She's ordering the pizza," Kellie whispered as if we hadn't heard it ourselves. "I didn't know she would order out when she asked us to dinner. It's Sunday." Again as if we didn't know.

Corina seemed fine with it, so we turned to the sister missionaries. Sora Campbell explained. "Many of the people here have not really embraced the idea of keeping the Sabbath. It's a challenge we face over and over again. We don't always know what it will mean when we accept dinner invitations. Our mission president counseled us to follow the Spirit in accepting invitations and to teach gospel principles while we are in the homes of the members and non-members alike."

Sora Barnes spoke up. "Sister Porter has asked us to give a family home evening lesson tonight, so this seems like a good opportunity to reinforce gospel teachings."

Corina had listened to this exchange with interest. "I don't really see the difference. If you look at the amount of work the workers at the pizza shop do compared to the amount of work my mother and grandmother put into a dinner when they invite guests over, I would say the pizza people work less. It is keeping Sister Porter from having to work hard to prepare a meal for all of us." She seemed satisfied with her explanation.

Sora Barnes and Sora Campbell looked at us as if to say, *Do you see the attitudes we encounter?*

I could see Corina's point and I wondered if we should accept any dinner invitations on Sunday. It wouldn't change the world, but it would make me feel better not to put anyone to a lot of work to feed me.

I had flashbacks of all the Sunday dinners I'd eaten that my mom or Barbara had worked hard to prepare. I knew they both did it out of love for their families, but I resolved that I would be more helpful in the future, so the burden would not fall so heavily on them.

Danielle had also invited her neighbor from next door. Christina Vulpes was about Danielle's age, also single, and not a member of the Church.

Before she arrived, Danielle explained that Christina often came over on Sunday afternoons to join them for dinner and listen to a lesson the missionaries had prepared. She declined to participate in the discussions, but was willing to listen to the family home evening lessons the sister missionaries presented. Danielle had invited her to church a couple of times, but Christina always had an excuse.

Christina loved all things American, so Danielle told us she would probably ask lots of questions about where and how we lived back in the States.

Danielle was right; Christina plied us with question after question. She was an intelligent woman with sharp black eyes and black hair that had a single streak of white down one side.

I mouthed "Cruella de Vil" to Tara when I was sure no one else saw me. Tara laughed and then we couldn't make eye contact with each other again for awhile for fear of breaking into a fit of giggles.

Christina stopped her inquisition of us periodically as she helped Alexi or Tomas. I noticed she was very good with the children and asked her if she had any of her own.

"No, Romania has enough children without me adding to the problem," she said sharply. Her abruptness surprised me.

Danielle tried to explain, "Christina doesn't like how the government allows parents to have children and then neglect to care for them. She thinks parents need to take more responsibility."

Christina studied me as if debating on whether or not to say what was on her mind. It was a quick debate. "I was dropped off at an orphanage as a child. I was there until I was ten. I was fortunate enough to get a job in the candy factory. I worked hard and studied all that I could. I learned how to make candy and had dreams of opening my own shop one day. Many years later I met a woman who was willing to help me with my dream. That does not happen often in Romania." She paused and gave Danielle a significant look. "I am thankful for the opportunity to have my little shop. It is my family. When I have need for more, Danielle shares her children with me. It is enough. I do not add to Romania's problems." I could tell by her body language she had said all she would on the matter.

As if on cue, Tomas and Alexi started asking Christina for chocolate. Christina smiled at them and asked Danielle if they could come with her to get some candy next door. Danielle agreed and Tomas and Alexi ran to the door, eager to get their treat.

While they were gone, Danielle told us, "Christina is a good woman. She's a little hard around the edges; I think growing up in an orphanage and on the streets makes you that way. She has a kind heart and helps me so much with Tomas and Alexi. The problem is, they always associate her with chocolate now, and she always gives in when they ask." She smiled fondly. "She gives me far too much credit. She had the drive to succeed in her own business, she just needed someone to put up a little money."

I was slow, but I figured out that Danielle had been the one to help Christina get into her own shop. It seemed that Danielle took orphans under her wing, no matter what their age.

The children returned with Christina, bringing enough chocolate for all of us. In my opinion it was a heavenly day—first pizza, then chocolate.

The sister missionaries gave a lesson on keeping the commandments. They covered keeping the Sabbath which we all could do a little better at. When they mentioned the love thy neighbor thing, as I glanced around the room at the eclectic group which included four orphans (counting me). I figured Danielle had that one pretty much nailed down.

chapter eighteen

The next couple of weeks fell into a pattern. Monday through Friday we spent mornings at the hospital, came home for lunch, stopped by the internet café for an hour when I could convince one of the others to go with me, then we would return to work at the orphanage.

I loved seeing Alin at the hospital and spent most of my time working with him. There was another child that seemed drawn to me, a little girl called Madalina. She was about five years old with a puffy face and squinty eyes. She clung to me and was naughty, especially when I paid more attention to Alin. I felt a bond with Alin that I didn't feel with Madalina. It didn't help that Madalina threw temper tantrums, would pinch Alin when she thought I wasn't watching, and pulled at my clothes and tried to chew on them.

The mornings at the hospital became a battle for me. As much as I loved Alin, I couldn't really stand Madalina. I referred to her in my head as the "devil child." I had lots of patience with Alin and many of the other children, but little for Madalina.

It seemed the less tolerance I had for her, the worse she became. One morning I was working with Alin in his room for a little while before I took him into the play room with the others. Madalina sneaked in, as she often did when I was working with him. He was responding so well, he was starting to reach for toys as I held them out. As I held one towards him, Madalina ran up and snatched the toy, then ran far enough away that I couldn't get it back.

I sternly reprimanded her, "Madalina, bring me the toy. Now!" My tone was mean and she responded tauntingly with "Engleză. Engleză," followed by a string of what sounded like gibberish, but I was pretty sure she was actually mocking and maybe swearing at me. She always called me "Engleză" which meant "English." I think she knew my name, but just tried to irritate me. I wanted to spank her; but, of course, I didn't.

I decided to ignore her, and turned my attention back to Alin. I picked up another toy to entice him with. When Madalina saw that I wasn't giving her attention, she ran back over and hit me with the toy she had snatched. I grabbed her hand before she could dart off. I pulled her over to the doorway, shoved her through, and slammed the door shut.

She stood there stunned for a moment and I told her, "Stay out until you can behave!" She probably couldn't understand all of my words, but they were loud and my tone was clear. She started wailing and threw herself down on the floor, banging her fists and feet. I ignored her, which was hard, because her shrieks were piercing.

I thought other workers might come running to see what the matter was, but none came, so I guessed they were used to Madalina in action. I turned my back on the window to the hallway, and continued to play with Alin. There were no other children in the room; they were all in the play area.

The racket quieted after a few minutes, and I glanced back at the window. Madalina stood with her tear-stained face pressed against the window, snot-nosed and even more squinty-eyed than usual. I tried to ignore her, I was glad to have her gone and didn't want her back inside.

She didn't leave her post at the window. She didn't try the door, which wasn't locked and I knew she could open. Whenever I looked over she was there, staring at me with her darting black eyes. *She deserved to be put out, she was so naughty*, I told myself. I knew if I invited her back in, she would start up again. She needed to learn a lesson.

It took about ten minutes of her pudgy little face squished against the window to soften my heart. She was five years old, I was twenty; last time I looked, I thought I was an adult. I said a little prayer asking for more patience and a forgiving heart and I beckoned her back inside the room.

She kept against the wall as she crept back in. She stood there, sniffing uselessly, and ended up using her sleeve as a tissue. Gross. I forced a smile and used a kinder tone. "Are you ready to be nice, Madalina?" She stared but said nothing.

I picked up the toy she had grabbed and clubbed me with. "Come here," I offered her the toy. "Let's play." She came closer but didn't take the toy. She picked up a thick string of wooden beads, colors faded with age and use. She tried to get Alin's attention with them, shaking and twisting them as she had seen me do.

Alin followed the movement of the beads and Madalina started chanting in her sing-song way. She dangled them close to him, and he slowly reached out for them. Just as he nearly touched them, she snatched them away and laughed maniacally.

Alin pulled back his hand and Madalina again offered the beads to him. He stretched forth his hand again and I saw in her eyes that she was going to pull them away again. Same old Madalina. I was about to reprimand her again, but I noticed as she jerked the beads back and cackled that Alin actually smiled at her. He seemed to like the keep-away game she was playing with him.

"Buna, Madalina!" Good. I praised her in her own language. She giggled and said "Buna, Engleză!" She played the game with Alin for a couple more minutes before they both lost interest. She put the beads down, looked at me slyly, and reached over and pinched Alin. He started crying and I silently prayed for more patience.

Later that day, I worked with the infants. It was hard work; it seemed like there were constantly babies crying or staring silently off in space, detached, lost in their own little world.

I was always glad to see Ileana, the supervisor who had befriended us. She was close to my age and her English was much better than most of the other workers'. I liked working with her because she always had interesting things to tell us and was curious about how we liked it in Brasov.

I told her how we were a little creeped out by some of the rude things yelled at us and stares we got from guys on the street. She taught me a little phrase to use if someone gave me the eye. Ce te uiți la mine miamuțo? (Pronounced chay tay oo-eet-zee la mee nay my mootzoe—she had to tell it to me several times.) It meant "What are you looking at you dirty monkey?" I loved it, and planned on using it often. I practiced the phrase over and over, asking her to help me with the inflection. She told me I needed to say it with more attitude. She laughed as I perfected my delivery of the line.

Just like at the hospital, babies were only changed twice a day at the orphanage. There was no money for conveniences such as wet wipes. Old receiving blankets were used as diapers, and we had to peel off the soaking wet layers, hold the baby over the sink so we could run water over his behind and legs, and scrub the skin clean with a bar of soap. Sometimes the babies were so soiled, the mess was dried on and it took some effort to clean them up. Their little bums were red from being in the dirty diapers; some even had open sores that bled. Diaper changes were traumatic for them, but their smiles lit up their faces when they were clean and dry.

There was a limited supply of disposable diapers available so usually receiving blankets were folded and placed inside of a disposable one. The disposable diaper was used over and over until it was too soiled to reuse. Once we got the hang of changing the babies, we discovered the workers in the orphanage didn't mind if we changed them more often. Some afternoons were spent changing diapers the entire three hours.

I really liked working with the babies, and when Ileana was on shift, time sped by. I fell in love with two baby girls—twins, who had been at the orphanage since birth. Daciana and Simona were about four months old. They slept in cribs next to each other and I think it helped them bond. They didn't show signs of detachment yet.

I did my fair share of taking care of all the babies, but I found myself playing with Daciana and Simona the most. I imagined that they were my own children, which was odd because I'd never really thought too much about having children. It was always something in the future—the distant future. As I played with these two little darlings I thought about Adam and me as their parents. I didn't realize it at first, but I was getting obsessive about it.

I asked Ileana about how hard it would be to adopt them. I questioned Danielle about the process she went through to adopt Tomas and Alexi. I talked to Tara about it. I even mentioned it to Adam in an e-mail:

> I have grown to love some of these children here. There are twin girls, Daciana and Simona, who are so precious. They are only four months old. They've been here since birth and I asked Ileana if she knew anything about their parents. Sometimes the parents drop off their children for a few months or even longer, then come back and get them later, when they can take care of them. I wanted to know if my two little angels might ever be picked up.
>
> Ileana said they aren't supposed to release any information about the children's backgrounds, so she couldn't tell me about the twins' parents. I begged her to just let me know if they might get reunited with them. She finally left their file out "accidentally" and I picked it up and read through it. Their mother was only twelve years old, and the father was listed as "unknown." I couldn't believe it, and it made me feel even sadder about these little girls. I'm pretty sure that they'll never know their birth parents.
>
> Ileana said if they do get adopted, they would most likely be split up. It's so discouraging to think about them being split up, or becoming like the older babies in the orphanage with failure to thrive.
>
> I want to do something more than play with them and cuddle them for a couple more months. I sometimes imagine they're our girls. (I know that's weird, but I do.) I think about adopting them. Would you ever consider it? I know—we aren't even married yet and haven't even discussed the possibility of adopting, but we both want children. Maybe it's the reason I'm here. Maybe we should be their parents.

After I'd sent the email to Adam, I worried about it. I opened up to Tara, and she told me to stop obsessing about things I couldn't change. She advised me to enjoy the time I had in Romania, share the love I could with the kids, but not take it so personally. How could you not take babies lying in their own filth, unloved and untouched for hours by another human hand, personally? It was a skill I didn't possess.

I hoped Adam didn't dismiss my feelings so casually. I eagerly checked my email the day after I sent the one about adopting. I had one from Adam and Lily. I read Adam's first.

To: kitcarson@yahoo.com
From: bridgerman123@hotmail.com
Subject: Only 61 more days!

Hi Kit!

I'm so glad you're having a good experience in Romania. I can tell you're coming to love those you serve. I understand that feeling from my mission. I think it's a reward for serving others—your own capacity to love grows.

I'm not against adopting—I just never thought about it being something I might do. I do want to be married, at least, before I consider it! Don't fall in love with the kids there so much that you don't want to come back. I'm counting the days until you're home and I figure we're down to 61. One month down, two to go.

Guess what? My dad got a full-time job! He's now the assistant store manager at the home improvement center. The pay isn't as good as his old job, but he said, "It's a lot better than what unemployment pays." Sounds just like him, huh? My parents say they can survive on the pay, plus they'll have benefits again. He says they have a really good retirement plan. I told him I'm too busy training for employment to worry about retirement. He said I'll be his age before I know it. That was encouraging. (That was sarcasm.)

I'm in a good routine with school. I'm keeping up with all the assignments and so far I have A's & B's. I'm not a brainiac like you, but at least my brain still works. I did have to cut back on my hours at work because of school. I still don't have a car, and it's going to take longer now to get one. In the meantime, I take the bus, walk, or hitch a ride with someone. I haven't given up riding my bike sometimes, but the weather forecast says it's going to snow at the end of the week, so my biking days are numbered. I sure miss the weather in sunny California now that it's getting cold. I feel a little bad about taunting you about the weather for the last two winters, but I'm sure I'll get over it.

How's the weather in Romania? Have you had to break out (or in) the long johns yet? At least you have plenty of those, thanks to your mom!

I gotta go. My ride's here. I love you, stay warm & write back soon!

Adam.

Well he wasn't excited about adopting, but at least he didn't think I was crazy. That was something. I opened Lily's next. She was mad again.

To: kitcarson@yahoo.com
From: lilyofthevalley16@hotmail.com
Subject: gotta vent!

Ok, Kit, I've tried not to rant and I've tried to be nice, but I am going nuts! About what? You guessed it—Ruth! That woman should be called "Delilah" instead of Ruth. I think she's a phony, but it's like I'm the only one who sees it. She weasels her way in around here like a, well—a weasel!

Ok, you know how my dad's been out of work? Well Ruth got the part-time job for him. She's like in charge of hiring or some kind of office manager. That was all good and everything, but she acts like she's my dad's boss and Adam's too! She's a manager there—that doesn't make her everybody's boss.

So she "put in a good word" with the general manager cuz they needed an assistant manager for the whole store. They hired Dad, so I should be glad, and I am. It's been really hard having my dad out of work. One reason is, I want a cell phone. I don't think that's too much to ask for—all normal girls my age have them. But, no, we're too poor, I hate it. I'm like a freak!

So it's good my dad has a job again, but Ruth came over to announce it to the family to make sure she got the credit for it. She was hanging out after my mom invited her to dinner (again) and the manager guy called when she was there to offer Dad the job.

Everyone was so excited, and Mom and Dad started hugging each other and the little kids were jumping around cheering. So Ruth goes and hugs Adam! That's right, and she probably would have kissed him too, if she hadn't have seen my glare! I tell you, she has infiltrated our family like a mole, and I can't stand her.

Then she offered to take our family out for ice cream to celebrate. Mom said no cuz it was too expensive, but Ruth "really wanted to do something to celebrate" so then she suggested she and Adam could go to the store to buy some ice cream and bring it home to eat.

Don't worry! I begged to go—I wasn't about to leave her alone with Adam. It's bad enough they ride to work together half the time. I think maybe she schedules as much time working with Adam as she can. She's a year older than him, but she doesn't care. I think she's man-hungry.

I went with them and I complained about not having a cell phone cuz I want to text my friends—normal teenagers can text each other. Adam told me to stop whining (which I wasn't whining, I was stating my needs). So Ruth said "How cute. Lily, I think it's cute that you want to text your friends. I'll tell you what. You can use my cell phone to text your friends whenever I'm over. We can share my phone!" Like I would share a dog bone with her! Although I did eat her ice cream later—I'm not stupid, you know. She talked like I was a little kid. I'm almost 15! I'm almost an adult!

Sorry for going on and on. I just get so frustrated and can't text my friends—as I've pointed out to anyone who will listen to me. Don't worry about it, I'm keeping an eagle-eye on the mole! I'd draw you a picture if I could on the computer, but just look up "mole" or "weasel" in the dictionary and you'll see a picture of Ruth! j/k!

Love, Lily

Wow! She was mad. I reread Adam's email; he didn't mention Ruth at all. I wondered if Lily was over-reacting. I could recognize that trait in a fellow drama queen. But I did remember Ruth from our one meeting and I could almost hear her say the things Lily mentioned. I fought down the flare of jealousy and the wave of homesickness that threatened to engulf me.

I read Lily's email one more time. Poor Lily. She was so full of teenage angst. Everything was a tragedy to her. I missed her and wanted to talk to her face-to-face. She was growing up and wasn't the same little girl who used to curl up by me on the couch and rest her head on my shoulder.

I smiled as I thought about her cell phone problem. I remembered when I took mine for granted and used it to text and call people at a whim. I thought I couldn't live without it, but I had—for a month already. The cell phone we had now could hardly be called such, even though technically it was a cell phone. Since we were all scrimping on money, we rarely used it; never to text anyone. It usually sat in its charger as I willed it to ring; hoping it would be Adam when it did.

He didn't call nearly as much as I wanted him to. We were able to hook up by phone about once a week, the same with instant messenger. Emails were the surest form of communication between us.

I replied to both Adam and Lily with fairly short emails. I didn't have a ton of new stuff to tell them. I did make sure to thank Lily for her "eagle eye" and to assure her that she wasn't a freak simply because she didn't have a cell phone—I told her there were plenty of other reasons she was a freak! Lily and I could kid around like that. She really was like a sister to me.

chapter nineteen

The phrase Ileana taught me was in the forefront of my mind, just hovering for the right opportunity to leap from my mouth. I seized the moment one morning on the way to the hospital as we walked past the creepy little fruit vendor. He was giving us the evil eye, as usual, regardless of the fact that he had a customer right in front of him.

That day I stared right back at him calling out loudly, "Ce te uiți la mine miamuțo?" He really let loose with a loud tirade that went on longer than ever before. I don't know what possessed me, but I just looked at him and laughed. He picked up a piece of rotten fruit and threw it at me; luckily, it missed. It almost hit Tara, though.

"What did you say to him?" Tara looked at me in disbelief.

"Yeah," Amanda joined in, "It sounded like swearing to me. He's really mad."

I was actually quite pleased with the reaction I got all the way around. I told them I had yelled, "What are you looking at, you dirty monkey?"

Tara and Amanda both laughed. Kellie didn't. "That was really rude, don't you think?" She sounded disapproving, but I didn't care.

"Yeah, it was," I agreed. "But it's also rude the way he always stares at us and yells at us when we don't buy anything. He needs a lesson in customer service."

Kellie came back with, "I don't think that lesson you just gave him helped. I'm afraid to buy fruit from him ever again. Who knows what he might do to it now."

Tara was still laughing, "Maybe we should be more afraid of not buying from him now. Especially if his aim improves! He might actually hit us next time!"

As we walked and laughed, we didn't notice the guy who was coming up behind us until he was right there, next to us. It was the customer from the Evil Flying Fruit Man.

I was suddenly a little nervous and tried to give him room to pass us, but he slowed down to keep in step with us.

"Engleză." He spoke directly to me. He didn't look much older than we were and he didn't look scary; unlike the majority of the guys who took notice of us.

I figured it was safe to reply, "Nu vorbesc româneste." I can't speak Romanian. That usually ended conversations before anyone got the wrong idea, but I added, "Engleză." Just restated the obvious; sometimes you had to do that with people.

"It sounded like you spoke it fine a couple of minutes ago, back there." He switched to English easily, never missing a beat. "Where did you learn to say that?"

I began to wonder if maybe I had underestimated the power of the insult of my new catchphrase if a total stranger would question it. "Why—is it bad?" I feigned ignorance.

"I think you know what it means. You said it with such feeling. You have been practicing very much if you don't even speak Romanian. Who taught it to you?" He persisted with his questioning.

My roommates were as puzzled as I was. He was attractive in an intense sort of way. His black eyes bored into my brown ones. I didn't answer him.

He asked yet another question. "Was it Ileana?"

That statement stopped us in our tracks. After a moment I was able to croak out, "Do you know her?" My mind frantically tried to piece together how he could possibly know she taught me that phrase.

He smirked at my discomfort. "I taught that phrase to her when she was five years old to stop a bully from bothering her. Ileana is my sister."

Now what were the chances I would use that phrase for the first time when her brother was close by to hear it? Life was so strange sometimes.

Tara, never one to let an opportunity of meeting a cute guy pass her by, extended her hand and said, "Hi, I'm Tara." Her sparkly smile captured his attention just like it had ensnared dozens before him.

"I am Marcel," he said, returning her smile with one of his own, which totally transformed his face. He was as handsome as Tara was beautiful. His black hair and eyes were a perfect complement to her bouncy blondeness and blue eyes.

He recovered first. "Do your other friends have names?" He said friends but he stared straight at me when he said it—and kept smiling. I found I was not immune to his good looks either. I could not see a resemblance to Ileana although I studied his face long enough to have memorized all of his features. The shadow of his beard combined with the way his eyes crinkled at the corners when he smiled made me think that he might be older than I first thought—maybe late twenties.

Tara made the introductions like he was her new best friend. "This is Kit, Amanda, and Kellie. My roommates. We're from the U.S. as you've figured out by now. We're here doing our practicum for school. The university. We're working at the hospital and the orphanage. That's how we know Ileana. We're students. Here visiting. And working."

Hmmmm. I had never heard Tara talk in fragments while babbling before.

"That explains how you know my sister. Tara. Kit. Amanda. Kellie." He nodded at each of us as he repeated our names, as if he was committing them to memory.

"Do you live around here? We haven't seen you before." Amanda spoke up before Tara could start blathering again. Tara seemed content just to smile at him and listen attentively to his every word. I nudged her and we started walking again.

"My other sister, Brigita, lives down that street," he pointed back from where we had come. "She is married. My mother thinks I am her errand boy. Mothers!" He said it as if the word itself explained everything. "Ileana and I—we live at home still. She works at the orphanage and I attend the University." He nodded towards Tara as he spoke.

"What are you studying?" I had to ask. It was rather silly how we each seemed to want a turn to speak to him. Somehow I wasn't surprised when he told us he was going to be a doctor.

"That's so cool!" Tara gushed, determined not to be left out. I noticed she had conveniently kept her place between Marcel and me.

I felt a little irritated at Tara. It was like she had to monopolize every guy. Not that I cared—I didn't. It was just kind of annoying; she was waiting for a missionary, after all.

I caught a glimpse of Amanda's face and she looked a little bothered, too. That meant Kellie felt it too, since she and Amanda often mirrored each other's feelings. We continued to silently listen to Marcel and Tara talk until we arrived at the bus stop.

His bus came first, heading a different direction than ours. By the time he boarded his bus, Tara had invited both him and Ileana to dinner at our house on Friday and he had agreed to come. Tara said she would tell Ileana the details at work.

When Marcel was gone, Amanda turned to Tara. "You should consider the rest of us, before inviting people over to our place and committing all of us."

Tara shrugged. "I knew we weren't busy, so it would be all right." It looked like Amanda wanted to give Tara a lecture, but she didn't. I thought Amanda wasn't really all that upset at the prospect of having Marcel and Ileana come over; she just liked things to be her own idea.

The morning at the hospital seemed to drag by. Even working with Alin didn't hold my attention like it usually did. Madalina was there, acting like a little hooligan. When I tried ignoring her, she wrapped both arms around my neck and started sucking on my neck. Disgusting! I pried her off of me and pushed her away telling her to stop. "Nu Madalina! Stai!" She stopped, but gave me her evil laugh and darted out of the room. Why was she such a terror?

One of the doctors stopped in to check on Alin and I asked her if she knew what was wrong with Madalina. Few of the doctors spoke English well and most of them ignored us, but this doctor was the exception.

"Madalina suffers from kidney failure. She has spent most of her life here at the hospital." The doctor must have felt chatty that day.

I seized the opportunity to find out more. "Where are her parents?"

"Her mother left her three years ago when she moved to another city. It is not unusual for parents to abandon their children with disabilities." The doctor spoke with disdain, but her voice softened at her next words. "Most children in Madalina's situation would cope by becoming withdrawn and detached. Madalina handles it by acting out. It is the only control she has over her life. Most of the staff has learned to live with her actions, as long as she submits to dialysis and takes her medications when required."

After I digested this information I considered Madalina in a different light. Her puffy face and yellowish skin no longer seemed so ugly to me. I vowed I would be kinder to her and try to give her good attention. I would really try to like her.

I knew I needed help with my resolve. I figured the first thing I could do was to stop referring to her in my mind (and to my roommates) as the "devil child." I didn't know what else I could do, but I did know a prayer would help me. I went into the bathroom where I could be alone. I locked the door (Madalina was known to burst in on people even in the bathroom) and knelt down.

I prayed from my heart. I really wanted to change my feelings about her. I asked for help to know what I could do for her, or even for just a seed of love that might expand to something greater. No great vision opened up to me, but I felt calm and knew I would have the help I needed when I really needed it. I just had to pay attention to the promptings when they came.

When I came out of the bathroom, Madalina didn't reappear. I spent the rest of the morning working with Alin. He recognized my voice and I could nearly always make him smile. His progress made me feel better.

During our break between the hospital and orphanage, I couldn't convince any of my roommates to go with me to the internet café. They just wanted to go home, eat lunch, and maybe take a nap before they had to go back to work.

We didn't get naps because the topic of conversation immediately turned to Marcel. It was kind of funny to think of the four of us trying to come up with a perfect menu for the dinner. I wondered aloud why it was such a big deal, and Kellie put it in perspective for me.

"It's the first time we've entertained at our own place. We want to make a good impression as Americans and as members of the Church. We already know Ileana a little bit, but it will be nice to get to know her and Marcel." Amanda nodded in agreement and Kellie went on. "Anya and Corina are great, but they're being paid to be nice to us, if you think about it. Ileana and Marcel are the first friends we've met on our own."

Tara had to add, "And, of course, as American Mormon women in Romania we want to make a good impression. Let's face it— Marcel is hot, and he might have friends!"

Amanda rolled her eyes at Tara's comment, but had to give her input. "You're crazy, Tara. Maybe just man-crazy, but crazy nonetheless. I feel bad for poor Eric. It'll be a miracle if you end up waiting for him."

"Oh don't be such a drag, Amanda!" Tara responded. "There is nothing wrong with flirting and getting to know guys while I'm still single. I love Eric, but we're not engaged. If it's still the right thing to settle down with him and get married when he comes home, I'll know it. I'm not worried, so you shouldn't be either. Stop scowling." She reached over to smooth Amanda's forehead, which was furrowed in a scowl then she continued, "I dare you to flirt with Marcel when he comes over. I'll even back off, I promise. Just loosen up and flirt with him! Come on!"

"You do scowl too much," Kellie said, siding with Tara against Amanda for once. "I think you like Marcel a little already. I second Tara's dare."

I decided to offer my opinion. "Go for it, Amanda. Tara has Eric; I have Adam; Kellie's stepping aside—he's all yours. Seriously, we all think you should do it." We all nodded decisively, wearing her down with our enthusiasm. The frown on her face even smoothed away on its own.

"It's decided then," Tara summarized. "Amanda gets Marcel." Just like that, we decided his fate as if he were an object to be given away at our whim. We didn't consider his freedom to choose, or the fact that he might already have a girlfriend. We had decided—that was enough. Operation Marcel had begun.

Kellie offered to cook the dinner and suggested homemade calzones. We were excited for the project we had undertaken.

When we saw Ileana at the orphanage Tara and I hurried over to tell her our news. "Guess who we met this morning?" Tara asked brightly, knowing Ileana would never guess.

"Who?" Ileana looked back and forth between us, knowing we were up to something.

"Your brother!" Tara announced triumphantly.

"Marcel? How did you meet him?"

I interjected with my part in the story. "I yelled at the Evil Flying Fruit Man. I used that 'dirty monkey' thing you taught me and he threw fruit at us. Marcel heard me say it, so he caught up with us and asked how I knew that line. He told us he's your brother and he taught it to you. You could've warned me, Ileana! I thought I'd offended some stranger."

"What a funny coincidence. Marcel must have been surprised."

"He was," Tara said. "We invited both of you to dinner at our house this Friday. He said 'yes' for both of you." Ileana seemed pleased by the invitation.

"Does Marcel have a girlfriend?" Tara asked.

Ileana shook her head. "Marcel is too serious about his studies to take time for a girlfriend. He is too serious about life. Are you interested in him, Tara?"

"No, not me; I'm thinking about Amanda. She is way too serious about everything too. They'd be a perfect match!" Tara said.

Ileana just smiled and said, "Good luck to her. I think he needs someone lighthearted to make him laugh more. But you will only be here until December. I do not think my brother will care for a . . . for a . . . what is the word?"

"Fling?" I supplied the word I was thinking would describe the situation we were plotting. It was all challenge and fun to Tara, but I don't think she considered the ramifications if they did fall for one another.

"Fling?" Ileana repeated. "No, I was thinking of 'flirt.' It is the same thing?"

"Sort of," Tara explained. "Flirting is having fun getting to know someone and letting them know you like them. A fling is more like when you both like each other a lot, but it can't last. It's like getting together for only a short time."

"Ah," Ileana looked thoughtful. "A fling then he would not like; but a flirt—maybe it would lighten him up. It could be a good thing for him."

"Exactly," Tara agreed, point made. I felt a little sorry for Marcel at that moment as I considered what was going on behind his back for his "own good." But who knows? Maybe a bit of a flirt would help both Marcel and Amanda.

I went over to find my twins. Simona was asleep, so I picked up Daciana. She was soaking wet and very stinky; I wondered if she had even been changed at all that day. As I took her to the sink to clean her up, I couldn't believe she wasn't crying.

When Daciana was dry, she cooed at me, which melted my heart. I cuddled her and found a place to sit and play with her. She wouldn't reach for anything yet, but her little face would crinkle into a huge toothless grin when I talked to her and made faces at her. She made little noises now and then with the effort of all that smiling. She was so darling, I hated to put her down. I had to drag myself away from playing with her to take care of other babies.

I laid her down in her crib next to Simona's, who was still napping. I changed two other babies and played with each of them a little before Simona woke up. When she started to cry, I hurried over to her before anyone else did. I lifted her out of her crib and when Daciana saw me, she started crying to be held again.

I quickly changed Simona, taking care to put ointment on her terrible diaper rash. Most of the babies had rashes, which was no wonder, considering how long they had to lie there in their soiled diapers. She screamed until the ointment began to soothe the stinging. By the time I finished changing her, she was calm.

I held her close to me and talked to her until I saw a smile. Then we went over to Daciana, who was howling her lungs out. I scooped her up and she immediately quieted down. I went back to my chair with both infants in my arms and spent some time bonding with my little angel babies.

Ileana came over with bottles for each of them. She took Daciana from me and, as we fed them, she gave me a little lecture. "You are spoiling these two. They will get too attached to you—and you to them. There will be three broken hearts when you leave."

"I know I spoil them, but I just love them so much. There's something special about them. It's like we feed each others' spirits. Do you know what I mean?" I couldn't explain it any better than that.

Ileana was quiet for a moment then said, "I think I know what you mean. I have felt a special feeling for some of them, but you learn not to get too attached. There are so many children that it would drain the workers if we let ourselves feel too deeply about any of them. You can see how difficult it is just to take care of changing them and feeding all of them with the staff we have. You learn to love them all a little, but none of them too much. Do you understand what I am saying?"

I did but felt so sad to think that most of these children would face a lifetime of being loved far too little. It made their lives seem so hopeless to me.

chapter twenty

When Friday came we hurried home at lunch to start on dinner prep. Kellie mixed the dough for the calzones—from scratch, of course, then started working on the filling. I asked her how she was able to get her recipes to turn out so well when the ingredients were so different. Kellie liked to keep her cooking secrets, but she divulged to me that there was a Romanian lady in her ward at home who had given her tips for substitutions and also some recipes adjusted for Romanian ingredients. No wonder Kellie's cooking was so much better than ours.

Tara insisted on giving Amanda a pedicure and manicure, as if she were getting her ready for a big date. I half-expected Tara to offer to do her hair, but she didn't, at least within my earshot. I was in a snit because I hadn't been able to talk anyone into going with me to the internet café for three days. They'd all been fixated on the dinner with Marcel—sometimes they added Ileana into their conversation almost as an afterthought.

I was irritated with the whole thing. I decided that if someone wouldn't go with me Saturday morning, I would go by myself, even if it meant breaking one of the rules we made for ourselves; nobody went out alone.

Even Tara was unsympathetic to me. When I grumbled for the fourth or fifth time about going to email Adam, she snapped at me. "For goodness sake, Kit! Write him a letter and stop whining about it!" That shut me up on the outside, but I was murmuring mighty loud on the inside. Tara had never spoken to me like that before.

I sulked off to my room and considered writing to Adam, but I didn't want to do anything she suggested after she had just talked to me that way.

They called to me when it was time to leave for the orphanage. I'd dozed off during my pout, so I missed getting anything to eat for lunch. Whatever filling Kellie had created for the calzones smelled great and made my stomach growl even more. I grabbed a granola bar and a banana to eat on the way.

The three of them chattered all the way there. They didn't seem to notice I wasn't joining in; or maybe they did and didn't want to deal with my "whining" anymore. I was determined not to say another word about going to the internet café, I would just go ahead with my plan the next morning. It would be broad daylight and I knew the way by myself. Then I could stay as long as I wanted to.

As if sensing my sour mood, Daciana and Simona were both fussy. Simona threw up all over me when I tried to burp her, and Daciana wouldn't quiet down no matter how I held her. I finally put both babies back. I was so frustrated, I just wanted to sit down and cry.

Ileana came over and gave me a little sympathy as I cleaned up my shoulder from a second baby barfing on me. (It was way too much to be called spit-up.) She suggested I go home a little early. I thanked her but told her I needed to wait for Tara, and I didn't want to take away from the hours she needed to meet her practicum requirements.

After I cleaned up, I went outside to the play yard to watch the older kids. They didn't have many toys, but made do with what they had. Several of them peered through the fence to watch a group of street children play some sort of game of keep-away. A few of the younger children played on the swings, but a lot of them wandered around playing in the dirt, talking to themselves and sometimes wetting themselves.

They were a grungy, sad-looking lot. There would be no parents calling them in to supper or tucking them in at night. I wondered if their dreams consisted merely of getting to the other side of the fence. It was hard to dream of things you couldn't even imagine.

What if I had been one of these children? I was born in America where babies are adopted quickly; but what if I had grown up like this? What if my mom and dad didn't adopt me and I spent my whole life never knowing if anyone cared about me? It would make me feel small and worthless. How will they ever believe someone cares for them? How will they ever believe in God—especially that He loves them and knows them? How will they ever know?

My thoughts depressed me. We couldn't speak about God to these children; it was part of the agreement. We were humanitarian workers—not missionaries. My young testimony burned within me and I cried out silently, How can I be truly humanitarian and not be a missionary? Faith in God was life-changing. I knew it, but couldn't share it. I felt helpless; why come here if I couldn't make a real difference in their lives?

When the time came to go home, I was no longer angry at my roommates, but I didn't feel like socializing at all. I was drenched in homesickness from head to toe. Self-pity has never been a good mood enhancer.

Tara sat by me on the bus, but quickly moved to another seat when she caught a whiff of me. "Kit, you stink! Did you take a bath in vomit? Yuck!"

"Yeah, unfortunately I took two barf baths. I'm sorry—I'll shower as soon as we get home." I guess I was used to the smell because it didn't bother me anymore.

"Don't take too long in the shower," Tara reminded me. "We all want a turn to rinse off before our guests arrive."

"Don't worry, I'll be quick." I wouldn't want to interfere with the party, I added bitterly in my head. I guess the murmuring was back.

I hurried in the shower as promised and tried really hard to shake off my lingering unhappiness. Even though I felt like spoiling the evening, I realized I was acting childish and decided I could try harder to be nice.

I finished getting ready and checked to see if Kellie needed help. She directed me to set the table, which took about two minutes. I went to see what Tara and Amanda were doing. Tara was actually fixing Amanda's hair for her! I had to leave the room before I said something rude.

Marcel and Ileana arrived a few minutes later. I was genuinely glad to see Ileana again, although I had reservations about Marcel. (I saw him as something of a victim in all this.)

Ileana gave me a kiss-kiss and told me I smelled much better. I laughed at that and Marcel leaned over and sniffed in my general direction. He said he agreed that the smell was better.

I stopped smiling and arched a brow at him. "Do I have to yell something at you in really bad Romanian?" I asked, surprised that he would be so forward.

"Only if you allow me to arm myself with fruit, as any dirty little monkey should do," he replied smoothly without a hint of smile.

"Good. As long as we understand each other." I took Ileana by the arm and led her in to sit down. Marcel followed, alone—but not for long.

Tara bounced in, dragging Amanda with her. "Hi, guys! I'm glad you're here!" Tara gave Ileana a kiss-kiss and Amanda stepped forward to do the same.

All I could think was *Wow*! Tara did some major makeover on Amanda! Now, it's not like Amanda was a dog or anything, normally. She just looked fabulous after Tara got through with her. Her brown hair was shining, twisted into some sort of cool knot in the back. Bronze eye shadow and subtle eyeliner made her hazel eyes look luminous. She wore a soft peach lipstick that matched her fingernails and glimmered in the light.

Marcel checked them both out. I think he liked what he saw. He may not have time for a relationship, but he sure seemed to have time to look. I felt a twinge as I wished I had done something more with my hair than the loose braid hanging down my back.

Kellie came out from the kitchen looking like a regular Betty Crocker. She was wearing a cute red apron that said "I Cook, You Clean" and her cheeks were flushed from the heat—or maybe the excitement. Her green eyes were bright with anticipation.

"It smells so good in here. What are you cooking?" Ileana asked Kellie. Marcel nodded appreciatively and Kellie beamed at the compliment.

"Calzones. It's a family recipe." Kellie winked at me as she said it. "Tara, show Ileana to her seat and Amanda can show Marcel to his. Kit, come help me serve." Kellie gave orders like it came naturally; I was beginning to believe it did.

I brought out the salad and Kellie followed with the piping hot calzones. Tara announced she would ask the blessing on the food. Ileana and Marcel followed our lead as we folded our arms and bowed our heads. After Tara's prayer, they murmured "amen" with the rest of us. I wondered what they were thinking.

Kellie's dinner was delicious, of course. There was little conversation as we ate; mainly just a few words of praise for Kellie's cooking. We finished quickly and Kellie commandeered my help with clearing the table and serving the dessert. Apparently I was the servant in this match-making drama. Oh well, better the servant than the cook—or worse yet, the femme fatale, which was totally beyond me.

Dessert was chocolate trifle, which was superb. I knew something of desserts because I'd eaten lots of them in my lifetime. I wasn't shy about helping myself to seconds and noticed Marcel followed my lead.

We lingered over dessert and talked about life in the U.S. versus life in Romania. It was fun to learn more about things that were different and things that were the same, but it became evident that Marcel was very serious about becoming a doctor and improving life in Romania. The thing that surprised me was how passionately he spoke about making a difference for the children, particularly the orphans.

Listening to Marcel talk about helping the children triggered something in me. I forgot about my roommates' matchmaking plans and my own frustration at not being able to go to the internet café. I saw Marcel as someone who cared, like I did, about the children. Unlike me, he was doing something about it.

I asked him so many questions, he probably thought I was psycho. I caught a disapproving look from Amanda at one point. I backed off for a few minutes, but Marcel kept drawing me back into the conversation. It turned out I had a wonderful time and I felt like Marcel and I had a lot in common.

By the time the evening was over, I had two out of three roommates glaring at me. Tara seemed to have gotten her sense of humor back. When Ileana and Marcel left I tried to go quietly to my room because I didn't want to deal with any of it. Tara stopped my progress when she said, "Kit, it looks like you've got yourself a Romanian boyfriend! What will Adam think?!"

Her tone wasn't irritated; it was amused. I vehemently denied her accusation. "You've lost it, Tara. Marcel's interested in what he can do for Romania's children. That's really the whole problem. We tried to set Amanda up with a guy who's already married to his dreams. He's not on the market—even if he was, you know how I feel about Adam."

Amanda had to share her opinion. "Well, you sure hogged the conversation, if you weren't trying to hit on him." Her sour look marred the perfection Tara's makeover had created.

Irritation washed over me, but I decided I could be the bigger person. "Amanda, I wasn't hogging the conversation, I was actually interested in what he had to say. I didn't get a chance to say so earlier, but you look beautiful tonight. I know Marcel really noticed you, I just don't think he has room for a relationship."

Although her face softened a little at my compliment, which was genuine, she still looked peeved. Kellie stood behind her, a reflection of her best friend's frustration.

I thought I should try to soothe their ruffled feathers. "Kellie, those calzones were the best. I loved the chocolate trifle, too. Do you think you might share the recipes? Please?" I had no intention of cooking them myself, but I figured my mom would do almost as well as Kellie with the recipe. If not, Barbara and Lily would both be willing to try.

"I'll think about it." Kellie offered. "I don't like to share family recipes, but really good cooks add their own touches anyway. I might give it to you; even if you are a conversation hog." They were so touchy. I gave up and headed for bed.

chapter twenty-one

The next morning I was determined not to say a word about going to the internet café. They were probably still mad at me, anyway. Kellie and Amanda were already up, but pretty much ignored me, and Tara was still asleep.

After I showered, I put on my long-johns underneath my jeans. October was definitely cold in Romania. I thought about Adam and wondered what he would be doing right then. Mentally calculating the time difference, I figured he would be sound asleep.

If I waited until evening to go, I might catch Adam online and could chat with him. He usually worked Saturdays, though, so I might be waiting a long time.

We had plans to go with Corina to the gypsy market that afternoon. By the time we got home from there, I was pretty sure my roommates wouldn't want to come with me to email or chat online. My best option was to go that morning.

I rebraided my hair while I tried to decide if I should leave a note for my roomies or if I should tell them where I was going. I sure didn't want a lecture from any of them. Besides, I would be back in plenty of time to go with them to the gypsy market.

I wrote a short note and tucked it in my pocket. I decided that if I didn't see anyone on the way out, I would just drop the note on the table. If I did see someone, I'd casually tell them where I was going. If they wanted to come, they could. I was just tired of asking them.

I heard the shower as I stepped out of my room. When I saw Kellie in the kitchen, her back to me, listening to her iPod, I decided to just drop the note on the table. I grabbed my coat and quietly let myself out the front door.

The day was clear and cold. I walked quickly and made it to the internet café without any problems. Vasilé was working as always. He looked disappointed when he didn't see Tara follow me in. We greeted each other like old friends and he got me set up on a computer.

I pulled up my email and logged on to IM—just in case. There were two emails from Adam; one from my mom; one from Adam's mom, Barbara; one from Lily; and some spam. A chat invite popped up on the screen from mmiklos@yahoo.com. *Who is "mmiklos"?* I wondered. My curiosity got the better of me. I decided I could always block the person if it wasn't someone I knew, so I accepted the invite.

I read through Adam's emails, savoring each one. He missed me as much as I missed him, judging from his email. I read the email from my mom and the one from Barbara. Barbara had attached a few pictures from Beth's family birthday party There was an adorable one of Adam wearing a silly little party hat. The next one was of Beth blowing out her candles. The third was of the whole Bridger family; including Hal and Barbara. I wondered who took it. The final one was a group shot of the whole family—except for Hal, who must've been roped into taking the picture.

I studied the last picture and couldn't contain my smile as I looked at Adam's family. I loved them all so much. There was Beth, the birthday girl, in the center holding her cake. Beside her were Travis, Sarah, and Lily. In the back row I saw Justin and Michelle, arms looped around each others' waists. Next came Barbara, Mark, Adam and—what?!?! Who was that next to Adam? Ruth Randall! I'd only met her once, but I hadn't forgotten what she looked like. The smile disappeared from my face in an instant.

I felt betrayed, seeing her there in the Bridger family picture. That was my place. How dare she? She stood there next to Adam as if she belonged there. Tears filled my eyes and threatened to spill over. Had I been replaced? I wiped my eyes and re-read the emails from Adam again, looking for clues.

No mention at all of Ruth. Who invited her? Was it Adam or Barbara? I quickly clicked on Lily's email. She would give me the truth, even if Adam wouldn't.

> To: kitcarson@yahoo.com
> From: lilyofthevalley16@hotmail.com
> Subject: It's me again.
>
> Hi, Kit. I'm going to try to send you a normal email. I know the last few I've sent have been raving. Everything just seems to rub me the wrong way lately. I love my family, but they are so darn perfect sometimes that it makes me feel like a misfit. I can't seem to do anything to please them. I'm not the best student, but it's not like I'm failing school or anything. I don't skip school like a lot of my friends do. I just can't make them happy and I can't talk to them anymore
>
> When I try to talk to Mom she is either busy with the little kids or that stupid Ruth is over here, hanging out like she's part of the family. Sometimes I think she is trying to take Janet's place. I miss Janet so much. She always had time for me and she never made me feel like I had to be perfect. Do you ever stop missing someone you love when they die? It's been over a year since Janet died and sometimes it still feels like yesterday. Do you ever feel that way? Sometimes I think people around here have forgotten her. I said that to Mom one day and I thought she was going to slap me. She didn't, but I wondered for a minute. I'm confused and I don't fit in anywhere.
>
> I miss you, Kit. Come home. I don't mean now, this instant, because I know you can't; but I really, really miss talking to you. You're one of the people who have made it easier for me to bear Janet being gone.
>
> Wow. I promised not to rant and now I'm making myself bawl sending you this pathetic email. I think I like it better when I'm a raving lunatic. So anyway back to the important teenage stuff. I still don't have a cell phone and probably never will. Okay, maybe that's an exaggeration because my parents did say that I could get one when I'm sixteen and get a part-time job to pay for it. So I guess my life will begin when I turn sixteen because then I can date and have a cell phone. If I can stand it until then.
>
> One more thing and then I'll go. We had a birthday party for Beth (who is now a Beehive can you believe it?)—a family party. And guess who shows up? Yep, Ruth the Mole burrowing in deeper and deeper. I don't care

if my mom did invite her, she is not family and I think she is trying to buy her way into Beth's affection. She gave her two CDs and a purse. A purse! Like our Beth will ever use a purse, except maybe to put frogs and snakes in. So my mom is taking pictures all during the party like she does and makes us all gather together for one of the pictures. Ruth sticks her nosey face into the picture. Yeah, I would send you one, but Mom said she already emailed some to you, so you'll probably be seeing a picture with a UFO (unidentified ferreting object—you know ferrets are related to moles!) I thought you might want a warning.

Okay I'd better go. Write back soon.

Love ya, Lily

I felt sick. It seemed clear to me that while I was here in Romania, Ruth was putting the moves on Adam. It was even worse because Barbara seemed to like Ruth so much. Maybe Barbara thought Ruth would make a better wife for Adam than I would. Ruth had always been a member of the Church, was the niece of a stake president, and was probably a lot more spiritual than I was.

I forced myself to reply to my mom's email because I knew she'd worry and end up calling me. I kept it short by telling her I was really busy but doing okay, and signed off with my standard plea for her to keep my brother Dave out of my things.

I also sent a short email to Barbara thanking her for the pictures and telling her I was doing pretty good but keeping really busy. I was sitting there trying to figure out how to reply to Lily and Adam when an IM message popped up on my screen. It was from mmiklos.

mmiklos: Hi Kit, thanks for accepting my invite
kitcarson: No problem. How r u?

I had no idea who I was chatting with. It was one of those situations where you figured the other person knew you, but you couldn't figure out who you were talking to, so you hoped they would give you a clue so you wouldn't sound totally lame. The clue came.

mmiklos: I was surprised to find you online. Ileana and I had fun last night. Kellie is a great cook. What r u doing?

Marcel! How did he get my email address? I vaguely remembered giving it to Ileana when I was at the orphanage; he'd clearly gotten it from her. I replied, not letting him know I just figured out it was him.

> **kitcarson:** I'm here at the internet café near our house reading and answering my emails. What r u doing?
> **mmiklos:** I was just going to run a couple of errands. One involved getting a cup of coffee. r u at La Strada?
> **kitcarson:** That's the one. Why?
> **mmiklos:** Can I join u? it will take me 20 min.
> **kitcarson:** Sure. I should leave in about an hour though.
> **mmiklos:** I'm on my way. La revedere.

Wow. That was weird. I sure didn't expect to hear from Marcel, of all people. It felt good to be noticed, especially when I seemed to be on the wrong side of my roommates and Ruth Randall was back home trying to take over my spot in the Bridger family.

With a little dose of confidence in me, I felt like I could reply to the emails from Lily and Adam.

> To: bridgerman123@hotmail.com
> From: kitcarson@yahoo.com
> Subject: I made it back to email you!
>
> Hey, Bridger! It took me a few days to get to where I could email you. My roommates have been caught up in life here and are pretty sick of me begging them to come with me so I can email you. So this morning I got up, got dressed, and came here all by myself! We had agreed to only go places in pairs, but this place is just a few blocks from our house and it's broad daylight. I left them a note. I'm kind of sick of always following their schedules. Tara is usually pretty understanding, but even she got tired of me asking and told me to get over it!
> I really miss you. Your mom sent me some pictures of Beth's birthday party. You were so cute in that little party hat! I'm glad your mom sent the pictures to me since you don't seem to think of things like that. I was a little disturbed when I saw in the one family picture that someone was standing in my place. Yeah, I'm talking about Ruth. What is she doing hanging around you so much? Has she forgotten that you're taken? I hope you haven't forgotten it! I'm not really

worried, but maybe a little jealous.

Lily has sent me some emails and she's struggling with things. I think she is really missing Janet and not having her to talk to. I don't want to break her confidences, but she really could use a listening ear (just not Ruth's, so don't get that idea!).

My friend Ileana taught me a phrase in Romanian to use when creepy guys stare at us.

I went on to tell him about the "Evil Flying Fruit Man" and meeting Marcel. I also told him about my roommates trying to fix Amanda up. I conceded I was in on it at first but thought they went way overboard. I realized I was rambling and finished up.

My email to Lily ended up reminding me of the one she wrote to me. I knew she was hurting about Janet, so I tried to give her some comfort. The more I wrote about Janet, the more I had to fight back tears. Her death had left a huge void in my life. Lily was right; Janet always listened and never made you feel stupid. One of the most important things she taught me was by her own example—she never made anyone feel bad, she always made them feel better.

I fumbled through my backpack and found a tissue to blow my nose. I figured I'd better shift gears or I'd never stop blubbering like a baby. So I started writing about how irritated I was that Ruth was in the picture with Adam. That got me all fired up and angry, although I was still near tears. After venting to Lily, I didn't feel better, I felt worse. I hit "send" then wished I hadn't sent it to her when I was in such an emotional state.

I heard the door open and looked up to see Marcel walk through the door. Oh great, I thought, of course he had to see me looking all splotchy and red-eyed. I chided myself—as if I cared how Marcel Miklos saw me. I dug for another tissue and took one last swipe at my nose.

"Good. You're still here, Kit. Thank you for waiting." He glanced down at the computer I was sitting at. "Are you still busy with your email?"

"No, I'm finished. I'll tell Vasilé and then we can go sit at a table." I talked to Vasilé while Marcel went over to the counter. I finished first and went to sit down.

I didn't realize what he was doing, but Marcel came over with two steaming cups of coffee. As he sat down, he put one in front of me as he asked, "Do you prefer it black or with milk and sugar?"

I bit my lip to hold back a smile. I inhaled the fragrant aroma, which appealed to me, but gently pushed the cup back towards him and said, "Neither. I don't prefer it at all."

He looked surprised. "You do not like coffee? I am sorry. I just assumed as an American you would prefer it. Let me get you tea. It will just take a moment." He started to stand, but I reached out and grabbed his arm.

This time I did smile. "No, Marcel. No coffee, no tea. I thought you knew I was Mormon." I was sure we'd made it plain last night.

Marcel was puzzled. "So you are Mormon? What is that to me?"

"Mormons don't drink coffee or tea. It's a commandment we follow. It's called the Word of Wisdom." I thought everyone knew that much about Mormons.

He considered what I said. "I am sorry. I hope I did not offend you." He looked so serious.

I could never resist messing with a person who was too serious. "Please don't offer me a glass of wine. We don't drink alcohol either."

His confusion showed in his voice and on his face. "I was not thinking of offering you a glass of wine."

This was kind of fun; for me, at least. "Don't offer me a cigarette either. I'll just say no."

"I do not have any cigarettes. I do not smoke." The light came on as it dawned on him I was smiling. "I think you are having fun at my expense."

Those words sent the silly grin sliding from my face. "I'm sorry. I was teasing you. I thought everyone knew that Mormons don't drink coffee, tea, or alcohol, or smoke." I felt even more ashamed because I had just been thinking about Janet, who never made people feel small.

Marcel saw the shadow cross over me. "It is fine, Kit. I speak English well, but I do not understand joking and teasing. I do not always understand it in my own language." He shrugged then asked if drinking water was permitted for Mormons.

"Of course it is," I laughed.

He went over to the counter and got a bottle of water for me. He settled down to his two cups of coffee and surprised me with what he said next. "So, Kit, tell me why you were crying when I came in?"

I briefly toyed with the idea of denying anything was wrong, but sensed he really wanted to know. "I was thinking about my friend Janet who died last year. Her little sister emailed me. She's having a hard time right now and asked me to come home." I brought my hand to my face to cover my quivering chin.

"I'm sorry you lost your friend; was it unexpected?" he studied me over his coffee cup.

"She was in a car accident. We were together. I survived, she didn't." It was still hard for me to talk about it. "I was close to their whole family. Janet's brother, Adam, is my boyfriend. Her brother Justin baptized me. In some ways I'm closer to her parents than I am to my own. Lily is like a sister to me. Their family are the ones that really taught me about the gospel and helped me believe in God—and to realize I was someone worthwhile." I gulped my water nervously. I hadn't meant to spill my guts to him.

"I see you miss your 'adopted' family. So I wonder what made you come to Romania, when your heart wants so much to be home."

His words confused me. I hadn't said anything about being adopted. "What? How did you know I was adopted? I'm sure I didn't tell you or Ileana about that."

"What did you say? I only meant the family of your friend cared so much about you as if they had adopted you into their family. Are you adopted?" His sharp eyes searched my face, his curiosity clearly piqued.

I realized what he was talking about then. "Oh. I understand now. I was confused because I really was adopted by my own family, but I don't tell that to a lot of people. To answer your question, I think that is one reason I came to Romania, because I wanted to help other children who had been abandoned by their parents. I felt a strong impression to come. It may sound silly to you and it used to sound silly to me; but I believe in God—a God that hears and answers prayers. I prayed about coming to Romania and got the answer to come. I don't know why, but I think I can help the children here, somehow." It was like my mouth kept opening and words just kept coming out. I never talked about myself like that to strangers and Marcel was, by most accounts, a stranger to me.

"I do not think you are silly, Kit. You are unusual. I could not come up with a reason why four American girls would come here at their own expense. Your friends explained about their school studies—what is the word?"

"Practicum."

"Yes, practicum. To me, it makes sense for them to come to further their studies. But for you, I cannot grasp what brings you to Romania. But now I think I may start to understand. You were an orphan once. You have a connection to these children."

I felt like he was analyzing me and it made me feel self-conscious. "I do feel a connection to them. You look like you're studying me for a research project. Do you think I'm crazy for praying about it? And then coming here because my prayer was answered?"

He shook his head. "I do not mock anyone's faith. Medicine is a science, it is true. But many good physicians will tell you that there is great power in a patient's faith and prayer. I do not claim to understand it, but I do not mock it."

I felt a rush of adrenaline and I hurried to speak up before I chickened out. "If you want to understand it, would you consider coming over to our house and listening to the missionaries? They can explain things so much better than I can."

Marcel drained his second cup of coffee. I wondered if he got the jitters from all the caffeine. He stacked the two cups, crumpled them and said, "I will come to learn more. My schedule is very full, though. It would have to be on a Sunday evening."

I was stunned. I had asked the missionary question and he had said yes! I assured him I could set it up for Sunday and asked him if I could call him with the time. He wrote down his phone number on a napkin and gave it to me. I folded it and put it in my backpack.

"Thanks, Marcel, for listening to me. You don't know how much I needed to talk to someone." I smiled at him. "I'm really glad you came this morning. We have a lot in common."

"I am glad too. We do have a connection, Kit, and I am happy you feel it." He reached across the table and tucked a wayward strand of hair behind my ear. "You are very beautiful."

Heat flushed my face. I was flattered, but suddenly felt self-conscious. "Uh, I really have to go now. Thanks for the coffee!" I gathered up my backpack and offered him my hand for a handshake.

He took it, squeezed it, and said. "I will walk with you. I need to go to my sister's house again. My mother has given me an errand and I am an obedient son."

He talked about Brasov as he walked with me to my street. When we said good-bye, I promised to call him. I couldn't wait to tell my roommates the news. I had just set up my first missionary contact!

chapter twenty-two

My elation was short-lived as I was greeted by three anxious roommates, along with Corina, who all appeared to be waiting for me.

"Why did you go out without us?" Amanda demanded. "You broke the rules, Kit." She spoke to me like I was an idiot. I didn't like it and felt my defenses prickle.

I forced my tone to sound neutral. "I only went to the internet café. I asked all of you to go with me several times this week, but none of you would. I needed to check my email. It was broad daylight anyway, so it really wasn't a big deal."

"There's no point in rules if you don't obey them." Amanda insisted. Clearly she was more concerned about rules than my safety. I rolled my eyes.

"Kit, you can't just go off by yourself. We were worried about you." Tara, on the other hand, really did sound concerned.

"Remember what happened to Amanda when that creep rode by on his bicycle." Kellie joined in.

"Yeah, and we were all together and it didn't stop him from grabbing her, did it? Seriously, you guys are making this into something big, and it isn't." I was annoyed. I had news to share and they all ruined it.

"Not only did you take off without us, but you made us all wait," Amanda wasn't ready to let it go. "Corina's been here for half an hour."

"We could've stopped on our way to the market. You didn't have to take off without us," Tara said.

"If I asked to stop by on the way, you would've said no or you would've hurried me the whole time. I am sorry I made you guys wait, but I'm not sorry I went." It felt good taking a stand, but I wasn't winning any popularity contests.

Amanda frowned. "Maybe we wanted to go too. We would've figured out a time. You shouldn't go out alone. We all agree on that, Kit."

Corina had listened to us silently, but suddenly spoke. "May I make a suggestion?"

We nodded and she went on. "It seems important that you stick together for safety reasons and it also seems important that Kit goes to the internet café more often. You can set a schedule of when you will go to the internet café and Kit will agree not to go out alone again."

It sounded simple when she put it like that. Tara said, "I think that's a good idea. If Kit wants to go more often than we do, we can take turns going with her. All four of us don't have to go every time." She turned to me. "Kit, I'm sorry I wouldn't go with you sooner. I was rude when I told you to get over it."

My heart softened. "Thanks, Tara. I'm sorry I broke the rule. It seemed okay at the time, but I do agree we need to stick together when we go out. If we could make a schedule it would really help, then I won't nag you all to go with me."

Amanda was already getting out a paper, ready to make the schedule. We figured out what days we would go and I was happy with the results. Amanda stuck the schedule on the refrigerator with one of the many magnets she must have stuffed her suitcase with. They were all handmade inspirational ones like "I never said it would be easy, I only said it would be worth it." A lot of Mutual activities and a couple years worth of Enrichment meetings were represented by Amanda's magnets.

I apologized again for making everyone wait, and we thanked Corina for her insight. We were gathering our stuff together to leave for the gypsy market when I remembered my news.

"Wait! I have to tell you something." I told them about Marcel sending the instant message and coming over to the internet café. After we got past the exclamations of disbelief, I recounted most of the conversation; I left out the part where I teased him and he told me I was beautiful.

When I got to where I asked him to listen to the missionaries, their mouths were all agape. Tara recovered first. "We have to call the sister missionaries! Do you think Ileana will come too?"

"When he said Sunday, did he mean tomorrow?" Kellie asked. "That's really soon. We should see if they're free for dinner. It's my turn to cook. I'll make potato soup with bread bowls."

"It's kind of funny that Marcel would just happen to IM you when you take off to the internet café by yourself. Are you sure you didn't arrange this last night?" Amanda wasn't enjoying the missionary moment. She had other things on her mind.

"When would I have arranged it? Do you think I'm lying about this? I don't lie, Amanda." I knew she liked Marcel and hoped he liked her, but I was upset at what she was implying. "Besides, why would I arrange to meet him there? You're just jealous and you have no reason to be."

"She's right, Amanda," Tara was looking up the number for the sister missionaries as we were discussing everything. "I think it was clear from last night that Marcel isn't really interested in a relationship and you don't really want one with him if you think about it. We're here for less than two months. What would you do when it was time to leave?" She picked up the phone. "It was fun to try to set you up with him, but this is really exciting. What if he joined the Church? Kit, do you want to call or do you want me to?"

"You call them. I'm really new at this missionary stuff." It was true. I still couldn't believe I had asked Marcel to listen to the discussions. It felt good to share the gospel.

Tara made the phone call. The sister missionaries already had dinner plans but they were available later in the evening. Tara arranged the time and ended the call. "Your turn, Kit. Call Marcel. Hurry!"

I pulled his number out of my backpack and made the call. It was his home number and Ileana answered. Marcel wasn't home yet, so I explained why I was calling and invited her to come along.

She agreed and promised to have Marcel call back if there was a problem.

"Why didn't you invite them for dinner?" Kellie asked. "Even if the sister missionaries can't come, I could cook for them. They really like my cooking."

"I thought about it, but felt a little strange inviting them again when they were just here last night. I guess I chickened out. Sorry."

Tara was still all smiles. "That's okay, Kit. You didn't chicken out on the important question! Will you still cook for us, Kellie? I love potato soup and bread bowls."

The appreciation for her culinary efforts worked because Kellie agreed and seemed to forgive me. Amanda was the only one who was still a little grumpy.

"We're never going to make it to the gypsy market if we keep dawdling. We've kept Corina waiting long enough." Amanda turned away from me and I guessed I was no longer on her best-friends-forever list (if I ever was). I don't think she believed I didn't have an ulterior motive.

Corina assured us she didn't mind waiting. I wondered if we should invite her over too, but since she didn't know Marcel and Ileana, I held back. I didn't want a big gathering to make them uncomfortable. I remembered how I felt when I listened to the discussions. I wouldn't have liked a stranger to be there.

We rode the bus to the area of town where the gypsy market was. Then we had to walk several blocks. We had seen gypsies during the month we had been there, but there was no describing the market.

The gypsies didn't look anything like they were portrayed in movies. There were no colorful clothes or brightly painted wagons. It looked like a bunch of beggars in gray ragged clothing selling piles of what I guessed were clothes on makeshift tables. Some tables were covered by shabby roofs; others were out in the open, cold air.

It smelled old and musty, even though it was mostly outside. We ventured in past the first few stalls; I couldn't imagine anyone would buy anything stacked on those tables.

The gypsies huddled by their heaps and looked at us suspiciously as we passed. A couple of them picked up some of their wares to display to us. The clothes we could see were worse than those my family threw away.

"Is this really the market?" I whispered to Corina. "Who would buy any of this?"

Corina defended herself. "I tried to tell you it wasn't anything good." That was true, but we hadn't taken it literally. Somehow we thought she was just being modest about the shopping opportunity.

"Is this how they earn their money? Where do they get these clothes, the landfill?" Amanda looked a little ill.

"They don't work. Gypsies will steal anything and gypsies will sell anything. What they cannot steal, they beg for." Corina's voice was filled with disgust.

I was shocked. I had heard some disparaging remarks about gypsies during the time we had been in Romania, but I didn't expect the near-hatred from Corina, who was usually so kind.

We decided to leave. It was disgusting and a little scary. Tara pulled out her camera to capture the moment. A wrinkled, toothless old woman noticed what Tara was doing and starting towards her yelling something we couldn't understand. Tara stopped in surprise and lowered the camera. As we backed up a couple of steps, we asked Corina what the woman was saying.

"She wants you to pay her for taking her picture," Corina said.

"For taking a picture with my own camera? I don't think so." Tara clutched her camera closer to her. We picked up our pace to get out of there.

As we reached the edge of the marketplace Tara suddenly lifted her camera and snapped a couple of pictures before any of us realized what she was doing.

The ancient crone chased after us, shrieking loudly as if we had stolen her prized possessions. We took off running and easily outdistanced her, but we didn't slow down for a couple of blocks.

We asked Tara why she did it and she said, "It was a challenge. Don't you think it was funny? I'll never forget her face—I've got a picture of it!" We shook our heads at her behavior then Kellie asked if Tara would send her a copy of the picture. Tara promised to send one to all of us.

On the way home Tara wanted to stop at the internet café. I'd already been there that morning, but I was willing to go again even if it wasn't on our new schedule. Kellie and Amanda agreed to stop too.

Vasilé wasn't working when we got there. I could tell Tara was a little disappointed.

"He missed you this morning when you weren't with me," I offered.

She perked up at that. "Did he ask about me?"

"He didn't have to ask, it was obvious by his face. He likes you a lot. He'll be devastated when you go home." I got her to smile again.

We had to take turns because there were only two computers that weren't being used. I didn't mind waiting since I wasn't really expecting any new email. I spent the time thinking about Adam and calculating how many hours had passed since I'd sent him the email that morning. It was possible I'd have a reply.

When it was my turn to log on, I pulled up my email and to my disappointment there wasn't one from Adam. I was surprised to see one from my brother, but my surprise turned to dismay when I read what he wrote.

To: kitcarson@yahoo.com
From: live2ski@yahoo.com
Subject:emergency

Kit. I know you're probably surprised to hear from me but you're the only one I can talk to about this. I heard Mom and Dad talking last night after they thought I had gone to bed. I swear I heard them talking about separating and getting a divorce. I'm serious. They haven't been fighting or anything, but they haven't been talking, either. I came home yesterday and Mom had been crying. I'm afraid to tell them what I heard. I don't think I want to hear the answer. What do you think I should do? Do you think I should just ask them? I'm sorry to put this on you, because I know it'll be a big shocker. Write back. I want your opinion. I'm really worried.

Dave.

I read the email again, stunned. He had to be wrong; even

Dave wouldn't kid about something like this. My parents couldn't be getting a divorce. They never fought; they were so calm. What could possibly be so bad as to cause a divorce?

I wanted to get up and run away from this horrible possibility. I knew I needed to answer Dave, but I had the fleeting thought that if I ignored it, or deleted it, it might go away. I made myself hit the reply button.

> To: live2ski@yahoo.com
> From: kitcarson@yahoo.com
> Subject:re: emergency
>
> You need to go to Mom and Dad and ask them about what you heard. Maybe you heard wrong. They might not want to tell you, but I don't think they'll lie to you. Please let me know what they say ASAP, no matter what.
>
> Kit.

My thoughts were racing. I didn't want to say anything to Tara or the others, at least not until I heard from Dave again. I didn't want to face any questions so I tried to compose myself before they noticed anything.

My head was pounding and my stomach churning, so it wasn't a lie to tell my roommates I was sick. When we got home, I went straight to bed, hoping I would wake up to find I'd just had a bad dream.

chapter twenty-three

I woke up early Sunday morning after a restless night. I couldn't get my parents off my mind. I couldn't wait another day to know what was going on. I calculated the time difference—it was still Saturday evening at home. I considered calling Dave. I was almost out of minutes on my calling card, but I needed to know what was going on.

I was the first one up and tried to be quiet. I opted to go outside to call him. Frost covered the world as far as my eye could see, but my shaking wasn't from the cold. I punched in the numbers and said a little prayer as I waited for Dave to answer.

"Hello?" His voice sounded distant, yet familiar.

"Hey, Dave. It's Kit." I tried not to let my teeth chatter.

"Hey! What's up?"

"Are you serious? You send me an email like that and you ask me what's up?" He was still the same lame brother I'd left behind.

"Oh yeah, I got your reply." It was hard to hear him because of background noise.

"So did you ask them?" I asked. "Speak up, it's noisy there."

"Yeah, let me step outside. I'm at Jake's house, he's having a little party." As he stepped outside, the noise faded.

"Dave, are you there? I don't have much time on my calling card. Did you talk to Mom and Dad?"

"Yeah, I did. It's what I thought."

"What do mean? Are they getting a divorce? Is that what you're saying?" I hoped I was hearing him wrong.

"Yeah, they're getting a divorce. They didn't want me to tell you, though. They're going to call you or something. Or maybe wait till you get home. Surprise!" He barked out a laugh that didn't sound funny. I didn't like his news or the way he delivered it.

"Did they tell you why? You're not making a lot of sense. What happened?" I'd been gone a month and my world was collapsing around me. A beep sounded in my ear letting me know I only had one more minute left on my calling card.

"They'll tell you." His voice switched to a high pitch that I guessed was intended to mimic my mother. "It's not your fault, dear. It's between Dad and me. We love you; that will never change." He snorted. "Yeah, right. Nothing will ever change. So I'm celebrating that nothing will ever change. With just me, my buddies, and some brewskies!" His speech was slurred, and it occurred to me that my little brother was most likely drunk or on his way to getting there.

"Dave! Listen to me. It's hard, I know, but don't get all crazy about it. Partying and drinking with your friends won't solve anything; it'll just get you into trouble. Promise me you won't do anything stupid!" A new fear crept inside my heart; I did love my brother, in spite of all the ways he annoyed me.

"Oh yeah, Kit. You got religion. Well, tell you what. You pray and I'll party. One of us is bound to be right. Don't worry, I'm not—" The line went dead. My time was up.

I stared at the phone in my hand. My family was disintegrating and I was half a world away. Oblivious to the cold, I sat down on the concrete step and let the sorrow engulf me and the sobs tear through my body.

When my heart felt as numb as my rear end was from sitting on the frozen cement, I went back inside. My head pounded and my nose was running. I slipped into the bathroom before any of my roommates saw me.

I got in the shower, trying not to think as I let the water pour over me. It worked for about thirty seconds. I cried some more and let the water wash away the tears.

As I toweled off I wondered how my parents would tell me. Would they call me or email me? Or worse yet, send a letter by snail mail. *Dear Kit, We regret to inform you that we are getting a divorce. We hid it so well you must be having a heart attack from the surprise. Hope you feel better soon. Don't hurry back because you won't have a home to come home to. Don't worry, it's between us and not your fault. We love you. Sincerely, Mom and Dad*

I was being dramatic, I knew, but how do parents tell their child they're getting divorced when the kid is half a world away? How did they tell their kids when they're only a room away? I didn't want to know, but I was going to find out.

My eyes were red and puffy, but I'd stayed in the bathroom long enough. I was glad to see that Tara was up and out of our room. Grateful for the few extra minutes of privacy, I got dressed.

I wore flowered long johns under my long black skirt. One thing we had learned in Romania was to worry more about warmth than fashion. At church, it was common to see women with thermal underwear or pants on under their skirts. Several just wore pants, too poor to also own a dress.

Many were single parents; several were the only members in their entire family. They were just trying to make it in a tough world, trying to stay true to their faith and hold on to hope amid discouraging trials.

I felt humbled. Even in my current circumstances, I was privileged in ways most people here only dreamed of. At least I still had parents, even if they weren't going to stay together; and more importantly, I knew where I could turn to for lasting strength.

I sat there and uttered a silent prayer; giving thanks and asking for help. When I stood, I felt stronger and was able to stand a little taller. It was only hopeless if I allowed it to be.

I was able to keep my emotions in check for most of the day. I was fasting and my headache grew worse throughout our meetings. On the way home, Tara let me know she had noticed something was wrong.

"Kit, you look like you're feeling awful. Does your head still hurt?" I nodded, unwilling to speak lest everything come tumbling out.

"I think you should lie down when we get home," she said. "Sleeping should help."

I took her advice and crawled into bed. I was exhausted enough that I fell asleep quickly.

Tara woke me a few hours later. "Kit, wake up. Marcel and Ileana will be here in half an hour. We saved you some dinner, if you want it."

I had slept in my clothes, but hadn't moved much so they weren't too wrinkled. I didn't really care anyway. I did brush my hair and put a couple of clips in it. I felt a little better and decided to break my fast.

After a prayer and a few bites of Kellie's potato soup, I decided I might live after all. My roommates were chattering excitedly about the upcoming discussion. The sister missionaries arrived first.

Marcel and Ileana came just a few minutes later. We'd told Sora Barnes and Sora Campbell a little about them. The discussion went well. Marcel and Ileana both listened with interest, asked several questions, and listened to the comments we made.

I actually didn't make many comments at all. I felt distant from the group, almost as if I were on the outside looking in. As the discussion drew to a close, Sora Campbell asked if we could meet again the following Sunday.

Marcel agreed and they set up another appointment. Kellie announced she would be serving apple crisp. I automatically got up to help. The phone rang; Tara pounced on it, then handed it to me. "It's Adam," she whispered loudly.

Feeling a surge of elation, I took the phone and headed to my room for privacy. I felt Marcel's eyes on me as I left, but I didn't care if I was being rude leaving for a few minutes—it was Adam!

"Hi, Bridger, is it really you?" I was afraid to hope.

"Yeah Carson, it's me. How are you doing? I have a few minutes before church so I thought I'd surprise you with a call. Are you surprised?" His warm voice filled some of the void in my soul.

"I am. I have been willing you to call me. Maybe the brain waves got through to you. I miss you so much." To my embarrassment, I started crying. Of course the tears weren't the silent, tragic kind; but the sobbing, hiccuping kind.

"Kit, what's wrong? I know you miss me, but this is something more." Adam's concern made me cry harder. I couldn't even get any words out for a minute.

"Kit, it's okay. Calm down, I'm here, you can talk to me." His words soothed me enough that I could at least manage speech again.

"Oh Adam, it's horrible!" The situation spilled out about my parents and Dave. I told him about my fear of having no family to come home to. I had the hiccups for real by then, so I had to repeat some of the things I said.

"Kit, I'm so sorry. I wish I was with you right now to hold you and let you know everything will be all right. I know it doesn't feel like it, but it will be okay. I promise."

"I wish you were here, too. Or better yet, I wish I was there. I think maybe I should come home. What do you think?" I wanted him to tell me what to do. I wanted him to say *Catch the next flight, I'll be there to meet you.*

Instead he said, "If you think you need to come home, then you should. But make sure it's for the right reason. It's normal to want to rush home to fix things, but the situation with your parents probably won't change if you're here or there."

"So you don't want me to come home?" Images of Ruth hanging on Adam's arm flashed before my eyes. Maybe he wanted me out of the picture for a while longer.

"Of course I want you to come home. I want it more than anything. But you worked hard to get there. You changed your school schedule, you felt prompted to go. I want you to do what you need to do. If you pray about it, the Lord will answer your prayer."

"I want to come home. No, I don't want to come home, ever again. I want you to come here. Will you come here?" I knew it was irrational even as I said the words, but I wanted things to go my way for a change.

"I'd love to, but you know there's no way I can. Just remember that I love you. Don't forget that, okay? I'll be here for you when you come home, though, you know that."

I wished I could know that for sure. I was worried about Ruth.

"Adam, are you dating Ruth?" I asked suddenly.

"What?" The confusion in his voice was sincere. "Ruth? No! Why would you even think that?"

"Your mom sent me pictures of Beth's party. Ruth was there, all cozy next to you. I think she likes you and wondered if you were dating her." It sounded petty, but I had to know.

"She was not cozy with me. She comes over for my mom, mainly. Her mom died last year and my mom's like a surrogate for her or something." Adam's voice and words reassured me.

"It sounds silly, I know, but when I saw the picture it felt like my place in your family—in your life—was being taken over by her. Then I found out about my family and I felt like there was nothing I could do. I thought I was losing both my families."

"Kit, you probably have more of a place in my family than I do. You should hear Lily go on about you. Justin and Michelle are always asking about you. Don't ever worry about not having a home; my whole family loves you."

The heavy weight lifted from me as I heard, and felt, Adam's words. "I love you, too. Thanks for listening to me. You don't know how much I needed to talk to you today."

"I had the feeling I needed to call you, even though I wasn't sure you'd be around. I needed it too."

We set up a time to chat online, which was easier now that I had a schedule of when we'd be at the internet café. I hung up the phone feeling better than I had all day.

I'd talked to Adam for about fifteen minutes and I could hear voices in the living room. I slipped into the bathroom and tried to repair my face so my crying wasn't so obvious. I hoped they hadn't heard me through the walls.

I knew I needed to join the others. To stall for a little more time, I went to the kitchen first to help myself to some apple crisp. While I was dishing up, Tara came in with some dirty plates.

"Are you okay, Kit?" she whispered. I guess my face was beyond repair.

"I'm fine now. You couldn't hear me in the living room could you?" I felt self-conscious at the thought.

"No, we couldn't hear anything. I just know you've been feeling bad since last night and I can tell you've been crying. Is it Adam?" Tara kept her voice low.

"No, everything's fine with Adam. I'll tell you later, okay?" I took a deep breath, pasted on a smile, and then went back into the living room.

I got a lot of glances, but thankfully no one said anything. I focused on my dessert, and tried to ignore Marcel, who kept watching me. As the conversation started sinking in, I realized they had continued on to the next discussion while I was gone. I thought that was a good sign.

I caught Ileana's eye and smiled at her. She smiled back and kind of nudged her head slightly towards Marcel. I ventured a look at him and he was still studying me. I smiled at him too, but he didn't return it. He just kept watching me like a germ under a microscope.

He answered the questions Sora Barnes and Sora Campbell asked him, but I could tell he was concentrating on something— or someone—else. Me. I was perplexed at his behavior and hoped no one else noticed it. Besides Ileana, of course, who had already pointed it out.

The sister missionaries were wrapping up for the evening. They confirmed next week's appointment and Sora Barnes wrote it in her little planner. Neither Marcel nor Ileana wrote it down. Sora Barnes offered to give them a reminder card or call.

Marcel waved her offer away. "We will remember to be here." He shook their hands and Ileana followed suit. Then he shook our hands and Ileana stepped forward to give us a kiss-kiss. When his hand touched mine, he squeezed a little tighter and leaned in towards me.

He said quietly, so only I could hear, "I would like to speak with you a moment, Kit. Alone."

I didn't know how to respond. We waved to the sister missionaries as they left. Marcel picked up his coat, but as Ileana reached for hers, he stopped her.

"Kit and I are going to talk for a few minutes outside." His voice was loud enough for all of us to hear. Ileana shrugged and put down her coat. My roommates stared at me.

I was curious to hear what he needed to talk to me about. I got my coat and we stepped outside. I could envision my roommates with their ears to the door.

"Do you want to walk a little?" I asked. I didn't want to go too far, but I didn't feel like worrying about who heard what.

"That would be good. You are puzzled Kit, yes? You are wondering why I would be so bold as to want to talk to you alone. I, too, am puzzled. Two times in two days I have seen you crying. I sense you are not a person who cries as easily as you laugh. So I ask myself, 'Why is she crying so much?' I have no answer so I am asking you. Why are you crying so much?"

That was the longest speech I'd ever heard from Marcel that didn't have to do with medicine or orphans. I was flattered. Although it wasn't really his business, I felt like I needed all the friends I could get.

"Yesterday it was because I missed my friend Janet, and her family. I guess you would call it homesickness. I already told you that. Today, it was, well—I got some bad news from home. My parents are getting divorced." I found myself tearing up again. I was a regular crybaby lately.

Marcel was armed this time with a handkerchief. He handed it to me. "Divorces happen all the time. It is hard, but it is more common these days. My parents, they divorced when I was a young boy. It felt like my fault but I later learned that it was because my father was selfish. Ileana was too young to remember. I was angry with my father. He left our family and never came back again. He is dead to me now."

He seemed almost nonchalant as he talked about it. They were angry words, yet spoken without rancor. "Do you still hate your father?" I asked.

"I don't hate him. He is nothing to me. I rarely think of him. You see, time passes and heals most wounds." He took my arm and stopped me, abruptly changing the subject. "You have spoken several times of Adam. Are you engaged to be married?"

"Adam and I aren't officially engaged. We do want to get married, though."

"Is he the reason you were crying tonight? Has he hurt you or maybe ended the relationship?" Marcel sounded almost hopeful. I actually laughed a little.

"Marcel, Adam is not the reason I was crying tonight." Then I thought of Ruth and my suspicions. "Well, maybe a little bit. There's this woman at work who likes him and she lives near him and hangs out with his family. So I was a little jealous about it, but that's not what made me cry. It's because of my parents. Divorce might not seem like a big thing to you, but it is a big thing to me."

A thought suddenly occurred to me. "Why do you ask, Marcel? Why do you care if Adam and I are engaged?" He couldn't have feelings for me, we hardly knew each other.

"I find you very interesting and need to know if there are obstacles I need to be aware of," Marcel said bluntly.

Well, so much for professions of undying love and him being overcome by my beauty and charm, I thought. Aloud I said, "Marcel, you make me feel like I am some problem you are trying to solve, or some new disease you are trying to isolate."

"Perhaps I am infected by you. I am not flowery of speech and I am not easily distracted by pretty girls." He got the flowery of speech part right.

We turned to head back to the house. We took a few steps and then he took my arm and pulled me to a stop again. He stepped close to me and looked directly into my eyes. I thought he was going to say something else, but then he leaned in and kissed me.

I was so surprised, I didn't even close my eyes. I just stood there, in shock, staring at his eyelids. I became aware of his lips, which were soft and warm. I had to admit it was pleasant.

Then it deepened into something more. His kiss became persistent and passionate. I suddenly realized my eyes were closed and I was responding to him in kind.

I pulled back, trying to regain my composure, "Marcel! What was that all about?"

His breathing was jerky, spasmodic. "Perhaps I am infected," he said, almost under his breath.

Shaken, in more ways than one, I hurried back inside, with Marcel only a few steps behind me.

chapter twenty-four

I shared Marcel's odd behavior with no one. I just told my roommates that he had seen me crying and wanted to know if he could help. Only my journal and I knew what really happened and I doubted my own recollection. If I hadn't written it down immediately, I would have convinced myself I had imagined it.

Marcel's actions surprised and puzzled me, but my own response was also a great source of troubling thoughts. Why would I react to a kiss from a guy who wasn't Adam? Did it mean I didn't really love Adam? I knew that I did, and I was ashamed of my response to Marcel.

My parents emailed me with the news. I received one from each of them. I rarely got emails from my dad and I didn't expect anything long or detailed. It didn't say a lot, yet it spoke volumes.

> To: kitcarson@yahoo.com
> From: paul.matthews@usu.edu
>
> Dear Kit,
>
> Dave told us he emailed you and you called him back. He was quite upset and I'm sure you are too. I want to clarify things for you. We tried to call you, but couldn't get through. Your mother and I have talked about divorce, it's true. However, we have not yet decided to pursue that course of action. We have agreed to a trial separation for a period of a few months. I will be getting an apartment and your mother

will remain in the house, which, of course, is your and Dave's home. The issues are complicated and we are trying to explore the options. We both love you and want you to know that it is no reflection upon you and Dave. You are an adult now and are certainly aware that relationships can be very complex. Please do not change your plans. We have agreed not to pursue anything final until after the first of the year. I don't expect you to fully understand the situation and we will talk more when you are home.

Love, Dad

My mother's email was a little more detailed and emotional.

To: kitcarson@yahoo.com
From: nmatthews@yahoo.com

Dear Kit,

I've tried to call you several times. It either wouldn't go through or you weren't at home. I'm so sorry that you are so upset. Dave talked to us about his email and your phone call. What he told you isn't entirely accurate. Your father and I are considering divorce. We haven't decided that is what we will do, but we have decided that Dad is going to move out and get his own place. So officially we are separating.

I'm sure it is shocking and devastating to you and Dave. It is for me too. While I'm not placing blame or pointing fingers, you should know that your father has instigated this. Well, so much for not pointing fingers. He has made some choices and apparently wants to make more. I am upset and not really in a frame of mind to go into specifics, nor do I think I need to discuss details with my children.

I'm hurt and I'm angry, I won't pretend otherwise, but that is between your father and me. It isn't where I envisioned I would be after 24 years of marriage, but there it is.

The important thing is to remember that Dad and I both love you and Dave. We want this to affect you as little as possible. I'm staying in the house, so your room will still be here just like you left it. Please stay and finish the program. Coming home early won't make a difference to how Dad and I end up, and you have sacrificed a lot to get there.

I will keep trying to call you to talk to you more. Remember, I love you.

Love, Mom

They didn't give me any details about Dad's "choices" so it was left up to me to guess. He was fifty-seven years old and I thought that was kind of old for a mid-life crisis. I wondered if he was having an affair. I just couldn't picture my dad doing that.

When my mom called she enlightened me a little. She said Dad was involved in a "relationship" but would not elaborate. I tried to push, but she started to cry, so I let it go.

I told Amanda and Kellie that my parents were separated, and talked to Tara in more detail.

"It's such a shock, Tara. I don't know what to do. I can't believe they're talking divorce." I blew my nose again; crying seemed to be my new pastime.

"I can't even imagine my parents divorcing. It must be hard." Tara offered sympathy and a listening ear.

"I'm afraid of how Dave's handling it. I know he's drinking and hanging out with friends who party all the time. He doesn't reply to my emails." I worried more about Dave than I ever had in my life. I felt like he was floundering and trying to mask his pain.

"You're doing everything you can. Keep praying for them and remember Heavenly Father knows your situation, Kit; He won't forget about you."

I forced a smile and said, "I know." Inside, I felt alone and hopeless.

In spite of my worries, the week flew by. I spent most of my hospital time with Alin and Madalina. Both were responding to me, and despite their totally different natures, I could see some parallels. Alin started smiling at me more and could almost sit without assistance. Madalina also brightened when she saw me, and there were fewer sly pinches or shoves from her.

Madalina saw my delight with Alin's progress and she mimicked it. I came in to find her in his room talking to him through the bars of the crib. He was looking at her and smiling.

"Buna, Madalina. You are helping Alin so much," I told her, uncertain of how much she understood. She jabbered in Romanian and hugged me around my waist. I caught myself actually thinking of her as being cute. It was a good change.

At the orphanage, I tried to take care of as many babies as I could, but I still had my favorite twins. I held them every chance I got. When I played with Simona and Daciana, it eased the pain in my own heart. Their eager eyes and sunny smiles radiated love that anchored deep into my soul. I didn't know how I could ever leave them.

Ileana didn't say anything to me about Marcel all during the week. I heard Tara ask her at least three times if we were still set for Sunday. They were coming for dinner as well as having the discussions.

I was a little concerned about dinner since it was Tara's and my week to cook. I was more leery of how Marcel would act around me.

Kellie relieved my worry about the food by offering to cook again and Amanda wanted to make the dessert, which she claimed was her specialty.

I was distracted all through church on Sunday. The sister missionaries called on me twice during Gospel Principles, and I had to be nudged by Tara both times.

"What is wrong with you? You're a million miles away today." She observed.

I didn't want to correct her and tell her my mind was only a few miles away and filling with dread, so I murmured, "Sorry," and tried to pay better attention.

When evening came, my stomach was doing flip-flops. Marcel and Ileana arrived, and I hid out in the kitchen under the guise of helping Kellie.

She sent me out to fill the glasses with punch. As I was filling them, Marcel came over and offered to help. Startled, I immediately slopped some punch over the side of one of the glasses. Marcel picked up one of the napkins and soaked up the spill.

"Kit, are you feeling better today?" His voice was low.

"I'm doing great, except I can't get the punch to stay inside the glass." I kept my tone light and hoped he wouldn't say anything about last week. He didn't; he just said enough to unsettle me this week.

"I understand. It is hard to hold a pitcher when you are trembling." Trembling? I was not trembling! I was just a klutz.

I thought I should set him straight, but was wary of saying too much right there. "Marcel, I'm not trembling. You mistook it for something it really wasn't." I hoped he caught my double meaning.

He smiled at me, and I was taken aback by just how dazzling his smile really was. It should be classified as a lethal weapon. He said, "I rarely mistake things. I am a scientist and I study things very carefully."

Kellie rescued me from having to answer by bringing out the main course of sweet and sour rice. It smelled great and tasted as good as it smelled.

Marcel left me alone during dinner, except for one point when he held his empty glass towards me and asked me if I would pour him more punch. "Yeah, over your head," I muttered under my breath, but his head was saved when Amanda expertly filled his glass.

We finished clearing the table just as Sora Campbell and Sora Barnes arrived. The discussion went smoothly, so smoothly in fact, an idea occurred to me.

Was Marcel feigning interest in the discussions just to be close to me? I tried to dismiss the thought because it seemed so vain, but I found myself watching him and Ileana and analyzing their responses. He caught me watching him twice and I quickly looked away.

Then I started to worry about him thinking I was interested in him because I kept looking at him. I tried not looking at him, but just listening to his responses. They sounded too polished. After last week, I doubted his motives. It was hard to think badly of Ileana, though. She appeared genuinely interested in what the sister missionaries were saying. I felt safe watching her. Then I caught Amanda's gaze on me. When I looked at her, she looked away. A minute later she was watching Marcel. It was all so confusing. I realized I could not possibly help bring the Spirit to the meeting with the directions my thoughts were going.

I considered excusing myself with a plea of not feeling good again. Who could feel good with all the undercurrents in that room? I didn't like intrigue and wasn't above taking the cowardly way out.

I listened eagerly for the discussion to draw to a close so I could escape. Then I mentally berated myself. *What kind of missionary am I, anyway?* I chided myself. *Not a good one, which is why I'm not serving a mission*, I rationalized back at me.

I heard Tara's voice and my name which got my attention. "What?" I asked without thinking.

Tara gave me a strange look and repeated, "Sora Barnes asked you if you would tell them your conversion story. I simply called you back from your trance." She gave the sister missionaries an apologetic look on my behalf. "Kit's had a rough week."

I felt self-conscious and offered a silent prayer. I wanted to share the gospel, I truly did. I just felt like I was so bad at it.

I launched into the long version, starting with my move from California to Utah. I told about Janet's friendship and meeting her brother, Adam, and their example of happiness living the gospel.

"I first felt the Spirit in the Bridger home. I learned I could have the constant companionship of the Holy Ghost if I chose to. I wanted to believe that Heavenly Father existed and loved me, even though I was abandoned at birth and often felt worthless." Nobody interrupted me so I continued.

"When Adam left on his mission he asked me to read the Book of Mormon and listen to the missionaries. I read the book, but put off the missionary part. I finally agreed to let the sister missionaries teach me and when I agreed to get baptized, I knew it was the right decision." It looked like Sora Barnes might start cheering, at that point.

"I was still afraid and lacked faith. I had accepted the gospel and was making changes in my life, but I experienced no mighty change in my heart. Then my friend Janet died in a car accident. I was left without my best friend and with a scar that would be with me forever." Without conscious thought, I pulled back my hair to reveal the long scar I usually tried to hide.

"That was when I turned to God, with real intent, to find out if He was really there for me. He is there and he makes the weak, strong; and can replace fear with faith." Eyes filled with tears as the

Spirit bore witness of the truthfulness of what I had spoken

When I finished my story, there was silence. I had spoken for about ten minutes straight. I would have never believed it possible. Sora Barnes looked at me and said, "Thank you for sharing your story, Kit." She then turned to Ileana and Marcel and said, "That warm feeling you are feeling right now is the Spirit telling you these things are true. Heavenly Father is real. He is the literal father of our spirits. He knows each one of us, as Kit has testified."

I thought she was going to challenge them to baptism right then and there. But she didn't. She challenged them to pray about the things they had learned that night and promised them their prayers would be answered. Sora Campbell gave them a reading assignment in the Book of Mormon.

Ileana and Marcel each had a dark blue Book of Mormon that the sister missionaries had given them the week before. Amanda presented them each with a red scripture marker, which she also seemed to have an endless supply of, judging from how many I'd seen her hand out at church already. Her year's supply was certainly met when it came to refrigerator magnets and red pencils.

Amanda then asked me to help her serve the dessert. I gladly went to assist her. In the kitchen she said, "Kit, your story is so amazing. You just told it so well, like you've practiced it a lot. Have you?"

"No. I nearly panicked when they asked me to tell it. It's so personal and I'm a little embarrassed that I didn't accept everything like I should have from the beginning. I've always been stubborn." I filched a crumb of carrot cake that fell on the counter. "This is really good, Amanda."

She smiled smugly and said, "Thanks. Kellie's not the only one who can cook." She must have realized how she sounded because she added, "She's just so good at it that I don't often get a chance to cook around her."

I thought a little more kindly of her, I almost felt downright charitable; then she opened her mouth one more time. "So Kit, you and Marcel seem to have a thing going. What exactly is going on? I saw the way he looks at you."

"Amanda, I've said it before, nothing is going on. He looks at me like I'm an interesting specimen. He probably looks at everyone like that; you need to just watch him more—if that's possible." Oops, that just slipped out. *Oh well, what's done is done*, I thought.

She looked like she might snatch my piece of carrot cake back in retaliation, so I moved it just out of her reach. "I'm sorry," I said, not wanting her to take a second lunge at my dessert, but I wasn't sincere and she knew it.

"You've got a lot to learn about being a Latter-day Saint!" She huffed past me but pasted on a smile as she went back into the living room with her tray full of real sweetness and her face full of fake sweetness.

"I'm glad I don't have to learn it from you," I said softly as I followed her back to the others.

I managed to avoid Marcel directly for the rest of the evening until it was time for them to go. Once again the sister missionaries left first. As Ileana and Marcel put their coats on and headed to the door, I hung back and gathered up the dessert dishes.

Ileana couldn't leave without giving us each a kiss-kiss on our cheeks. She stepped back inside towards me to give me mine. She said, "Kit, thank you for telling us how you came to accept the gospel. I will pray about it. I would like to be like you, not afraid to ask."

"I understand being afraid, Ileana, but don't be. Even though it's hard, it is worth it." I sounded like a refrigerator magnet.

As she stepped away, Marcel moved closer. "I came for a kiss-kiss, too," he spoke softly again, so only I could hear. I was trapped holding the dishes, but attempted to side step him. I didn't want him to know how he affected me, so I tried to dissuade him.

"The only kiss-kiss you'll get from me is up side your head with these plates," I smiled sweetly as I spoke, careful to keep my voice low.

"Last week your lips spoke differently." He stepped aside to allow me a clear path past him but kept looking at me intently.

"Ce te uiți la mine miamuțo?" (What are you looking at, you dirty monkey?) It was the only thing I could come up with, and I couldn't even say it with attitude. Amanda was moving our way. I hoped he wouldn't say anything that she could use against me.

"You need to learn more of our language. I would be happy to teach you," he said as Amanda linked her arm in his.

"I would love to learn more of your language," she said brightly as if the remark was meant for her. "Kit, when you take the dishes to the kitchen, would you mind wrapping up some carrot cake for Marcel and Ileana to take home with them?"

I had spent the night trying to stay away from Marcel, but something about Amanda butting in irritated me. "No problem, Amanda." Then looking at Marcel I added, "Marcel, do you want to come and show me how much you want?"

He followed me into the kitchen and Amanda followed him. I'm not sure who was more frustrated, Marcel or Amanda. I thought it was funny and considered stirring things up a little more, but I refrained.

After setting the dishes in the sink I said, "Amanda, you can help Marcel with the carrot cake, I really need to get to bed. My head has hurt most of the day. Good night, Marcel. Good night, Amanda."

I was pleased as I went to my room. I just needed to put my irritation with Amanda aside. She liked Marcel, and she could be the answer to my problem with him. As long as I kept her for a chaperone, nothing could happen.

chapter twenty-five

A couple of days later, when I made it back to the internet café, I had a lot of emails. Dave had sent me one telling me he was sorry for acting like a jerk on the phone and that the only difference at home he noticed was that Dad wasn't there for dinner anymore. He sounded like he had accepted their separation a lot better than I was able to. Maybe if I was there it wouldn't seem so awful to me; but then again it might be even worse, seeing the evidence face to face.

My mom emailed me again, checking on me, telling me not to worry. She said they were going to counseling. That sounded like a good sign to me, so maybe it wasn't hopeless. There was no email from my dad which didn't surprise me. He usually let my mom handle stuff like talking to the kids.

Part of Lily's email made me laugh, but another part angered me:

> Adam must've tattled on me to Mom because I got a lecture about spreading gossip. Since Ruth's name and your name came up in the conversation, I figured out that Adam had squealed on me. I didn't mean to make you feel bad, I just wanted you to know what was going on. Is it gossip to tell the truth? Maybe I colored the truth a little because I like you SO much more than I like Ruth. So I told Mom I'd apologize to you for making you worry and I would try not to gossip anymore.
> I figure I can still tell you about family gatherings, like Sunday dinner. Justin asked how you were

doing and Adam told him your parents were separated and it was hard for you. A certain person who wants "her people to be my people" (that's the only clue I'll give) said, "Oh, that's so sad. Well, at least they weren't married in the temple." Michelle started crying because her parents are in a similar situation to your parents (only worse) and her parents were married in the temple. Justin got mad and said, "Maybe you should be more sensitive" and Adam said, "Married in the temple or not, it's heartbreaking for everyone involved." And the certain person who is not a member of the family was really embarrassed and I wanted to laugh, but I didn't because Michelle really felt bad. Then Ruth (oops I said her name) tried to leave and my mom tried to get her to stay, but she left. I was glad she left. Justin and Michelle were glad too. I think everyone was glad except my mom, who hates to have anyone feel bad even when they say really stupid things.

I hope none of that made you feel bad. I thought it might cheer you up that her true colors are starting to show.

It seemed Lily couldn't stop gossiping, but I was glad she would tell me things others might want to keep from me. I couldn't believe Ruth would make such an insensitive remark. Marriage was sacred—even if it wasn't a temple marriage.

I also felt sad for Michelle. She had always seemed like she had the perfect life: beautiful, wealthy, a really good-looking husband (I could say that because Adam and Justin looked so much alike). It made me realize that even people who appeared to have everything had their share of burdens.

Adam's email talked about his mid-term grades, which were pretty awesome, and he told me he was able to start saving some money now that his dad was back at work and he wasn't contributing to the family anymore. I wondered if he would have a car by the time I got home. It was only a few weeks away. I was on the downside of my Romania experience.

The next email surprised me. It was from Marcel.

To: kitcarson@yahoo.com
From: mmiklos@yahoo.com
Subject:I want to talk to you.

It is important that I speak with you about the things that are on my mind. I have been thinking a lot about you and I am afraid you may have the wrong impression about me. You know I am very busy and I am frustrated that we have not had an opportunity to speak without being interrupted.

It may seem to be a game that we play, but to me it is no game. I can laugh when you are clever enough to push Amanda at me so you can escape, but I really would like a time to talk to you about what I see the future bringing to us.

My schedule is full and Sundays are usually my only free day. I have some time on Thursday night. Will you meet me at the internet café? I promise I will not buy you coffee or tea or wine. (You see I remember the joke.)

Your friend, Marcel

I wasn't sure what to do. I couldn't keep avoiding him if he was taking the discussions at our house. I also didn't want whatever was between us to interfere with his decision of accepting or rejecting the gospel. I even found myself avoiding Ileana at the orphanage, which made me sad because she was my friend.

Logically speaking, what was wrong with meeting him here? I could hear him out, set him straight, and, hopefully, we could remain friends. I was only going to be in Romania for five more weeks, it wasn't like it was a lifetime commitment.

I hit reply and agreed to meet him on Thursday.

I promised my roommates I wouldn't go out by myself again so I decided to bring Tara into my confidence. That night in our room, after making her promise not to say anything to anybody, I told her everything that had happened with Marcel, including the kiss, except for how I had responded.

"Omigosh, Kit! I can't believe it. Amanda kept insisting there was something going on between you and Marcel, but I thought she was just jealous. I saw him stare at you a lot, but I had no idea he kissed you! How was it?"

"It was so sudden I didn't even close my eyes." It felt good to confide in a friend.

"You just stared at him? Was it a peck or a long kiss?" Tara always had to dig in the details. I felt just guilty enough about it that I wanted to share the burden with someone else.

"It was just a kiss, you know, nice at first and I did just stare, I was so startled. But then . . ." I trailed off.

"Then what? Tell me!" I thought she might fall off the edge of her bed.

"Then it got more intense. Really intense. And I kissed him back." There, I said it out loud.

"You kissed him back! Kit! Then what?"

"Then we came back into the house and I've tried to avoid him since then. He makes it kind of hard. He says things to me, quietly, so no one else can hear. Now he wants me to meet him on Thursday."

"I'm glad you told me. I can't believe Amanda was right. She would just die—but don't worry, I won't say a word to her." Tara loved intrigue and she was happy to be a part of it. "Of course I'll go with you. What time are you meeting him?"

Tara and I got to the internet café before Marcel did. We ordered soft drinks and sat at a little table. I thought about checking my email, but felt weird about it. I didn't want to be surprised with anything and lately my email had been full of surprises.

Vasilé was working and was excited to see Tara. Her eyes lit up too and I knew I didn't have to worry about her hanging out with me when Marcel came. I was right. As soon as Marcel came through the door, Tara was off to talk to Vasilé.

As Marcel sat down I was aware of his black hair curling around his ears and collar. Now, why would I notice that? I found myself looking at his mouth, remembering that kiss. Uncomfortable with the direction of my thoughts, I shifted my gaze back to his eyes.

"I am glad you would come tonight. I see you brought Tara." He nodded in her direction and she waved at him and flashed him a smile. "I was concerned you would not want to meet me."

"Well, I'm not going to go walking in the dark with you, that's for sure." I said. "I'm curious to hear what you have to say."

"I am very serious about my studies to become a doctor. You know I have plans for improving health care here in Brasov and all of Romania. I particularly care about the orphans and homeless children."

"I think what you are doing is wonderful, Marcel." Romania needed more people like him.

"I rarely thought about dating or having a long-term relationship. After my father left my mother, I had ruled out marriage for me. I saw no point to it. I would be married to my work of making life better for the children of Romania."

I shifted uncomfortably and wondered where this was leading.

"When I met you and your roommates and got to know you at the first dinner at your house, I felt a stirring. You were someone who also cared about the children. I could hear it in your voice and I could see it in your eyes."

What I was hearing in his voice and seeing in his eyes was charming and unsettling at the same time.

"When I found out that you also were an orphan, I knew you had come here for a reason. You told me that you felt there was a reason you needed to come to Romania. We share the same love for the children. We both want to make their world better for them."

I nodded, unable to speak, my heart fluttering.

"Then you invited me over to hear the missionaries speak about God and His plan of happiness for mankind. Here in Romania there is not enough of happiness and there is too much suffering. I thought if there was a God, He had forgotten about Romania. Then I heard your story, your 'mighty change of heart' and I knew that you were sent here, by God, to help me. To help us."

I felt the same way; that I had come for a special purpose. I just wished I knew exactly what it was. Marcel's next words caught me off guard.

"You are only here a few more weeks. There is no time for flowers and dating. You are intelligent, spiritual, and you understand what it is like to be abandoned. When I kissed you I felt something—something for myself that I had never hoped to feel. I know that you felt something, too. You are the perfect wife for me. I am asking you to be my wife. To stay in Romania with me; with the children."

I frantically tried to process it all. When I agreed to meet Marcel, I thought he might express his interest in pursuing me—I sure didn't expect a proposal of marriage.

I struggled to find the words. I felt flattered, yet couldn't imagine he was really serious. I felt those piercing black eyes delve almost to my very soul. There was a connection; I couldn't deny it. I wanted to say, *No, you're wrong. I don't belong here. I belong at home, with Adam, with my own family.* But there was a part; a sliver of my being that cried out: *This is why you are here, Kit! This is the man who can help you change the world. Your family is broken, but you can build a new one here and help heal other broken children.*

My silence encouraged him. Marcel leaned over to me and took my hand. "Kit, it is so much to think about, I know. Do not give me an answer right now. Think about it. Pray about it. I can promise you this—if you say yes, you will never have to doubt me. I will stay with you and never leave you."

I didn't say no. I couldn't say yes. I was confused, but one thought came to me clearly and I told him. "Marcel, there's something I have to know. It's important to me. Are you listening to the discussions just to be near me, to win me over? Or do you really want to know if the gospel is true? I need to know how you feel about that."

I think his answer was truthful. He said, "At first I agreed, not just to be near you, but to understand you more. I needed to know you more. Then as I listened, especially when you told your story of conversion, I knew there was something there. That something is bigger than me, bigger than you. I want to know more."

"So if I say no to you, here tonight, you'll still listen to the discussions?" It was a test, but I had to know his level of commitment.

"Ileana and I both want to know more. I say the issues are not connected, yet they are connected because you were sent here, and through you the message of the gospel is being given to us. I cannot promise I will join the Mormon Church, but I will listen. Please, do not say 'no' tonight. Please consider it."

He held my hand tightly and fervently gazed into my eyes. I was riveted by the magic of the moment. I was drawn to him in a way I couldn't explain. I agreed not to say no.

Relief flooded his features. I realized I had just committed to considering his proposal and I had to add some conditions of my own. "Marcel, if I am to think clearly about this, I need you to not pressure me and confuse me. Please let's keep this between us, for now. Amanda already thinks there's something going on with us; you have to realize she likes you a lot and wants you to like her too. It's already strained between us; I don't want more fuel being fed to that fire."

"I understand. You want me to not steal kisses from you, even though you are willing to return them. You want me to not make you tremble when you fill glasses. You want me to not watch you with longing. I do not know if I can comply." He spoke with soberness of face, but those words must have been chosen to tease me. "But, I will try."

"Marcel, I'm serious. I don't want to feel like I have to keep up my defenses every time you're around me." I felt a communication problem here.

"Kit, I am serious too. You do not need to raise your defenses around me."

"Then why do you tease me with talk of kisses and trembling?" I wanted him to admit he was messing with me.

"I only speak the truth." He said the words simply, which only infuriated me more.

"Okay. Forget it. There's no point in even considering anything between us. You are just trying to push my buttons, and I don't like it." I tried to stand up, but he held my hand fast.

"I do not know what you mean by 'push your buttons,' but I am not trying to anger you. I just do not see why we should deny that we both liked our kiss. And you *were* trembling. Please sit down." Again, I really could detect no guile in this man, but his words were laced with an arrogance which I didn't like.

I leaned over the table and looked directly into those mesmerizing eyes. "I was *not* trembling. Get that out of your head. I was nervous, so I spilled the stupid punch. Get over it. I just want you to give me some space and time if you really want me to consider what you have said tonight." Having said my piece, I sat down again.

He slowly smiled. I could forgive almost anything when I saw that smile. His tone changed; it softened. "I will give you some space. But there is not a lot of time. We have only a few more weeks."

He moved his chair around the table so he was sitting close to me. "May I at least kiss you, here where it is discreet?" His face was nearly touching mine.

"No!" I pulled back; or at least tried to pull back. My chair tipped with the sudden movement, I overcorrected and literally fell into his arms. He seized the moment and kissed me anyway. I knew I'd regret it, but I returned his kiss, again.

chapter twenty-six

Tara pestered me for information about my conversation with Marcel and I told her that he wanted a serious relationship, but that's as much as I would tell her. She witnessed the kiss, though, and teased me about it.

When she teased me a second time I told her I'd seen her kiss Vasilé too, and even though I'd seen nothing of the sort, she turned so red I knew I'd inadvertently hit pay dirt. It was nice to have ammo. I didn't need Tara's heckling to distract me.

I didn't think I could seriously consider Marcel's proposal, yet over the next week it consumed my thoughts. As I sat at the orphanage playing with Daciana and Simona, I envisioned them as my children as I had before, but it was Marcel's face, not Adam's, that flashed in my mind when I pictured their father.

That bit of fantasy upset me. I had never felt so disloyal in my life. I needed someone to talk to. My parents weren't the kind I could turn to even when they weren't half a world away and immersed in their own problems. The people I usually talked to were Adam or his mom, Barbara. Obviously, I ruled them out even if they weren't in a different hemisphere.

That left Tara. I'd asked Marcel to keep things quiet, but I knew I could trust her not to tell anyone else. The one problem with Tara was she liked to ask so many questions and I had plenty of my own that were unanswered, I didn't need more.

As I fed Daciana, I noticed a new baby on the end. He was

wailing loudly, and I wondered if anyone would tend to him. He looked to be about a year old. He had darker skin than the other babies and had a lot of black hair. Several workers walked past him, none paid him any attention.

I finished with Daciana and put her back in her crib with Simona. I went over to the little howling boy and lifted him out of his crib. I had to hold him at arms' length because he was so soiled. He looked like he hadn't been changed all day, and he smelled like it too.

I took him over to the sink where we cleaned the babies, and I changed and washed him from head to toe. He screamed the whole time, but once he was dry he stopped screaming but kept whimpering. I fixed him a bottle and he greedily sucked it down.

He was a sweet little boy, once he was clean with a full tummy. I asked one of the workers if she knew his name. "Pali," she said, barely glancing at him.

I played with Pali and rocked him a little bit. He was like a cuddly little teddy bear. He fell asleep and I put him in an empty crib while I changed the bedding in his. Usually the workers knew a little about the children; I would have to ask about him.

As other babies needed my attention, I forgot about Pali. The rest of the day flew by and I was thankful I was so busy I couldn't worry too much about my dilemma with Marcel.

The next day when I got to the orphanage, I noticed Pali wailing loudly in his crib. That wasn't strange in and of itself, because there were always babies crying; but he was soaking wet, and very dirty again.

I repeated my efforts from the day before. Again Pali responded to me, smiling and grabbing my face. He was so easy to entertain when he wasn't wet or hungry. He would even sit in his crib and watch silently as long as he was clean and fed.

I noticed again that the workers seemed to avoid him. I stood at his crib playing with him when Ileana walked by. I called her over.

"Ileana, why do the workers ignore Pali? Nobody seems to pay any attention to him."

She gave me a puzzled look and said, as if she were stating the obvious, "He is a gypsy baby."

"I don't understand why that makes a difference. He's just a baby and needs care. Look how cute he is." As if on cue, Pali flashed his happy little grin.

Ileana looked at me as if she was trying to understand what I was saying. In a surprised tone she asked, "You love all the babies, don't you, Kit? Even gypsy babies?"

"Of course I love all of them. It doesn't matter if they're gypsies. They all need love." As she walked away, I puzzled over the deep prejudice that the Romanian people felt against the gypsies. And how could they blame a baby?

I noticed Ileana talking to another worker and they both looked my way. I wondered if I had broken some code by showing a gypsy baby loving care. I didn't care if I had; Pali needed attention just like any other baby.

They gave me no indication that they were upset; on the contrary, I noticed that most of the workers stopped ignoring Pali. Even one of the workers who spoke little English and rarely spoke to me smiled at me and said, "You love all babies." I smiled back and agreed with her.

By the end of the week things were still strained between Amanda and me, and she said she was too tired to go to the internet café even though it was her turn. I was glad because, at that point, I would rather not go at all, than go with her.

I really did need to check my email though, since I'd put it off all week long. I had avoided going since I hadn't talked to anyone about Marcel's proposal and I didn't know how I could email Adam or Lily when I felt like I was carrying around a huge secret. I decided I would tell Tara the rest of the details; I was desperate for her opinion. I asked her if she would go with me between our hospital and orphanage shifts, and she agreed.

As we walked there, I told her I needed to talk, but she had to promise not to tease me and not tell anyone else about it. Her curiosity showed on her face as she agreed.

"When I told you that Marcel wanted a serious relationship with me, I didn't tell you how serious. He asked me to marry me and stay in Romania." I watched her face for her reaction.

She didn't disappoint me. Her jaw dropped open. "Shut up! Are you kidding me?"

I shook my head. "I was shocked, to say the least. He was really sincere. He thinks I was inspired to come so we could meet and I could introduce him to the gospel. He thinks we could help a lot of children. He even asked me to pray about it. Here's what's even stranger; I agreed to think about it. That's all I've been thinking about the whole week long. It's crazy."

"Really? Why didn't you tell me? I'm your best friend." She shook her head back and forth in disbelief.

"I made Marcel agree not to tell anyone. I thought since I made him promise, then I probably shouldn't tell anyone either. But I can't stand it. I need to talk about it."

"You're not seriously considering it? I mean, you love Adam. You guys are practically engaged. You've told Marcel about Adam, right?" Tara responded pretty much like I knew she would.

"Marcel knows about Adam. Adam doesn't know about Marcel. I feel so disloyal even thinking about it."

"So why are you thinking about it? Just tell Marcel no. He's hot and everything, but you don't really want to live here in Romania, do you? We're talking permanently here, Kit."

"That's what I keep telling myself. Believe me, I'm not forgetting Adam. But there's a reason I had to come here and maybe this is it. Look, I made a list of the pros and cons. Don't laugh. I have to write things down." I pulled out the paper I'd kept tucked away in my journal.

Tara took it from my hand as we reached the internet café. "Let's go in where it's warm."

I agreed. Inside we sat down at a table. I was glad Vasilé was not in sight; I had Tara's full attention and wanted to keep it. She opened up the paper and laid it on the table. I read it upside down as she studied it.

Marcel
- *I could help the orphans in Romania*
- *I was inspired to come to Romania*
- *We could make a difference in Romania*
- *My family has fallen apart; home won't seem like home*
- *Maybe this is where I'm supposed to stay*

- *Marcel is investigating the Church*
- *I could adopt Daciana & Simona*

<u>Adam</u>
- *I love Adam*
- *Adam loves me*
- *Ruth is after Adam*

She finished reading and looked at me. "This is your whole list?" I nodded and she went on. "Do you really want my opinion?"

"Of course I do. That's why I told you. This whole thing is so crazy that it's making me crazy too."

"I think it's kind of romantic and everything, but look at your list. There's something really huge on Adam's side. It's called 'love.' I think that's the answer right there. You haven't mentioned anything about Marcel loving you or you loving Marcel. Don't you think that's kind of important?"

"I think that's so important. It's true, I don't love Marcel and he hasn't said he loves me, but there was something there when I kissed him. Like some major potential exists, you know what I mean?"

Tara snorted, "I liked kissing Vasilé, but that doesn't mean I'm going to marry him. Kit, finding Marcel's kisses exciting only means you're human. Have you ever heard of lust? Don't confuse lust with love."

"I'm not saying I love Marcel. I'm only saying there's a feeling that could grow. I don't think it's about lust on Marcel's side either. He's not a person who lets himself be driven by that kind of thing. He wants to make a difference in health care and conditions for orphans. He's the one who suggested I pray about it. The thing that's really nagging me is—what if this is why I'm here? What if the Lord really did want me to come here to find Marcel and stay in Romania?" I felt like I was pleading my case before a judge.

"Have you prayed about it?" Tara asked.

"No, not specifically. I'm afraid of the answer," I confessed.

"Kit, I can't tell you what to do. I understand the excitement of a Romanian romance, but this is your life. You do need to pray about it. I'll tell you one thing, though. One of my institute teachers warned us about one person getting revelation for another when it comes to dating. He said there are plenty of stories where a guy told a girl she should marry him because he prayed about it and it was revealed to him. When it comes to who you're going to marry, you're entitled to your own revelation, and you'll get it." Tara's insights made perfect sense to me and I was glad I had confided in her.

"You don't think I'm nuts for considering it, though?" I wanted reassurance.

"I don't think you're nuts, but I am surprised. You've always been absolutely sure about Adam. I'm surprised that anyone—even someone as hot as Marcel—could tempt you away from him. It just goes to show you that we're all human. Even you, Kit. So cut yourself some slack." Tara got a glint in her eye. "Now, not to change the subject, but tell me more about this Ruth person and why do you think she's after Adam?" Her mischievous grin rubbed off on me, so I told her I'd tell her if she got us some hot chocolate.

After I dished the dirt on Ruth and how Lily kept me up-to-date, I decided I should check my email. We didn't have a lot of time before we needed to leave for the orphanage.

There were three from Adam and I read them in order. The first two were his normal emails, going on about school and telling me he missed me and loved me. I felt badly that I hadn't responded; especially when I read the third one.

> To: kitcarson@yahoo.com
> From: bridgerman123@hotmail.com
> Subject: Where are you?
>
> Hey you! I'm starting to get worried. It isn't like you to just ignore my emails. I hope you're okay. You haven't been carried off by the gypsies have you? I'm more concerned that you're sick or stressing out about your parents.
> Please, either email me or call me. I've tried calling once this week but it wouldn't go through for some reason. I'm thinking I might call your mom if I don't hear from you soon.
> Don't make me get on a plane to Romania! I'm worried-can you tell? Something just seems like it's not right.
> I love you, Adam.

I felt awful. I wasn't sure what to say. I read emails from my mom which were depressing, mainly because nothing had changed with her and my dad. There was also one from Marcel, which I ignored for the moment. I went on to read Lily's email.

> To: kitcarson@yahoo.com
> From: lilyofthevalley16@hotmail.com
> Subject: Alert!
>
> Okay I know this is gossip, but it's gossip you need to know about (don't say you heard it from me). I was walking home from a young women's activity last night and when I got near the house I saw Ruth's car. She was giving Adam a ride home from work (I'm guessing). They were sitting in front of our house talking. I saw Ruth lean over and hug Adam. Then I saw her KISS him! On the mouth—not the cheek! So much for sisterly affection! I ducked behind the neighbor's hedge cuz I didn't want them to see me. Adam got out of the car right after that, so maybe she was kissing him goodbye. I don't know. Come home, Kit! I don't want Ruth to be my sister-in-law! Hurry!
>
> Love, Lily

I was stunned. How dare he kiss her! Or she him—however it went. And he was acting all worried about me. Of course he never said one word about Ruth in his emails to me. I really didn't know what to do. And to think, I was filled with guilt because Marcel had kissed me! I still had four weeks left before my flight home; it wasn't like I could just hop on the plane tomorrow.

Well, Adam could just worry some more. I thought about not replying, but I didn't want him calling my mom. Then I had an idea. I couldn't get Lily in trouble for gossiping so I had to be discreet.

> To: bridgerman123@hotmail.com
> From: kitcarson@yahoo.com
> Subject:no need to worry about me
>
> I'm sorry I haven't written you all week. Don't worry, the gypsies didn't carry me off. It was the dark-eyed Romanian who proposed to me and wants me to stay here forever that distracted me! Things are really busy here. There's lots going on at the hospital and orphanage. I'm not really getting along with Amanda lately either. She makes little remarks that make me feel like I'm not good enough.

I am worried about my parents. Sometimes I just want to stay here and never have to face the situation. Just when you think you know somebody, they surprise you.

Let me know how things are going. I hope you get a car soon so you don't freeze on your bike or have to hitch rides with dangerous people!

Don't forget about me. I haven't forgotten about you.

Love, Kit
P.S. I miss you, I hope you still miss me.

I re-read the message. Was it too obvious that I was trying to make him jealous? I wondered if he would read between the lines or just figure I was joking. I briefly wondered if he felt guilty for kissing Ruth. I hurried and hit send before I changed my mind; Tara was ready to leave.

We hurried back to our house to grab some lunch and I told her about Lily's email. She shook her head and said, "I don't believe it! Lily must have seen wrong."

"I don't think she would tell me that unless she was positive. She isn't mean-spirited. I know Ruth is after Adam; I'm just upset that he apparently let her catch him."

"Like you did with Marcel?" Tara said slyly.

I felt my face flush red. "I don't think it's the same thing. He doesn't have to take rides from her if he knows she's chasing him. It would be like me seeking Marcel out after he made his intentions known. I told Marcel to back off."

"Maybe Adam told Ruth to back off. Lily said he got out of the car right after that. You should give him the benefit of the doubt. You'd want him to do the same for you. What if someone told Adam they saw you kissing Marcel? Would you want him thinking the worst?" Tara's defense of Adam made sense even though I wanted her to take my side.

"Well I already sent the reply, so I can't take it back," I grumbled.

Later on I remembered the email from Marcel. I wondered what it said. I'd been so upset about Lily's report that I never went back to read it. Maybe it was a retraction of his proposal. I hoped so; that would make things a lot easier.

chapter twenty-seven

I spent the next couple of days doing a lot of soul-searching. I felt like my world had turned topsy-turvy. There were a couple of things I'd been certain of before coming to Romania. One of them was the solidity of my parents' marriage. I never examined the issue openly—there was never a need for me to do so. It had always been there, like a solid foundation.

The other thing I had been sure of was that Adam and I would get married. We agreed not to get engaged yet, and we talked about the trials of being apart for three months. I hadn't really been concerned about leaving him to come to Romania; I knew I would miss him, but he would be there when I returned.

Things were different now. My parents lived in separate dwellings; carrying on separate lives. I had received a proposal of marriage from Marcel; Ruth and Adam were having some sort of relationship that exceeded friendship.

I never thought I would seriously contemplate staying in Romania. As I battled the twin demons of my parents' separation and Adam's apparent inconstancy, I looked around me, trying to picture living in Brasov permanently.

I briefly toyed with the idea of staying on as Danielle had; a single woman living in Brasov and adopting some orphans. That would make a difference in the lives of a few. With Marcel's proposal, I felt like I was being offered the chance to make a difference in the lives of many.

Marcel's intensity was appealing, in its own way. He had a single-minded interest in making changes that would affect generations. He wanted to include me in his crusade.

When I'd returned to the internet café the next day, there were no new emails from Adam, but I read the email from Marcel I had neglected. It consisted of just a few words that stuck in my memory.

> Kit, we spoke of many things when we met. I did not tell you how I feel about you. You have brought sunlight to my overcast life. How can a person live without sunlight?

His words moved me. He claimed he was not flowery of speech, but that email told me differently. There was no "I love you," which I'm not sure I would have believed. I was fond of Marcel, I was intrigued by him—but I knew I didn't love him. However, I also thought I could easily grow to love him.

I knew I loved Adam and he always made me laugh. One problem was that it was hard for me to believe that someone like him could actually love someone like me. He was a spiritual giant—fed from birth by a faithful, religious family; and I was a spiritual infant. I felt like I would never be on the same level he was.

Perhaps that was why I was so quick to believe there was something between Adam and Ruth. Ruth also came from a spiritual family—after all she was the niece of a stake president and named after a biblical stalwart. She probably had multiple ancestors that crossed the plains with Brigham Young.

It occurred to me that in Romania, I felt like I was the spiritual giant. The sister missionaries had looked to me to share a testimony-building experience. Marcel and Ileana saw me as a person with strong faith and investigated the gospel because of me. At the orphanage and hospital the children saw me as someone who loved unconditionally. I liked the way it felt to be treated as if I were faithful and spiritual.

In Utah, I was treated like someone special as I investigated and joined the Church; but after I joined, I was just one of thousands. At places like Enrichment, Sunday School, Institute, and Relief Society, it was just assumed that I suddenly knew everything I needed to know to understand what was being talked about.

I remembered the awful incident at Enrichment where I had worn my mother's sleeveless wedding dress to an activity highlighting temple weddings. In my ignorance, I hadn't known how inappropriate the cut of the dress was; yet I still remembered the comment, "Don't you know what temple-ready means?" I didn't know at the time; I was still trying to fit in, but the whole thing made me want to never return.

In Romania I felt like I wouldn't be judged or found lacking. I never felt inferior; except maybe when it came to the language, which I was slowly learning.

I was different and could make a difference in Romania. I was unique, yet lost in the multitudes in Utah.

I poured out all my feelings into my journal. I felt relieved, but still confused.

When Sunday came, we ate dinner with just the four of us roommates. Tara and I got to cook, and our spaghetti and green salad was a far cry from the food Kellie had been cooking for us.

That night the missionary discussion went smoothly. The sister missionaries were excited to hear that Marcel and Ileana were praying and reading the assigned scriptures. I was excited to see that Marcel kept his promise and had backed off his obvious pursuit of me.

He backed off so well, in fact, that I started to wonder if I had imagined the whole thing. There were no sidelong glances; no remarks with double meanings; no singling me out for questions.

When the subject of temple marriage came up, Marcel listened attentively. He asked where the nearest temple was. Sister Campbell told him it was the Kiev Ukraine temple. I confess I watched him and he never so much as glanced at me during that whole discussion.

The missionaries had another appointment to keep, so they didn't stay long. We offered some cookies and hot chocolate to Ileana and Marcel. Our discussion turned to the children in the orphanage.

"Daciana and Simona are my favorites. I think they're kindred spirits—maybe we were triplets, separated at birth. When I'm with them, I feel renewed, like anything is possible. I want to take them home; I wish there was a way." My roommates had heard me say this kind of thing before.

Tara commented, "I don't know how you're ever going to leave those twins, Kit. Maybe you can smuggle them home in your suitcase."

I'd had that impractical thought myself. Marcel chose that moment to make his first direct comment to me. "Maybe you could stay here in Romania and adopt them yourself." His gaze lingered only for a moment, but it pierced me to the heart. Had I discussed my hopes of adopting the twins with him? I had mentioned it to Ileana, but I doubted she and Marcel would have had a discussion that included my wishes for those two motherless babies.

I felt the impact of his unspoken words. *Kit, stay here, marry me, and we will adopt those two baby girls you have fallen in love with.* I also knew at that moment Marcel would be willing to join the Church and take me to the temple.

I could start a new life; apart from the old one. I would be far away from the turmoil tearing my family apart. I wouldn't have to wonder why a guy as wonderful as Adam would settle for me. I wouldn't have to feel insignificant and unable to help.

I was not a material person. I didn't care that much for clothes, jewelry and nice homes. But could I be happy in a poor Romanian apartment or house? It was one thing to make do with the inconveniences for three months, but a lifetime?

"I don't know if I could live in Romania forever," I said in reply to Marcel's statement about the twins. Then I asked Ileana and Marcel if they had ever considered living in the U.S. Ileana said she would like to visit there and see some of the famous landmarks, but would not want to live there. Marcel's answer was enlightening.

"If I could follow my dreams, part of that dream would be to study medicine in the U.S. as well as in Romania. I would like to implement ideas from the U.S. and Canadian healthcare system to provide better healthcare here in Romania. If I could hold dual citizenship here and in the U.S., I would be able to accomplish much, much more."

Amanda said, "It sounds like you need an American wife."

As her words sunk in, suddenly his proposal made so much

more sense to me. It wasn't about being swept off his feet by me; it was about forging a partnership. I wondered if I told him no, would he pursue Amanda, who was obviously interested in him. I felt a little flare of jealousy.

"Are you volunteering for the job?" I asked Amanda. I expected her to get angry at me for putting her on the spot like that, but she laughed and looked directly at Marcel.

"Maybe I am. But Marcel, you need to know that I will only get married in the temple, so you'll need to get baptized soon."

If astonishment could be measured and paid in gold, we would have all become instant millionaires. Never would we have imagined Amanda practically proposing to Marcel if he got baptized.

I could tell that Marcel was uncomfortable. I felt partly to blame for her comment because I did deliberately bait her so I spoke up. "Marcel shouldn't get baptized just so he can get married. He should get baptized because he wants to."

I realized I had just told Marcel he should get baptized. I felt my face go crimson and I ventured a look at him. He was smiling at me. I wished he wouldn't do that; I had already discovered I wasn't immune to that charm.

"It sounds like you and Amanda are taking over for the sister missionaries. I think I will let them teach me more before I decide. I cannot speak for Ileana." He turned to his sister.

Ileana said, "Oh, now he wants me to speak! When we began to listen to the missionaries, Marcel was the one who wanted to go slowly. Now he wants to always speed things up. He has even spoken to our mother, who I thought would never listen. Marcel says he needs to learn more, but acts like he has made his decision."

Marcel grinned at his sister's words. "You blame me, Ileana, when you are the one who agreed to go to the Sunday church meetings."

"You guys are going to go to church next Sunday? Why didn't you tell us?" This came from Tara, but we were all surprised. Somehow we thought we were the conduit for Ileana and Marcel to learn the gospel.

I was glad the marriage talk had passed and I think Amanda was, too. She had looked slightly embarrassed at her bold comments.

I meant to talk to Marcel alone about them. I needed to know if he wanted to marry me, or if any American woman would do.

When it came time for them to go, Marcel gave me a casual hug while he slipped a piece of paper into my hand. I glanced around to see if anyone else had noticed, but was pretty sure no one else had.

I read the note in my room. It simply asked me to meet him at the internet café Tuesday afternoon. I would have to make sure Tara could go with me. I didn't want to be alone with him, but I was determined to find out his true intentions.

chapter twenty-eight

On Tuesday Tara and I arrived at the internet café a few minutes late and Marcel was already there. Vasilé was working and, as if on cue, Tara flitted over to talk to him. I went over to join Marcel at the table; he already had a bottle of water for me and I noticed he was drinking the same. That brought a smile to my face.

"What? No coffee?" I asked him straight out as I sat down.

"No more coffee. I have recently learned it is not good for the body. You will find I am an excellent student. When I learn something is right, I take it very seriously."

"I'm glad you're taking the Word of Wisdom seriously. I won't have to worry about you buying me coffee anymore." For some reason, I wanted to lighten his mood which I sensed was somber. My attempt met with failure, so I quashed my own light-mindedness. "It is true, you know."

"What is true?" He demanded clarification.

"All of it. The Restoration of the Gospel, a Heavenly Father who loves us, Jesus Christ as our Savior, living prophets—it's all true." I don't know why I needed to tell him; it was like bearing my testimony again. I just felt like he needed to hear it.

He silently considered my words then asked a question. "What about the part about eternal families? Do you believe that is true?"

"Of course," I was quick to answer. But a silent little voice argued in my head: *Do you really believe families are eternal?* It was a question I didn't want to face head-on.

While my parents were together, I told myself I could hope for the day when they would accept the gospel. Now that it looked like divorce was in their future, I felt like I was kidding myself to hold out hope that my parents would even stay together, much less join the Church and have our family sealed in the temple.

I thought briefly of my birth parents; wherever and whoever they were. That was strike one. Now my adoptive parents were separated, and even though they said a divorce would have nothing to do with me, I felt like this was a big strike two where my role in a family was concerned. What would strike three be—Adam dumping me for Ruth? Finding out he wanted someone as spiritual as he was? Someone who never doubted?

"Why do you look so sad, Kit? What is the matter?" Marcel reached for my hand, so I quickly took a drink of my water.

"I'm sad thinking about my family. They aren't members of the Church and we haven't been sealed together as a family. If I believe in eternal families, it's hard to know I'm not a part of one. I feel like I don't belong anywhere anymore." There, I said it. I shared one of my biggest insecurities with Marcel. I wondered what he would say.

"You cannot change what your parents do, but you can choose what you do. Perhaps it is time to create your own family. Your own eternal family." His inflection added meaning to the words he spoke to me. He was including himself in that family.

"Marcel, that's what I thought I was going to create with Adam. You have to know that I love him and I want to marry him. I'm just worried that he doesn't want to marry me anymore." I twisted my hands around the empty water bottle. "His family has belonged to the Church since the pioneer times. I feel like I don't measure up to them. This other girl I think he's seeing, she's probably a better mate for him than I am. I'm sure you don't want to hear all of this, do you? I can't imagine you want to hear how I feel about another guy."

"No, I would rather talk about us. You need to know that I find you to be the perfect mate for me. I have discovered that I have been missing two very important things in my life—you and the gospel. Now I have found both." He waited for the words to sink in.

I wasn't sure I was hearing him right. "You mean you're going to get baptized? Is that what you are saying?"

"Yes, I have prayed about it and it is the right decision for me. I have not spoken to my family about it yet, but I believe Ileana will make the same decision. That is one reason I want the missionaries to meet my mother. I hope she will understand better if she feels what we feel when they teach."

"She will, Marcel; it's the Spirit that teaches."

"You need to know that I am not making this choice to win you over. I am making this choice because I am learning for myself that there is a God. Whether you decide to stay here in Romania with me, or to go home to Adam, I still must choose to start on the path that will lead me back to God."

He finished talking and I was speechless. I had a glimpse of what it must have felt like the day I'd told Janet and Justin I was going to get baptized. A feeling of joy just enveloped me; to be a part of bringing the gospel to someone else!

I seized both of his hands in mine. "Marcel, I'm so happy! Thank you for telling me!"

"I hoped you would be happy. As the missionaries have taught me, it is the first step towards the temple, and towards a forever family. Kit, I am here for you. We can begin our own family unit here and we will be sealed in the temple. Together we can make a difference to so many; to heal them physically and feed them spiritually."

I was caught up in the intensity of the moment; his eyes burned with the fervor of a new convert, and his lips spoke the words that made me think I could feel whole again. He leaned in to kiss me. I sensed it, even before he was close enough. I instinctively moved towards him. A phrase came to my mind, unbidden; *dual citizenship*. As the words entered my conscious, the spell was broken. I pulled back.

"Marcel. I have a question for you. Did you propose to me so you could gain dual citizenship? Would any American woman do?" I had to know the answer.

Something flashed in his eyes that I thought might be annoyance. "Kit, I would not take any American woman. I never thought I would marry. I mean *never*. I will not deny that becoming an American citizen through our marriage is appealing to me. You are the perfect one for me. If I had enough time, I would show you."

"Then tell me. How am I the perfect one for you?" He would have to take time to tell me, even if he couldn't show me.

"Both of us want to help the orphans of Romania. Who better than a Romanian doctor and an American orphan? We both have great intellect. We both want to change the world. You have brought the gospel of Jesus Christ into my life. We can learn together and teach others together." He leaned in close to me again and caressed the backs of my hands.

He continued in a softer voice. "You are beautiful and you tremble when I am around. I like it. I think you do too. Stay here with me. Forget about your broken family. I will be your family. Forget about Adam. I will be your husband. You will never have to doubt me."

"Do you love me, Marcel?" I burned with the need to know.

"I am beginning to know what love feels like. As time passes, our love will grow."

He moved in again to kiss me, but I turned my face away at the last moment. His gentle kiss landed on my cheek. I thought he might be irritated, but he simply pressed his lips to my cheek and stroked the other side of my face with his hand. I heard him murmur, "Give me a chance, just give me a chance." I forgot about my protests and my problems for the moment and enjoyed his warm embrace.

A shadow fell upon us. It was Tara. "Sorry to break this up guys, but Kellie and Amanda are about to walk in the door. Thought you might like a warning." She turned to head them off.

I jerked back, not wanting them to see me there with Marcel. Marcel let me go and I swear he smirked as he glanced at the door. I quickly said, "I'll talk to you later. I've got to go check my email." I hurried over to a vacant terminal and fumbled through my backpack, hoping they hadn't noticed anything.

Marcel wandered over to the counter and spoke to Vasilé in Romanian. Vasilé laughed and I wondered what the joke was about.

Amanda saw Marcel as she and Kellie approached Vasilé. "Marcel! What are you doing here?" She looked past him directly at me and I felt myself go twenty shades of red. "What a surprise, you happened to run into Tara and Kit here."

"I know from Ileana that you four often come here in between your shifts. It is no surprise to see you, only a pleasure," Marcel said smoothly. Amanda ate it up. I fought back the surge of irritation. Whether I was irritated at Marcel's glib remark or Amanda's eager attitude, I didn't know.

I ignored them and asked Vasilé why the computer wasn't working. "Because you must pay first; you know this." He made a remark to Marcel in Romanian and they both laughed again.

My face still aflame, I went to the counter to pay for my internet time. Amanda stepped closer to Marcel on his opposite side. I deliberately stepped closer to Marcel and leaned across the counter to pay Vasilé. I shoved a little as I reached across, causing Marcel to have to step even closer to Amanda.

"Oh sorry, Marcel," I said innocently, "I didn't mean to get in your way."

"You are never in my way, Kit," he said loud enough for all to hear. Then soft enough for only me to hear he added, "You are my way."

Startled, I stared for a second then said the only thing I could think of. "I hope you're reading the scriptures, Marcel. We're hoping for an announcement of your baptism soon."

"I'm hoping for an announcement of my own," he said. "I must go. I will see you ladies another day. La revedere!"

Amanda walked him to the door and I returned to my computer. I needed to stay away from that man for a few days. I was getting far too confused.

I logged on to my email account. I was so glad to see an email from Adam. I felt a wave of guilt as I opened it. I had just let Marcel kiss me, again, and here I was excited Adam had written me. What kind of player was I?

I shoved back the guilty feelings with a reminder that I had been straightforward with Marcel about Adam. I never even hinted that I cared more for Marcel than as a friend. I even "turned the other cheek" when he tried to kiss me. I had nothing to feel guilty about. *You haven't been straightforward with Adam about Marcel. And you didn't tell Marcel that you wouldn't marry him. You've even thought about it—far too much to put it off as a harmless flirt. What game are you playing, Kit Matthews?*

Ignoring the voices in my head (one of which sounded a little too much like my mother) I read Adam's email. His words made me wonder why I ever doubted him.

> To: kitcarson@yahoo.com
> From: bridgerman123@hotmail.com
> Subject:I miss you I miss you I miss you I miss you I miss you I miss you infinity
>
> Of course I miss you! What a silly question to ask! I am so glad you're two-thirds through your trip. I can't wait to see you again. There's so much to talk about, so much to catch up on. I'm glad for email, because it's so much faster than snail mail and I remember how hard it was waiting for a letter from you while I was on my mission. It's not the same as being together in person, though.
>
> Email me back and let me know some times when you'll be online so we can IM. I'm dying to hear your voice. I'm dying to see your voice (and if you wonder what that means, just realize I'm imagining your voice coming from your lips . . . your lips from your face . . . your face from your head . . . and so on). Bottom line–I want you here!
>
> And let me just mention that if there are any dark-eyed Romanians proposing to you, they will soon be black-eyed Romanians (under the age of eight exempt, as they are not yet accountable for their actions). Just the thought makes me jealous, but I suspect that was your motive! Don't make me get even with you!
>
> It's cold here in Cache Valley. Then I checked out the temperatures online for Brasov and let me just tell you, "Keep your long-johns on, and better you than me!" Ha ha, I was gloating at you the last two winters too. It seems like I'm always in the milder climate. Sorry to gloat, it's just the way it is!
>
> I have to give a talk in my student ward this Sunday. Pray for me. Ruth is giving a talk, too, so pray for the both of us. My family wants to come and

listen but I told them to stay away. I wouldn't have
even said a word to them about it, but Ruth has loose
lips.

Speaking of church, do you understand the talks
and lessons any better? Do the sister missionaries
still translate for you? How did the discussions go
with your friends, Marcel and Ileana? Are they serious
investigators?

Write back soon. I gotta go. I love you and miss
you.

Adam.

I was frosted at the part where he and Ruth were speaking
together at church, like they were a couple or something. And how
would he know if her lips were loose? What I wanted to pray for
on her behalf wasn't really something a person should mention in
prayers, so I'd have to let Adam down on that one. After all, I wasn't
a saint.

Ignoring my uncharitable feelings about Ruth, I answered
Adam's email.

To: bridgerman123@hotmail.com
From: kitcarson@yahoo.com
Subject: Ha ha! You have to talk in church

Just so you know, I think it's funny you have to
talk in sacrament meeting. That's one thing I can gloat
to you about. Not speaking the language pretty much
saves me from that same fate. I'm picking up some of
the language, but not enough to say anything meaningful.

I've been worrying a lot about my parents lately,
as you might guess. I always hoped someday they would
join the Church. I feel like a failure as a missionary in my own home. Maybe I should have concentrated
more on my family and less on the other side of the
world.

Ileana and Marcel are still investigating the
Church. . .

I made no mention of what else Marcel was investigating.

I think they will announce their baptism dates
soon. I can't really take credit for it, but at least
I've been of help in bringing the gospel to someone,
even if it isn't my own family.

I miss you so much. I didn't think this trip would

be so hard. I would go crazy without Tara to talk to.
Since she's waiting for Eric to come home from his mission, she and I have a lot to talk about. She's probably
sick of me talking about my family's problems. When you
go to the temple again, will you put their names on the
prayer roll? I don't know what else to do for them.
  Let me know how your church talk goes and I hope
you get a really cold spell in Cache Valley and a big
fat inversion! That's what gloaters deserve.

  I love you. Kit.

There was an email from my mom attempting to keep things
light-hearted and upbeat, but I sensed a false bravado in her words.
I felt so sad for her; but even more sad for me.

There was another email from Lily. I read it and gasped out
loud. A couple of people looked over at me, but none were my
roommates.

To: kitcarson@yahoo.com
From: lilyofthevalley16@hotmail.com
Subject:This is the worst one yet!

  Ruth was over here last night (as usual) and after
dinner and the dishes (which she always volunteers to
help with cuz she wants to impress everyone) she and
Adam went into Dad's office to use the internet. That
alerted my radar, so I hung around close so I could hear
most of their convo. I couldn't see anything (I had to
keep my cover). Adam said "What do you think of this
one?" She said "I like it a lot. But look at the price.
That's way too much." He said "I'm not worried so much
about the price; I just want to get the right one."
  I'm thinking, oh they're looking at cars, so I
keep listening. Ruth said "It can be the right one and
still be a good deal. You don't want to buy something
like this online anyway. You need to see it before you
buy it." Adam's like, "I know, I just wondered if you
thought it looked good and was a good deal."
  Then she goes, "I think Salt Lake has a much better
selection than here in Logan. I told you my uncle
down there can get you a great deal. Let's go look on
Saturday. I'm off work and you work the early shift so
we could get down there in time to have my uncle show
you what he can do. My aunt makes the best homemade
cinnamon rolls in the world! I'll call them and let them
know we're coming. I know she'll make some for us. She
knows how much I love them! What do you think?"
  Adam agreed and then they planned a trip to Salt

Lake together! I'm all thinking I'll try to butt in, so I'm trying to think of a way.

Anyway, they go back to the family room where everyone else is. I ducked into the bathroom so they didn't see me. So I go into Dad's office because I'm curious to see what kind of car he was looking at. I pull up the history and go to the last website he was on. Guess what? It wasn't cars they were looking at; it was engagement rings! I'm not kidding. Adam was looking at engagement rings with Ruth!!!! Why would he do that? They're going to go to Salt Lake together to look at rings on Saturday.

Remember when Justin and Michelle took off to Salt Lake to look at wedding rings? They came back engaged! I'm worried sick! Do you want me to confront Adam? I don't know how this happened; I've tried to keep them apart. I've been crying and trying to figure out how to tell you, but I knew that you would want to know.

Can you come home sooner? I think this is a major crisis. Sorry to be the one to tell you.

Love, Lily.

Stunned, I tried to process her email. She had to be mistaken. There was no way Adam and Ruth would be getting engaged. No way. I pulled up his last email and re-read it. Lily had to be wrong. Adam would never say he loved me and get engaged to someone else. He just wouldn't.

Lily was right about Justin and Michelle coming back from Salt Lake with an engagement ring, but that was the day after they got engaged. I remembered it clearly because they had stranded me at an activity and taken my car to Salt Lake. Justin had proposed to her that day and they were gracious enough to return my car before they actually went ring-shopping the next day. Lily did exaggerate a little and was prone to drama.

I didn't think she would outright lie, though. Why would she tell me something like that unless she had really overheard it? Maybe she pulled up the wrong website when she went back to the computer.

The very idea of Adam and Ruth being engaged was ludicrous. A sick feeling came over me as I realized that if I said yes to Marcel, he would want to buy me a ring as soon as possible. At least I thought he would. And to think I had never given Adam a hint about Marcel. Maybe the idea wasn't as farfetched as I thought.

Tara came over and told me we had to leave or we would be late. I logged off as thoughts still swirled in my head. I wished I could know what was really going on with Adam and Ruth. I could just email him and ask him, but that wasn't the kind of thing I could talk about via email or IM. Maybe I would ask him when we talked on the phone again.

I was glad Marcel had already left the internet café. I needed to sort things out and I knew I needed to be away from Marcel when I did it.

chapter twenty-nine

Wednesday morning I woke up with a fever and a terrible headache. I took ibuprofen and went back to bed. My roommates went to work and I dozed off and on. My dreams were fitful, involving Adam, Marcel, and Ruth. They were dreams I was glad to wake up from.

Tara checked on me when they came home for lunch. Body aches had set in by then and I took more medicine. My roommates left and I wished my mom were there to take care of me. The fever persisted for a couple of days and my roommates tried to get me to go to a doctor.

"No way. I'm not going to go to someone who I can't communicate with. I'll get better." I stubbornly refused to go, even when my throat was sore and I felt like my head would explode. I asked them to go get me some cold medicine.

They called Corina to go with them. She came with a jar of soup for me. Her mother and grandmother could always be relied on to provide us with something to eat. She also brought homemade mazurka, a scrumptious almond pastry that was my favorite. I knew I was really sick when it didn't even appeal to me.

Corina also brought a small bottle of medicine that smelled like something from a cow pasture. Her grandmother said it would cure fevers and most illnesses. I was desperate enough that I took some. I didn't feel nauseated until I swallowed that concoction.

"Do not worry," Corina soothed me. "It does not taste good, but it does work."

It cured my desire to drink anything else her grandmother might send over, but the next morning I woke up without a fever. The body aches and sore throat remained, but not as severe. I was impressed enough to take another dose of the vile stuff.

I felt a huge improvement by Saturday, except for a nasty cough that settled in my chest. I could live with that; at least I could think straight again.

Kellie, Amanda, and Tara all went out with Corina for the day, leaving me alone. My thoughts turned to my dilemma; Marcel versus Adam. Was staying in Romania the right thing to do?

I wanted to do what the Lord wanted me to do. I fervently wished I'd taken Janet's advice when she urged me to get my patriarchal blessing. I was still too new in the Church at the time and didn't understand its importance, but if ever there was a time I wished I had a blessing to guide me, it was then.

I turned to the scriptures for comfort and direction. I had received an answer to prayer before by turning to the scriptures; I knew it was possible again. Notwithstanding my sincere efforts at praying and searching the scriptures; no answers came to me.

I had confided the entire thing to Tara. I tried to leave out nothing. She knew about Marcel's plans to get baptized; his promise to take me to the temple; Lily's email about Adam and Ruth going ring-shopping together; and Adam's continued profession of love for me.

She agreed that there must be some misunderstanding about the Adam and Ruth thing. To her the answer seemed simple: go home to Utah and marry Adam.

I didn't confide in her my darkest fears—that I wasn't good enough for Adam; that I would never be a part of an eternal family; and that I was afraid if I didn't stay in Romania I might be letting the Lord down. Things like that seem silly or ungrounded when you voice them to a friend; but those feelings are real, they run deep, and they haunted me in my attempt to make the right decision.

I prayed again for what seemed like the hundredth time. I thumbed through the scriptures; looking for the answer I needed.

Again nothing came. It was hopeless.

A folded paper fluttered out of the back of my scriptures. I picked it up and unfolded it. It was a small copy of *The Family: A Proclamation To The World* given to me in a Relief Society meeting months ago.

Looking at the title, I almost crumpled it up, I was that discouraged. Somehow in the recesses of my troubled mind, it registered that I was holding scripture—revealed by our latter-day prophets. I began to read through it, for no particular reason.

More than halfway through it, in paragraph seven, a part caught my eye. It talked about how true happiness in a family can only be achieved when based upon the teachings of Jesus Christ. It then went on to explain how successful marriages are based upon several principles of the gospel, such as faith, prayer, repentance and forgiveness. Those in a marriage relationship must also have respect for one another, love, compassion, and a willingness to work together.

What I had just read was nothing new to me, nor would it be new to the majority of the families in the Church. It would be new to my family, however. I felt strongly that I needed to bear that same testimony that I had found in Cache Valley and given voice to in Brasov, to my own parents and brother. I knew, without a doubt, that I needed to go home and do that very thing.

I felt peace. It wasn't the answer I had been looking for. Indeed, the question I had been asking seemed irrelevant given this illumination of my own role in the current crisis my family was experiencing. I knew at that moment that I could tell Marcel no. I knew that regardless of whether or not Adam was with Ruth, I needed to go home.

With my mind at ease for the first time in several weeks, my weary body settled down to sleep. I was ready to let the healing begin.

Sunday morning came and although I got a good night's sleep, the cold had settled deeper into my chest. Spasms of coughing erupted, causing pain in my chest and making it hard to breathe. I stayed home from church and considered taking more of Corina's grandmother's brew. I braved one more dose, but it seemed to have cured all it was going to in my body, because the coughing grew worse.

My roommates came home from church talking about Marcel and Ileana.

"They both came and stayed for all three meetings," Amanda announced. "They came to Gospel Principles with us. It was a really good lesson. The Spirit was so strong—I just know they're going to get baptized soon."

"Marcel asked where you were," Tara informed me. "I told him you were sick and refused to see a doctor."

"Yeah, Corina was there and told them about her grandmother's elixir," Kellie added. "Marcel and Ileana were familiar with it—it's some kind of folk remedy."

"We told them you only had a cough now," Amanda continued. "So they're still coming over for their next discussion." I erupted into a fit of hacking. "You sound awful, Kit. Maybe you should stay in your room when they come. You wouldn't want anyone else to get sick, would you?"

Somehow, I didn't believe Amanda cared how I was feeling. I didn't think I was contagious since none of them had gotten sick. I was too weary to argue, so I took some of the store-bought cold medicine and went back to bed.

I was awakened by a knock on my door later that evening. I was surprised to see Marcel's face. He came into my room, followed by Ileana. A spell of coughing erupted as I tried to talk to them.

"You are going to see a doctor," Marcel said firmly. "I have heard your cough and I can tell by the way you sound that you are very sick."

"Tara said you will not go to a doctor," Ileana said. "She said you are afraid to go."

"I'm not afraid," I wheezed. "I just don't know who to go to and I'm afraid—" I realized what I'd just said.

"There are competent doctors in Romania," Marcel sounded displeased. "There is a clinic by the university that is open seven days a week. We are going there now." He turned to Tara. "Get her coat. I will carry her out if necessary."

Tara complied and I was too weak to protest any further. She came with Marcel and me to the clinic.

When the doctor examined me, I got a lecture about waiting so long to come in. "You have bronchitis and your lungs are not as clear as they should be. I should admit you to the hospital. You will get a breathing treatment and start on antibiotics. I will see you again on Tuesday. If you have not improved, you will go to the hospital."

The breathing treatment eased the pressure in my chest; I felt like a weight had been lifted. They gave me a shot and filled the prescription next door. Tara and Marcel helped me to the taxi even though I felt good enough to walk on my own.

When we got home, I just wanted to crawl back in bed. I turned to Marcel and said, "Thank you for taking me." I tried to smile, but the effort was feeble.

"You are not an island, Kit. Let others help you. I am here for you." The concern in his voice was mirrored in his face.

"I know, Marcel. Good night." I turned from him and as I went to my room I heard him whisper:

"I will always be here for you."

chapter thirty

The antibiotics worked their magic and I was able to go back to the hospital and orphanage on Thursday. I was glad to see Alin had not forgotten me as he greeted me with waving arms. It took me until Friday to realize that Madalina was nowhere to be seen. I asked one of the doctors about her, and she told me that Madalina was in intensive care, suffering from end-stage renal failure and the outlook was bleak.

I asked about a transplant. I knew they were relatively rare in the U.S., and I knew even before the doctor answered that the possibility for Madalina was virtually nonexistent. Of course, I thought, I've come to accept that this is a place where parents will abandon their children; why would I consider an organ might be available for one of these lost children when their own parents don't even stick around?

I felt resentful but didn't want to give up. I found the doctor again. "If we could find a donor, would a transplant save her life?" I had a wild thought that maybe I would be a match.

The doctor's answer dashed that farfetched idea. "Even if we had the perfect kidney, there is no place in Brasov for transplant surgeries and there are no funds to pay for it. We don't even have proper emergency room equipment!" She wandered off, shaking her head in exasperation, and I still felt helpless.

I got permission to visit Madalina in intensive care. I could not believe how she had deteriorated. I had only been gone one week. I was ashamed to think I had been so caught up in my own problems that I couldn't remember how long it had been since I'd last seen her.

It was clear to me that Madalina wouldn't be around much longer. How absolutely sad it was that she was dying alone in a hospital room with no parents or family around her. I asked one of the nurses if they had been able to contact Madalina's mother, but she shrugged and said they had no way to find her.

Although she couldn't hear me, I promised Madalina that I wouldn't leave her to die all alone. Her skin was more yellow than ever before and her face was puffy almost beyond recognition. I wished she would wake up and call me Engleză again. I stayed with her until my shift was over. "I'll be back tomorrow," I told her as I left.

When we got home, I told my roommates about Madalina. They were sad but none of them had interacted with her like I had. I told them I wanted to spend as much time with her as I could during the next few days.

Kellie tried to give me some practical advice. "Kit, I don't mean to sound insensitive, but there's nothing you can do for her. Your staying by her won't make a difference to the outcome and it's just going to make you feel even worse. Maybe you could spend more time with the children who can respond to you and know you're there."

I know she meant well, but it seemed so cold. "Kellie, no one should have to die alone. She's a little girl who's already been abandoned by her parents. She might not know I'm there, but I'll know I'm there. I'm going to spend as much time as I can there this weekend and next week. And the next, if necessary."

"Isn't this the little girl you used to call the 'devil child'?" Amanda asked. "Why the change of heart?"

I cringed at the memory of the thoughts I'd harbored and shared about Madalina. "Maybe I'm feeling guilty, I don't know. I really have been trying to learn to love her, even before this. I just think about how sad it is—her life has been so short, most of it in the hospital, it makes me think 'What was the point?' I mean, who will even remember her?"

Tara saw that I was struggling with this and sought to comfort me. "Kit, there's a scripture—in the Doctrine and Covenants I think—that says that little children are saved in the celestial kingdom. That's where she'll be going. I'll bet she has family and friends who are waiting there for her."

Amanda recited, "Section 137:10 'And I also beheld that all children who die before they arrive at the years of accountability are saved in the celestial kingdom of heaven.' I guess she's not a devil child after all, is she?" Amanda's knowledge and memory of the scriptures was amazing, but her lack of tact was equally so.

"Stop reminding me I said that." I said irritably. I tried to soften my tone. "Thanks, you guys, for trying to help. I'm going to spend some time with her anyway. I just want you to know where I'll be. I don't expect any of you to go with me; I'm telling you because we agreed not to go off alone."

"I don't think you should go to and from the hospital alone after dark, even if we know where you are," Kellie admonished me.

"I'll be careful, but I can't promise not to travel alone when I don't know how long I'll be with Madalina." Being careful was the most I would commit to.

I kept my word regarding Madalina, and I spent Saturday at the hospital with her. I borrowed some children's books that Kellie and Amanda brought with them and read to her even though I didn't think she could hear me. I contacted the elders and they came and gave her a blessing. She didn't even stir, but I thought she looked more peaceful afterwards.

Tara showed up in the late afternoon with a sack lunch for me. I went out with her to one of the dimly-lit waiting areas. We sat on an ugly brown vinyl couch and I ate while Tara tried to cheer me up.

"Kellie sent these chocolate chip cookies." She fished a plastic bag out of her backpack, took out a cookie and bit into it. "I wish she'd share the recipe. I think it's a little selfish of her not to. Of course that may be the only thing that's keeping her from being translated! Ha ha, I'm funny. What're you going to do about Marcel?"

I cleansed the peanut butter from my palate with a swig of soda. I grabbed the bag of cookies from Tara before she ate them all. I took one and appreciatively sank my teeth into it. It *was* selfish of

Kellie not to share her recipes with us.

"Aren't you going to answer me?" Tara nudged me with her foot.

"I'm enjoying my food. Thanks again for bringing it." I kept the cookies out of her reach while I answered her. "I'm going to tell Marcel what I should have told him a few weeks ago." I bit into another cookie, in part because they were so delicious and partly to torment Tara a bit.

"Okay . . . what's that?" She reached past me to snag another cookie. I figured I should share, since she did go to the trouble of bringing them to me.

"I'm going to tell him 'Thanks, but no thanks.' His offer is tempting, but I need to go home."

"You've decided to marry Adam, then. You go, girl!" Tara's hand went up to "high five" me.

"I decided that long ago. I just hope he still wants me. It'll be devastating if I go home to find out Lily was right—he and Ruth are engaged. But I have to go home, just the same."

"He wants you. Take my word for it." Tara said confidently. "How long were you going to stay today? I want to go to the internet café. We haven't been there since you got sick and I need to check my email. I can't believe you haven't wanted to check yours."

I drained my drink and started putting the trash back in the bag. "There's no change in Madalina. The nurse told me she could be like this for days or weeks. Or hours. I should stay." I wadded the bag into a lop-sided ball and tossed it towards the garbage can. I missed.

Tara retrieved it for me. "Come with me now. You can come back tomorrow after church. You need a break." She was right. The hospital was a depressing place.

We stopped by the house to see if Amanda and Kellie wanted to go with us. They didn't, so I thanked Kellie for the cookies, and Tara and I helped ourselves to a couple more on our way out.

I had emails from Adam, Lily, and my mom. The two from Adam were short. They pretty much said that he missed me, loved me, and wondered why I hadn't replied yet. I sent a long one back to him giving him the details of my illness, but that I was recovering nicely.

The one from Lily was short also. She told me that Adam and Ruth had gone to Salt Lake together and had come home without a car, but Adam was being pretty secretive. She assured me she was keeping her eyes and ears open. I tried not to let her email bother me, but I was really glad I was going home soon.

My mom's email talked about a few trivial things and then she spent a paragraph or two expressing concern about how I was dealing with things. She wondered if I would consider going to family therapy with them when I came home—or individual counseling if I needed it. Like I was the one who needed counseling!

I replied that I would try to keep an open mind about everything if they would do the same and not make any final decisions without me being home. I told her I loved her, Dad, and even Dave. This trip had helped me appreciate them much more than I ever had before.

I kind of expected an email from Marcel, but there wasn't one. He hadn't stopped by or called to see how I was doing, either. Ileana had asked how I was doing when I got back to work, so I guessed she must have passed it on to him. I assumed he would be in church the next day. I wondered if he would announce his decision to get baptized

Tara was reading her email and gave out a screech. I leaned over towards her. "What's wrong?" I asked.

"Did you get an email from Tarom-Romanian Air? About our flight home?" She sounded panicked.

"No. I don't see anything. Let me check my junk mail, maybe it got filtered. What's wrong?" I quickly scanned my junk folder as I waited for her to explain.

"All flights from Bucharest to New York have been cancelled indefinitely. Our flight home has been canceled! They said we have to contact the airline to make alternative travel arrangements." No wonder she was alarmed.

I saw the email in my junk folder. I opened and scanned through it. We printed it off and paid Vasilé for the pages we printed. We were in such a hurry to leave that Tara didn't even take time to flirt with him.

We showed the email to Amanda and Kellie when we got home. Kellie took charge and called the airline. After several recordings, she eventually got through to a live person who only spoke Romanian. Although we had all improved in the language, none of us were fluent enough to explain the situation and figure out what to do.

We called Corina for help, but she was at work. We knew we would see her on Sunday so we forced ourselves to calm down and be patient.

The next morning we were greeted with the first snowfall of the season. Although there wasn't a lot on the ground when we woke up, snow was in the forecast for most of the day.

The buses were running slower because of it and we were a few minutes late for church and missed choir practice completely. We weren't the only ones who were delayed because of the weather and people trickled in throughout sacrament meeting.

We saw Sora Campbell and Sora Barnes sitting with Ileana and Marcel. We sat in the row in front of them. I had a terrible time concentrating; I thought I felt Marcel's eyes boring into me throughout the meeting.

I knew I needed to talk to him, but I didn't know when I could do it. Maybe I should've sent him an email. That would be cold, especially after he took me to the doctor. After the meeting was over, Amanda jabbered at Ileana and Marcel as we walked to Gospel Principles class. She motioned for Marcel to sit by her, which suited me fine. Instead, he waited until I sat down then sat next to me. Tara nudged me once and winked.

I noticed Corina had joined us for the Gospel Principles class. That was a first. I strongly suspected it was because of Marcel. There were ten of us in the class, and I wondered if we outnumbered the Gospel Doctrine class.

"Are you feeling better, Kit?" Marcel whispered to me.

"Much better. Thank you again." I really wanted to talk to him and tell him my decision, but I didn't know when or where we could meet.

"You are looking well," he said. I could tell Amanda was straining to catch what we were talking about. Fortunately, class started and I listened attentively to Sora Milcu's lesson. I was acutely aware of Marcel's presence next to me and was relieved when it was time to go to Relief Society.

Listening to Amanda and Ileana talk, I gathered the discussion would take place at Ileana's house that evening.

"Would you like to come to dinner?" Ileana invited. "We would like to return your hospitality. My mother would like to meet all of you." I was certain she looked at me when she said that.

"We would love to," Amanda quickly accepted for us. Ileana made a point of inviting Corina, too.

After lunch, I couldn't stop thinking about Madalina, so I told Tara I was going to take the bus over to the hospital. She reminded me we were leaving for Ileana and Marcel's at five. I planned on being back by then.

At the hospital, I pulled a chair next to Madalina's bed and settled into it. I talked to her about the snow and church and how the buses were all late. She was unresponsive. Her color was worse, her breathing labored. I sensed her time left was short.

I sang softly to her, through all the hymns I knew, which wasn't that many. I didn't know if it calmed her, but it sure calmed me. I held her hand and spoke to her in a kinder tone than I had ever used with her when she was conscious and full of mischief.

"Madalina, I think it's time for you to go. When you get to the other side, I know you'll have some family and friends there waiting for you. Will you do something for me? I know you're going to make it to the celestial kingdom, because the scriptures promise it's true. When you get there, or on your way there, if you see anyone who knows me, will you tell them to help out all they can with my family? We really need some extra help, so if there's anything you can do when you get there, will you? I'm so sorry I called you a 'devil child.' I was wrong, I just didn't understand you. I hope you forgive me." I wiped the tears from my cheeks and had to find a tissue for my dripping nose.

I came back after I used the restroom and took up my post by her bed again. I leaned against the hard chair, closing my eyes. I must have dozed off. I'm not sure how long I slept in that uncomfortable position, but I woke with a start. The room was dark, daylight had faded. I went to turn on the light and looked at Madalina.

Sometime during my sleep, she had passed through the veil. The sound of labored breathing had ceased and her round face looked at peace. I knelt by her bed to offer a prayer, *Dear Father, Please bless this little one and welcome her home. Help her find peace in thy arms. Please forgive me for being mean to her sometimes. I'll try to do better. Please, please don't forget about all the other little children who suffer and are alone. Help us all to feel thy love. In the name of Jesus Christ, Amen.*

I arose and went to find the nurse on duty. I held in my emotions until I sank onto the ugly brown couch. Leaning against the unfeeling, cracked vinyl, I let the tears erupt. My jumbled thoughts turned into another prayer, more anguished this time. *Why is life so hard and short for so many? Why would you send a child into this world, to be abandoned by her parents and left to suffer and die alone? I couldn't even help her! I came here to help—I didn't even make a difference.*

Eventually my sobs subsided. I sat there quietly, wanting answers, willing God to give me answers. It seemed when it was time for someone to die, there were no clear cut answers. It wasn't even Madalina, the person, I was mourning so much—in all honesty I hadn't had the patience or desire to know her like I did Alin or the twins. I was grieving over the situation, how hopeless it seemed for those children abandoned by the ones who should love them most of all—and seemingly abandoned by that Heavenly Father who gave them life.

Words came to my troubled mind: *Be still and know that I am God.* I felt the soothing comfort wash over me with such magnitude, which had only happened to me once before, shortly after Janet had died. I felt a sense of peace that let me know that we had not been abandoned by that God who gave us life; He knew each of us and watched over each one of us. It gave me the strength I needed, if only I could store up that feeling and recall it whenever my faith faltered.

Feeling emotionally drained, yet spiritually renewed, I left the hospital and caught the bus back home. My roommates weren't home when I got there, having gone over to Marcel's house. They had left me a note, asking me to call Corina's phone when I got home so they would know I was all right.

I didn't want to disturb them, but I also didn't want anyone thinking they needed to come and check on me, so I called Marcel's house and asked for Tara.

"Madalina's gone," I found myself crying into the phone. "She died a little while ago."

"I'm so sorry, Kit. Would you like me to come home, so you're not by yourself?"

"No, I'm fine," I sobbed. "She died while I was asleep. I couldn't even stay awake for a little while."

"I'm coming home right now," Tara said.

"No, don't. I just wanted you to know I made it home safely. I need to have some time to myself tonight. I really am okay."

After I hung up the phone, I realized that both Madalina and I had made it home safely—we just went to different homes for now. I picked up my journal and wrote for awhile, trying to capture the experience of the past few days.

chapter thirty-one

I was asleep by the time my roommates got home, but Amanda eagerly announced the news to me the next morning at breakfast.

"Marcel and Ileana are getting baptized! They told us last night!' Amanda couldn't have been more excited if she was announcing her own engagement. You would think she had personally found and taught Marcel and Ileana herself.

I wanted to gloat a little and tell her I already knew, but then she'd want to know how I knew and that was none of her business. "That's great," I managed to reply. "Have they set a date?"

"Well they want to do it next Sunday evening. When we told them we didn't know for sure when we'd be leaving because of our flight cancellation, they wanted to make sure we'd still be here. Of course the sister missionaries were excited. They're meeting with the elders tomorrow night, to introduce them."

Tara wandered in and said in a teasing voice. "Yeah, Amanda's really excited. She volunteered to give a talk at the baptism. She'd probably baptize them herself if she could, huh, Amanda?"

"I do not wish I could baptize them! I take priesthood responsibility very seriously, Tara, and you should too!" Amanda always got indignant when she thought Tara was being too light-minded; which was fairly often, in Amanda's book.

"I know you do, I was just messing with you. See how easy it was? Lighten up, cousin."

"You're light enough for both of us, Tara," was Amanda's retort.

I ran interception since Kellie hadn't come in yet. "What did Corina say about our tickets?"

"She called last night before we went over to Marcel and Ileana's house. They said we need to go to Bucharest to figure it out." Amanda said.

"We have to go all the way to Bucharest? What about online or over the phone? It'll take a whole day to go there and back!" I couldn't believe it.

"The airline said that in order to have our tickets honored, we needed to bring them in, in person, to get new flights booked. They don't seem to be real big on customer service." Kellie answered as she came in to grab some breakfast. "But Corina said she'll go with us if we go on her day off, which is Thursday."

Kellie asked me how I was feeling, so I told them about Madalina and how I felt like our small time of service wasn't really making a difference. Talking about it made the waterworks start up again and before I knew it, all three of my roommates were hugging me and telling me all the things I needed to hear; like Heavenly Father noticing if a sparrow falls and how we never know what influence we have on other people. Their kindness made me cry even harder.

"Thanks, you guys. I don't know why I'm such a crybaby," I blubbered. Amanda went and got some tissue, Kellie kept patting my back, and Tara ran to our room and brought me some chocolate. All three gestures helped. I was so thankful for them at that moment.

After I got control of my senses, we finished getting ready for the day. We were running late for work at that point and Amanda and Kellie left before Tara and me. I noticed Tara was dawdling and I prodded her to hurry.

"Don't panic, Kit. There's a reason I let them go on ahead. I wanted to be able to talk to you alone. Apparently I'm now the go-between for you and Marcel."

As we walked to the bus stop, she filled me in on the prior evening's events.

"We met Marcel and Ileana's mom. I think she was a little suspicious of our motives at first. She's a little afraid of American influence on her children—even though they're adults. It was a good thing Corina was there. The missionaries speak pretty good Romanian and all, but Corina is from here, so she was able to talk to Marcel's mom."

"So is their mom taking the discussions, too?" I was sorry I missed meeting her.

"Not yet. I think she will though. It's kind of cool to realize I understand Romanian better than I used to, even though I still can't speak it very well. So when their mom said 'Which one is she?' I was able to figure out what she was saying." Tara chattered on.

"What do you mean? What was she talking about?" I asked.

"Not what, but who. She was asking about you, of course. I knew it and Corina could understand everything. Amanda was picking up on it too. So I told them you were at the hospital with Madalina. When Marcel translated, his mom just broke out in a big grin and said something I didn't understand, but I'm pretty sure she likes you even though she hasn't met you. So you probably won't have any problems with your Romanian mother-in-law." Tara smiled with satisfaction.

"That's for sure. I won't have a Romanian mother-in-law. I already told you that."

"Yeah, but nobody's told Marcel—or his family. I think they all love you. So I'm supposed to tell you that Marcel wants to see you at the internet café tonight. I told him it would have to be tomorrow unless he wanted Amanda and Kellie to come hang out too. So he's all set for tomorrow night at 6:30. We'll go straight from the orphanage so we won't be out too late. You have a day to practice what you're going to say when you break his heart." Tara laughed at her own cleverness. "I could see myself getting into this predicament, but never you, Kit. It's pretty funny!"

"I don't think it will break his heart. He just decided we were a good match. I don't think he loves me." I said it to reassure myself as much as Tara.

"Well, look on the bright side. If we can't get a flight out of Romania, you've got a husband and in-laws ready to take you in. The rest of us will have to fend for ourselves."

I was glad when we got to the hospital, so I didn't have to listen to Tara's teasing for a while. I went to see Alin first. He was happy to see me and I was able to take him to the playroom. I played with him and several other children but was acutely aware of Madalina's absence.

When we got to the orphanage, I went to the babies as usual. When I stopped to see Simona and Daciana, there was only Daciana in her crib. I scooped her up and looked around to see who had Simona, but couldn't see her anywhere.

Feeling panicked I tried to find Ileana. I found out from one of the workers who spoke a little English that Ileana had left for the day. I figured she might also know about Simona. Pointing to Daciana, I asked her where Simona was.

She apparently understood what I was asking and went to look at Simona's file. "Simona familie. Unu saptamana." I guessed she meant Simona went with a family for one week. Like books in a library, sometimes prospective parents would "check out" a child for a short time. Danielle had explained that she had done it when she was ready to adopt Tomas and Alexi.

"Why only Simona? Why not Daciana, too?" I couldn't imagine one without the other. How could someone split them up?

The worker shrugged, whether to say she didn't know, or didn't care, or both, I could only wonder.

Daciana seemed to be taking the separation better than I was, because she cooed and smiled just like always. I wondered if she would grow up never knowing she was a twin. The thought made me sad, which compounded the feelings of helplessness.

Amanda and Kellie went to the internet café that evening and invited Tara and me to come. Tara went with them, but I went to bed early that night, hoping to sleep away the despondency that hovered around me. I was dreading talking to Marcel, although the more I thought about it, the more I was ready to put Romania far behind me.

Tuesday seemed to drag by and I alternated between anxiety and excitement. I was anxious to talk to Marcel and be done with it; and I was excited to hear from Adam, since I hadn't checked my email in several days. Then I felt anxious again as I imagined another email from Lily, filled with news I wouldn't want to hear.

I wanted to talk to Adam so badly and hoped he would be online when I was. I wanted to tell him about Madalina and Simona. I also wanted to tell him about the upcoming baptisms, assuming Marcel didn't call it off when I dumped him. I reminded myself that if he did, then he was getting baptized for the wrong reasons and should wait anyway.

Tara saw that I was nervous so she refrained from hassling me. Usually I could see the humor in most situations, but I was a little too close to this one.

When we arrived at the internet café that night, there was Marcel waiting for me. Tara went directly over to Vasilé, as if it were scripted. I took a deep breath and went over to join Marcel.

"Kit, how are you doing? I am sorry to hear about your little friend. I wanted to be with you, so you were not alone." He took my hand.

"Thank you, Marcel." Not wanting to start crying again, I changed the subject. "I understand you have some exciting news. You've decided to get baptized! That's wonderful!" I truly was excited for his decision to join the Church.

"I have you to thank. Ileana and I are both so grateful to you." Happiness radiated from his face.

"Have you and Ileana decided what day?" I did my best to ignore the charisma he emanated. "I hope it's before we leave." There, I had opened up the fact that I was leaving with the others.

"Oh, it will be before you leave. We are trying to set it up for Sunday evening. We have to meet with the branch president. You have disrupted my schedule, Kit, and all my careful plans."

I was about to disrupt his careful plans even further. "Marcel, I've given your proposal a lot of thought. I've prayed about it and I know I need to return home. I can't marry you. I'm sorry." I gave his hand an apologetic squeeze.

He held on to my hand. "I knew you would want to go home. I have prayed about it too. But do not confuse your need to go home with the need to tell me 'no.' We can make plans. I realize you want to finish your schooling and I need to work harder to save money to provide a home for us. Don't say 'no' to us, iubita."

I guessed he'd just called me sweetheart or something like that.

I wished he would just accept my answer. I was flattered and there was a part of me that wanted to keep him hanging on—just in case things didn't work out at home. I stifled that thought and knew I couldn't give him false hope.

"Marcel, please understand—I love Adam. I plan on marrying him when I get home. I never meant to lead you on. You are very attractive and if I stayed, I would consider it, but I'm not staying, and I don't plan on ever coming back." There. He had to understand that.

His smile disappeared and he leaned forward to be closer to me. He said softly, "Please understand me. I will not give up until I see that you are married to me or to another. I know you say you love Adam, but you have been apart and perhaps things have changed."

"We've been apart before and things only changed for the better! Adam and I are going to get married; you need to accept that. There are so many other choices for you, Marcel. Better choices." I sounded confident, but inside still felt unsettled—what if things had changed? Well, Marcel would never know my hidden doubts.

I knew I had to end the conversation, but needed to let him know that I wanted to be his friend. Saying that sounded so trite, but I had to say something. "Look, I've heard it's very common for converts to care very deeply for those who introduced them to the gospel. Maybe that's what you're feeling. I do care about you; just not in the way you want me to. I want to be your friend; I really do."

"Do not ever minimize my feelings for you," Marcel's voice had a distinct chill to it; one I'd never heard before. "I know what I feel." He smiled again, but this time it looked forced. "I will accept your friendship, Kit. But I can hope for more."

He stood up abruptly and said, "La revedere." He was gone in an instant and I was left alone, feeling like it hadn't quite ended the way I hoped it would. I wondered if I was still invited to the baptism.

Feeling some relief—after all my conscience was now clear—I paid for my computer time and logged on. I checked my email and there was one from Adam, but no others. I felt a little forgotten but it had only been three days since I checked my email last. I also

checked to see if Adam was online, but he wasn't. I eagerly opened
his email.

> To: kitcarson@yahoo.com
> From: bridgerman123@hotmail.com
> Subject:Hey, my favorite scout!
>
> I had a little time between classes and thought I'd
> check to see how you were doing. I'm sorry you were
> sick. I wish I could have been there to take care of
> you.
> It's kind of funny that it is so cold in Brasov
> this winter! I think you affect the weather. We've had
> a warm spell here, very strange for Cache Valley in
> late November.
> So it's just over a couple more weeks before you'll
> be home! I can't wait to see you and talk to you in
> person. The only bad thing is that finals are the very
> next week and I have to study—so I'm kinda bummed
> about that.
> I'm excited to see all of your pictures; my mom
> wants to see them too. She wants to have a coming home
> (homecoming?) party for you. She is doing a lot better
> with her depression. I think having my dad back at work
> is a big relief to her. Ruth also seems to be good for
> her, she visits her a lot. It's like Ruth was provided
> just at the time my mom really needed someone.
> Lily talks about you all the time—even more than I
> do. She's always following me around saying "Remember
> when you and Kit did this . . . ?" and asking when
> we're getting married! She is funny, but she's giving
> my parents fits with her attitude. She sure can be a
> brat.
> Thanksgiving is practically here. It's my first one
> with Justin in four years! He'll actually have competi-
> tion for my mom's pumpkin pie, and the turkey, and the
> stuffing, etc. (Sorry if I'm making you hungry!) I'll
> really miss you this Thanksgiving, I'm glad the time
> has passed pretty quickly.
> Well, I've rambled on and on. I have to get to
> class. See you soon! I love you.
>
> Adam.

Even though he mentioned Ruth in his email, I thought it was
pretty clear that Adam still loved me. I felt the urge to get home
grow stronger and stronger.

When I replied to Adam, I told him about Madalina's death,
Simona's "test drive" at a prospective home, and Marcel and Ileana

getting baptized. I told him about our flight home getting cancelled and that we were waiting for a resolution.

Tara had apparently finished flirting with Vasilé and came over to my computer station. "So how did it go with Marcel? Did you tell him?"

"Yeah, I told him. Are you ready to go?" I started to log out.

"What did you tell him?" Tara pressed, snapping her chewing gum.

"I told him 'no'," I said as I gathered up my backpack.

"Duh, I guessed that by the way he stomped out of here. How did he take it?"

"You just said you saw the way he stomped out of here. That's how he took it. Oh, and he said he wasn't giving up hope for something more than friendship. I told him I was going home to marry Adam. I couldn't have put it more plainly than that."

"Wow. Is he still getting baptized? Do you think he'll invite you to the baptism now?" Tara wondered aloud the same thoughts that had crossed my mind and it made me laugh.

"I'm pretty sure he's still getting baptized. I don't think that has to do with me—at least he claims it doesn't. As for being invited to the baptism, well, I'm pretty sure Ileana will invite me, even if Marcel is mad at me."

Tara brought up another thought I'd had earlier. "I think Amanda's pretty sure there's something going on between you and Marcel."

Irritated, I replied, "There isn't anything going on between us—nothing besides friendship. I made that clear to him. Amanda can have him."

"I think a marriage proposal could be construed as something going on. You should tell Amanda and Kellie about it. You know, what they imagine is probably a lot worse than what really happened." Tara's advice was probably good, but I didn't like the thought of having to explain my actions to anyone, and Amanda in particular.

"Has Amanda said anything to you about it?" I asked her.

"Not anything more than what she's said in front of you. Mainly innuendo about how you arrange to meet Marcel; stuff like that."

"Maybe I'll tell them. I just don't like how Amanda judges me.

Maybe she doesn't mean it, but it makes me feel like I'm not good enough for her. Sorry, I know she's your cousin."

"She's my cousin, and I love her, but I know what you mean. She does have a self-righteous streak. That's one reason I always push her buttons. It's my way of letting her know that I don't have to measure up to her standards. If I let my feelings get hurt by her little remarks, I'd have a big chip on my shoulder. So I just laugh it off. You've heard her call me light-minded." Tara laughed. "I try to find the humor in life and try to have fun. If that's light-minded, then so be it. I know what my values and beliefs are; I don't have to prove them to anyone—especially Amanda."

As we hurried through the frigid wintry night, I reflected on Tara's assessment. She was confident and self-assured; she did know her values and beliefs. I knew she had a strong testimony of the gospel and wasn't afraid to share her feelings with others. Tara was a good friend and could also teach me a thing or two about taking myself too seriously. It seemed I'd forgotten to laugh at life lately. That was enough to bring anyone down.

chapter thirty-two

We took the train to Bucharest on Thursday. I was so grateful Corina came with us. It took us two and a half hours one way on the train then we had to take a bus to the airline office. If she hadn't come along, it would have been much harder to find our way.

The workers helped us rebook our flight home. Although the airline no longer flew directly to New York, it did fly to Paris, London, Berlin and a number of other European cities. It was tricky trying to figure out which route would be best.

Our best option was to fly to Paris and from Paris to New York. The flights that met our criteria (that the airline would pay for) were one week earlier than our original flights home. That meant we had to re-book our flights from New York to Salt Lake.

When it was all finished it sounded fairly simple, but getting it handled took over an hour. The airline personnel did not seem to be trained in customer service, that's for sure. Corina was soft-spoken, maybe a little too much so; when the agent told us we would have to pay a fifty dollar change fee per ticket, Amanda got riled up.

She instructed Corina to tell the agent that we wouldn't be paying any change fees because it was the airline that instigated the changes, not us. When Corina translated Amanda's words, she was missing the, "Oh no you will not!" tone that Amanda had mastered. Evidently Amanda's tone needed no translation, because the rep changed her story and said no fees were due.

I was thrilled to be going home a week earlier than planned. Now that I had made a decision and it felt right, I wanted to move forward with it. I couldn't wait to email Adam and my family that I would be home sooner.

We found a place to eat before we had to catch the train home. Our luck was such that it took longer than we thought it would, so we were rushing to the train station to make the train back to Brasov.

Even Corina got confused as we rushed through the train station. It was a much bigger station than the one in Brasov and we were trying to hurry and look for the right train at the same time. I noticed a man who looked like he was in his mid-thirties watching us as we searched. He looked a little scruffy, but not scary. He approached us and asked—in English—if he could help us.

We told him we were looking for the train to Brasov. He said, "Follow me, I'll show you, you'll have to hurry." We followed him and I saw another man about the same age kind of following along beside us as we hurried to make the train.

Just a short way down the terminal we found the right train. We hurried to show the conductor our tickets as we thanked the man for his help. He blocked our entrance to the train. "Ten dollars," he said.

"What? Are you kidding?" I asked incredulously.

"No. Ten dollars for taking you to the train. Pay or you won't get on." He looked very menacing. We looked to the conductor for help; he turned away to answer someone else's question. The extortionist's partner closed in behind us.

Corina said something to him in Romanian to which he replied. She said to us, "It's only ten dollars total, not ten dollars each. Maybe you should just pay him so we can get on the train."

Astounded that she would suggest that we pay this man who led us maybe two hundred feet, I decided I'd had enough. "No!" I said in the man's face. "We did not agree to pay you and we were almost to the train anyway. We won't pay you anything and you can't stop us from getting on the train! We have tickets. Move!"

I turned to my roommates and said, "Just push past him. There are five of us. He can't stop us." Emboldened, we all shoved and got past him. He started yelling awful things at us and followed us onto the train.

The conductor calmly ignored the situation and merely said, "Tickets." We showed him our tickets and he let us board. Kellie and I were the last two on board.

Scruffy Man still yelled at us as we tried to scurry away from him. He grabbed at my backpack and I had to stop to pull it away from him. Kellie stopped with me.

"Let go! Leave us alone!" I yelled in his face. The conductor asked him for his ticket. He glanced at the conductor then back at us. He hocked up a huge gob of spit and spat right at us.

It hit me in the side of the face and some sprayed Kellie. Incensed, I lunged for him, wanting to punch him in the face. Kellie and Tara pulled me back and the conductor shoved Scruffy Man off the train.

With filthy mucus running down the side of my face and in my ear, it sank in to me what had just happened and my knees went weak. I thought I might pass out. Amanda shoved a wad of tissues at me and I tried to clean up the foul mess. Kellie was doing the same.

People on the train stared at us, but said and did nothing. What could they do, really? Kellie received an indirect hit and she didn't seem as upset. When my roommates saw that I was really shaken up, they led me to my seat and forced me to sit down.

I was nauseated and thought I might lose it right there on the train. I couldn't stop thinking about that gross man demanding money and then spitting in my face. I asked if anyone had a wet wipe. None of us did, but Amanda supplied more tissues and suggested I go to the restroom or "water closet" to get some soap and water.

In the tiny compartment I scrubbed my face, ear and hair as best I could. Overwhelmed by the confrontation, my emotions let loose, and I started sobbing. Maybe I just should have paid the ten dollars, I thought. Who's ever felt such degradation? Who can understand how horrible it feels?

A quiet thought came to me. *Jesus has felt it all.* I felt it deep inside. I knew who had felt the horror of being spat upon and much,

much more; the Savior. Never before had His suffering touched me in such a personal way.

There, in the smelly toilet compartment of a train, after being spat upon by a petty blackmailer, I gave thanks for the experience that brought me a little closer to my Savior. I entered the water closet feeling soiled and humiliated, and left it feeling clean and grateful. What a difference the still, small voice can make.

My roommates were glad to see I had calmed down. I didn't want to talk about it right then, so we focused our conversation on our change of plans for leaving. It suddenly dawned on us that we were leaving in ten days.

Thanksgiving was a week away. It wasn't a holiday in Romania, which surprised us at first because we were pretty certain the world revolved around America. Danielle, being from the States, had invited us to celebrate Thanksgiving at her apartment so we wouldn't miss out on a traditional dinner.

Our new flights left on the Monday following Thanksgiving. We couldn't believe it was so close. Discussion turned to Marcel and Ileana's baptism. We all hoped it would be the coming Sunday, although none of us had heard anything.

When the subject of Marcel came up, Tara nudged me with her foot. I knew she wanted me to tell Amanda and Kellie about his proposal, but I didn't know if I wanted Corina to hear it. So I gave Tara the lifted-eyebrow look and she backed off.

I decided I would talk to Amanda and Kellie when we got home. I didn't want them to hate me, but I knew that Amanda wasn't one of my big fans anyway. She would really be mad if, after the fact (like back in America), she found out. Plus, I honestly didn't know what Marcel would do or say when I saw him again.

On our front door were two envelopes. One was addressed to Amanda, Kellie, Kit & Tara; the other one was to me only. Amanda pulled them both from the crack of the door and handed me the one with my name on it. She gave me a questioning look. I knew I had to tell them, just as I knew the note I held in my hand was from Marcel.

Amanda tore open the one that was addressed to all of us. It was an invitation to the baptism of Ileana and Marcel Miklos on Sunday evening. We screeched in excitement. Actually, they screeched and I smiled, silently wondering if I could escape to my room to read the note I held privately.

Eagle-eyed as ever, Amanda turned to me and asked, "So what does your personal letter say? It is from Marcel isn't it?" Her saccharine tone didn't fool me at all; I saw the feral glint in her eyes.

"I haven't opened it yet, Amanda," I said waving it towards her. "It probably is from Marcel, but I really wanted to talk to you guys about something. About Marcel, actually."

I told them how Marcel had taken an interest in me—I stressed it was because of our common interest in the orphans of Romania. He knew I was an orphan, and was adopted, and I seemed to share a lot of the same ideals he did.

I mainly watched Amanda as I talked and she was not very good at masking her feelings. A smug look appeared on her face at first, but as I went into details of our meetings at the internet café and the events leading up to Marcel's surprise marriage proposal, that look was replaced by shock mingled with disbelief. I also saw a flash of anger mar her features.

Tara sat nodding in approval as I told my story. Kellie pretty much shook her head in disbelief. When I finished, of course it was Amanda that spoke first.

"I knew it! I knew there was something going on between you two!" She crowed triumphantly. "Didn't I tell you guys they were meeting secretly?" She looked to Tara and Kellie for support. Kellie nodded, Tara just smiled.

"What did you do to get him to propose? Isn't it enough that you have a boyfriend in Logan? What do you do, collect them everywhere?" Amanda's words were harsh, but I wasn't too surprised.

Although she usually riled me up with her accusations, I tried to remain calm. "I didn't do anything, Amanda. I was not out man-hunting. You might note that it wasn't me all dressed up like a prom date when we decided to try to fix you and Marcel up."

That reminder didn't help soothe Amanda. "Marcel probably doesn't even want you in particular. I think he would settle for any American wife. And I think you're a total player. At least Tara only flirts with guys. You lead them on until you wrangle a marriage proposal out of them. Do they even know about each other?" She was determined to fight about this.

"Well, if he only wants an American wife, then he might propose to you next. You heard me, I told Marcel no. I think you are being judgmental and unreasonable. I shouldn't have even told you." I gave Tara a look saying, *See where your suggestion got me?*

Kellie had something to say. "Is he joining the Church because of you?"

I appreciated the change of direction. "No. He said the decision was his own. And Ileana's, as well. She sure wouldn't be getting baptized because of her feelings for me."

"So, what does your note say?" Amanda asked again.

"I don't think that's really your business," I replied. I wasn't inclined to share anything else with her.

"Oh, so you're still hiding stuff from us. How much haven't you told us?" She demanded suspiciously.

"For Pete's sake, Amanda! Give it a rest! You're just jealous. Do you tell me about every conversation you've had with a guy? All two of them?" That last remark was low, even for me and Amanda, but that woman shattered my calmness like a brush hitting a mirror on a bad hair day.

Amanda lunged at me and I'm not sure what she would have done, but I dodged out of the way. Tara and Kellie stepped between us.

Tara tried to reason with us. "You two need to stop before you say or do things you'll regret. We're all tired. Kit was just trying to let you two know what was going on. It's over anyway. We're going home in ten days. Let's not ruin the time we have left together."

I huffily marched to my room. I heard Amanda slam her door as she went to her own. I sat on my bed and looked at the envelope in my hand. I tore it open. It was from Marcel, just as we all suspected.

> *Dear Kit,*
> *I have cleared my schedule Tuesday evening. Please spend it with me. I want to have time with just the two of us to enjoy our time here together before you go. I will meet you at the internet café at 3:00. Please come.*
> *Love,*
> *Marcel*

chapter thirty-three

I emailed my parents about our earlier arrival time. I wanted to surprise Adam by just showing up early, but I'd already told him about our flights being canceled. Then I figured out a way, without really lying, just by omitting a couple of things.

I told him that our flight from JFK airport had to be changed because we were flying from Bucharest to Paris to New York. I told him my arrival time was 4:30 instead of 2:45. I just neglected to mention the date had changed as well. I told my mom what I was doing, just in case he talked to her—which was possible, but unlikely.

Sunday was eventful to say the least. We quickly ate dinner and hurried back to the church for the baptism. I recognized the elders from when they gave Madalina a blessing. Ileana looked nervous; Marcel just looked calm. Their mother came to watch the baptisms, and introductions were made to the branch president and his counselors.

Marcel brought his mother over to meet me. It was awkward—in part because she spoke very little English and I spoke very little Romanian; but even more because I wondered if Marcel had told her I was the one he had proposed to. I wondered if she was sizing me up as a potential family member or if she was mentally cursing me for breaking her son's heart. I was glad when we were interrupted and I could quietly sit down with my roommates.

Amanda wasn't asked to give a talk during the services, much to her disappointment. She kept an eye on me and Marcel. Things had been tense between the two of us since I'd told them about Marcel; I was pretty sure she was still angry with me.

After the baptismal service, refreshments were served in the cultural hall, courtesy of the Relief Society. Corina was there and helped the sister missionaries introduce Ileana and Marcel to the branch members. It was fun to see such strong support from the branch and to watch them bask in the attention they received. They looked truly happy and seemed to have the support of their mother—I noticed their married sister did not come.

We helped clean up and when we were finished, Marcel and Ileana were still there talking to the branch president and his wife. They were getting ready to leave so we went to tell them good-bye.

When Ileana gave me the inevitable kiss-kiss, she whispered to me. "I am so happy you introduced us to the gospel, Kit. We are now sisters in the gospel. I wish you would have chosen to be my sister in another way."

I pulled back and looked into her eyes. "You know? Marcel told you?" I was surprised; I thought Marcel would keep it to himself. She nodded and hugged me again.

Marcel came up to me next. I was keenly aware of him as he took my hands and leaned in for a kiss-kiss. I was also acutely aware of Amanda watching us, standing just a few steps away.

"Congratulations, Marcel. I'm so happy for you." I said as he properly kissed me on the cheek. His lips were warm on my face and I tensed up, afraid that he might make his kiss less than proper.

"Thank you," he said softly. "Did you get my note? Will you be there?"

"I got it, but I'm not sure there's a point in coming. I've told you how I feel." I spoke quietly then stepped back, but he kept my hands in his and leaned towards me.

"Come. Please. I'll be waiting." He pulled back and dropped my hands.

I glanced at Amanda. I wondered if she could hear our conversation. I noticed that Tara had stepped in, effectively blocking Amanda's view and, I hoped, her hearing.

I talked to Tara later that night and told her that Marcel wanted me to meet him on Tuesday. She thought that one last meeting would be fun and romantic.

"Romantic is not what I need from Marcel. Besides, he wants me to meet him at three and I'll be at the orphanage then." Sometimes I thought Tara wasn't the best person to get advice from when it came to guys, but she was really the only one I had to talk to about this.

"So skip the orphanage. It's our last week here. You'll probably never see Marcel again. Why not have a little fun? Just stay in a public place."

"Why? Do you think he would attack me? That's just silly. He would never hurt me." Tara had me thoroughly confused.

She just laughed. "I didn't mean he might attack you. I meant stay in a public place so he won't start kissing you. You seem to get a little weak and confused when he kisses you." Her dimples flashed. "That's just what I've heard, anyway!"

"Well, if I go—and that's a big if—I don't want Amanda to know. I'll never hear the end of it."

"Just tell her you're not feeling well or that you're tired. Or don't tell her anything. We can go to the internet café together after lunch and I'll leave straight from there. I want to see Vasilé again before we leave and I don't know when I'll get the chance." Tara plotted eagerly and sucked me in with her enthusiasm.

Tara and I went to the internet café at lunch on Tuesday and when she left for the orphanage, I just stayed there to wait for Marcel.

He showed up a little before three and his face lit up when he saw me. I think he doubted I would come. To tell the truth, I doubted I would come up until the last minute. I was still wearing my Care Bear scrubs, the ones I'd worn to the hospital that morning.

He sat down and looked more animated than I had ever seen him. Usually Marcel looked intense and focused, but he seemed almost jovial that afternoon.

"I wanted to spend time with you before you go. We have always spent our time together almost secretly. I know you are going home, but I want to have a day where we are just two people—a man and a woman, enjoying each other's company. We are not trying to save the world or anyone in it." He glanced at my attire and continued. "I want to show you Bran Castle. Ileana told me you have not been to see it yet."

Bran Castle. The name brought back the memory of my brother, Dave, tossing a paper at me telling me to visit Dracula's Castle. I had read that it was traditionally, although not actually, the home of some count that Bram Stoker's Dracula was based on.

I did want to go there. My roommates and I had tried to figure out a day or time to go, but it never worked out. It qualified as a public place—it was now a museum. I thought it would be safe and fun.

"We'll take the bus?" I verified. A bus was a public place too.

"Yes." He reached out his hand and I took it. He led me out the door to the bus stop. A couple of transfers later we were on our way to Dracula's Castle.

The day was cold, but the sky was a majestic blue expanse above us as we stood high in the castle gazing over the courtyard and the countryside spreading out below us.

It was one of the most beautiful places I'd ever seen. We opted for a guided tour, and Marcel threw in tidbits of information he had learned being a native of the area. Several times I caught other tourists listening to his inside scoop on the castle.

He turned his million-watt smile on a group of middle-aged American women and I thought they might swoon. We spent the better part of an hour with those ladies, answering all their questions. I thought they might ask him for his autograph.

One of them told me, "You are a very lucky young woman to have such a handsome boyfriend. And he is so kind and sweet. Hold on to him, young lady."

I told her he wasn't my boyfriend, just my friend, and she winked at me and said she was sure I could change that!

Marcel was thoroughly charming. He was a gentleman and tried nothing more than holding my hand, which was very pleasant and not too intimate.

There was a restaurant very near the castle and we stopped there for dinner. They had delicious meatball soup and crusty bread. I was starving; we had done a lot of hiking in and around the castle.

"Thank you, Marcel. This has been a wonderful evening." I looked around, enjoying the atmosphere. "I'm so glad I got to see this. You were better than the paid guide. Those women should have paid you."

"It has been a pleasure for me as well. My biggest regret is that we do not have more time to know each other in this way. There is more to Romania than poverty and orphans. There is beauty here too. It is made more beautiful by your presence, Kit."

His compliment embarrassed me. I felt like he had crossed the line again, although he still acted like a gentleman. My guard was up—Marcel had warned me he wouldn't give up easily.

"I need to get home. My roommates will get worried about me." I reached for my coat. "I don't want to deal with Amanda. She's jealous, Marcel. I think she wants you—maybe you should propose to her." I threw it out there lightly, in part to see how Marcel would react.

His faced tightened momentarily, then he relaxed and smiled. "I do not care about Amanda. You know it is you I care for. Do not offer a dandelion when there is a rose for the taking."

"This rose has thorns, Marcel. Don't forget it." He apparently needed a warning.

"I am aware of your thorns. The rose is more desirable because of its thorns."

Wow, he was waxing poetic and rather romantic. It was a side of Marcel that I had rarely seen. I liked it better than his intense, insistent side. I figured we'd better get out of there. So I stood up and put my coat and gloves on; when he saw me head to the door, he followed.

During the bus ride home, we talked about school, how much time we each had left to finish our degrees, and a little about the branch in Romania.

"There is one thing I cannot understand or like about the branch," Marcel stated.

I wondered what it was, because Marcel had not been negative or critical about anything regarding the branch, the Church, or any of the people. I asked him what he meant.

"The gypsies. I saw that there are some gypsies that come to the meetings. They are allowed to come. I do not like it."

I thought he must be kidding. "Marcel, are you joking? You really don't think gypsies should be allowed in church?"

"No, not in the same church as everybody else. They belong with their own kind. I am bothered by it." He was serious.

I had encountered prejudice against the gypsies several times— I thought about Pali at the orphanage and how the workers would ignore him. I never, ever guessed that Marcel would feel that way. He claimed he wanted to help the children—and there were a lot of gypsy children that needed help.

I had to speak out. "Marcel, I know that the gypsy people have a bad reputation and a lot of people regard them as thieves and beggars, but they are children of God, just like you and me."

"They are not like me. It is an insult to compare me with them." He was adamant.

"I'm not asking you to be their best friend; I just think you need to acknowledge them as Heavenly Father's children. They were created by Him, they are people too. They can't all be bad. Besides, anyone should be welcome at church if they want to come. I mean, it is church. There, of all places, they should be welcome."

"You have not lived around them or you would think differently."

I could tell by his tone that I was fighting a losing battle; I could not change his hard heart with regards to the gypsies. I felt like my eyes were opened to yet another side of Marcel—a side I didn't care for at all.

We spent the rest of the bus ride in silence. Fortunately, we were almost home. He walked me home since it was dark. Although he reached for my hand, and I let him take it, it felt like a bond was broken.

When we reached my street, he turned to me and said, "My feelings for you have not changed. I wish only the best for you. If you decide differently, I will be here."

"Thanks, Marcel." I stepped forward to hug him, and we clung to each other for a moment. I savored our last embrace and felt a surge of sadness I hadn't expected. "You are a good friend, and I'll never forget you. I hope you find what you're looking for."

He gave me a kiss-kiss on my cheeks and said, "I already did, but she is not for me." As he walked off, I wondered if I would ever see him again.

No one—mainly Amanda—said a word to me about where I had been. I was glad for that. I was at peace with the whole Marcel thing; we had fundamental differences, most likely due to our respective cultures, that couldn't be easily overcome. I felt certain that a common desire to help the orphans and passionate kisses were not enough to overcome the gaps; even if I hadn't been in love with Adam.

It was amazing to me the difference two weeks could make. I had actually considered staying in Romania just a couple weeks prior, and had felt that my prayers weren't being answered as I struggled with my decision. Now it seemed perfectly clear to me—home and Adam were waiting.

On Thanksgiving morning we worked at the hospital and took the afternoon off so we could go to Danielle's for dinner. We had chicken instead of turkey, but at least it felt like a holiday. We talked about our Thanksgiving traditions at home and told Tomas and Alexi the story of the first Thanksgiving.

I pulled Danielle aside at one point and told her about Simona and Daciana. Simona had come back from her trial visit, and Ileana told me that paperwork was in the works for the family to adopt her. I was worried about Daciana, so I asked Danielle if she was considering adopting more children. She told me she wasn't sure the time was right, but I begged her to take Daciana at least for a weekend visit. I hoped Danielle would fall in love with her like I had. Danielle said she would do it, but couldn't promise anything more.

All the talk of home made our homesickness worse. When we got back to our house we anxiously awaited calls from home. It still felt strange that our evening was their morning.

My mom called me and I was surprised that my dad was there too. They were spending Thanksgiving together, which I thought was a very good sign. I talked to both of them and I could almost imagine everything was fine.

Tara got a call from her family, and Amanda got a call from

hers. No call came for Kellie and she told us her family wasn't real big on tradition; they were bigger on saving money and they knew she'd be home in a few days.

The phone rang once more and it was Adam. "Hey, Carson. How's Turkey Day in Romania?"

"I'm missing my favorite turkey—you!" I teased. "Tell me everything about the day so far at your house."

"Everything? There's not much to tell yet, it's only eleven AM" he complained.

"I did it for you last year and the year before. Describe what's cooking; the dinner and the desserts. Especially the smells—I love the way your house smells on Thanksgiving."

He described it, in not-so-great detail (like a typical guy), but I closed my eyes and imagined I was beside him. "I wish I was there." I said.

"For the food?" he asked. "Didn't they feed you today?"

"For you and the food." I clarified. "I'm just so excited!" It was a big struggle to not tell him I would be home in four days. "Adam, I have a favor to ask."

"Your wish is my command, sweetheart."

"Will you please call me on Monday at 8 PM your time?" I wanted to make sure he would be home when I showed up on his doorstep.

"I will if you want me to. Isn't that kind of early for you though? It'll be like 6 AM your time. What's up?" He sensed I was keeping something from him.

"Nothing's up. I think my roommates are waiting for calls tonight and I want to talk to you longer. So Monday night at eight, right?"

"Okay, I'll talk to you then. I love you, Kit."

"I love you, too, Adam. Happy Thanksgiving." I hung up and reminded myself that I would see him in four days. Four days!

Friday was our last day working at the hospital and orphanage. We had an ally in Ileana. Even though it was prohibited to take pictures, she agreed to distract a couple of the other workers so we could take some. Tara took some shots of me holding Daciana and Simona. I also got one with Pali and me. We took pictures of the rows and rows of cribs, and the children playing on the playground.

It was bittersweet to tell them goodbye. I lingered with the twins, cuddling and kissing them. I prayed they would be adopted by good families.

We spent Saturday packing and cleaning. Our scrubs all went in a pile for Ileana to distribute to the workers at the orphanage. I held back the Care Bear scrubs, wanting to keep a set as a souvenir. Then I thought about how I wore them when I went with Marcel, and I decided to cut all ties and put them in the pile.

We put our long johns in a pile, along with quite a few of our other clothes. Those would go to Corina, to give to the branch members. We also packed up our extra food to take to Corina's family.

Amazingly enough, during our packing, Kellie managed to make a double batch of her famous chocolate chip cookies. She sorted them into four plates; one for Ileana and Marcel, one for Corina's family, one for Danielle and her kids, and one for us.

We spent Saturday evening delivering and visiting. We stopped at Ileana and Marcel's first. I was relieved to find Marcel wasn't home. We visited for a while with Ileana, who translated most of the conversation to her mother. When we gave her the scrubs, she cried. She thanked us over and over.

She hugged us each about five times and couldn't stop crying. She asked what she could do for us. We shrugged, embarrassed. We didn't expect anything in return. She insisted there must be something. It came to me then, simply and clearly, so I spoke up.

"Just keep caring for and loving the orphans. That is what we want. We have to go home, but it helps to know that you are there watching over them." I meant those words even though they sounded trite, and I fought tears. To lighten the moment I motioned to the cookies Kellie had given them. "And also eat some cookies; chocolate always makes me feel better!"

A few hugs later, we were on our way to Corina's. Her family greeted us and immediately started trying to feed us. We told them we had other dinner plans and just wanted to stop and tell them good-bye. We gave them the clothes and long johns and the bags of food we brought for them.

They didn't start crying, but they pelted us with hugs and kisses. Corina walked us to the street. "Thank you for the clothing. You know there is a great need for these things. I'll see that they are given out."

"You're welcome," Tara said. "Thank you for your friendship. You are far more than a tutor to us. We'll miss you."

Corina looked like she wanted to cry. "Please come to choir practice one more time."

"We will," Amanda said, and we all nodded in agreement. I even refrained from complaining about getting up early.

Our last Sunday in Romania was packed with a spiritual punch. It began when the branch president invited the four of us to bear our testimonies. We spoke in English, with Sora Barnes holding a microphone to translate for us. We each spoke of how we knew the gospel was true and how our testimonies had been strengthened in the past three months.

Tara spoke of how our service in Romania had helped her learn to love others; Kellie mentioned the love we had felt from the people in the branch; Amanda marveled at the miracle of missionary service; and I testified that we are all children of God—regardless of our family circumstances in this life.

Our hearts were full as we were greeted by virtually all the branch members after that meeting. Two of the young women, who were sisters, showed us their "new" thermal underwear that they wore under their dresses. We understood the words "Corina" and mulțumesc (thank you) in their exuberant gushing.

Apparently it hadn't taken Corina long to distribute some of the things we gave her. I also saw one of the sisters we sang with in choir proudly clasping a blue leather hymnbook which I recognized as having belonged to Amanda.

Ileana and Marcel were there with their mother. We joined them in the Gospel Principles class. I wondered if Marcel would ignore me, but he actually smiled at me, although he didn't invite me to sit next to him. I returned his smile, happy to know I wasn't leaving an enemy behind.

After the meetings were over, there was one more round of hugs and kisses. There was an awkward moment when Marcel and I faced each other. He stepped in to give me a kiss-kiss. "La revedere, iubita," he whispered. Good-bye, darling. I looked once more into those dark, intense eyes. I stepped away and the moment passed.

Amanda saw the smiles and kiss-kiss, most likely misinterpreting them, judging from her sour look, but I didn't care. We were going home the next day, and I wouldn't have to be roommates with her ever again. Things were definitely looking up.

Anya stopped by that evening and walked through the house which was looking pretty bare again. She collected the extra keys and instructed us to leave the last one on the table when we left the following morning.

Anya was nicest when we first met her, and when we were leaving. The in-between part was iffy; she always seemed impatient and irritated with us. Tara observed that it was probably the nicotine fits she suffered from because Amanda had asked her not to smoke around us. Whatever the cause, we all breathed a sigh of relief when she signed off on their practicum papers and left.

chapter thirty-four

I didn't sleep well that final night in Romania, feeling too much excitement at the prospect of finally going home. From the looks of them, the other three had the same problem. Anya had promised to send a taxi to take us to the bus station and she apparently remembered because a car was out front, honking, at 6 AM.

My suitcase was noticeably lighter than when I came, and I hoped my mother would understand about giving away my scrubs, long johns, and that magnificent first-aid kit she had procured for me. It had found a home at the orphanage along with several other items my roommates and I decided we could easily replace at home.

Even with the few souvenirs I purchased, I had plenty of room in my luggage. That roominess felt good. I asked the others if they noticed that their suitcases were emptier and they all said "yes" with big smiles on their faces. However small our contributions were, it felt satisfying to know they were so needed and appreciated.

The main thing I remember about the trip home was that it was long. Getting up at 5 AM was early enough, but by the time we arrived at the Salt Lake airport at 4:30 PM, local time, a lot more than eleven and a half hours had passed. With the time difference, we had been up for almost twenty-four hours and we were exhausted.

My mom was already at baggage claim. She was the only one waiting for me, but she hugged me tightly then held me back at arm's length to look at me. I wondered if she thought she'd hugged the wrong person. Tara and Amanda had about twenty family members to greet them who immediately mobbed them.

Kellie came over to give me a hug. "I'll miss you, Kit. I'm sorry you and Amanda had issues, but overall I think we all got along pretty well."

I hugged her back and said, "Yeah, I'll miss you too. I really want you to email your chocolate chip cookie recipe to me. And any others you'll part with."

She grinned and said, "I'll think about it. Good luck with Adam."

Tara waved at me through the crowd and motioned with her hand as she mouthed the words "Call me." I nodded and was saved from having to say good-bye to Amanda by the timely arrival of my bags.

My mom insisted on taking my bags for me and chattered in a chipper voice all the way to the car. It was strange being back in Utah with my mom, and I felt almost like I was watching the scene from a distance; like I was there in third person, simply observing the situation rather than actually living it.

"Are you hungry, dear?" she asked, then answered for me. "Of course you are. Airlines don't even really serve food on planes these days. Where shall we stop to eat?"

Before I could give my input, she started again. "Let's see. Where could we go that's not too far off the freeway. I'm not that familiar with the Salt Lake area. What sounds good?" I opened my mouth but, again, she was too fast.

"We'll just drive north and see what looks good. I'm sure we'll find something." At that point I just started to laugh. She had carried on the entire conversation without me.

She glanced over at me. "What's so funny?" She didn't even seem to realize what she had just done. I enlightened her.

She turned a little pink. "I am so sorry, Kit. I'm just used to talking to myself. I guess I started answering myself without realizing it. Now, where would you like to eat?"

I waited for a moment, just to make sure she wanted to hear from me and not herself. "I want a huge, thick milkshake. And a cheeseburger and french fries. I am starving and I've been craving real American fast food."

She frowned. "I'm not sure where to go."

"That's okay. I know exactly where. It's a little ways off the freeway, but it'll be worth it." I gave her directions and leaned back in the seat. It felt good to be back in Utah. My mom's little chat with herself had broken through some of the awkwardness we had both felt at the airport.

As she drove, she said, "I want to hear all about your trip. Everything. You weren't nearly as descriptive as I'd hoped for in your emails. I hope you took lots of pictures."

"I took tons of pictures. I don't know where to start, so you'll probably get random stuff as I think about it."

"Well, start with today. Tell me about the trip home. Let's see, you've been in Brasov, Bucharest, Paris, New York, and Salt Lake—all today! That's amazing by itself." Her words made it sound more exciting than it really was; after all, I was either in train stations or airports in every city she mentioned. It wasn't exactly sightseeing, but I tried to remember all the details to share with her.

It wasn't too long before I had a huge caramel macadamia nut shake in my hands—and mouth. I alternated spoonfuls of ice cream heaven with big bites of my cheeseburger and fries. I savored the taste, textures and smells. My mother just shook her head as she nibbled on a salad.

When we were back on the road, I decided to ask her bluntly about one of my foremost concerns. "How are you and Dad doing?"

She thought for a minute, as if choosing her words carefully. "I'm doing well; your father appears to be doing well . . ." she trailed off.

"Just tell me the truth. I want to know how things really are." She might have been able to put me off while I was half a world away, but it was much harder to do so when I was sitting next to her in the front seat of a car.

"The truth. Well, the truth is we're both doing fine, just not doing fine together." She didn't seem forthcoming; I would have to take the initiative.

"What does that mean? You're both fine, just not together. Have you already given up on the marriage then?"

"We're not to that point—yet. But it is a very real possibility that we're going to divorce. It's something we have to face; and if that time comes, our family will survive." She sounded very resigned to the inevitability.

"Our family will survive? You can't break up a family and then say it will survive. That's an oxymoron. A divorce means the end of the family." Disillusionment reared its dreary head to mar my happy homecoming.

"Kit, I know this is hard for you, but you're being a little dramatic. The family will survive. It will be changed, it's true, but it won't cease to exist. The marriage is the only thing that will be dissolved. You will still be our daughter and Dave's sister. I will still be your mother and Dad will still be your father." I knew she was trying to soothe me and make me see reason.

I needed to change tactics. "But the marriage isn't over yet, right? I mean, you guys were together on Thanksgiving. That's a good sign, isn't it?"

"We did have a nice Thanksgiving. In part, we were together for you and for Dave. You need to understand that we are not making this decision lightly. You're already in college and Dave is graduating from high school in the spring. We're less and less involved in your lives. Soon you'll each go your own way for good. Your father and I have a right to think about ourselves and our own happiness."

"Have you considered that maybe you can have happiness together? That you don't need to get divorced to be happy?" I didn't know how to introduce the idea I wanted her to consider.

"Of course we've considered it. It isn't like we woke up one morning and said, 'Oh look, we'll be happier apart; let's separate'. This was a long time coming. Your father simply was the first to take action." For the first time in the conversation I heard bitterness creep into her voice.

"You said you guys were going to counseling. Is it helping?"

"It is helping, although perhaps not in the way you wish it would. We're adjusting to the situation. I think counseling will benefit you too." Her voice was bland again.

"Mom, what if there was a way to save your marriage and to save our family. Not just save it—heal it. Would you be willing to try?" I uttered a silent prayer for help.

"There is no magic cure. I know you would like to believe there is, but there isn't," she said gently.

"But there is," I insisted, "I know there's a way. Will you just listen?"

"Kit—" She sounded a little exasperated and I cut her off.

"Mom, I'm willing to try counseling. You and Dad should be willing to try whatever it takes to save your marriage and our family. Will you please consider listening to the missionary discussions? I promise, the Church is true and Jesus Christ has the power to heal us. Say you'll be willing to try it. Please!" Emotion overcame me and tears spilled onto my cheeks.

My mom patted my hand and said. "Religion isn't the answer to everything. We've let you choose your own path; you need to let us do the same. We haven't forced you to believe as we do and I'm sure you wouldn't want to force your beliefs on anyone else." She fished a tissue out of her purse and handed it to me. "You're tired from all the travel. Let's not discuss this anymore for now. Maybe you could take a little nap while I drive."

I blew my nose and turned away from her. I could help convert strangers, but my own family wouldn't listen to me. I didn't know what else I could do.

chapter thirty-five

I dozed off and awoke to find us pulling into our driveway in Logan; I spied my blue car as we pulled in. Still groggy, I grabbed my backpack and staggered inside as my mom brought in the suitcases.

My house looked the same as when I'd left it nearly three months before. I eagerly went up to my room and saw that it, too, looked like I had just left it the day before. There wasn't even a trace of dust.

I looked at my watch. It was 7:15. I'd told Adam to call me at eight. I had to hurry! I had time for a quick shower, but not enough time to wash my hair too.

I started the shower and picked out some clothes. My closet reflected the excess we took for granted in America. I pulled out one of my favorite pairs of jeans and an ivory sweater.

I felt refreshed after I had showered and dressed. I carefully applied my makeup and stressed about my hair for a few minutes. I decided to leave it loose, the brownish-blonde waves falling to the middle of my back. Adam liked it best that way and claimed he saw no point in the hours girls spent straightening their hair. It was a girl thing, I guessed.

I bounded downstairs at 7:45 yelling, "Mom, where are the keys to my car?" grabbing my black leather coat out of the closet in the front room.

She stepped out of the kitchen with them and asked, "You're going out tonight? I thought you were too exhausted."

"Remember, Mom, I told you I was going to surprise Adam. He's not expecting me until next week. I told him to call me tonight. I've got to hurry if I want to get there before he tries to call me." I grabbed the keys and hurried to the garage.

I pulled up in front of the Bridgers' at five minutes before eight. I couldn't stop smiling as I imagined Adam's surprise. Come to think of it, they'd all be shocked. I hoped I could see his face before the horde of younger siblings ruined my surprise by yelling out that I was there.

I took a deep breath and rang the doorbell. I could hear feet running for the door. It was always like that at the Bridger house. The younger kids practically trampled one another to get to the door first. I heard laughing and squeals and I swore I heard Adam's voice say, "Oh no, you don't!" just as the door opened.

The door wasn't the only thing hanging wide open as Adam caught sight of me. From the appearance of his arm around Ruth Randall's waist, it wasn't his siblings he was racing and wrestling to the door. His jaw dropped as it dawned on him that it was me standing there, he released Ruth so abruptly she almost fell into my arms—if my arms had been outstretched.

They weren't, and she was lucky she caught herself.

"Surprise," I said quietly, trying very hard not to let myself jump to conclusions. Unfortunately for me, I had slept very little in the past couple of days and I couldn't control where my mind leapt. The vision of Adam holding Ruth around the waist, combined with their laughter, wouldn't dissipate. I felt on the brink of tears again.

"Kit!" That's all Adam could say. He didn't even ask me to come in.

Ruth scrambled back inside after she saved herself from a face plant on the doorstep. She stood behind Adam and whispered, "Invite her in, Adam!"

By then, the horde had descended in truth and there were squeals of "Kit! You're back!" Several hands tugged me inside. I swallowed the lump in my throat.

"Hi!" I said with forced cheerfulness. "Are you guys surprised?"

As they clamored around me, Adam seemed to recover his faculties. He stepped towards me to put his arm around my waist. I stepped away from his reach. He would not hug me just after hanging all over Ruth. He gave me a questioning look.

Struggling to put on a happy face in front of the entire Bridger clan, I briefly explained that I just arrived home and had left out the date change of my flight in order to surprise Adam. He was definitely surprised.

"I can't stay long; I'm exhausted from all the travel, so I guess I'll go. I'll talk to you all tomorrow." I turned to leave and there was a general clamor protesting my departure. Adam grabbed my hand and wouldn't let me pull away.

"We're having family home evening," Lily piped up. "You're lucky you missed the lesson." She rolled her eyes. "Now we're playing charades. We're teams. Adam and Ruth are on a team, but I'll bet you can be Adam's partner." She gave me a direct stare like she was trying to tell me something.

"Thanks, but I'm too tired to play games tonight. I really should go." I couldn't deal with the issue of Adam and Ruth together in any form; I needed to get out of there.

"I'll walk you to your car." Adam said. He grabbed his coat from the closet and turned to the others. "Go ahead and finish the game without me. I want to talk to Kit for a few minutes."

I was glad he wanted to talk, but I was a little afraid that I couldn't keep my jumbled emotions in check.

Before I could get into my car, behind the protection of the steering wheel, Adam pulled me to him and encased me in his arms. "I am so glad you're home, Kit. I've missed you so much."

I pulled back and looked up into his warm brown eyes. I should have said, "I missed you too." Instead, I blurted out, "It didn't look like you were missing me too much."

Adam said, "What is that supposed to mean?"

"I saw the way you had your arms wrapped around Ruth's waist. I heard you guys laughing. I'm not blind or stupid, Adam." The hurt and betrayal felt crushing.

"What? That was nothing. We were playing a game and we'd just drawn a card that required us to act out something stupid. We were both standing, so we raced to the door. It was nothing more than that." He stepped back and jammed his hands into his pockets in frustration.

I was shivering and opened the car door. "Let's get in. I'm freezing." We both climbed in and I started the engine. "If it was only tonight, I would believe that. But she hangs out at your house all the time. She rides to work with you. I know you've kissed her." All my doubts and insecurities bubbled up and I cursed myself for coming.

He looked confused. "What are you talking about? I never kissed Ruth. There's nothing going on."

"Don't lie to me, Adam. Lily saw you two kissing in her car and she told me. It doesn't take an expert to figure out why she hangs out here all the time."

"First of all—she kissed me. One time, in the car. That must be what Lily was talking about. I set her straight and told her I wasn't interested in her for more than a friend, and that you and I were together. That was the only time." His defenses were up.

"So you did kiss! Why did you lie about it? What else are you keeping from me?" I demanded.

"What am I keeping from you?" he asked incredulously. "Let's talk about betrayal, Kit. What about you keeping things from me? You tell me about this Marcel guy who is supposedly investigating the Church, but you conveniently leave out that you met him secretly, dated him, and he even proposed marriage to you! I think you're the one who has explaining to do." I'd never heard his voice so tight with anger, especially directed at me. How did he know about Marcel? There was only one possibility I could think of.

"Who told you that stuff about Marcel and me?" It had to be Amanda—Tara would never do that to me, and Kellie was never riled up like Amanda was.

"Yeah, your roommate told me. She sent me a nice email," he said, voice dripping with sarcasm. "I think I can remember some of it verbatim. 'Someone needs to tell you that Kit is seriously dating a guy named Marcel who is investigating the Church. I wouldn't tell you, except it's to the point that he has proposed. She said she told him no, yet they are out on a date together right now. A secret date. I just thought you should know.' Yeah, that's pretty much what it said. And it was sent last Tuesday—not even a week ago."

"Amanda hates my guts! She'll do anything to put me in a bad light. She wanted Marcel for herself. She's just being incredibly mean and spiteful." I was practically yelling. If Amanda had been there just then, I would have decked her. I was shaking with anger and adrenaline.

"Yet, you're not denying that you dated Marcel. Did he propose to you?" Adam matched my volume and tone.

"It's not like it sounds."

"Did he propose to you?" He asked the question again, emphasizing each word.

"Yes! Is that what you want to hear? He kissed me too!" Adam clearly wasn't interested in my explanations. My head was pounding; I wished I was anywhere but there.

"And you're worried about Ruth and me. That's a little hypocritical, don't you think?"

"You act like you and Ruth are all innocent, but I know you went to Salt Lake together! I know you went ring shopping together! Why don't you just be honest with me? I'm not good enough for you, am I? I never was—I don't have the Mormon pioneer pedigree; I wasn't named after a mighty woman from the Bible. You probably would have been relieved if I had stayed in Romania and married Marcel! Just admit it!" I poured out my deepest fear; there it was, out in the open.

Adam just shook his head and said softly, "I can't believe you really think that way. I did go ring shopping with Ruth. But you were wrong about my intent. The ring was for you, Kit. Maybe I was wrong about it—about us." He opened the door and climbed out of the car, slamming the door behind him.

I was stunned. I didn't know what to do. Should I chase after him and beg him for another chance? My sleep-deprived brain and pride told me he should be the one begging me. I put the car in gear and drove off. I decided surprises were way overrated.

chapter thirty-six

I went home and did what I should have done in the first place—I went to bed. As I shook off my coat, my mom figured out by my expression that things hadn't gone well with Adam. She asked if I was okay and I told her I just needed to sleep and to please not wake me unless the house was on fire.

My mind kept spinning as I lay in bed, trying to figure out what had gone wrong. I despised Amanda more than I did Ruth at that moment. I thought about calling Amanda and giving her a piece of my mind, but I realized that would just give her satisfaction.

I tried to clear my mind so I could sleep. I calculated how long I'd been awake. It was more than twenty-four hours. It was no wonder I couldn't think straight. As I drifted off, I mentally berated myself for being so impatient.

It was noon before I woke up. I was starving and mortified as the events of the previous night came flooding back.

Two things stood out in my mind: one, Adam had purchased the ring for me; and, two, he now wondered if he had made a mistake. I was a world-class moron.

It was glaringly clear to me as it had never been before—Adam was the man I loved and wanted to marry. I had let suspicion and self-doubt creep in for too long. Adam was worth fighting for. I just had to figure out how to get him back.

My mom was at work and I had no idea where Dave was. I

hadn't seen him since I got home. Considering the time, I assumed he was at school. I checked the caller ID to see if Adam had, by some stroke of good luck, called. There were no calls.

I dug my cell phone out of my backpack. I had recharged it before we left and used it to call my mom from New York. There were no calls from Adam on it, either.

I took a bubble bath and lingered in the tub for an hour while I tried to figure out what to do. I thought about calling Tara, but I really wanted to do this on my own.

Bathed and beautified, I still had no ideas at 3 PM. I decided I needed some help. I got down on my knees and offered a sincere prayer. The only thought that came to me as I asked for help was to be patient. I arose thinking *Oh great, the one thing I stink at—patience.*

I heard Dave come in from school so I went downstairs to see him. He greeted me with his usual finesse. "Eeeew, look what the cat dragged in!"

For once I ignored his remark and went over and gave him a big hug. "I'm so glad to see you and to be home." He actually let me hug him and half-heartedly returned it.

After about two seconds, he pulled back and said, "Who are you and what have you done with my sister?" He gave a dramatic pause then added, "She's still in Romania, I hope."

"Sorry, Dave, it's me, I'm home, and I love you!" I couldn't say why I felt cheerful and loving towards him, it had never happened before. I didn't fight it; I just kept talking to him.

As he fixed a snack, I asked him about how things were really going at home. He reiterated that it wasn't that much different than before, except Dad didn't come home at night.

"He does make an effort to hang out with me now. He's actually gone with me to a couple of USU basketball games. Maybe he's trying harder to be a father."

"That's good then. What about Mom—how's she doing?" My mom had put on a happy face every time she talked to me, I wondered if Dave saw the same thing.

"You know, she's not around as much. She went back to work full-time. She drags me to counseling once a week, so get ready for that. She cried a lot at first, but now it's like she's over it and moving on." Dave shrugged. "I'll be outta here in a few more months, so I don't think about it all that much."

"It just seems weird to me, that they're not together. I haven't even seen Dad. I wonder if he'll even call me or anything." I really missed my dad at that moment, and it hurt that he wasn't there to welcome me home.

Dave shook his hair out of his eyes and washed his last bite of sandwich down with a swig of milk. "Oh yeah, I'm supposed to tell you that Dad's taking you and me to dinner tomorrow night and he'll pick us up at six. Well, I gotta go to work. Catch you later." He grabbed his keys and went out the door.

It dawned on me he grabbed keys. That meant he was driving a car. I ran to the window to see him pulling away in a white Honda Civic. Well, that was a change from three months ago. I didn't get my car until graduation. I always thought he was more spoiled than I was.

A few minutes after Dave left, I heard a knock at the door. I answered it and there in front of my face was a huge bouquet of flowers. Standing behind the massive floral arrangement was the one person I wanted to see the most—Adam Bridger.

My heart was racing and I opened the door wider. He peered around his offering and said, "Special delivery."

Of course I invited him in. I took the flowers from him, then I had to peek through them to see him. I didn't want to walk away from him, so I put them on the couch—crushing a few petals, I'm sure—then turned to face him. I was not going to blow it this time. He was looking at me and his gaze told me he felt pretty much the same way I did.

"I'm sorry," we said at the same time.

"Jinx, you owe me a Coke," I was slightly faster than him.

We reached towards each other and before I could say anything witty or moronic, we were hugging and kissing. The brief thought fluttered through my mind, How could I have ever doubted this?

After a few minutes of swapping saliva—I blame my brother Dave for my crude way of putting things—we pulled apart, but kept holding hands.

"Come help me put these in water." I motioned to the bevy of blossoms covering the sofa. "Did you rob a funeral parlor?" I asked as I gathered them up.

"Nah, I just bought all the fresh flowers the store had. I'm glad you like them. I have to confess, this many flowers was not my idea. My mom and Lily put me up to it. They even pitched in to pay for them. Not very romantic, huh?" Adam was so cute, confessing in his forthright way.

"Well, Lily should pay for some of them. She's partly to blame and she probably knows it." Without Lily's emails I wouldn't have jumped to the wrong conclusions. Of course, being older and supposedly wiser, I should have realized that she saw things extremely one-sided. "I wonder if you can send a bill to Amanda?"

"Lily admitted she had sent some emails to you 'reporting' the things she had seen. She really did see the things she told you, she just took them out of context. For what it's worth, I think she's sorry. I can't speak for Amanda, though." Adam pointed to some weedy-looking flowers in the bouquet. "I think these are stinkweeds. These should be the new lily."

"No, look at all these lilies that are already in the bouquet. They're colorful and make it more interesting. These stinkweeds are the 'Adams' of the bouquet," I tested him to see if his sense of humor was back.

"You're calling me a stinkweed, woman? I think it takes one to know one." It was back. I could tell Adam truly wasn't mad at me anymore.

"Then stinkweeds can be our official flower. We were both stinkers last night. I am really sorry, Adam. I was planning on telling you all about Marcel. It's a strange story and I just couldn't tell it through email or IM." I found two vases that my mom had stashed up high. We managed to stuff all the flowers in.

"We have a lot to talk about, Kit. But I have to say one thing to you right now. I love you. You're the one for me, so don't ever worry about anyone else." His words thrilled me.

"I love you, too. Haven't we waited long enough to get married?" I wanted him to know how much I cared about him and to get everything out in the open.

"Are you proposing to me, Kit Carson?" He asked with a wink and a mischievous grin.

"Cap'n Bridger, for a mountain man, you're pretty dang smart," I played along. "But I haven't got a ring," I added in an innocent tone.

"It just so happens I have one here in my pocket. I keep it for emergencies. You never know when you're going to need it to seal a deal." He reached in his jeans pocket and pulled out a little ring box.

He got down on one knee and said, "Kit Matthews, I, Adam Bridger, do hereby accept your proposal of marriage and offer you this ring as a token of our bargain."

"Are you sure it's a good bargain?" I asked. "Once I take it, you're as good as mine." I loved his silly playfulness.

"I'm already yours. We just need to set the date." He took my hand and slipped the ring on my finger. It was a beautiful marquise diamond in a platinum setting.

"It's gorgeous, Adam! Omigosh! We're engaged!" I squealed and flung myself into his arms. He caught me and held me like he would never let me go. I was just fine with that.

After a few more passionate kisses, we tore ourselves away from each other and decided we'd better go somewhere public, yet private enough that we could talk about things alone, before we told anyone else our news.

We got ready to leave and Adam informed me I would have to drive, that Barbara had dropped him off at my house with the flowers. I thought that was hilarious.

"Your mommy had to drive you to my house and drop you off so you could propose? How cute! It's kind of like your first day of kindergarten, isn't it?" I didn't mind driving, I just loved teasing him.

"Well, fiancée, I had a choice—buy a car or buy my girl a ring. I chose the ring. Besides, my girl already has a car. When we get married, I get her and the car, too!" Adam gave me a sideways glance, grinning at me. "It's not a Lexus—but hey, it beats walking!"

I smacked him lightly up side his head. When Justin married Michelle, she had a Lexus. "Well, Bridger boy, you didn't keep up with Justin on this one. He married into a Lexus, you're marrying into a Chevy!"

"It isn't a contest, but if it was, I'd win because the Chevy comes with Kit Carson, famous scout. The Lexus came with Lexus Barbie and I've never been into Barbie dolls."

"I'm relieved to hear that. I've never been into Barbies either. Let's go get pizza." I was suddenly ravenous.

While we ate our pizza, I marveled at how a good night's sleep could make such a difference. We opened up about Marcel and Ruth and I didn't even have to fight off defensiveness. Adam wasn't at all happy that a good-looking Romanian had tried to marry me, but he understood it better when I told him the whole story.

He reiterated that Ruth had initiated the kiss, and he had told her quite bluntly that he wasn't interested. She had apologized and been on good behavior since then.

We both agreed that if, in the future, someone emailed us or told us something about the other, we would be straightforward and go directly to the source.

After we had cleared the air and apologized to each other a couple more times, Adam suggested we talk about more important things—like a wedding date. I couldn't believe we were really, truly setting a date!

We had to work around our school schedules. We considered the second week in March, during spring break. Or we could get married in May, after school ended. May was the logical choice when considering housing, but I sure didn't want to wait that long. I was delighted when Adam spoke up first.

"Kit, I really don't want to wait until May. If it's just because of housing, then we can find something in March. It won't be student housing, true, but we can make it work."

"I don't want to wait until May either. But I remember when Janet was planning her wedding and listening to Michelle and Justin plan theirs; it seems like you need four to six months to get everything done. I don't even know all the stuff we need to do."

"Well the only things we need to do are set a date, get our temple recommends and get married! The other things are fluff in my opinion." Adam said. "Of course, it's the fluff that women seem to like, so we'll do what you want."

"You make it sound so simple. I'd pick what you just said about getting our recommends and getting married. I don't care about fluff. I don't think our moms will go for that, though." I couldn't even guess how my mom would react, given the recent changes in her life.

"We both want to get married in March, so let's plan on March. Our moms will have to deal with it! The thing is, we'll have to look at a calendar so we know the specific dates for spring break. We can do that when you take me home, if you don't mind stopping in for awhile."

"I'm fine with that. Now we have to decide who we're going to tell first!" The waiter stopped by to drop off the bill. I reached for it, but Adam snatched it out of his hand before I could get it.

"You proposed, I get to pay for the engagement dinner," he said, pulling out his wallet. The waiter told us he would be our cashier.

"We just got engaged!" I said, flashing my ring in front of our waiter. He smiled indulgently and told us congratulations as he took Adam's debit card.

"There. I just told the first person; you get to tell the next one." I wanted everyone to share in my happiness.

On the way out, Adam held the door for a group of women who were coming in the restaurant. They looked at him and said thank you. He grinned and said, "We just got engaged!" They exclaimed over my ring and wished us well. He turned to me and said, "Tag, you're it!"

chapter thirty-seven

On the drive back to his house, we discussed when we would tell our families. Adam said we should tell my parents first and I explained that I wasn't going to see my dad until the following night, and I didn't actually know where he lived. Adam suggested we go tell my mom, find my dad and tell him, and then go tell his family.

That meant we needed to bypass his house for the moment and go back to mine. I guessed my mom would be home by then, considering it was almost six. She was, and I asked him if he wanted to share the news, or if he wanted me to.

"She's your mom and it's your turn, anyway." Adam opened the door for me.

My mom was in the kitchen cooking something and watching the news on TV. She smiled as we walked in. "Hello, you two. Are you hungry? I was just starting some spaghetti, and I was trying to decide how much to cook."

"No, we just ate. We had pizza." Should I just blurt out my news? I wondered. I gave Adam a questioning look. He nudged me.

"I thought you'd probably eaten. You seem in better spirits tonight, Kit. Things always look better after a good night's sleep. I haven't seen you around in a while, Adam. I'm guessing we'll be seeing more of you now that Kit's home." That was the opening I was looking for.

"Mom you're going to be seeing Adam a lot more, that's for sure," I stretched out my hand and turned it so the diamond sparkled as the light hit it. "We're engaged."

She took my hand and looked at the ring. "I can't say I'm surprised. I guess congratulations are in order. Have you set a date yet?" She would have won an award for containing her enthusiasm— if she felt any at all. She was being polite, but I could tell she was disapproving.

"In March. We have to check to see when spring break is." I tried not to let her lack of excitement dampen my own, but it was hard.

"March? Of next year? That's less than four months away! I think you should consider a longer engagement. You can get to know each other better that way." She would have thought a twelve-month engagement was too short.

"Mom, we've known each other for three years. I'm pretty sure we know each other well enough." My mother had a way of making me feel defensive. I just wanted her to be happy for us.

"You've known each other for three years, but you've only actually dated a few months of that time. You've been apart for over two years. A marriage relationship is much different than dating." I think she realized she was lecturing us, because she tried to lighten it up. "Of course, Adam, my hesitation has nothing to do with you, personally. I think you are a wonderful young man. I just don't want you two rushing things. You have your whole lives ahead of you."

"Don't worry, Mrs. Matthews, I know you're just looking after Kit's best interest. We have that in common—we both love Kit." Adam always knew the right things to say. I probably would have gotten into an argument with my mom if he hadn't been there.

"I know, Adam. Just don't get your heart so set on marrying in March, that you overlook what's really best for the two of you." I knew she meant well, but she was pushing my buttons and I had to get out of there.

"Mom, we want to go tell Dad. Do you have the address of his apartment?" I blurted out.

She sighed. "Did Dave tell you that you two are having dinner with him tomorrow night? You can tell him then and save yourself a trip."

"I want to tell him tonight, with Adam. Besides, I want to see where he lives now." She hesitated again and I said, "I can just call him to get the address; I just thought you knew it. Never mind."

I turned to leave the kitchen and tugged on Adam's hand so he'd follow me. My mom's voice stopped me. "Kit, I'll give you the address. Just be prepared. He might have his lady friend with him."

Lady friend? I thought. She tried to keep her voice neutral, but I could tell she was struggling. I stood there dumbfounded. The possibility of my dad seeing someone else was so disturbing. "He's still married," I choked out, in a half-whisper.

"Tell that to him." My mom didn't bother hiding her bitterness with that remark. She snatched a piece of paper from the memo pad by the phone, jotted down an address, and held it out to me.

"Thanks." I mumbled, still stunned as I let Adam lead me to the door.

When we were in the car I turned to him, overcome with the reality of what my mom had just revealed. He held me close and let me cry it out. I vented to him in between my sobs.

"This is supposed to be one of the happiest days of my life. I can't believe my dad has a girlfriend. I knew they were separated and my mom even told me he was in 'a relationship' but I didn't expect this. It's like they've given up on their marriage. I don't even want to go over there. I don't even want to talk to him!"

Adam listened to me wail and found a tissue for me. There wasn't a lot he could say. He mainly listened and said, "I'm sorry." It was a huge comfort to have someone to cry to, who would just listen to me.

"Adam, when I was in Romania, I prayed and prayed without getting any specific answers. The one answer I finally got was to come home. My family needed me. Now I'm here and they don't need me at all. They're all going their separate ways. I thought I could make a difference if I shared my testimony with them—that maybe if they knew about the gospel, they would be willing to try to keep our family together. My mom wouldn't even listen when

I tried to tell her. And it's pretty clear my dad is living his own life—one that doesn't include the family." After blurting it all out, my tears were drying up and I felt drained.

"Kit, maybe you don't need to convert your family; maybe you just need to be here as a source of strength and a good example. We never know what effect we are having on others. They may not be in a position to hear or accept the gospel now, but who knows what seeds are being planted?" Adam's words made me feel better.

Sometimes I felt like I had to do it all myself, and if I didn't succeed the way I thought I should, then I was a complete failure.

Adam stroked my hair as he comforted me. "We don't have to go over to your dad's tonight. Wait until tomorrow to talk to him. This is our night—a night to be happy and celebrate."

"You're right. I'm not going to let my family ruin this night for us." I sat up straight and announced. "I want ice cream. Let's go get some first, then we'll go tell your family." Maybe it was a flaw that I self-medicated with ice cream, but it sure was soothing; physically and mentally.

After a huge helping of ice cream drizzled with caramel and hot fudge in a chocolate-dipped waffle cone, I felt the excitement of being engaged return (or maybe it was the sugar rush I felt).

"You know what?" I asked Adam, enjoying the silky texture of the ice cream on my tongue.

"What?" The chocolate smudge on his chin indicated he was enjoying his hot fudge brownie sundae and I had a brief flashback of the time he'd eaten disgusting bubble gum ice cream on our first date, which made me smile.

"We forgot to look up the spring break dates for March. We still don't have a specific date set."

"We'll tell my family, then we'll go online and pick a date."

"When they stop mobbing us," I added, reveling in the vision of the Bridger clan's reaction.

I was not disappointed. When we walked into Adam's house Lily was quick to greet us. "Are you guys all made up?" she asked eagerly.

"Yeah, we're all made up," Adam told her, "Thanks to your flowers, Lily." I noticed he didn't make any disparaging remarks about the part she played in our troubles; I tried to follow his example. I had a big soft spot for Lily, so it wasn't too hard.

I gave her a big hug. "We're all made up, Sis," I whispered. She hugged me back and said she was sorry for any trouble she'd caused. It took a couple of seconds for what I said to sink into her brain.

"What!" She shrieked. That noise brought most of the family running to the living room.

Barbara asked, "Lily, is everything okay? Why did you scream?"

Lily looked at me and asked loudly, "Did you just call me 'Sis'?"

Before I could answer, Adam cleared his throat and said, "May I introduce my fiancée, Kit Matthews." He held out my hand with a flourish to show off the diamond on my third finger.

The uproar was quite gratifying. Lily and Beth announced they'd been hoping for it and talking about it all afternoon. Hal and Barbara congratulated us and gave us each a big hug. Mark wasn't around, but Travis and Sarah were jumping around, asking tons of questions.

Barbara asked if we'd decided on a date and we told her March. "That's not very long. We have so much to plan!" Her enthusiasm was a sharp contrast to my own mother's reaction.

As if she read my mind, Barbara asked, "Have you told your parents yet?"

"We told my mom. We haven't talked to my dad yet." Adam squeezed my hand as I answered.

"I'll bet she's excited. You're her only daughter. It is so special to prepare for your daughter's wedding. Not that a son isn't fun," Barbara smiled at Adam. "Daughters are just different. I'd be happy to help however I can. Please tell your mother."

"Thanks, I will," I said, desperately wishing to myself that my own mother was like Barbara. I brightened a little as I realized that in a few short months, I would truly be a part of this wonderful family.

Adam and I escaped long enough to look up dates on the computer. We decided on March 12. Three and a half months. I felt like pinching myself to make sure I was awake.

Adam called Justin to tell him. He put it on speaker phone.

When Justin answered, Adam said, "Hey man. Guess what?"

"You and Kit are engaged." Justin said matter-of-factly. Michelle must have been listening in because I heard her say, "It's about time!"

"How did you know?" I asked Justin. "It just barely happened a few hours ago!"

"Well, I heard you got home last night, surprised Adam, and left in a huff. Then Mom, Lily, and Adam bought a carload of flowers, and now you guys are calling. It wasn't rocket science." Justin loved to steal our thunder.

"So what do you think?" Adam asked his brother.

"What my wife said—it's about time. Now we can all get a break from Adam whining about how much he misses Kit. Waaaaaahhhh!"

"Is that how you sounded?" I asked Adam.

"Pretty much," he ceded. "Thanks for blowing my cover, Brother. I'll return the favor someday."

Barbara was animated the rest of the evening, talking about wedding plans and what she'd planned for Janet's wedding and what Michelle and Justin did, and on and on. Adam looked at me a time or two, rolling his eyes, and I just laughed. I liked hearing Barbara sound so happy again. It felt good to talk about Janet openly. I knew she'd be thrilled for us, if she were there.

When I got home at midnight I was exhausted, but I took the time to write about the day in my journal and to give a prayer of thanks for the wonderful way my life was going.

The next day when Dave got home from school I told him my exciting news. He tried to act interested and said "Good job," but I could tell he was antsy to play video games.

I followed him downstairs to the family room and pestered him a little more. "Does Dad have a girlfriend?"

He glanced at me as he unwound the controller cords. "I don't know. If he does, he hasn't introduced her to me. Mom and Dad are still married, Kit." He said the last part like saying "Duhhhh".

"I know they're still married and I want them to stay that way. It's just, last night when Adam and I were telling Mom about our engagement, we wanted to go tell Dad and she made some comment that his 'lady friend' might be there." I picked up the other controller. "If you play something non-violent, I'll play with you."

"You gotta realize that Mom's kind of bitter when it comes to Dad right now. She acts like she's okay, but she makes her little remarks. I just try to ignore it. Do you want to play a racing game?" He grabbed for the case.

"Yeah, racing's okay." I sat down. "So you don't think it's like Dad's dating someone seriously, then?"

"I don't think so, but you never know. Ask him. He'll pick us up in a couple of hours." He started the game and I spent the next hour trying not to get motion sick as I raced through the streets in a decked-out Mustang.

When Dad picked us up, he gave me a huge hug and told me how glad he was to see me. He actually looked better than he had in a long time, since before his heart attack almost two years prior. Whatever he was doing, it seemed to be agreeing with him.

He let me pick the place to eat, so I opted for a big juicy steak. Dad asked me about Romania, but I told him there was something I needed to tell him first. I put my left hand on the table, waiting for him to notice my ring.

After a few seconds of silence, he asked, "What was it you wanted to tell me?" He was totally oblivious to the clue I was giving him, so I drummed my fingers on the table, to see if he would notice. He didn't. "Well?" he asked expectantly.

Dave spoke up in spite of his mouth being full of half-chewed bread. "Her ring, Dad. She wants you to notice her ring." He took a gulp of soda to wash down his food.

Dad noticed the ring then. "I'm assuming this is from Adam and not some boy you met in Romania?"

"Of course it's from Adam! We're getting married on March 12th." I waited for his reaction.

"Wow! This is big news. My daughter's getting married! Are you happy? Of course you are. Congratulations, sweetheart." He gave my hand a squeeze. "I suppose this wedding thing is going to bankrupt me. You'll want a big shindig, I'm sure."

He was as geeky as ever. "A shindig? I don't think people even use that word anymore, Dad. Don't worry, I don't plan on bankrupting you." I decided I'd be up front with him. "The wedding ceremony will take place in the Salt Lake Temple. The reception will be the main cost. And the dress. And the photographer."

"Listen to her!" Dave piped up. "You'd better give her a budget or she'll break you. And you can't even go to the wedding!" His timing and comments were unhelpful, as usual.

"I'm aware that only members with recommends can attend ceremonies in the temple, son." He turned his gaze on me. "Have you told your mother yet?"

"She knows we're engaged; I haven't specifically told her we're getting married in the temple." I was a little nervous about her reaction.

"If she has a hard time with it, Kit, realize that it isn't just this; she's dealing with a lot right now." My dad was trying to be helpful, but his comment just brought up the issue of their separation. The waiter brought our food and we spent the next few minutes in silence.

I broached the subject again. "I know Mom's dealing with a lot. What I want to know is 'why'? Why are you two separated? I thought you were happily married." I couldn't keep the accusing tone out of my voice.

"Our marriage wasn't 'unhappy.' To tell you the truth, for many years I thought our marriage was about as good as any marriage was. After my heart attack, I did a lot of soul searching. I realized there were things I wanted to do. Things I needed to do."

"And divorce was one of them?" I asked bitterly.

"Your mother and I don't have a lot in common. I love teaching; she misses California. She's been after me to move back there since we got here. I like it here in the mountains; I like this valley, and I like teaching at Utah State. I can't explain it specifically, but our differences are just too great. I think we can both be happier apart."

It sounded like a big cop-out to me. "So, do you have a girlfriend, Dad? Is that what it's all about? Is this your mid-life crisis?"

He smiled rather sadly. "It isn't about another woman. As far as mid-life crisis goes—I think I'm well past mid-life. The heart attack gave me that wake-up call. I do have a female friend, it's true. She is not the cause of all this, though."

"Yeah, but it sure isn't helping matters." My steak had lost its flavor and I was in no mood for dessert, even though Dave inhaled his.

When we got home, Dad walked with me to the door, while Dave lumbered ahead, texting his friend. Dad put his arm around me. "Kit, I don't expect you to understand, but please know that I do love you. I want us to have a relationship and it'll be tough to get through these next few months. Don't give up on me. I'm not some kind of monster."

"I just want my family to be together, Dad. I can't make you love Mom, but I can still hope, can't I?" I gave him a hug and went inside.

chapter thirty-eight

Adam's family had planned a welcome-home party for me, but I had spoiled their plans by coming home early. Instead of canceling their plans, they just modified them and on Friday night I walked into the Bridger house and was greeted by a huge cry of "Surprise!" Justin and Michelle were the first to step up and hug me.

The family room was decorated with streamers and balloons. I could smell the aroma of delicious things and saw that Lily and Barbara had been busy baking. I was really shocked when I saw my mom there. They had also recruited Tara to come, along with a few friends from the ward.

It was all so perfect, or so I thought. Then I heard a perky voice say, "Sorry, I'm late. Did I miss the big surprise part?" It was Ruth. Ruth Randall. I wondered who invited her. It was, after all, my party. I glanced around to make sure Amanda wasn't hiding around somewhere to totally ruin my night.

Adam distracted me with a hug and a kiss. "Are you surprised?" He asked. I assured him I was and returned his embrace.

I could smell pizza and I realized Hal had arrived with about ten of them. Mark and Dave followed with plates and napkins. They even convinced my brother to come! Now that was a miracle. Of course, being friends with Mark probably helped a little.

We ate and talked and laughed. I avoided contact with Ruth.

Even though Adam had explained everything, I still didn't like her. I felt like she had ulterior motives. I imagined Adam wouldn't like it if Marcel had shown up to the party.

Tara and I started telling stories about Romania. I was so glad she came. I wished I had brought my camera and laptop so I could show them all the pictures we took. I said something to Adam about it.

"Your wish is my command, milady," he bowed gallantly, then reached down by the end of the couch and pulled out my laptop bag and camera.

"What? How did you get that?" I turned to my mom, who was smiling smugly.

"There are still secrets safe from you, my dear!" Adam gave me a mock leer.

Adam and his dad hooked up my computer to the TV so we could display the pictures for everyone to see. I took a few minutes to download the photos from my camera. I was excited to see them all.

We spent the next couple of hours looking at the pictures with Tara and me explaining each one. I'd forgotten some of the pictures I'd taken—like the gross dogs that were everywhere on the streets and the Evil Flying Fruit Man. I didn't have one of the gypsy market, but Tara told the story anyway.

There were pictures of Marcel and Ileana at their baptism, both smiling broadly. The next one must've been taken by Corina, because it had the four of us roommates with Marcel and Ileana. Marcel's arm was around my waist. I quickly clicked past that one and chose not to look at Adam right then.

When we came to the pictures of Madalina and Alin, I felt a stab of pain in my heart. I quickly said they were children from the hospital, but I couldn't elaborate. The baby room in the orphanage brought gasps, as did the pictures of the babies themselves. I pointed out Daciana and Simona, feeling a twinge of homesickness for them.

When a picture of Pali came up, the subject of the gypsy people surfaced again. I told about the deep prejudice that the Romanians had against them. It was hard to explain how those feelings permeated even the members of the branch. It was one of the things about Romania I was glad to leave behind.

After we were finished with the pictures, the talk turned to the engagement. I had called Tara to tell her, but she hadn't seen the ring. She squealed and hugged me and told me how happy she was for me. We were both so excited, we fed off each other and got even more excited.

Justin and Michelle crowded in to look at the ring. Justin said, "Looks good. Nothing I'd ever wear . . ." and Michelle elbowed him. Michelle was very gracious and told me how excited she was we would soon be sisters. Of course she quickly added "in-laws." But that was just Michelle. I could be offended or laugh. I just laughed.

Ruth came up next to congratulate us. She hugged me and I endured it. I held out my hand to show her the ring and she said, "I've already seen it. Adam and I got it from a guy my uncle knows. A different uncle—not President Lant. Aren't you excited?"

I was excited, and I loved my ring; I just wished Ruth had no part in it. I pasted on a smile as she babbled on for a couple more minutes. Luckily for me, she couldn't stay long.

Adam sensed my uneasiness around Ruth and he kept my hand tight in his and whispered, "I love you" a couple of times. I knew I'd have to get over my negative feelings towards Ruth; it seemed she was unofficially part of the Bridger clan.

I caught Barbara watching me as I frowned at Ruth's departing back. I hurried to put a smile back on my face and tried to forget about her.

The next day when Mom and Dave were both gone, I got a call from Barbara. She asked me if I had some time to spend with her, just the two of us. She wanted to take me to lunch.

I readily agreed—food and Barbara were two of my favorite things. She picked me up and we went to a nearby restaurant. After placing our orders, Barbara asked me if I had enjoyed the party. I assured her I had and thanked her again for all the effort she put into it.

"Kit, we are overjoyed to have you as part of our family. You're already like another daughter to me. I feel like Janet was taken from me too soon, so the Lord blessed me with two additional daughters—you and Ruth." Barbara was so kind and sincere; but she was also perceptive. She saw the shadow pass over my face at the mention of Ruth's name.

She continued on. "I can tell you have some hard feelings towards Ruth. I don't expect you to know and love her as I do, but you also need to know that there is nothing to fear from her. She is no threat to you and Adam."

I shifted uncomfortably. "I know that. Adam has reassured me and I believe him. I'm just bothered that she hangs out with your family so much. Doesn't she have her own?"

Barbara asked gently, "Don't you have your own?"

I felt ashamed. Why was I so possessive of the Bridger family? Adam, I could understand; but the rest of the family had stepped in when I desperately wanted and needed the kind of family mine could never be. "I just don't want to share you guys, I guess." I sounded like a petulant three-year-old, but those were my feelings.

I continued on. "I got to know your family through Janet and Adam. I had a reason to hang out and get to know you guys. I think Ruth must have a reason for lurking about all the time. I know you invite her, but there has to be a motivation. Wouldn't she want to hang out with people her own age? It makes me think she still wants Adam and is just biding her time." I was embarrassed to admit these things to Barbara, but that's what I was thinking.

Barbara responded with, "There are reasons she comes over and fits in so well. I want to explain some of those reasons, to help you understand." She pulled a handful of papers out of her purse.

"These are copies of some of my journal pages. I want you to read them, because I think it will help make some things clear." She pushed them across the table to me. "I'm going to go to the restroom and give you a few minutes to read through it."

When she left, I looked at the sheets she handed me. They were partially filled pages, selectively copied, with a range of dates. I started reading through the pages.

April 3

I have never felt days as black as these. I wish I could explain it or understand it. I just know it is a terrible feeling. I feel so hopeless and so down. It seems I can only feel despair. The worst thing about all this is I don't have a reason to be this way. I know I am very blessed. That makes it all the more horrible, because I am ungrateful on top of everything else.

Most people think I am still grieving about Janet's death. I know she is in a better place. I miss her, but the rawness of the grief has passed. Grief is something identifiable, something I can deal with. My testimony of the gospel buoyed me up through those awful days and months after Janet died. This is more than grief. I don't know how my testimony can help with this. I know, logically, my testimony is there. I just can't feel it anymore.

I almost feel like the Spirit is no longer with me. That makes me think that I must have sinned to drive It away. But I mentally go through, checking off what I do, and I am doing everything I have always done. I pray, read my scriptures, keep the commandments, we have family night—yet I still feel nothing. What have I done? What can I do?

April 25

Hal made a doctor's appointment for me. I couldn't even do that for myself. I went today and Dr. Evans said I am suffering from depression. Depression—I always thought it was something you could just snap out of if you tried hard enough. Dr. Evans gave me some medication and said if it doesn't work, we'll try another. That's not very encouraging. Nothing is.

May 13

I hate depression!!! Is it even real? Is it just an excuse I've invented because I'm lazy? I tried taking the medication the doctor gave me and I even gave it two weeks. The side effects are awful. I am dizzy and have dry mouth. A side effect was listed as "vivid dreams." They are vivid and they're horrifying. I'm not taking this stuff anymore. There has to be a better way.

May 15

I spent the morning in bed sleeping. I spent the afternoon curled up in a chair crying. The kids came home from school and I couldn't help them with their homework. I didn't even care about their homework. I just wanted to be left alone. It's like there is a wall of lead that surrounds me and nothing can permeate it, except despair. I am a terrible mother. I cry even more when I think of the effect this is having on my family. I truly am worthless.

July 25

I wonder sometimes, why didn't God just take me instead of Janet? She was a wonderful person; I was always amazed that such a strong spirit came as my daughter. She strengthened us all. I can strengthen no one, not even myself. Why am I even here? I just want to cease to exist.

Sept. 10

President Lant's niece, Ruth Randall, stopped by today. She helped Hal get on full-time at the home improvement center. She has been kind enough to drop by here and there. She came today when she knew I'd be home alone. I was really feeling down, as usual, and wanted to just fade away.

She is friendly and energetic, but I think it is a brittle sort of energy. Like she keeps herself busy to avoid herself—strange I know. She talks a lot. She was in a serious mood today and told me she had something to tell me. She said her mother had died in February of this year; she was suffering from depression and committed suicide. Nobody in the family really knew what to do and Ruth felt guilty that she couldn't help her own mother.

Ruth started crying and told me how much she misses her mother and would do anything to turn back the clock, to change things. She said she knew I had lost a daughter last summer and felt like I could understand her.

After she stopped crying she looked at me and said very frankly, "Sister Bridger, I can tell you are suffering from depression too. Can we help each other?"

That started both of us crying. We hugged each other, and for the first time in a long time I felt like maybe I could help someone instead of being such a drain on everyone. When she left, I thanked Heavenly Father for listening to both of us.

Sept. 13

Ruth brought me a folder full of information on depression. She studied it extensively after her mother's death, trying to understand what had happened. I guess I was ready to try to understand more about it myself. I asked her how she knew I was suffering from depression; I thought I had masked it pretty well. She said that was how—that she could see my depression mask—she called it a "flat face."

Ruth encouraged me to go back to Dr. Evans and try a different medication. They had a cancellation and he got me in immediately. I was open with him and he gave me another medication to try. He also made me promise to start counseling again. He wants to see me in two weeks. I think he wants to make sure I don't quit this medication too.

Sept. 28

I was reading through my journal from the past few months and it scares me that I was so down. I'm not cured by any means, but the meds I'm on now are much better than the first one I tried. I don't cry all the time, which is huge for me. I'm actually feeling something besides despair. It's not just the medication; I know the counseling helps too. And I thank God for Ruth Randall. She truly was an answer to my prayers.

She isn't a surrogate for Janet, although Lily has accused me of that. She is someone who offered me answers and compassion—and someone who truly needed me too. She seems changed too. She is more relaxed and less full of nervous energy. The Lord truly does know each one of us.

I finished reading Barbara's journal pages and sat there trying to absorb what she just shared with me. That Barbara, the one example I looked up to and tried to emulate, suffered from such despair for so many months—in silence—broke my heart.

Adam had told me Barbara was battling depression, but I never really thought about it much. She had looked sad and lost weight, but I was one of the many who attributed it to Janet's death.

I would never recognize a "flat face;" I was too self-absorbed. Compassion for Barbara and Ruth washed over me, along with shame for being so selfish and judgmental. The petty jealousy I felt towards Ruth vanished when I considered the loss of her mother.

As the tears spilled down my cheeks, I battled to regain composure before Barbara returned. What must she think of me? I wondered. I looked up as she approached the table and took her seat.

"Barbara, I'm so sorry I wasn't there for you and that I've been so spiteful about Ruth. I wish I could have helped you." I wanted her to know that I would do anything for her.

"Kit, the Lord provides the means for each of us to get through the trials we face. Ruth has helped me through my trial of depression and I have helped her through her trial of losing her mother. It doesn't diminish anything you and I have shared. You were there for me after Janet died; you'll never really understand how much you meant to our family during that time. Especially to Lily. She needed exactly what you could give her." Barbara handed me a tissue.

I handed Barbara's journal pages back to her as our food came. She smiled at me. "I shared these personal experiences with you, not so you would feel sorry for me, because I really am getting better. I wanted to share my testimony of hope with you. The Lord always provides a way. Sometimes we are the instruments, sometimes others are."

When Barbara took me home, I thanked her for lunch and for sharing her experiences with me. Then I went inside and recorded them in my journal before the tender feelings passed.

chapter thirty-nine

I enrolled in school, we reserved a sealing room in the temple, and I concentrated on making plans for my wedding. I wasn't even that excited for the Christmas season because I had too much to look forward to, and thinking of Christmas made me remember my fragmented family.

I spent the next week pretty much by myself since Adam was either studying for or taking finals. He still had to work as well. I had a lot of time on my hands so I went to the bookstore in the mall where I worked before, and they agreed to give me some hours during the holiday season.

As I roamed the mall on my break, I was reminded vividly of the times I'd spent there with Janet and our friend, Claire. I wondered whatever happened to Claire. I'd never heard from her since she took off to California with her old boyfriend. I wondered if she even knew about Janet.

Browsing through the Hallmark store where Janet and Claire used to work, I realized that it was there that Janet and I had looked through her book of wedding dresses. She had teased me about choosing a temple-appropriate dress when I wasn't even a member of the Church yet.

During one break I went to the bridal store in the mall and looked at all the dresses. One of them reminded me a lot of Janet's dress—the Cinderella gown she was going to be married in and ended up being buried in. I shuddered at the memory.

I started feeling paranoid, like I didn't want to pick out my dress because I was afraid I'd jinx things. I told Adam about it and he laughed and said, "There's no such thing as a jinx." I knew that but still fretted about something happening.

Adam and I started temple prep classes on Sunday. The elder's quorum president gave me a copy of the manual and I read through it in one night. I thought about Adam's comment right after we got engaged. *The only things we need to do are set a date, get our temple recommends and get married.* I wondered if it was proper to elope to the temple.

My anxieties were further fed when I came home from work one night to find my mom and dad both at the house arguing. I'd walked into the middle of it, and they quickly pulled me into it.

"Kit, come here," my mother commanded. She'd been terse with me ever since I told her Adam and I were getting married in the temple and we wouldn't compromise. She thought I was being inconsiderate. I thought she and my dad could write the book on being inconsiderate.

I went to the kitchen reluctantly. My parents were both angry as evidenced by their red faces.

My mom turned and faced me. "Kit, I've decided to take a job offer I've had in Ventura. I'm moving on January second, and you're welcome to come with me or stay here." She pivoted back towards my dad. "There! I've told her. No big deal. She's getting married anyway."

"What kind of mother announces, a couple of weeks before Christmas, that she's moving away from her family in less than a month?" My dad snapped at my mom. After those words sunk in he added, "Why are you going now? Won't they hold this job for you until Kit is married and Dave is graduated?" My dad was yelling—he rarely yelled.

"Right, like you haven't done anything to upset anybody in this family. It's no secret our marriage is through. I told you I have a chance at a partnership in this firm. It's a chance I gave up once to move to Utah, right after Christmas, I might add." She took a breath and turned to me. "I'll fly back for your wedding, of course.

Or should I say reception—since I can't come to the wedding. I'll
fly back for Dave's graduation as well, assuming he doesn't want to
come with me."

It sunk in. My mom was moving back to California—in like,
three weeks? I didn't think life could get any crazier and now this.
I ventured to ask a question. "Mom, what about the house? Where
will Dave and I live?"

"I've explained to your father," she emphasized the word 'father',
"that he can move back into the house with you and Dave until
you're married and Dave graduates. Then he can put it up for sale,
for all I care."

"Nora, I've signed a lease at my apartment." Dad paced the
floor. "This is crazy. I can't believe you're running off to California.
I just think you're being rash." My dad was trying to make her see
reason, but it wasn't working.

"I don't care what you think, Paul. I'm going. I'm sure you'll
figure something out. I'm going to bed. Good night." She stomped
upstairs and I heard a door slam.

"Is she serious?" I asked my dad.

"It sounds like it. Don't worry about it, Kit. We'll work
something out. I'm sorry you had to walk in on it." He picked up
his coat and keys. I followed him to the door and gave him a half-
hearted hug. Why was everything such a mess?

I felt just sick about the state my family was in. I prayed for
help, to know how to hold my family together. My mother remained
adamant about moving and my father placed an ad to sublet his
apartment. Dave opted to stay in the house with Dad and me. He
seemed distant and unaffected. I felt powerless and hopeless. In
despair, I continued to pray, seeking some form of comfort.

Comfort came in a very unexpected way—through Michelle,
of all people. Adam and I went to a Christmas concert at USU with
Justin and Michelle. During intermission, she and I joined the long
line for the ladies room.

We made small talk, as usual; then I suddenly felt prompted
to ask her a very personal question. "Michelle, how are you able to
handle your parents' divorce?"

Michelle wasn't offended and opened up to me. "There's nothing to prepare you for having your world turned upside down. We were the 'perfect LDS family.' There's no such thing." She shook her head. "After all the Sunday school lessons and family home evenings, you find out your own parents don't practice what they preach."

"Did you have any idea it was coming?" I asked.

"I pretended I didn't. They tried to keep it from us, but now I look back and I see the signs. They tried to hold it together for the sake of the kids." Tears came to her eyes. "So they waited until the kids were all grown up before they split. It seemed like they conveniently forgot about being an eternal family—if they ever believed it at all."

"I'm sorry to stir it all up for you. I'm just having a really hard time with my own parents separating. I hoped someday they would join the Church and we could be sealed together, but now that's been dashed." I wiped my own eyes. "I feel cheated. Like their choices have robbed me of eternal blessings. Did you ever feel that way?"

"That's exactly how I felt. Like they'd thrown out their covenants and robbed our family of all the blessings we'd been promised. I felt helpless."

"Has anything helped you? I don't know what to do." I didn't think I'd ever be asking Michelle for advice.

"After one really rough day, I asked Justin to give me a blessing. I was promised I would find peace in the words of the Lord. I searched the scriptures for something to give me hope."

"What did you find?"

"I didn't find anything until one day I came across a talk about divorce given by Elder Dallin H. Oaks in general conference in April 2007. It was exactly what I needed to hear. I have a copy at home I can bring to you, or you can find it on lds.org."

I told her I would call her if I couldn't find it. Later that night, I found the talk and read through it several times. I was amazed at how much it touched my troubled heart and buoyed up my spirit. One passage in particular touched me.

> Whatever the outcome and no matter how difficult your experiences, you have the promise that you will not be denied the blessings of eternal family relationships if you love the Lord, keep His commandments, and just do the best you can.

When young Jacob "suffered afflictions and much sorrow" from the actions of other family members, Father Lehi assured him, "Thou knowest the greatness of God; and he shall consecrate thine afflictions for thy gain" (2 Nephi 2:1–2). Similarly, the Apostle Paul assured us that "all things work together for good to them that love God" (Romans 8:28)."

I felt a surge of something—something I hadn't felt in a while. There was hope. I knew the Lord always keeps His promises and I knew I loved the Lord; I felt I had just been promised the blessing of an eternal family relationship. It was enough.

The next day I called to set up an interview with my bishop. I had some things to discuss with him. He knew very little about what was going on in my family since I was the only member and I'd been gone for three months.

He was able to see me almost immediately. I asked him a lot of questions and he gave me answers and some very good counsel. Part of that counsel was to share with Adam many of the things I had shared with him. Then he asked if I would bring Adam over to meet with him the following evening.

I called Adam and told him I needed to talk to him immediately. We talked for hours as I opened up my heart to him in a way I never had before. I voiced my fear about something happening to prevent us from getting married and how I kept reliving the horror of Janet dying just four weeks before her own marriage.

Adam already knew I was worried about my parents, but I hadn't told him I was afraid of marriage in general—I was fearful that no marriage could stand the test of time. I confessed my feelings of inadequacy of being a good wife. Surprisingly, Adam admitted he was worried about being a good husband.

I told him about the talk I had with Michelle, and how she had told me about the conference talk that was an answer to her prayers and later to my own. I felt some measure of peace regarding my family although things were still very much up in the air.

The subject of our wedding came up. "Do you mind if I make a few changes to our wedding plans?" I knew what his answer would be.

He said, "Make whatever changes you want, Kit, except you

can't change the bride, the groom, or the temple!" I took him at his word.

I then told Adam about the meeting with my bishop, and his request that Adam meet with him. He readily agreed, then I assured him not to worry; I'd already met with the bishop once. I think my admonition for him not to worry made Adam a little concerned.

The next evening I picked Adam up for his appointment with my bishop. On the way there I thought I should let Adam know what was going on.

"Last night you said I could make some changes to our wedding plans. After talking to you and my bishop, I've come up with some pretty big changes."

"Like what?" I detected a hint of alarm in his voice.

"Don't worry—they're good changes. Remember how I told you I was getting paranoid, especially considering Janet and the way my parents are fighting. Being around my parents makes me feel disillusioned about marriage. My mom's not into planning a wedding and neither am I. The only thing really holding us back is not having money for a place to live. Right?"

"That's a big part of it," Adam said slowly, not sure where I was leading him.

"With my dad moving back into our house when my mother moves back to California, it leaves a perfectly good apartment empty. The middle of their separation is not the most joyous time to be planning a wedding. I don't want all the fluff. I just want to get married as soon as possible. I'd do it tonight if we could." I blurted it out so fast that Adam shook his head as if to clear his ears.

"What? Are you serious? You want to get married now?" Adam was stunned, to say the least.

"You said it yourself; all we need is a recommend, a date, and a temple to get married in. The rest is fluff, which I don't want— frankly, the fluff scares me. My family can't come to the wedding anyway, so why wait?" I glanced at him to see his reaction, it was still sinking in. "We can have a reception afterwards; like an open house thing at your parents' house. That way my parents, your extended family and friends can come by. It saves money, time, and my sanity. A perfect plan, if you ask me." It sounded perfectly sane to me.

I was glad I'd prepped him before we met with the bishop. I didn't want the bishop to think I had a reluctant bridegroom on my hands.

Adam digested it all for a few moments. "You've already met with your bishop. Did you tell him your plan?"

"Yes. He said it could be done. He was the one who suggested the open house afterwards so family and friends wouldn't feel left out. He wanted to meet with you, though." I wondered if he thought I was nuts. I think the bishop did, at first.

"You really want to do it this way?" Adam asked.

"I really do. But I want you to be good with it, too." I held my breath waiting for his answer.

A huge smile split his face and he said, "I'm great with it! Let's do it." I had to pull over to the side of the road so I could let him know my reaction to his answer. It involved me crawling over to his side and smothering him with kisses. He liked my response.

And so it happened—Adam and I "eloped" to the Salt Lake Temple four days after Christmas. Hal, Barbara, Justin, and Michelle attended the ceremony with us.

My parents, although resistant when I told them the new date, realized I was serious. They came to the temple with Dave, and waited for us with the younger part of the Bridger clan. They all greeted us with hugs and kisses as we came through the doors as Mr. and Mrs. Adam Bridger. I was thrilled to see Tara waiting there with them; holding my bouquet, standing next to the photographer, who happened to be young, handsome, and flirting with her.

It was a beautiful day for December in Salt Lake City. There was freshly fallen snow, no inversion, and an azure sky to complement the rest of the picture-perfect day. The sunlight sparkled on the snow like thousands of tiny diamonds.

I didn't have a Cinderella gown; mine was simple, but elegant; straight off the rack at the temple. I had a beautiful white fur cloak draped around my shoulders to keep warm. I laughed when I saw my bouquet of lilies had a few sprigs of our "stinkweed" tucked here and there.

Adam changed into a black tuxedo for the pictures and looked amazingly handsome, especially when he flashed his Bridger smile at me, which he did all day long. I thought my heart would burst with joy at the thought of seeing that smile every day for the rest of my life—I corrected myself—for all eternity.

We had a luncheon at The Garden restaurant at the top of the Joseph Smith Memorial Building. We even had a wedding cake—an ice-cream cake compliments of Justin and Michelle. Adam and I stood hand-in-hand at the windows, looking out over the temple, drinking in the beauty of the day.

His parents surprised us with an envelope that contained the exact sum of money Adam had contributed to his family during the time Hal was out of work. My dad gave us the keys to his apartment and told us the rent was paid through the end of the school year. My mom hugged us both tightly and cried; I thought some of them were tears of joy. Then she gave us the reservation information for the Marriott Hotel and the honeymoon suite; her gift to us.

As a special gift to me—Dave kept all smart-aleck comments to himself, and he even smiled for all the pictures! I saw Lily checking him out when she thought no one was looking and it made me a little nauseated; but then I remembered that Lily was fifteen and boy-crazy.

Adam and I couldn't stop smiling. He whispered in my ear, "Are you happy, Mrs. Bridger?" My pulse quickened at those words and I answered him with a shower of kisses.

I pulled back and said, "Unbelievably happy, Mr. Bridger!" He replied with a passionate kiss of his own, and at that moment I felt we were the only two people on the face of the earth—a glorious earth full of hope and promise.

I could count on one hand the number of perfect days I've had in my life and this day would be number one. It was everything I had hoped for—and a little bit more.

having hope
Questions for book clubs and other groups

1. Would the story have been as effective if the setting was in America instead of Romania? Did you feel you experienced a taste of Romania? Why or why not?

2. Were the characters believable? How did you feel about Marcel? Do you think he truly cared about the orphans, or was simply playing on Kit's sympathies?

3. What recurring themes surfaced throughout the book? What are some examples? Are they true to life?

4. Can you relate to Kit's turmoil about not knowing if she's following God's will? About her family not fitting her ideal of a perfect family?

5. Did you agree with Kit's decision about whether or not to stay in Romania? Would you have chosen differently?

6. Why did Kit believe the things Lily emailed her about Ruth and Adam? Why did Adam give Kit the benefit of the doubt when he received the email from Amanda?

7. Did the book end the way you expected?

About the Author

Terri Ferran grew up in a small Colorado town that offered little in the way of entertainment. She escaped through reading (and later on a Continental Trailways bus), and although the town didn't have a library, she eagerly anticipated the coming of the Bookmobile and would check out stacks of books at a time.

When she was fourteen she discovered one of her favorite books, *Gone With the Wind*. She started reading it on the bus on the way home from school, and read straight through until she finished it at 4 a.m. the following morning.

She moved to Utah as a high school senior, where she joined the LDS Church and met her husband, Tod. Quietly dreaming of becoming a writer, Terri took the secure route and majored in accounting at Utah State University. She is a CPA who spent many years in public accounting and was the CFO of an automotive dealership group.

She finally got brave enough to quit working in the safe world of numbers to pursue her dream of writing and also to spend more time with her children.

She has had several magazine articles published and is excited to be living her dream of writing in real life.

Terri and her husband are the parents of six children: three boys and three girls. When she's not busy writing or doing mom things, Terri still loves to read, but she can usually be found doing laundry, washing dishes, running errands, napping, eating chocolate, or exercising (not necessarily in that order).

0 26575 52330 0